ANGELMASS

BOOKS BY TIMOTHY ZAHN

The Blackcollar

A Coming of Age

Cobra

Spinneret

Cobra Strike

Cascade Point and Other Stories

The Backlash Mission

Triplet

Cobra Bargain

Time Bomb and Zahndry Others

Deadman Switch

Warhorse

Star Wars: Heir to the Empire

Cobras Two (omnibus)

Star Wars: Dark Force Rising

Star Wars: The Last Command

Conquerors' Pride

Conquerors' Heritage

Conquerors' Legacy

The Hand of Thrawn

Book 1: Specter of the Past

Book 2: Vision of the Future

The Icarus Hunt

Angelmass

TOR®

A TOM DOHERTY ASSOCIATES BOOK | NEW YORK

ANGELMASS

TIMOTHY ZAHN

This is a work of fiction. All the characters and events portrayed in this novel are either fictitious or are used fictitiously.

ANGELMASS

Copyright © 2001 by Timothy Zahn

All rights reserved, including the right to reproduce this book, or portions thereof, in any form.

A Tor Book
Published by Tom Doherty Associates, LLC
175 Fifth Avenue
New York, NY 10010

Tor® is a registered trademark of Tom Doherty Associates, LLC.

Edited by James Frenkel

Book design by Gretchen Achilles

ISBN 0-312-87828-1

Printed in the United States of America

To my mother:
The first angel in my life

ANGELMASS

There were two of them waiting as Jereko Kosta climbed awkwardly up the ladder through the shuttle hatch: a young ensign and an equally young crewer second class, both clothed in shiny black and silver Pax military uniforms, the glistening red and blue threads of the *Komitadji*'s insignia pattern swirling with arrogant pride across collarbone and shoulder. "Mr. Kosta," the ensign said, his hand twitching halfway into an automatic salute before he seemed to remember the man facing him was a civilian. "Welcome aboard the *Komitadji*. Commodore Lleshi's compliments; he'd like to see you on the command deck immediately."

Kosta nodded, fighting against a strange fog of unreality as he looked around the docking bay's spotless gray walls and ceilings. The *Komitadji*. He was actually aboard the *Komitadji*. "Understood," he said, trying to match the ensign's neutral tone and not entirely succeeding. "I have just the two bags . . . ?"

"They'll be stowed aboard your ship," the ensign assured him as the crewer brushed smoothly past Kosta and disappeared down the ladder into the shuttle. "If you'll follow me, please?"

The slidecar door was in a protected alcove in the docking bay's rear wall. The ensign ushered him in and keyed a switch, and they started up toward the center of the ship.

Toward the center of the *Komitadji*.

It was, Kosta thought, like being aboard a living legend. Not even the crystal-walled towers of academia had insulated him from the stories of the huge ship's military victories; and even if they had, the eight weeks of intensive training he'd just finished would have quickly remedied any such omission. Practically every one of Kosta's military trainers had had his or her favorite story to tell about the *Komitadji*, stories that were invariably told with a sort of grim glee. For the military, as well as most ordinary Pax citizens, the *Komitadji* was a symbol of pride and glory and power. A symbol of the protection and strength that was the Pax.

To be traveling the corridors of a legend would have been impressive enough. To be traveling the corridors of a ship that had achieved such legendary status in barely five years of active service was truly awe-inspiring.

The trip to the command deck seemed to take an inordinately long time, even for a ship the *Komitadji*'s size, and to be unreasonably complicated besides. It added an extra tinge of nervousness to Kosta's already mixed feelings about his place in this mission; and it was only as they switched slidecars for the third time that it finally occurred to him that the inefficiency was probably deliberate. On a warship, it didn't pay to make critical control areas too easy to get to.

The command deck, once they finally arrived, was just as Kosta had pictured it: a long room filled with consoles and black/silver-suited men and women working busily at them. He looked around, hoping to spot the captain—

"Kosta?" a voice boomed down from above him.

Kosta craned his neck. At one end of the room a small balcony-like ledge jutted out over the command deck. An older, silver-haired man stood at the railing, gazing down at him. "Yes, sir?" Kosta called back.

The other jerked his head fractionally and turned away. Wordlessly, Kosta's escort led the way to a lift platform beneath the rear of the balcony. The memory-metal cage wrapped around the platform, and a moment later it opened again on the balcony.

The older man was waiting for him. "Kosta," he nodded gravely in greeting, his eyes flicking up and down in quick evaluation. "I'm Commodore Vars Lleshi. Welcome aboard the *Komitadji*."

"Thank you, sir," Kosta said. "I'm—well, it's . . ." He broke off, feeling suddenly like an idiot.

Lleshi's mouth twitched in a faint smile. "Yes; it *is* big, isn't it? Did you get your final briefing below?"

"Yes, sir," Kosta nodded, trying to shake the feeling of being the new kid at school. "As much briefing as they thought I should have, anyway."

Lleshi eyed him. "They were a little short on details?"

"Well . . ." Kosta said hesitantly as it occurred to him that sour-mouthing a military prep unit to a officer of that same military might not be a smart thing to do. "They kept it a bit on the light side," he said, toning his comments down to something tactful. "I get the feeling I'm supposed to play a lot of this by ear."

"You were expecting a script?" another voice put in scornfully.

Kosta turned, his throat tightening reflexively, to see a thin-faced man in a painfully neat, totally unadorned gray civilian suit striding toward him from one of the command boards at the balcony's side edge. "I—ah—I'm sorry?" he asked, floundering for words.

"I asked if you thought you'd be getting a script for this," the other repeated. "You've just undergone the finest intensive-training course money can buy. I'd have thought the absolute first thing they would have beaten into you is that spies play nearly *everything* by ear."

Kosta took a careful breath, fighting against the old automatic submission urge. This man wasn't his adviser, or his dean, or his department chairman. "I'm sure they taught me as best as they could in eight weeks," he said. "Perhaps I'm just not good spy material."

"Very few people are naturally that way," Lleshi cut in, throwing a brief glance at the other man. "But on the other hand, this isn't your average spy mission, either. As Mr. Telthorst has a tendency to forget. For secret information, you send a spy. For secret academic information, you send an academic." He favored Kosta with a tight but reassuring smile. "And for twenty years' worth of secret academic information, you send an academic with a knack for digging nuggets out of froth."

"That person being you, we all hope," Telthorst said sourly. "Otherwise this whole thing will be nothing more than a colossal waste of money."

Kosta gazed at him, again fighting against the urge to apologize. But at least now he finally had the man pegged. "I take it, Mr. Telthorst, that you're the *Komitadji*'s Adjutor Corps representative."

There was a faint sound from Lleshi that in a lesser man might have been a snicker. Slowly, Telthorst turned his head to look at the commodore; just as slowly he turned back to face Kosta. "I am not," he said, quietly and distinctly, "a representative of any kind. I am a fully qualified Adjutor, authorized to sit at Supreme Council meetings and to advise the government on any and all matters dealing with the financial and economic well-being of the Pax, or of any group, sub-group, world, nationia, district, or sub-district within it."

His glare turned colder. "Including such totally inconsequential matters as the academic debts incurred by tridoctorum students from small towns on minor worlds of backwater planetary groups. *Your* debts, Kosta, and whether they will be canceled or not."

"I'm sorry," Kosta managed, wishing he'd kept his mouth shut. The veiled power lurking beneath that icy disdain was every bit as intimidating as the *Komitadji* itself. "I didn't mean any disrespect."

"I trust not," Telthorst said. He looked again at Lleshi. "And I, in turn," he added grudgingly, "didn't mean to imply you were unprepared for your mission. You understand that liberating the people of this so-called Empyrean from their alien domination and bringing them under Pax enlightenment is going to be a very expensive proposition. My job is the same as that of every Adjutor: to make sure the Pax gets its money's worth."

"I understand," Kosta said, his reflexive fear fading into a rather annoyed nervousness. He was about to risk his life in enemy territory, and all Telthorst could think about was how much money it was costing. "I'll do my best not to waste the Pax's investment in me."

Telthorst's forehead creased, just a bit— "I'm sure you'll do fine, Kosta," Lleshi put in before Telthorst could speak. "But enough talk. Your ship is in the Number Six cargo hold—you'll be taken there directly from here. You know how to handle it?"

"Yes, sir," Kosta said. He did, too, after a fashion, though almost everything the ship would need to do should already have been pre-programmed into it.

"Good," the commodore said. "Remember that you're not to leave the cocoon for a minimum of twelve hours after you've been dropped. That's a *minimum*—if Empyreal ships are still poking around you'll obviously need to sit tight longer. Just take your time and don't panic. You should be totally undetectable inside the cocoon, and if we do our job properly they'll never even notice you leaving the *Komitadji*. We should also be getting a data pulse from the automated sleeper drop on Lorelei as soon as we arrive, provided we're grabbed by the proper net and our timing is on mark. If there's time, I'll dump a copy to you before you're dropped. Once you're down, go to the coordinates programmed into your ship's computer and pick up the final current-conditions compilation, the false identity papers that should be waiting for you, and the access information for your credit line."

"A very *limited* credit line," Telthorst put in. "Keep that in mind, and try to find ways to be economical."

"Yes, sir, I will," Kosta said, trying not to grimace. Money again. With Adjutors, it was always money. "If that's all, Commodore," he added, "I'll get down to my ship."

Lleshi nodded. "Go ahead. And good luck on your little trip to heaven."

"Thank you." Kosta looked the commodore square in the eye. "I won't fail, sir."

"Scintara Catapult Control, Commodore," the man at the communications board called up to the balcony. "We have signal green."

"Acknowledged." Lleshi gave his status board a leisurely scan. Ship's rotation was at zero, energy weapons charged and ready, missiles loaded into their tubes and stand-by armed. Everything in place for a little jaunt into enemy territory. "SeTO?"

"All green, Commodore," Senior Tactical Officer Campbell reported from his console. "Alpha and Beta both. Ship and crew at full battle stations."

Peripherally, Lleshi saw Telthorst swivel around from his observer's console at one side of the balcony. "Beta?" he asked, a suspicious overtone in his voice. "What's Beta?"

"It's a simulation run," Lleshi told him. "Fighters at station; that sort of thing. We *do* intend an eventual invasion of these systems." He eyed the Adjutor, noting the other's tight-lipped expression. "Your last chance to get off here if you'd rather," he offered.

Telthorst returned his gaze without blinking. "*Your* last chance, Commodore, to not risk this ship."

Lleshi looked back at his board, fighting back a flash of very unprofessional anger. Zero hour was *not* the time to reopen old arguments. They had no choice but to use the *Komitadji* on this, for reasons Telthorst already knew. "Helmsman: Move us into position."

"Yes, sir."

A visual representation of the focal point of Scintara's hyperspace catapult sat directly in front of the *Komitadji* on the helm display: a hazy red ellipsoid hanging in space, undulating slowly as its three axes rhythmically fed from and into each other. In the early days of catapult travel—and it was a thought that always intruded into Lleshi's mind at this point—a ship that didn't fit entirely within that focal area risked leaving pieces of itself behind while the rest was thrown across the light-years. Without the discovery of paraconducting metal, a ship the size of the *Komitadji* would never have been possible.

Such a wonderful thing, progress.

The proximity alarm trilled: the *Komitadji*'s bow had touched the focal ellipsoid. "Stand by," Lleshi ordered. "Scintara Catapult, you have the timer. Launch at T-zero."

Scintara acknowledged. Thirty-eight seconds later, with a metallic stutter of stress from the paraconducting underskin, the stars abruptly disappeared from the viewscreens.

Lleshi took a careful breath, mind and body slipping automatically into full combat mode. It was nearly three hundred light-years from Scintara to the Empyreal world of Lorelei: just under six seconds of hyperspace travel. "Stand by," he murmured, more from habit than any expectation that his crew wasn't ready. He settled himself . . . and, as abruptly as they'd disappeared, the stars were back.

"Location check," he ordered. The nav display had sprouted multicolored relative-V arrows now: many of the "stars" on the visual were, in fact, asteroids. But that didn't necessarily put them in the right net—all the nets around Lorelei seemed to be deep in the system's extensive asteroid belts. "If we're in the right net, key for data retrieval."

"Focused pulse transmissions from the planet, Commodore," the comm officer reported. "We're in the right net. Copying now."

"Campbell?"

"Tactical coming up now, sir," the SeTO said. "Defenses as expected."

Lleshi nodded, his eyes on the tac display . . . and it was indeed as expected. Arrayed in a rough triangular pyramid two hundred kilometers on an edge around the *Komitadji* were four small ships. Each of them carried the pole of a hyperspace catapult; together, they guarded the center of the net field that had—somehow—snatched the *Komitadji* from its original hyperspace vector and deflected it to this precise point. Any three of those ships, acting together, could throw the *Komitadji* right back out of the system, in any direction they chose.

And if they did so immediately, young Kosta might as well not have bothered coming aboard.

"Message, Commodore," the comm officer announced. "They remind us the Empyrean has closed its borders to ships of the Pax, and request that we state our business here."

Lleshi smiled tightly. So the first part of the gamble had succeeded: the *Komitadji*'s sheer size had caught the Empyreals off guard. Even now they were scrambling to recalibrate their catapult as they tried to make the invaders waste time with useless conversation. He threw a glance in Telthorst's direction, saw only the back of the Adjutor's head. "No return message," he said quietly. "Attack pattern Alpha."

The *Komitadji*'s lights dimmed slightly as, on the tactical, four lines of blue light lanced out, one focused on each of the distant catapult ships. Behind the laser beams four yellow plasma jets boiled out; following right on their heels the red lines of a dozen Spearhawk missiles shot similarly outward. Lleshi was pushed back into his chair as the *Komitadji*'s engines roared to life, driving the ship away from the center of the pyramid. The Empyreal ships moved to stay with them, the Spearhawk missiles shifting vectors in turn to match the movement. The *Komitadji*'s computers refocused the lasers, launched new plasma clouds—

And a second later, almost in unison and at least thirty kilometers out from their targets, all twelve Spearhawks exploded.

"Premature detonation; all missiles," Campbell reported. "Plasma and lasers having no discernible effect; catapult ships still tracking us. Second Spearhawks away."

"Data pulse retrieval complete," the comm officer called as another set of twelve Spearhawks appeared on the tactical, arcing toward the defenders. "Copy dumped to cocoon."

Behind the four beleaguered catapult ships eight similar spacecraft had now appeared on the tactical, emerging from cover behind various asteroids. Back-ups, already starting to configure themselves into catapult arrangement.

"Cocoon launch on my command," Lleshi ordered, frowning with concentration as he watched the second group of Spearhawks climb toward their targets. With the detonation codes already computed by the Empyreals, this set ought to go considerably closer to the *Komitadji* than the previous ones had—

In twelve simultaneous flashes, they did . . . and surrounded by light and fire and expanding clouds of debris, the *Komitadji* was momentarily hidden from enemy view. "Cocoon: launch!" he snapped.

The *Komitadji* didn't lurch—it was far too big for that—but Lleshi imagined he could feel the dull thud of the explosive springs as their cargo was blown clear of the Number Six hold. "Third Spearhawks away," Campbell called.

"Fire Harpies," Lleshi ordered. "Random minus one pattern."

"Acknowledged. First Harpies away."

On the tactical the twelve Spearhawk trails were abruptly joined by fifty more, bursting outward from the *Komitadji* like the time-lapse flowering of a strange and exotic plant. Almost lost among them was the tiny spot drifting with maddening leisure from the *Komitadji*'s starboard side. "Hard aport," Lleshi ordered. "Draw the catapult focus away from the cocoon."

He was pushed into the side of his chair as the helmsman complied. With plasma and missile debris blocking their view it took a few seconds for the Empyreal ships to notice the maneuver and move to match it; simultaneously, the Harpy missiles began exploding. "They've found the Harpies' code," Campbell said. "Second Harpies ready."

"Focus forming," the helmsman called. "Five seconds: mark."

"Hold second Harpies," Lleshi ordered. If Kosta and the cocoon weren't in the clear now, wasting another batch of expensive missiles on what was little more than a fireworks display wasn't going to make the difference. "Stand ready for catapult."

And with the usual stuttering from the hull, the universe vanished.

Automatically, Lleshi started counting the seconds; but he'd barely begun when the stars returned. The stars, and a dull red sun barely visible to one side.

Carefully, he let out a quiet breath. That had been the final gamble of this phase of the operation, and now it too had come up clean. "Secure from battle stations," he ordered. "Location check, and scan for the cocoon."

"Location computed, Commodore," the navigator said briskly. "We're fifty-four point seven light-years from the Lorelei system; running a hundred thirty million klicks out from the local sun. I'll have an orbit profile in a moment."

"No trace of the cocoon within inner scan limit," the scanner chief added. "Shifting to midrange, but looks like a clean drop."

"Good. Get us some rotation, and have engineering start putting the kick pod catapult together."

The weight warning trilled through the command deck; and as the huge ship started almost imperceptibly to rotate, Lleshi turned to look at Telthorst. "You see now why we weren't all that worried about risking the *Komitadji*."

The Adjutor gazed back, his eyes hard. "Two hundred million kilometers further and you wouldn't be in a position to gloat," he said pointedly. "Our vector would have passed straight through that star out there and we'd all be very, very dead."

"Agreed," Lleshi nodded. "Which I imagine is why it took the Empyreals so long to get rid of us. Laser-point precision on top of a fast field reconfiguration."

Telthorst looked at the dim star on the viewscreen. "I suppose they expect us to be impressed by that."

Lleshi shrugged. "*I'm* impressed. Aren't you?"

The Adjutor looked back at him, his lip twisted in contempt. "Impressed, Commodore? Impressed by a people who've become so sheep-like that they won't kill even in their own defense? You're too easy to please."

"Am I?" Lleshi countered, the slow unprofessional burn starting again. "Those Empyreals were risking their lives, Adjutor—make no mistake about that. If those Spearhawks had hit them they'd have died, with or without those fancy sandwich-metal hulls of theirs. In my experience, sheep seldom come equipped with that degree of courage."

Telthorst's expression didn't change . . . but abruptly Lleshi felt a chill in the air. "Admiration of one's opponents is said to be a useful trait in diplomats," the Adjutor said softly. "The same doesn't apply to soldiers. Bear in mind, Commodore, that we're not dealing with *men* here. We're dealing with men under alien control. There's a considerable difference."

"I'm aware of what we're up against," Lleshi said, keeping a firm grip on his temper. "But then, that's why we're here, isn't it? To rescue our fellow human beings from these dangerous angels?"

The lines around Telthorst's mouth deepened. "Don't mock me, Commodore," he warned. "I may not profess admiration for their soldiers the way you do. But *I* wasn't the one who set up a dry scorch run, complete with a full complement of fighters and Hellfire missiles ready in their launch tubes."

Lleshi swallowed a curse. He'd hoped that in all the excitement Telthorst would have forgotten about the Beta simulation. Not only hadn't he forgotten, he'd obviously even taken the time to monitor that part of the exercise. "My orders are to subdue the Empyrean and bring it under the Pax umbrella," he said stiffly. "I intend for my crew to be ready for any contingency that may arise in the act of carrying out those orders."

"I applaud your foresight," Telthorst said. "Just remember that the operative word is 'subdue.' Not 'destroy'; 'subdue.'"

"Understood," Lleshi growled. No, of course the operative word wasn't "destroy." You could put an Adjutor into a cold sweat simply by suggesting something with cash value or money-making potential might be damaged. "Let me remind you in turn that that was the main reason we chose the Kosta feint over the other scenarios Spec Ops suggested. If he *isn't* caught, he may be able to provide us with valuable information on the angels."

Telthorst snorted. "Of course he'll be caught. Isn't that the whole purpose of a feint? To get caught?"

Lleshi nodded reluctantly, feeling a twinge of discomfort. Dangerous situations were hardly anything new to him, and he'd had his fair share of ordering men onto what were little more than suicide missions. But always before they'd been *military* men, who had known what they were getting into and had had the best possible chance of getting out alive. Not a civilian with barely eight weeks of training.

Especially not a civilian who'd been lied to straight from square one about what his contribution was expected to be. "He may get lucky," he said.

Telthorst eyed him thoughtfully for a moment. "Perhaps. I'd like a copy of that Lorelei data pulse."

Lleshi caught Campbell's eye, nodded. Wordlessly, the other stepped over to Telthorst and handed him a data cyl. "Thank you," the Adjutor said, getting to his feet. "If you need me, Commodore, I'll be in my stateroom."

He went to the bridge lift platform; paused there. "By the way, you'll want to do a complete survey of this system," he added over his shoulder. "As long as we have to leave a functioning catapult here anyway, we might as well see if there's anything worth coming back for."

"Thank you," Lleshi said. "I *am* familiar with standing orders."

"Good." For a moment Telthorst let his gaze drift leisurely around the balcony, as if to remind them all who was ultimately in charge of this operation. Then, without another word, he disappeared down the lift plate shaft to the lower command deck and left.

Bastards, Lleshi thought after him. *Carved-ice bastards, every one of them.* He turned back to his console, keyed for an engineering status report. Work on the kick pod catapult was already underway, with an estimated completion time of five days.

At which point they would be able to send word back to the Pax that

Kosta's drop had been successful. And the Empyrean would be on its slow, leisurely way to defeat.

"Tell engineering that as soon as the kick pod is away they're to put triple shifts on the main catapult construction," he instructed the comm officer. "I want it ready in four months."

"Yes, sir."

With a grimace, Lleshi keyed for a copy of the Lorelei data pulse. To be trapped out here for four months, only marginally in touch with what was going on with his task force, was going to be an unpleasant exercise in patience. But for the moment, at least, he possessed information that no one else in the Pax had. Plus five days to decide how much of that information would go out with the kick pod.

Settling himself in his seat in the ship's slowly returning gravity, he began to read.

The timer pinged quietly, and Kosta looked up from his reading. The twelve hours Lleshi had insisted on were up, and a careful look at the displays showed no Empyreal ships within inner scan range.

It was time to go.

Unhinging the control cover, he turned and then pressed a button; and with an awful racket of explosive springs he was shoved back into his seat as his tiny ship was thrown forward through a tunnel that magically appeared in the rock-textured surface of the cocoon. He held his breath, waiting tensely for the inevitable enemy fighter ship that must surely have been skulking behind an asteroid waiting for him.

But nothing. Not as the tiny ship oriented itself; not as it began its pre-programmed flight inward toward the Empyreal world of Lorelei; not even as Kosta breathed a sigh of relief and dared to relax. The gambit had worked, and he was on his way. Heading to Lorelei, and a rendezvous with a little auto-mated spy system the Pax had managed to set up before their last talks with the Empyreal leaders broke off some months back.

And after that it would be on to Seraph. To Seraph, and Angelmass.

Staring out his viewport at the distant crescent of Lorelei, Kosta felt his stomach tighten. *I won't fail,* he'd told Lleshi confidently. But now, far from the bright lights and purposeful men and women of the *Komitadji,* the words echoed through his memory like so much empty bravado. He was alone now, in hostile territory, facing an enemy possibly more alien now than it was human.

A little trip to heaven, Lleshi's last words echoed through his mind. It had been something of a running gag, that, during Kosta's training: the fact that the breakaway colonists who'd founded the Empyrean a hundred eighty years ago had chosen an ancient term for the highest reaches of heaven.

Question was, had the choice of that name indeed been purely coincidental? Or had it been an indication, even way back then, of the angels' subtle influence on people's minds?

There were all sorts of questions like that hanging over this mission. Questions currently without answers. Questions he, Kosta, was supposed to find answers for. Overwhelming, deep, impossible questions . . .

And then, as the enormity of the whole thing once again threatened to drown him, the image of Telthorst's face floated up into his mind. That face, and all that contempt . . .

"Forget it," he said aloud to the memory, the sound of the words echoed oddly by the displays curving around in front of him. If Telthorst expected Kosta to land on his face just to accommodate the Adjutor's preconceived notions, he could forget it.

The pep talk helped a little. A flashing light on his console reminded him that the cocoon's escape tunnel was still on standby; keying in the proper commands, he watched as the false asteroid sealed itself up again and then went inert. Briefly, he hoped *inert* meant exactly what it said, then put it out of his mind. Surely the masterminds behind this mission had understood that if the Empyreals came across a ship berth disguised as an asteroid it would be a dead giveaway that the Pax had slipped in a spy.

And with that chore out of the way, the ship was back on automatic, where it would remain until they reached Lorelei. Keying one of the displays for a continual status report on his course, Kosta returned to his reading. The data pack Lleshi had sent down to him was far more extensive than he'd expected, and it was going to be a bit of a push to get it all read in the five days before planetfall.

But he would manage it. If for no better reason than that Telthorst probably didn't think he could.

The cocoon remained inert for six hours more, until Kosta's ship had passed beyond any theoretical possibility of detecting a change in its status. Six hours of totally wasted time; but the vast network of computers and sensors and fabricators built deep inside the rock was patient, and its designers had considered it absolutely imperative that Kosta believe he had left nothing behind him but an empty shell.

Quietly, stealthily, the network activated itself and began to look around. Even without its inertial memory to guide it, the sensors would have had no difficulty locating the center of the net fields which had caught the *Komitadji*.

The hive of Empyreal ships buzzing around the area would have been all the indication it needed.

Quietly, stealthily, the sensors reached out, delicately probing and studying. It would take time—considerable time—for it to achieve its programmed goal.

But the network was patient.

CHAPTER 2

"Your attention, please," the cool, middle-class voice came over the spaceport softspeaker system. "The twelfth and final shuttle for the spaceliner *Xirrus* has now arrived at Gate Sixteen. All remaining passengers should come to the check-in counter at this time for pre-flight confirmation and boarding. Repeating: your attention, please—"

Seated at the far end of the waiting lounge, half hidden behind a large decorative vase, the girl hunched a little deeper into a contour chair that felt too large for her and watched as the last group of passengers gathered their things and walked over to join the line at the check-in counter. She brushed the freshly blonded hair carefully away from her face, feeling a familiar tightness squeezing her throat. In a minute she would have to get up and join them. And if Trilling Vail was watching from hiding, like she was . . .

She took a deep breath, an acid tightness swirling in her stomach. It was the same feeling she always got when she was getting ready to score a track and suddenly had the impression that the targ was onto her. The horrible demand of a crucial decision: whether to keep going, and hope her twitches were wrong, or to pop the cord, lose all the prep time, and look for a targ who would more easily part with his spare cash.

Should she pop the cord on this whole crazy idea? It still wasn't too late to do that, she knew. She could get up right now and walk out of the spaceport and try to bury herself somewhere on Uhuru instead of going off to a whole new world.

Only she couldn't. Trilling had friends everywhere on Uhuru. Sooner or later, he'd catch up with her. On Lorelei . . . well, at least she'd have a head start.

Maybe. Reaching into her pocket, feeling the same tingling in her fingertips that she always got when handling merchandise that had cost her blood and sweat to get hold of, she slid out the precious piece of threaded plastic. *Chandris Lalasha*, the name at the top said, and for probably the hundredth time she wished she had had the time and money to have a new ID made up. She hadn't used the Lalasha surname since she was thirteen, a year before she met and moved in with Trilling. But if he got into the spaceline data listings the *Chandris* part would be a dead giveaway.

She snorted to herself. *If* he got in, hell. *When* he got in. Trilling was the one who'd taught *her* how to crack into fancy computer systems. Her only chance was that he wouldn't expect her to do something this crazy, or at least that he wouldn't think she could get enough money together this quickly to spring for a spaceliner ticket.

But, then, who knew how Trilling's mind worked these days?

Unconsciously, Chandris tightened her grip on the plastic card. She'd heard a kosh brag once about how he'd killed someone with a spaceliner ticket. She wondered if any of that story had been true.

The line was beginning to shrink now, the passengers showing their tickets to the reader display and attendant and disappearing down the boarding tunnel. Chandris licked her lips, wincing at the unfamiliar tart/sweet taste of expensive lipglow, and got to her feet, heart thudding in her ears as she went over and joined the line. This was it; and it was Trilling's last chance to stop her. She'd sat over in that corner for four hours straight, watching every single batch of passengers as they headed down the tunnel, making sure that Trilling hadn't slipped aboard. If he didn't make this last shuttle she would be safe. At least for now.

She reached the reader and the attendant standing beside it. "Hello," the man greeted her. For just a second his eyes skipped down across her, taking in her bright blonded hair, her even brighter lipglow, her probably botched attempt at an upper-class outfit.

And when he looked back up she could sense his quiet amusement. "And you are . . . ?"

"Chandris Lalasha," she growled, thrusting her ticket at his face and then waving it over the reader.

"Nice to have you aboard, Miss Lalasha," he smiled. "You heading off to college?"

"That's right," Chandris said shortly. "On Lorelei." The reader pinged acceptance of her ticket, and she stuffed the plastic back into her pocket.

The attendant shook his head, a smile on his face. "Thought so. I never cease to be amazed at how inventive you college kids get with your travel outfits. Have a nice flight."

"Thanks," Chandris muttered, heading down the boarding tunnel and hoping the sudden heat in her cheeks didn't show. She'd done it again, damn it all—taken offense at an insult that wasn't even there. The same touchiness that had kept her stuck in the Barrio and out of the upper-class areas in New Mexico City where the really major tracks were. Or so Trilling had always told her—

The muscles in her back stiffened, mind suddenly snapping back to where she was. She twisted around, half expecting to see Trilling walking behind her, his shining eyes glowing, his scarred lips grinning their crazy animal grin at her.

But there were only a couple of last-minute passengers in sight, and no sound or commotion coming from the check-in counter around the corner.

She turned back, breathing again, and continued down the tunnel. At the end of it waited the shuttle, an oversized plane sort of thing with rows and rows of contour chairs. Choosing one that would allow her a clear view of the door, she let the straps curve into position around her and waited. Trilling's absolute last chance . . .

Five minutes later, the door was slammed shut with a dull thud . . . and as the shuttle rolled away from the terminal, she felt her muscles unknotting for the first time in hours. For the first time in months. Finally—finally—she could dare to hope that she was free of Trilling Vail.

And all it had cost was leaving the only home she'd ever known.

The trip up to the spaceliner took about an hour. An hour, for Chandris, of absolute magic.

She had ridden on a regular plane once before, but at the time had been too preoccupied with keeping inconspicuous to really appreciate it. Now, though, it was different. The wispy clouds breaking in front of the shuttle like white nothing; the buildings and hills and forests beneath them; the sensation of flying itself—she drank it all in, pressing her face tightly against the cold plastic of the window so as not to miss any of it. The ground kept receding, the highest clouds cutting off most of the view, and presently she noticed the deep blue of the sky above them was fading into black. The dull roar of the engines faded away to a throaty whisper, leaving her bouncing gently against her straps.

She spent the next few minutes with fists and teeth clenched tightly, fighting a gut-twisting nausea and a horrible feeling that she and the shuttle were falling back toward the ground. Then, strangely, both stomach and brain relaxed and she was able to concentrate again on the view outside her window. Overhead, stars were visible in the black sky, even though the sun could still be seen off to one side. She marveled at the novelty of that for a while, shifting her attention back and forth between sun and stars.

Presently, above and ahead of them, she got her first glimpse of the *Xirrus*.

It didn't look like much at first; a sort of toy or model, its shadowy shape outlined by strings of little lights. But as the shuttle kept getting closer, and the shape kept getting bigger, it finally dawned on her that calling a ship like that a flying city wasn't nearly as much puff-talk as she'd always thought.

Pressing her nose against the cold window, she smiled to herself. If there was one thing the Barrio had taught her, it was how to survive in a city.

They arrived at the *Xirrus* a few minutes later, to the accompaniment of a lot of clanking and the sudden return of weight. Joining the other passengers, she climbed a steep set of fold-down stairs through the roof of the shuttle and found herself in a large room with a huge layout diagram of the *Xirrus* covering one wall. Her ticket listed her cabin number; glancing once at the diagram to get its location, she headed toward the rear of the ship.

Her roommates were already there when she arrived: three of them, middle-class as all get out, chattering away about college and other middle-class things as they moved around the room stuffing lockers full of clothes and generally checking the place out. Silently, Chandris stepped through the activity toward the fourth bed, where her small suitcase had already been deposited, and the conversation waffled a little as the others checked her out. What they saw made the conversation waffle even more. "Nice travel outfit," one of them commented from behind her, the dry tone sparking umphs of not-quite giggles from her companions. "Design it yourself?"

Chandris turned to look her straight in the eye. "Sure," she said coolly. "Had to. It's one of the requirements."

The other seemed taken aback. "Requirements for what?" she asked.

"Where are you going to school?" Chandris countered.

"Uh—Ahanne University on Lorelei," the other said, looking even more confused.

Chandris shrugged. "Well, there you have it, then."

She turned back to her unpacking, watching their quiet confusion out of the corner of her eye and revising her class estimate downward a little. *Real* middle-class types—or at least the middle-class types she'd scored tracks on—would have dumped right away on that kind of skidly-talk. These puff-heads must be freshly moved up, smart enough to imitate middle-class mannerisms and speech but too dumb to really know what the hell they were doing.

For what she needed now, they would do nicely.

"Oh, come *on*, Kail," one of the others said into the silence, giving a little snort of derision. The proper reaction, Chandris thought scornfully, only about a year too late. "Look at her *luggage*, for gritty'sake. Probably paid for her ticket with table tips."

The third girl giggled. "Yeah," she said slyly. "Or else a more *personal* kind of service work."

She gave a warbling whistle, a pretty good imitation of the come-on hookers sometimes used in the Barrio, and all three laughed. "Girls, girls," the first admonished, her voice mock-severe. "I'm *sure* we've got her all wrong. I'll bet she's just *so* incredibly smart that she doesn't even *care* that she dresses like a sfudd. Probably gonna major in catalytic nuclear drive or politics or something equally frizzly."

Chandris kept quiet, fighting back the awful temptation to turn around and pull the little puff-head's face off by the roots. One of the girls whispered something else, eliciting another mass giggle, and the conversation resumed where it had left off. With Chandris pointedly excluded.

She stayed in the room another half hour, pretending to arrange and re-arrange her meager wardrobe in her locker and enduring the snide comments not quite directed her direction . . . and by the time she left, she had it down pat. All of it: every repetitious bit of slangy, every silly gesture, every bad joke, every word of gossip and school talk and clothes talk.

Everything that would let her pass herself off as one of them.

For a while she just wandered, poking around the edges of her section's public areas—dining rooms, lounges, recreation rooms and the like—and just generally getting a feel for the ship. The corridors themselves were pretty well deserted, most of the passengers who were out and about seated in the lounges getting a head start on their socializing. The delicate aromas of alcohol and other traditional reeks tugged at her, and more than once she was sorely tempted to join in and put off her exploring until morning. It wasn't like she was short on time—they'd told her when she bought the ticket that it would take the *Xirrus* six or seven days to get to Lorelei.

But she resisted the temptation. Long experience had taught her that mass confusion was the best cover for scoring tracks; and the day when twelve shut-tles ungorged themselves of new passengers was probably going to be as con-fused as things got up here.

Besides which, if she didn't get busy and make other arrangements, she was going to be stuck spending at least one night with those puff-headed snobs back in her room.

From the different sizes of staterooms and cabins that the big floorplan had shown, it had been pretty obvious that the upper-class sections were the ones furthest forward. Directly behind them had been a narrow blank area; be-hind that the middle-class cabins, another blank area, and finally Chandris's own lower-class section. Another blank area ran up through the core of the ship, connecting with the ones separating the passenger sections.

Blank areas on floorplans and maps were almost always worth checking out. Giving herself a quick orientation, she headed off toward the nearest to take a look.

It was surprisingly well hidden. There were no abrupt flat walls or red-lettered warnings anywhere advertising forbidden territory; nothing but smoothly curving corridors that kept passengers moving along in blissful ignorance that there was anything else lurking behind the scenes.

Without having seen the floorplan, it might have taken Chandris all of ten minutes to find a way in. With the floorplan, it took her two. Sometimes the tracks scored themselves.

She'd expected it to be either a section of crew quarters or else part of the *Xirrus*'s functional areas. It was, in fact, a combination of the two: a large room filled with machinery and pipes and bundles of wires, but with a pair of short door-lined corridors leading off of it. A handful of men and women were visible scattered around the room, moving around the machines or sitting at consoles, their conversation masked by the dull hum that seemed to come from everywhere at once.

For a moment Chandris watched the activity, gauging her chances of getting past them without being seen. If she could, it ought to give her a way into the middle- and upper-class sections without having to use the usual connecting passageways. That could be useful, especially as the passageways had probably been designed to keep nowies like her back here where they belonged.

It was worth a try, anyway. Keeping close to the wall, trying to watch all the workers at once, she started forward.

"You, there—miss?"

Chandris's heart skipped a beat; but her face was all innocence as she turned around to face the man walking toward her. About forty, she estimated his age, with an open, unsuspicious kind of face. "Yes?" she said.

"Sorry, miss, but passengers aren't allowed in here," he said. "This part of the ship is for crewers only."

"Oh," Chandris said, letting her face fall a little. Not the kind of man who'd accept a sexual advance, she decided, at least not from a sixteen-year-old girl. But he might fall for the right mix of kid sister and eager student. "I'm sorry," she said, face and voice in her newly acquired middle-class college student role. "I just thought that—well, you see, I'm going to be studying catalytic nuclear drive in college and—" she waved at the room with a self-conscious shrug— "well, I just wanted to see what it was like in here."

Dead center score. His eyes widened, just noticeably, and when he spoke there was a new admiration in his voice. "You're kidding. Really? Which college are you going to?"

"Ahanne University on Lorelei," she told him, watching his face closely. His forehead seemed on the edge of wrinkling—"At least to start with," she added before he could say anything. "I'm hoping to transfer somewhere else after a couple of years."

"I'd hope so," he said with a little snort. "Ahanne's starship engineering program isn't worth beansprouts. You'll want to do your last two years at either Lanslant University or else Dar Korrati on Balmoral."

"I tried to get into Dar Korrati," Chandris said. "But they said the only scholarships they had left were for transfer students with high enough grades." She gazed into his face for a split second, then looked down, letting her shoulders sag slightly. "It's kind of scary," she confessed.

"Yeah," he agreed, and she could hear the sympathy in his voice. She held her pose, waiting for him to flip his mental coin . . . "Well, look, I guess it'd be okay, just this once. Come on—I'll give you a quick tour."

She gushed some appropriate words of thanks and then shut up, letting him do all the talking as he led her around the room, pointing out this and that and gabbing about a lot of stuff that made no sense whatsoever. But that was okay. Every word he said was going into her general mental grab bag of useful information, maybe to be pulled out someday.

"—but since they decay within a few microseconds, we have to keep making new ones," he commented as they passed an untended console. "The actual equipment is a little further forward, but we've got a monitor here to keep tabs on it." He pointed to a free-standing display a few meters away.

"I see," Chandris said; but her eyes were on the console right beside her. Lying on top of it, looking as if it had been casually dropped there by someone with more urgent things on his mind, was a flat plate that looked like a hand computer. Worth maybe a couple hundred on the open market . . . and she was going to be hitting Lorelei flat broke. "Which one of those lines is the actual production rate?" she asked her guide, gesturing toward the distant display.

"The blue one on top is flux rate," he said, pointing. "Red is particle temperature, green is interface transfer, and that heavy black line shows the confinement profile. Now, this thing over here . . ."

Taking her upper arm in a big-brotherly sort of way, he led her toward yet another giant incomprehensible machine. It was, Chandris reflected, just as well she hadn't tried a sexual approach on this one. A hand around her waist, instead of on her arm, would hardly have failed to notice the hard lump that had suddenly appeared hidden beneath the waistband of her skirt.

In all the tour took nearly twenty minutes. When it was over Chandris thanked the engineer profusely, let him escort her back through the door to the lower-class section, and said a warm and grateful good-bye.

Two minutes later she was back, slipping in through a second entrance she'd spotted across the room during the tour. Hidden from view of the crewers by a long thick pipe he'd called a catalytic-balance slifter, she made her way forward. The other end of the room opened onto a short corridor lined with unlocked doors; choosing one, she went inside.

The room was small and, inevitably, filled to the ceiling with equipment—pipes and pumping sorts of stuff this time. Turning on the dim overhead light, she pulled out her newly acquired toy and sat down cross-legged on the floor to take a closer look.

It was a hand computer, all right. An expensive one, too, from the look of it. She turned it over—

"Nurk it," she muttered to herself. Stamped into the back of the casing was the *Xirrus*'s logo. A ship's computer, then, tied into the *Xirrus*'s central nexus and hard-programmed only with ship's data and business. On the open market, worth just fractionally above zero.

For a moment she glared at the flat little plate, letting her annoyance at it subside. It wouldn't have brought in *that* much money; and anyway, it would probably have taken her forever to locate a safe buyer in an unfamiliar market. Besides, it wasn't like the thing was *completely* useless.

It took her a minute to locate a wall power plate, and another minute to pry the back off the computer with her little pocket multi-knife. The computer's ID register . . . there it was. Snapping out two of the knife's blades and the specially insulated screwdriver, she eased one of the blades into the lowest voltage socket on the plate and brought the computer's ID register up to lightly touch the other blade. There was a small spark, hardly visible; carefully, she shifted the knife point to two other spots on the instrument, with similar results. She gave it a quick examination, then pulled the blade from the socket and folded the knife back up. Assuming she'd done it right, the computer would now still have full access to the ship's central nexus, but the nexus wouldn't be able to either identify the particular computer she was using or to keep any record of which files she pulled up.

It was a trick that for years she'd had to pay Trilling or someone else to do for her. One day he'd foolishly let her watch.

She replaced the back cover and keyed the computer on. First on her list of things to do was to pull up a set of the *Xirrus*'s floorplans—a *real* set, including all the crew and equipment areas. She leafed through them, memorizing each with a glance, and by the time she was through she'd found half a dozen ways to get from one end of the ship to the other without anyone having a ghost's chance of spotting her.

Second on her list was to find a place to stay, preferably one that would be a step up from her present cabin and roommates. Hunting around a little, she found a passenger accommodations list, which after a little study yielded the information that there were sixteen empty cabins on the ship, three of them fancy staterooms in the upper-class section. A crewer roster was next, with particular attention given to which servitors were on duty at the moment and which cabins they were assigned to.

And finally came the triskiest part: coaxing the nexus to give her the general passcode for servitor entry into the passenger rooms.

It took awhile, but the people who'd set up the *Xirrus*'s security hadn't been very bright. In the end, she got it.

And that was that. She could return the computer now, her tampering a cinch to be missed until long after she disappeared into the barrios of Lorelei. And in the meantime she could mingle with the people in the upper-class section whenever she liked, scoring whatever tracks she could. Preferably with people who wouldn't be stopping at Lorelei; if they didn't notice their losses until afterwards, it would take that much longer for them to howl the police onto her tail.

On idle impulse, she keyed the computer for the *Xirrus*'s itinerary. Not that it really mattered; but the next stop after Lorelei was—

Seraph system.

She stared at the display, stomach suddenly fluttering. Seraph system. The place where angels came from.

She leaned against the wall, watching all her neat plans twisting themselves into skidly-talk with new possibilities. Angels. Things only politicians and rich people could get—she remembered a news story once that had talked about them, with a big security type from the Gabriel Corporation opening up a box and handing over a chain and pendant to a High Senator type, who turned around and put it around another High Senator type's neck. The chain had looked pretty classy, at least from the one close-up she'd seen, and she remembered trying to sit down and watch more. But then Trilling had started yelling about something, and she'd yelled back, and somehow she'd never gotten around to finding out more.

But the angels came from Seraph system—that much everyone knew. They were made out in space by something called Angelmass, and a whole bunch of little ships went out there every day to bring them back.

Little ships. With little crews . . .

Don't be stupid, she growled at herself. They'd been turning out angels for years. By now they must have filled in every single gap in their security.

But if they hadn't, and if she could somehow crack into the system . . .

She rubbed her finger over her lower lip, stomach acid swirling again with indecision. It might be a total waste of time, sure; but even if scoring an angel turned out to be a popped cord it might still be worth continuing on to Seraph just to throw Trilling that much farther off her trail. And it would be easy enough to do. With the stuff she'd already pulled out of the computer—

The thought stopped short. The computer, whose circuits she'd just scorched, secure in the knowledge that no one was likely to notice for the six or seven days till they got to Lorelei.

But if she continued on to Seraph, which the computer said would take another five or six days after that . . .

She smiled tightly. *No one ever gets anywhere if they never take chances.* Trilling had said that a lot, usually when puffing some particularly trisky job he wanted her to do. But even Trilling was right sometimes. And if she really *could* pull this off . . .

Abruptly, she got to her feet. First thing would be to get the computer back without being seen. Not necessarily to the same spot; people never remembered where they left things, and in a place like this they'd probably assume someone else had borrowed it.

And after that, it would be time to rearrange her accommodations. Before, getting access to the upper-class section had just been something she wanted to do. Now, it was something she *needed* to do.

Trilling had always said that her touchiness would never let her fit in with upper-class society. She was about to find out if that was true.

CHAPTER 3

Chandris's goal when putting her outfit together had been to try and end up with something that would look upper-class without costing money she didn't have. She'd been rather pleased with the results, or at least she had been until those puff-heads back in her lower-class cabin had started giggling.

A single pass by one of the upper-class lounges showed her why they'd giggled.

It was a humiliating moment, not to mention a dangerous one. Luckily, it was also very quickly over. A really good look at the expensive outfits wasn't necessary; all she needed this time through was to get the style of uniform worn by servitors in this section. That knowledge in hand, she slipped back through the nearest crewer door and made her way down to the maids' quarters. With the work schedule and cabin assignment information she'd read off the computer, it was simple enough to locate an unoccupied room. One of the general passcodes got her inside, and she began her search.

There were, as she'd expected, several different types of uniforms for the different parts of the ship, and she had to raid a dozen rooms before she found a maid's uniform that was both the right style and the right size. Fifteen minutes later, having changed in a conveniently isolated emergency-battery room, she returned to the upper-class section.

No one gave her a second look as she slipped silently past wandering and chattering passengers; very few gave her even a first look. It was the perfect camouflage, particularly for someone like Chandris, who had played the role so many times before that she had the mental attitude and body language of a servant down cold. Even in operations a lot smaller than a spaceliner, she'd sometimes blended into the identity so well that other workers had totally missed the fact that she was a stranger. On a ship this size, assuming she was careful, they didn't have a hope of fingering her.

She reached one of the empty staterooms without incident and let herself in. The place wasn't as flat-out luxurious, somehow, as she'd expected it to be, but it stomped the snot out of her own cramped cabin. More important to her plans at the moment was the fancy computer system built into the entertainment center, a system that should give her access to the ship's public library. Pulling out her pocket knife, she stepped over to it—

And stopped short. "Nurk," she muttered. She'd expected it to be a floating nexus-connect type like the hand-held job she'd used earlier. Instead, it was hard-wired in through the entertainment lines.

Which pretty much popped the cord on the uncoupling trick she'd used earlier. If she wanted to get into the library without the computer howling up a stink, she was going to have to do it from a room that wasn't supposed to be vacant.

Mentally, she shrugged. No big deal—she'd planned on mingling with the paying passengers anyway. It was high time she got started.

The room had been fully made up, with an impressive selection of fluffy towels laid out in the bathroom. Taking two of the larger ones, she folded and stacked them for carrying and slipped out of the room. Given the crowd in the lounge she'd passed earlier, it seemed likely that most of the rooms along here would be vacant. An ideal time to go shopping.

It was a more difficult search than the hunt for her maid's uniform had been. Not only did she have to find clothes that would fit her, she also had to find them in closets so bulging that there would be a good chance the owner would never notice the loss. Upper-class people, she'd always heard, were so rich that they threw their money away on everything they saw. Unfortunately, the image didn't seem to apply to spaceliner passengers. Up and down the corridors she went, hitting stateroom after stateroom: knocking, apologizing about having the wrong room if there was an answer, letting herself in if there wasn't. And she was just about to concede defeat and move down to the middle-class section when she finally scored.

It was a huge room, easily twice the size of the vacant one she'd moved into an hour earlier. With twice the storage space, too; and every bit of it stuffed to the throat. A family of five, judging from the various sizes represented, with the teenage daughter taking more than her fair share of the closet space. Chandris sorted through the dresses, chose two of the plainest layer-style ones, and folded them up inside her towels. An equally bulging jewelry box beckoned from the top of one of the dressers, and for a moment she was tempted. But only for a moment. An upper-class teen might not miss a dress or two; but *everyone* kept tabs on their jewelry.

She took the dresses back to her borrowed room, added a third towel to her pile, and returned to the hunt. Her newly changed luck held: the very next stateroom she tried contained not only too many dresses, but too many shoes as well. Neither set was exactly her size, but close enough. Again selecting a layer-style dress, she hid it and a pair of shoes inside her stack of towels and went back to her room.

There, using her knife and the compact sewing kit she'd brought from her luggage, she set to work stripping the various layers of the dresses apart.

There'd been a girl from the Barrio once who'd swiped a fancy outfit during a score and gotten cracked two days later when the original owner spotted her wearing it on the street, and Chandris had no intention of doing something that puff-headed herself. The alterations took her nearly two hours; but when she was finished she had combined parts from the three dresses to form three entirely new and—hopefully—unrecognizable ones.

Altering herself was next. First step was to get the damn blonding out of her hair, returning it to its natural shiny black. She cleaned her face and hands next, getting rid of both the cosmetic stuff and the underbase that had lightened her skin into line with the blonded hair. Redoing the makeup was easy enough—from what she'd seen, the upper-class women aboard the *Xirrus* used far less makeup than was common among middle-class or even Barrio women. Possibly because they didn't need to try and make themselves attractive; more likely because they could afford to go with cosmetic surgery instead. Still, as Trilling used to say, vanity had its uses, provided it was in other people.

Redoing her hair was a little harder. Most of the women she'd seen while hunting for clothes had been pretty free with the frostsprays, fancy holdings, and jeweled clips, none of which Chandris had available even if she'd known how to fasten them in. Fortunately, she'd also spotted a few who had simply put their hair into elaborate braidings, and she'd passed close enough to one of them to get a good look at the pattern. Actually recreating it was trickier than she'd expected, but with persistence and several false starts she finally got it more or less right.

And now came the easy part. Giving herself a careful examination in the long foyer mirror, she keyed off the lights and left the stateroom. With the outer woman transformed from lower-class scorer to upper-class leech, it was time to do the same for the inner woman.

Earlier, she'd given herself a leisurely half hour to learn how to play a newly middle-class college student. Now, wandering between the various upper-class lounges, she had her new role down in half that time. Part of that was sheer necessity—she hadn't eaten since late morning, and was starting to feel the familiar pangs of hunger—but mostly it was that the mannerisms of these people were genuinely less complicated. Perhaps, she thought once, their money and power did their talking for them.

A fresh rumble ran through her stomach; but fortunately the solution was already close at hand. He was hovering not quite obviously at the edge of her vision, and had been there since the second of the lounges she had visited. Around fifty years old, he was wearing an expensive-looking jacket and jeweled neck clasp and the look of a man on the hunt.

Under other circumstances she would probably have let him make the first move. With her stomach starting to hurt, she wasn't in the mood to be patient. Drifting toward him, her eyes turned elsewhere, she shifted direction with smooth suddenness and bumped gently into him. "Oh!—excuse me," she said, looking up into his eyes. "That wasn't very graceful of me, was it?"

"Don't worry about it," he said, smiling a hunter's smile back at her. "Spaceliner travel does that all the time to people. Shifting engine thrusts throw the pseudogravity off, and all."

She raised her eyebrows fractionally and returned the smile. "You sound like someone who travels a lot."

It was an obvious setup line, and he grabbed it with both hands. "More than I wish, sometimes," he said. "My company's headquartered on Seraph, but we're also heavily involved in Lorelei asteroid mining and Balmoral orbital refining. Makes for a busy schedule. Stardust Metals—you might possibly have heard of us."

"Don't be modest," she chided gently. "Of course I've heard of you." She hadn't, actually, until she'd caught a passing reference ten minutes earlier. But he didn't need to know that. "And what is it you do for them?"

He grinned, the hunter's smile again. "Mostly try to keep them as profitable as possible," he said, offering his hand. "I'm Amberson Toomes; part owner and CMD."

She raised her eyebrows, higher this time. "Really!" she said, wondering what the hell a CMD was. "I'm impressed."

He shrugged modestly. "Don't be. Most of the people here are considerably more important than I am."

"If importance is judged by how well you ignore strangers, they're definitely more important than you," she said ruefully, dropping her eyes a bit. "I've been walking around for—oh, I don't know how long—and you're the first person who's bothered to speak with me."

He patted her shoulder. "Don't judge them by first night out," he warned. "Anyway, you haven't exactly been working hard to elbow your way into conversations."

She let her lip twitch in a coquettish smile. "And how would you know that?" she challenged. "Unless you'd been watching me, that is."

He smiled back. "I might have noticed you," he acknowledged. "But only because I happen to like looking at beautiful women."

"Flatterer."

"Connoisseur," he corrected with a slight bow.

She laughed. "My name's Chandris Adriessa," she told him. "I don't suppose that in and around all that looking you happened to find the dining room?"

"I did indeed," he said, gently but firmly taking her arm. Not big-brotherly, like the engineer had, but like a hunter who's caught his prey. "All six of them, in fact. Come; I'll show you which one's the best."

He insisted from the start on charging her dinner to his bill, a gallantry she accepted with a maximum of verbal gratitude and a minimum of token protest. The issue had never been in doubt, of course; no one at this end of the ship seemed to use money or cards, and she could hardly charge her meal to an unoccupied stateroom. But by making the offer up front he saved her the trouble of maneuvering him into doing so later.

The food was good enough, though not as filling as she might have wished. As they ate she worked at getting her companion talking about himself, with an eye toward filling in some of her ignorance about upper-class life.

No hard task, as it turned out. Toomes was a braggart—a refined and cultured braggart, but a braggart just the same—and after the first couple of questions all Chandris had to do was listen and nod and act fascinated by it all. By the time he remembered his manners and began asking her about herself, she had everything she needed to puff him a convincing spider web of lies, right down to a convoluted story about how her parents' manufacturing firm on Uhuru had made enough the past year on superconductor contracts to send her to college on Seraph.

Not that he was in any shape to notice small slips anyway. It was clear even before they got to the dining room that Toomes had gotten an early start on the *Xirrus*'s supply of reeks, giving him a slight mental haze that the alcoholic drinks he'd washed his dinner down with had made even hazier. It was a personality type Chandris had had more than her fill of back in the Barrio: men who measured themselves by how much they could drink or sniff or swallow before their brains were so nurked they couldn't see straight.

She'd lost track of how many evenings Trilling and his friends had ruined for her with those stupid contests of theirs. It was only fair that, just this once, it should work to her advantage.

And so she talked, and listened, and kept the floaters and relaxers and drinks coming; and by the time they headed back to his stateroom he needed to hold onto her arm to keep upright. She got the door unlocked and maneuvered him to the bed, sitting him down there and helping him off with his jacket and neck clasp.

He was fumbling with the fasteners on her dress when he fell asleep.

She took his shoes off and, with some effort, managed to get him straightened out on the bed. For a moment she considered stripping him all the way down, then decided against it. If he woke up thinking he'd already scored he might drop her back at square one and go looking for someone more challenging. Better to keep him dangling, at least for another day or two, before considering any alterations to the script.

Kicking off her own ill-fitting shoes, she snared a chair and pulled it over to the room's computer terminal. A minute later she'd pulled up the *Xirrus* library's complete index of articles pertaining to spaceship operation. With Toomes snoring gently behind her, she called up the first article on the list and began to read.

CHAPTER 4

"... But first I'd like to clear up any questions about how I see this new job you're sending me off to do. The first duty of a High Senator, it seems to me, is to the whole Empyrean. Not one district or another, not even one world or another; but to all the people."

The man on the screen paused, and Arkin Forsythe took a moment to let his eyes trace out the other's face. A care-lined, middle-aged face, with receding sandy hair, blue-gray eyes, and an oddly intense set to the square jaw. A serious face; a face whose strong aura of professionalism formed a perfect counterpoint to the casual, common-man pattern of his speech. A face that would inspire loyalty in some and contempt in others, but nothing in between.

Across the room, there was a knock on the door. "Come," Forsythe called, tapping the freeze button and looking up. The door opened, to reveal Ranjh Pirbazari. "Have you a minute, High Senator-elect?"

"Sure, Zar, come on in," Forsythe waved him over, noting the data cyl in the other's hand. "What have we got?"

"The official follow-up report on that Pax incursion out in the belt three days ago," Pirbazari told him, crossing to Forsythe's desk and handing him the cyl. "They've done some more analyses of the ship and the battle, but there's nothing really new in the way of fresh data. They were able to pull a name off the bow, though: the *Komitadji*. It was the name of some guerrilla or mercenary group in the Balkans, I'm told, sometime in Earth's distant past."

"Mm," Forsythe said, eyeing the slender cylinder distastefully. Official follow-up reports, in his experience, were nearly always a waste of time for everyone concerned. "Any fresh excuses as to why it took them so long to kick the damn thing out of the system?"

Pirbazari shook his head. "They still say the catapult simply wasn't designed for anything that big, and that it took them that long to recalibrate." He hesitated. "I'd have to say, though, that that's probably more an explanation than it is an excuse. There's really no way anyone could have anticipated the Pax having a warship that big. Certainly they never showed anything even approaching that size during the contact negotiations. From everything I've read about the incident, EmDef did as well as could be expected under the circumstances."

Forsythe nodded, still not happy but experienced enough to recognize a dead-end when he found himself driving down one. Finding tails to pin the blame on was standard political instinct; but Pirbazari had twenty years of Empyreal Defense Force service under his belt, and if he said they'd done all they could then they probably had. "Subject closed then, I guess," he grunted. "Any fresh ideas as to what the Pax was trying to prove with this stunt?"

Pirbazari shrugged. "Number one theory is still that they've decided to escalate their little psychological pinprick campaign and wanted to see what kind of reception they could expect if they sent in a warship and started shooting. Second place goes to the possibility that they wanted to map out the net's physical configuration and figured that using a ship outside our normal catapult range would buy them more time to study it."

"Or maybe they wanted to drop something and hoped all the noise and smoke would hide it?"

"If they did, it worked," Pirbazari said dryly. "EmDef had ships quartering the area for several hours afterward and none of them picked up anything but normal asteroids. If anything *was* dropped, it had to have been pretty small."

"Or else shielded like crazy," Forsythe said.

"True," Pirbazari agreed. "Still, we're talking an awful lot of trouble and risk just to smuggle in a spy or two. Especially given that they've already got either a spy or data-sifter system in place here already."

Forsythe nodded sourly. "One at the very least. I don't suppose there's anything new on that data-pulse transmission?"

"Only that the timing of the pulse, with the *Komitadji* 'pulting in just in time to intercept it, meant they had the whole thing carefully planned out," Pirbazari said.

"Still no idea where on Lorelei the pulse originated?"

"No," Pirbazari conceded. "And if they haven't been able to backtrack it by now, they never will. Whatever this phase-and-relay scheme is the Pax is using, it's a real charmer."

"It ought to be," Forsythe growled. "They had five months to set it up before we kicked them out. For all we know they could have smuggled in an entire fifth column."

"Yes, sir," Pirbazari murmured.

Forsythe eyed him, noted the quiet battle of current and former loyalties in his expression. "I'm not blaming EmDef for that," he told the other. "It wasn't their fault that we had Pax ships and people swarming all over the place. The High Senate had no business holding those useless talks in Empyreal space in the first place. They should have insisted on neutral ground."

Pirbazari's face cleared, loyalties back in line again. "None of us liked it very much either," he admitted. "I have to say, though, that I really don't think more than a handful of Pax spies could have gotten past us."

"A handful could be enough." Forsythe looked at the cyl still in his hand, set it down on the desk. "Well, I'll take a look later. For whatever it's worth."

"Yes, sir." Pirbazari nodded to Forsythe's left. "Your father?"

Forsythe looked over at the still-frozen image on the screen. "Yes. His spaceport speech, the day he left Lorelei to take his own High Senate seat."

"I remember that day," Pirbazari mused. "My parents watched the speech at home, my father grumping the whole time about how he was going to make a hash of the job."

Forsythe snorted gently. "A confident sort, wasn't he?"

"Yes, sir," Pirbazari said. "But he was wrong about a lot of other things, too."

Forsythe smiled, feeling the bittersweet tang of memory in his throat. "He was an expert politician," he said, more to himself than to Pirbazari. "A lot of people never understood that, or else never believed it. But he was. He understood the checks and balances that make a government function—understood them better than anyone I've ever known. He knew that you had to make trades and deals and compromises if you wanted to get things done. And he *got* things done."

For a moment the room was silent, and Forsythe could almost see his father standing there in front of him. Laughing and joking one minute, teaching him some little secret of politics the next. "Speaking of speeches," Pirbazari said into the quiet, "you're scheduled for a broadcast in half an hour. Shall I go down to the studio and make sure everything's ready?"

The vision faded, and his father was once again just an image on a display screen. "No," Forsythe said. "I'd rather you go take another stab at talking EmDef into doing that landing check we asked for. If the Pax ship *did* drop a spy, he's got to come down sometime."

"Yes, sir," Pirbazari said, his tone markedly less than enthusiastic.

"I know it's probably a waste of time," Forsythe agreed with the other's unspoken thought. "I've already had it politely explained to me that EmDef hasn't got the manpower to sand-sift all the mining and cargo ships buzzing around Lorelei system. But if we nag them enough they may agree to at least a partial check. If only to get us off their backs."

Pirbazari smiled faintly. "It's nice to work for someone who understands how people operate, sir. What about the studio prep?"

"Ronyon can do that," Forsythe told him, picking up his call stick and tapping Ronyon's button three times. "Let me know how it goes with EmDef."

"Yes, sir." With a little bow, Pirbazari turned with military precision and left the room.

Forsythe looked back at the display, his frustration with EmDef shading—as frustrations always seemed to do these days—into an echo of old bitterness. Yes, he understood how people operated; but then, he'd learned about people and politics from a master. A man so able and competent at working through the system that by the end of his second term he was already being called the most effective High Senator Lorelei had ever sent to Uhuru.

And then, without warning, the system had been pulled out from under him.

His father had fought it, of course. Had argued long and hard that the newly discovered angels were far too incompletely understood to be loosed on anyone, let alone those men and women most directly responsible for the Empyrean's well-being. But the reformers were too strong, the optimism too soaring, and the tales of rampant political dishonesty and greed too deeply entrenched in popular mythology. The public clamor for the Angel Experiment had grown steadily louder . . . and as it did, all those who had originally opposed the plan quietly melted to the other side. Even the media, who normally salivated over the slightest hint of a controversy, just as quietly mutated into an Empyrean-wide cheering squad for the experiment.

Until, at the end, his father had stood alone. And when they'd handed him his angel, he'd handed it back. Along with his resignation.

It was the last hard, no-win decision of his political career. Perhaps the last hard, no-win decision that had been made in the High Senate chambers in the eighteen years since then.

Few people seemed to have noticed that. But Forsythe had; and this whole net-and-catapult method of dealing with the Pax's increasingly impatient thrusts into Empyreal territory was just the latest example of the High Senate's collective vagueness. It was all very well to claim, as they frequently did, that the Pax mentality was one of conquest instead of destruction; that it would prefer to absorb the Empyrean as it had all the other far-flung Earth colonies that had been sent out over the past three hundred years. It was a reasonable assessment, as far as it went.

But to then assume that such territorial ambitions would be discouraged simply by having some of their ships 'pulted away and trapped out in space for a few months was naive in the extreme. The only way to stop a bully was to give him a bloody nose.

And the perfect chance to do just that had been sitting in Lorelei system three days ago. A tiny change in the catapult vector, and that huge Pax warship could have been sent straight through the center of a star and been gone forever. A serious bloody nose, indeed.

But the High Senators who wrote EmDef's policies wore angels around their necks, as did the local commanders who carried those policies out . . . and men who wore angels never lowered themselves to something as crude as killing.

So they had taken their time, and done their calculations carefully, and sent the Pax warship somewhere where it would be safe. Someday, it would be back.

But before then, Forsythe would be a High Senator himself. A High Senator, with an angel of his own hanging around his neck.

Or perhaps not.

There was a diffident tap on the door. "Come," Forsythe called.

There was no response. Forsythe looked up, annoyed; and then it clicked, and he reached over to his call stick and tapped Ronyon's button twice. The door opened, and the big man came almost shyly into the room. His thick fingers traced patterns in the air—*You want me, Mr. Forsythe?*

Yes, Forsythe signed back. Deaf since birth, Ronyon could read lips reasonably well, but one of Forsythe's standing rules was that his inner circle use hand-sign language with Ronyon whenever possible. Like all skills, signing went rusty with disuse, and Forsythe didn't want his people losing this particular ability. It was often very handy to be able to hold a private conversation across a crowded room. *I'm going to be giving a speech in half an hour,* he told the other, *and I want you to go down to the studio and make sure everything's ready. Can you do that?*

Ronyon's droopy eyes widened, his slightly slack lips curving into a smile that was pure puppy-dog eager. *Yes, Mr. Forsythe, yes,* he signed, his fingers moving excitedly. *You mean all by myself?*

Forsythe suppressed a smile. *Yes, Ronyon, all by yourself,* he answered. It was one of the few stable points in the otherwise shifting ground of Forsythe's world: no matter how simple or menial the job, you could always count on Ronyon to jump on it with all the enthusiasm his eight-year-old-child's mind could generate.

And that was a *lot* of enthusiasm. No one had ever figured out whether it was the task itself that excited him so much, or the more subtle concept of having been entrusted to do something right. *Mr. Mils is down there now,* Forsythe continued. *You know how everything is supposed to be, right?*

Ronyon nodded. *I can do it,* he signed, the child's eagerness changing into a child's determination. *I can.*

I know, Forsythe signed, and meant it. Unlike many of the more "mature" personalities he'd dealt with over the years, Ronyon had none of that particularly infuriating brand of false pride that kept a person from admitting when he was in over his head. As a general rule, if you sent Ronyon to do a job and didn't hear anything further from him, you could assume it would get done right. *Better head downstairs, then. We can't keep the people of Lorelei waiting.*

Yes, Mr. Forsythe. With one last happy smile, Ronyon turned and hurried out.

There were still occasional quiet moments when Forsythe wondered why he had kept Ronyon on. Big and bulky, with a face that was considerably less than photogenic and the mind of a child lurking behind it, Ronyon was hardly someone who fit the usual image of a politician's inner circle. Originally, it had been little more than a symbolic gesture on Forsythe's part: the big important planetary representative taking the time and effort to reach out to those even modern medicine couldn't do anything to help. As a campaign ploy it had been remarkably successful, despite the loud denouncements from critics who'd proclaimed it to be nothing but shameless emotional manipulation. He'd gone on to win that election, and had never lost one since.

But that had been over fifteen years ago. Why, then, was Ronyon still around?

Shrugging to himself, Forsythe keyed his intercom. "Mils here," a familiar voice answered.

"This is Forsythe. How are things going?"

"Just doing the final lighting checks, High Senator–elect," the other replied, sounding his usual harried self. "We'll be ready in five minutes."

"I hope so," Forsythe warned. "Because I've just sent Ronyon down to make sure you're doing your job right."

Mils chuckled. "Well, we'd better get cracking, then," he said, mock-serious. Mock-serious, but with noticeably less tension in his voice than had been there a moment earlier. "I wouldn't want him mad at us."

"I should say not," Forsythe agreed. "I'll be down shortly."

He shut the intercom off. Perhaps that was it, he thought: the fact that Ronyon *was* so out of place here. With his childlike enthusiasm and loyalty he was like a gentle breeze blowing through the stagnant sewer gas that so often seemed to be the essence of politics. His father, Forsythe remembered vividly, had utilized that sharp sense of humor of his to break the tension that so often threatened to overwhelm himself and his inner circle. Perhaps Forsythe's subconscious had compensated for his own lack of that particular gift by hiring Ronyon.

For a moment he gazed at the image of his father still frozen on the display, a fresh swell of an old determination flowing through him. Once, a

Forsythe had resigned from the High Senate rather than accept the mind-numbing influence of an angel. With ingenuity, and a little luck, perhaps this Forsythe could have it both ways . . . and in the process prove to everyone that his father's warnings had been right all the time.

Switching off the display, he gathered his notes and headed for the door. The people of Lorelei were waiting.

CHAPTER 5

"That's good wine," Chandris said, watching closely as Toomes picked up the oddly shaped bottle—a caraffa, he'd called it—and poured a little more into her glass. His hand, she saw, wasn't shaking yet; but it *did* take him just a shade too long to get the bottle lined up properly on her glass. A bit more encouragement on her part, and it would soon be safe to let him take her back to his stateroom. "Very sweet and mild," she continued, sipping at her glass. "You really ought to try some."

He smiled lopsidedly at her. "It may be a little out of fashion, my dear," he said, "but in my humble opinion Guliyo wines are strictly for young ladies like yourself. *This*—" he raised his glass— "is the proper drink for a proper man."

"Oh, I didn't mean to suggest it wasn't," Chandris said, smiling back. "I *certainly* didn't mean," she added in a lower, more sultry voice, "that you were somehow less than a real man. I know better than *that*."

He grinned, his old hunter's smile combined with a sort of smug satisfaction as he reached across the table to lay his hand on top of hers. Chandris let him stroke it, continuing to smile on the outside even as she fought back a sudden nervous shudder on the inside. If Toomes ever suspected she'd been scoring him for a fool the whole time, or that his entire sexual performance with her these past two weeks had consisted of pawing her clothes off and then falling into a reek-induced stupor . . .

Stop it, she ordered herself harshly. Of course he didn't know—how could he? Besides, he'd hardly have continued throwing money away on her this whole time if he had any memories that contradicted the coy but admiring hints she always dropped the next morning about his supposed performance. Nerves—that was all it was. Nerves, and maybe the fact that she'd never done anything like this before. Quick zippers had always been her score: a few hours with the track, maybe a day or two at the most, then a fast chop and hop. Scoring the same track for two weeks straight had been a lot harder than she'd ever imagined it would be.

But it was almost over. Just one more night to endure, and tomorrow the *Xirrus* would reach Seraph. She'd ride a shuttle down with Toomes, give him one final kiss good-bye, and that would be the end of it. Chop and hop.

With her free hand she picked up her wine glass; and as she lifted it her gaze drifted across the dining room behind Toomes—

She froze. Four tables over, *that man* was being seated.

The sip of wine went down the wrong way, and for a minute her body shook as she fought to clear her lungs without a loud coughing fit. "Chandris?" Toomes frowned, tightening his grip on her hand. "You all right?"

She nodded, still coughing silently, furious at herself for doing something so stupid. Between spasms she threw another quick glance at the other table, wondering if he was watching.

He was. As he had been, off and on, for the past week.

He'd come aboard at Lorelei, and as far as she'd been able to tell had kept pretty much to himself. Nothing much to look at; a couple of centimeters taller than her, if that much, with dark hair and eyes. He was a few years older, too, probably somewhere in his early twenties. And if it hadn't been for one small problem she would probably have joined with everyone else in not giving him a second thought.

The problem being that, like her, he didn't belong here.

He wasn't nearly as good at faking it as she was, either. She'd seen him make lots of mistakes, mistakes she'd learned to avoid her first day in this part of the ship. Little things, most of them, but stuff that any really upper-class person would know without having to think about them.

She'd taken to watching him. And found that he, in turn, seemed to be watching her.

Ship's security, she'd thought at first, looking for a passenger named Chandris Lalasha who hadn't gotten off at Lorelei like she was supposed to. It had seemed the most likely explanation, particularly since she couldn't find any way to check up on her attempts to erase that identity from the *Xirrus*'s computer. As a result, she'd wound up wasting several hours of precious late-night study time in Toomes's room setting up contingency hiding and escape plans.

But the days had gone by, and the mystery man had continued to keep his distance. In fact . . .

Deliberately, she looked at him. For an instant their eyes met, before he wrenched his gaze back to the menu and pretended mightily that he hadn't been looking at her at all.

Chandris looked back at Toomes, a hard knot settling into her stomach. He was probably just new to the upper class, that was all. New to the upper class, interested in her, and too bashful to breathe straight. That was probably it. Really it was.

But the knot refused to go away.

Abruptly, she drained her wine and stood up. "Can we go now?" she asked Toomes.

A flicker of surprise, then the hunter's smile was back. "Sure," he said, polishing off his own drink and getting to his feet. Maybe he was reeked enough, maybe not; but at the moment Chandris didn't care. She just wanted out of here. And if it meant having to endure more than just Toomes's pawing hands for once, she could handle it.

Taking his arm, forcing an unconcerned smile onto her face, she led him out of the room.

Keeping his head bent over the menu as if he was looking at it, Kosta watched surreptitiously as the woman and her escort left the dining room. *Damn it all,* he cursed himself silently. *Talk about looking guilty. Why don't you just stand up, announce that you're a Pax spy, and be done with it?*

He took a deep breath. *Relax,* he ordered himself. *Just relax.* He had no proof, after all, that she was even remotely connected with Empyreal security. She hadn't approached him, or sent anyone else to approach him, and with the voyage ending tomorrow morning she was rapidly running out of time to do either. No; whatever her reasons for watching him, they were probably something totally innocuous. Maybe he reminded her of someone she knew. Or maybe his table manners were even worse than he thought.

He took another deep breath and forced himself to focus on the menu, wishing yet again that he hadn't insisted on going upper-class in the first place. The theory had seemed solid enough at the time: since most scientists and students would probably be riding in cheaper sections of the ship, the passengers up here would be less likely to recognize that he wasn't part of the Empyreal scientific community.

Or so the logic had gone. It had never occurred to him that the upper class would be so homogeneous in dress, behavior, and style that he would never really feel like he fit in.

He ran his eye down the menu's price list, an unpleasant warmth rising to his cheeks. Yes, it had been logical . . . but down deep, he couldn't help but wonder it had really been quite that neat and tidy. If perhaps the *real* reason he'd wanted to go upper-class had been a private desire to poke a figurative finger in Telthorst's annoying preoccupation with the Pax's money.

It was a worrying—hell, a downright *scary*—thought. Because he was in enemy territory now, with his survival balanced on his ability to keep his mind completely and unemotionally on his mission. Indulging in childish displays of pique or sport, even mild ones, could land him in an Empyreal jail cell. Or worse.

The waiter—a *human* waiter here, not simply an intercom plate—appeared at his side. Hoping desperately that he would pronounce everything right this time, he began to order.

CHAPTER 6

"Your attention, please," the voice came from overhead. "Shuttle number one has now docked; repeating, shuttle number one has now docked. All passengers holding debarkation cards for shuttle one may now prepare to board. The officers and crew of the *Xirrus* thank you for traveling with us, and we hope to see you again in the near future."

Don't hold your breath, Kosta thought back at the speaker as he picked up his travel bag and went over to join the line forming at the shuttle bay door. Not if he could help it would he ever fly this or any other Empyreal spaceliner again. Between that woman and his own superheated imagination his nerves were already shot to hell, and the mission had hardly even begun. When the time came to get back to Lorelei, he vowed, he'd charter a private ship or something and to the laughing fates with the expense.

Unless, of course, Commodore Lleshi and the *Komitadji* got here before that. Which would leave him stuck on the ground smack the middle of a war zone . . .

Superheated imagination, he chided himself, and put the thought firmly out of his mind.

The stairway linking the *Xirrus* to the shuttle seemed steeper going down, somehow, than it had a week ago when he'd been going the opposite way. An illusion, of course; just the same, he took it a shade more carefully than he probably needed to.

He was two steps from the bottom when he saw her.

Sitting between two uniformed men in the front passenger row.

Looking straight up at him.

For a single, horrible instant Kosta's brain froze, momentum alone getting him the rest of the way down to the shuttle deck. Those uniforms the men were wearing—vaguely like those of the *Xirrus*'s officers, but at the same time markedly different from those he'd seen while aboard. And the look the woman was giving him wasn't like anything he'd seen on either crew *or* passengers. It was cold and hard, and more than a little accusing.

He'd been right all along. She was indeed Empyreal security.

Run, was his first, frantic instinct. But there was nowhere to run to. *Fight, then.* His right hand twitched around the handle of his travel bag, aching to drop it and haul out the tiny commando-issue shocker hidden in his side pocket. Shoot all three—get to the command deck and hijack the shuttle—

With a supreme effort he forced his hand to hang onto the travel bag. Forced his feet to start walking. Forced his throat to relax. *Until they actually haul out their weapons and restraints and tell you you're under arrest,* his instructors on Scintara had told him over and over again, *always try to brazen it out.* Easy enough for them to say, safely tucked away in a Pax military base; but the more his brain unfroze, the more he realized that he really had no alternative.

Directly behind the trio was an empty aisle seat; with only a brief hesitation, he lowered himself into it. *You want brazen?* he thought darkly back at the memories of those instructors. *Fine; I'll give you brazen.*

It wasn't until after the shuttle had detached and was on its way down that he remembered on a conscious level something else they'd taught him: *Whenever possible, try to get above or behind your opponents.*

Perhaps, he thought, they'd trained him better than he'd realized.

The trip seemed to last forever. None of the three people sitting in front of him paid him the slightest attention. For all anyone could tell, they might have been totally unaware he was even there.

Not that that was any comfort. If they didn't feel the need to keep close tabs on him it probably meant they had plainclothes backups somewhere behind him. *So much for taking the high ground,* he thought once. But there was still nothing to do but sit tight and wait.

Eventually, they reached ground, landing on the kind of glidestrip Kosta had seen back at the Lorelei spaceport. From what he could see through the windows there seemed to be about as much traffic here as there had been at Lorelei, though both ports seemed to have both space- and aircraft sharing the same facilities. That was a new one on Kosta; on even sparsely developed Pax worlds like Scintara the air and space fields were kept strictly separate. The Empyrean, he decided, must have far less of either kind of traffic than the Pax.

Though considering there were five Empyreal worlds to the Pax's thirty-six, that was hardly a startling revelation.

The shuttle came to a slightly bumpy stop at the terminal. A second bump a moment later heralded the arrival of the ramp, and Kosta tried to prepare himself for whatever action was about to be necessary. Another small thump and a whisper of fresh air, and the door was open. Retrieving his travel bag from beneath the seat, swallowing once to clear his ears, he joined the rest of the passengers in standing up and traffic-jamming the aisle.

The woman and her companions were first in motion, the other passengers, not surprisingly, yielding them the right of way. Kosta took advantage of the gap to slide in directly behind them. Travel bag gripped tightly in his left hand, he followed them up the covered ramp, fighting hard to quiet his heart.

They went down the ramp together, the three of them still ignoring him. Kosta felt his back itching, and it took all his willpower to keep from turning around to see if there was a gun pointed at it. They reached the last bend, rounded it—

And came in sight of the two police officers waiting there.

There was no doubt of who they were—the Empyrean used standardized police uniforms, recognition of which had been part of Kosta's second day of training. Nor was there any doubt as to who they were after. Their eyes were pointed his direction, the amused half-smiles creasing their faces clearly meant for him.

Brazen it out. Brazen it out. Clenching his teeth, Kosta forced himself to keep walking toward them, his hand slipping of its own accord into his pocket. His fingers found the flattened half-cylinder of the shocker; clicked off the safety . . .

"So, Lieutenant," one of the police said, stepping up to the three people walking ahead of Kosta. "This is your ghost stowaway, eh? Looks solid enough to me."

Kosta nearly ran the group down as the universe abruptly tilted around him. Somehow, he managed to sidestep them without a collision and kept walking, his face burning with equal parts relief, adrenaline rush, and embarrassment. It hadn't had anything to do with him at all—none of it had. *She* was the one all the official attention was focused on, not him. No wonder her escort hadn't seemed to notice him.

In fact, now that he thought about it, it could very well be that all those strange looks the woman had given him aboard ship might have been her wondering if *he* was Empyreal security watching *her.*

So much for the expert spy's first brush with danger, he thought, feeling like a complete fool. It would have served him right if he'd fallen down those last two steps on the shuttle and broken his stupid leg.

His right hand, he noticed suddenly, was still gripping the shocker in his pocket. Carefully, he slid the weapon's safety back on and withdrew his hand, feeling a fresh bead of sweat as he realized what he'd nearly done to himself. If he'd pulled the shocker and started shooting . . .

Relax, he ordered himself. *So you're not an expert spy; you knew that going in. Learn from it, and then forget it.*

Ahead, he could see a line of low tables arrayed across the end of the roped-off area he and the other passengers were walking through. Customs, they'd called it at Lorelei; entrypoint formalities, by whatever name. Kosta's own travel papers were forged, of course, and from the beginning of the mission he'd anticipated this moment with a certain dread. Now, with all his adrenaline already used up, he found himself striding almost nonchalantly toward the tables. Even fear, apparently, was a relative thing. Reaching into his inner coat pocket, he pulled out the papers—

And nearly dropped them as a sharp yelp of pain came from behind him.

He spun around, fresh adrenaline flooding back into his bloodstream, suddenly frozen fingers fumbling with papers and travel bag in a mad scramble to get to his shocker. The woman stowaway was charging straight toward him, weaving in and out of the crowd of befuddled passengers with all the skill of a professional linegainer. Behind her, partially blocked by the confusion in her wake, he caught just a glimpse of the two police officers bent over in obvious agony and the other two men belatedly in pursuit.

Should I stop her?—but even as the automatic question popped into his mind it was too late. A flash of blue and silver in his face, a gust of perfume-scented wind, and she was gone, brushing his arm just enough in passing to knock the papers from his hand.

"Hey!" he shouted reflexively, diving for the papers before they could get trampled or lost among all those feet. He got one, and was bobbing for a second—

The heavy body didn't quite slam into him, but it didn't quite manage to stop, either. "Get out of the *way!*" a voice snarled in Kosta's ear. A pair of hands grabbed his shoulders and pushed, killing what was left of his balance in the process. He managed to let go of his travel bag in time to break his fall, and with a flurry of uniformed pant legs they were gone.

"You okay?" another voice asked as a hand gripped his arm and helped him to his feet.

"Yeah," Kosta said, looking at the man. One of the *Xirrus*'s other passengers, he vaguely recalled the face. "Thanks."

"No problem. What all did you drop?"

"I think this is everything," another man offered into the conversation before Kosta could answer. He held out a fistful of papers.

"Thanks." Kosta took the papers and leafed quickly through them. "Yes, they're all here."

"Craziest thing I ever saw," the first man commented, craning his neck to look over the crowd. "What was that all about anyway?"

"I heard someone say she was a stowaway," Kosta said, shuffling his papers into some semblance of order and picking up his travel bag. His left wrist stung where he'd broken his fall, but nothing seemed to be broken. "Where'd she go, anyway?" he asked, trying to peer ahead through the crowd flowing around them.

"She jumped over one of the customs tables," the second man told him. "Vaulted, rather. Real nice move."

"Couple of ship's security people took off after her, but they'll never catch up," the first man said. "Not with the crowds out there."

"Not at the rate she was going," the second added dryly.

"Anyway, thanks," Kosta said, taking a step away. "Both of you."

"No trouble," one of them said with a wave as they retrieved their own cases.

Kosta moved back into the flow of passengers toward the customs tables, feeling a fresh sense of rather limp relief. So now there was an escaped stow-away loose in the terminal attracting the bulk of official police and security attention. If he'd arranged it himself he couldn't have come up with a better diversion. Well worth a sore wrist and a few scattered papers.

A strange tingle went up his back. Those men back there. Those busy, important men, who'd taken the time and trouble to help a stranger . . .

No. No; surely not. It was the politicians who were supposed to be under angel control. Surely the Empyreals didn't have so many of the things they could afford to hand them out to run-of-the-average businessmen.

Still, he couldn't help wondering if he'd still be scrambling around on the floor for his papers if this had happened at the Scintara spaceport.

Even without everything else that had led up to it, Kosta decided afterwards, he would probably have found the customs formalities anticlimactic. As it was, they verged on the deathly boring.

There was no baseline computer check of his identity, as would have been done at any Pax spaceport. No retina comparison against the one on his passport; no layer-scan of his papers, his travel bag, his clothing, or his body; no stress-monitored questions about his business in general or his reasons for coming to Seraph in particular. They checked his passport, confirming that his face matched the picture grained into it, glanced over the rest of his travel papers, and ran his travel bag through a simple contents scan.

And that was it.

"Thank you for your patience, Mr. Kosta," the official smiled, doing something to his passport that looked like a standard stamp-encoding procedure and handing everything back across the table. "I hope you have a pleasant stay on Seraph."

"Thank you," Kosta nodded, relief mixing with an odd sense of disappointment. After all the effort that had gone into getting him into Empyreal space, he'd expected their internal security to be a little more impressive. Particularly here in the center of the angel hunting and processing industry, an industry that was supposed to be vital to the Empyreal way of government.

Unless they didn't have any choice in the matter. If indifference to personal safety was in fact a side effect of Seraph's proximity to Angelmass . . .

He forced the thought from his mind. There was no point in letting his imagination run wild. Not when he would soon be able to start digging out the facts for himself.

He eased into the wide cross corridor beyond the customs tables and joined the flow of pedestrians. There were more people than he would have expected, clearly a result of the Empyreal habit of combining air and space travel facilities. Not an especially smart configuration, to his mind; it didn't take a military genius to see that it left their entire off-ground transport vulnerable to a single, carefully targeted attack. Peering over the crowd as best he could, he kept an eye on the guidelights leading to the terminal exit and headed off.

It was a longer way than he expected, but a well-designed system of el-ramps and slidewalks made the trip easy enough. Within fifteen minutes he'd reached the main lobby area, a large, high-ceilinged space that seemed to be mostly glass and tile and a type of stone that reminded him of marble.

And people, of course. Lots of them, streaming in from several corridors like Kosta's as well as in from outside through the wall of glass doors he could just barely see at the far end. Clutching his travel bag tightly, keeping to the less populated strip immediately along the side wall, he worked his way around toward the exit doors.

A group of small shops opened off to his side; beyond them was a long wall decorated by a strange but interesting sort of sculpted mural. After that was a set of Empyreal-style public washrooms: gaping open doorways whose sole concession to privacy was a set of flimsy baffle screens, and Kosta suppressed a shudder as he passed. Of all the adjustments he was still having to make to the Empyreal culture, this was already proving to be the hardest.

He was past the washrooms and walking alongside another sculpted mural when he suddenly became aware that there was someone walking beside him.

He turned his head sharply, his hand twitching at the same time toward his hidden shocker.

Apparently twitched a little too violently. The slender teenaged girl walking there jumped in reaction, startled eyes widening at him as she seemed to sink back into her skin. "Sorry," Kosta apologized, his face warming with embarrassment. "Didn't mean to startle you."

"'S okay," she said, her expression still tight. Some of her long black hair had fallen across her cheek, and she reached a hand up nervously to brush it back over the shoulder of her white dress.

A nervous, vulnerable type . . . which made Kosta feel all that much worse. "No, really," he insisted, feeling like a complete fool for the second time in less than an hour. A new personal record. "I'm a little jumpy today, I guess. First time in a new place—you know how it is."

Her face softened, just a little. "Yeah. Guess I do."

"Well . . . bye." Awkwardly, he turned away and headed again for the distant exit.

He got maybe three steps. Then, to his surprise, she was back beside him. "So, uh, so it's your first time on Seraph, huh?" she asked hesitantly.

"Yes, it is," he confirmed, frowning back at her. And instantly regretting it as she seemed to wince back from the expression. "You?" he added, striving to look less threatening.

She shook her head, a jerky motion. "No. I mean, I was here once before with my parents. But I was only five, so I guess that doesn't count."

He smiled. "Probably not." He glanced up at the people detouring around them. "You know, we're probably blocking the road here."

"Oh! I'm sorry," she breathed guiltily. Hunching over a little, she started toward the exit again.

Taking a long stride, he caught up with her. "I didn't mean we had to run," he said.

She glanced at him, a somewhat sheepish smile on her face. "Sorry," she apologized again. "I guess I'm a little nervous today, too."

"That's okay." For a minute they walked in silence, as Kosta searched furiously for something else to say. "So where exactly are you headed?" he asked at last.

"A little frontier town," she told him. "Safehaven. It's about four hundred kilometers from here. You've probably never heard of it."

"No, I haven't," he admitted. "What's out there? For you, I mean."

"A new job. I'm going to be helping put in a new catalytic fusion generator."

He cocked an eyebrow at her. "You seem a little young for that."

"Oh, I won't be doing anything important," she shook her head. "Just some of the simple stuff. My uncle runs the project, and my parents thought it would be good experience."

She launched into a complicated and increasingly animated description of family connections . . . but Kosta wasn't really listening. They were almost to the exit now, and for the first time he saw that each of the glass doors was flanked by a pair of uniformed police officers.

Who were looking carefully at each person who passed them.

Relax, damn it. It was certainly conceivable that they were looking for him, that his travel papers had caught a delayed flag. But the odds were far higher that all they wanted was their escaped stowaway.

The girl beside him had stopped talking, and belatedly he realized that she'd asked him a question. "I'm sorry," he apologized. "Mind on other things. What'd you say?"

"I asked where *you* were going," she said. "—Ow!"

"What?" Kosta asked as she stopped suddenly, hand groping for his shoulder.

"Bent my ankle," she said with a grimace. "I twisted it two months ago and it sometimes still goes out. Always at the worst times."

"That's usually how it works, isn't it?" Kosta craned his neck, trying to look over the crowd. "Do you want me to try and find you one of those carts?"

"No, I'll be all right in a minute," she said. "If I could—I mean, just hold onto your arm . . . ?"

"Sure," he said, stepping close to her. Her hand groped unsuccessfully for a good grip on his elbow. "Let's try this," he offered. Bracing himself, he slipped his arm around her shoulders. "Lean some of your weight on me."

"Yes—that's good," she said, putting her own arm around behind his back. "Thank you."

"No problem," Kosta assured her. "In step; let's go."

So; here we are, he thought as they set off, feeling a not entirely uncomfortable heat rising to his face. Not that he'd never been this cozy with a woman before, but there was something embarrassing about holding onto a stranger like this right out in public view. Even when he was just being helpful.

Not that anyone else watching would know that. Her ankle must not have been all *that* bad; even when he concentrated on it he could hardly detect her slight limp. Anyone else would just assume they were being very, very friendly.

And yet, even as he fought against both the awkwardness and the guilty pleasure of her body pressing against his, he became aware that there was something poking insistently at the back of his mind. Wispy and unidentifiable, but at the same time triggering the skin on the back of his neck.

A breeze ruffled his hair, jerking him out of his concentration. To his mild surprise he found they were outside, with one of the glass doors turning just behind his back. Distracted by too many other things, he'd completely missed their obviously uneventful exit.

"Thank you again," the girl said, deftly disengaging from his arm and giving his hand a quick squeeze. "I really appreciate it."

"No problem," Kosta said again, stumbling over his tongue a little. "Can I—do you need help getting anywhere?"

"No, thank you," she said. "My ankle's fine now. Anyway, don't you have to go back in and get the rest of your luggage?"

He blinked. "Oh. Right. I guess I do."

She smiled, somehow managing to look both shy and impish at the same time. "Thank you again." She turned to look out over the rows of line cars parked along the curb, the breeze brushing her hair up against Kosta's face as she did so.

And abruptly, it clicked. Her hair—that *perfume*—

She was already walking away from him. Dropping his travel bag, he took a half dozen quick steps and caught up. She started to turn at the sound of his footsteps; grabbing her arm, he spun her the rest of the way around and took his first real look at her face.

She was the escaped stowaway.

For a handful of heartbeats he just stood there and stared, his hand frozen to her arm, his head spinning with the unreality of the transformation that had taken place.

It wasn't just her hair, though that showed no trace of the fancy braidings he'd invariably seen her wearing aboard ship. It wasn't even her dress, though how and where she'd managed to find a replacement for that blue and silver thing she'd been wearing he couldn't even begin to guess.

It was her; *she,* herself, had changed. Changed from a serene, confident, pampered upper-class young woman to a slightly helpless, very vulnerable teenage girl. Her posture, her expression, the way she moved her hands, even the texture and lines of her face—all of them were totally different.

"I don't suppose," she murmured into the brittle silence, "there's much point in asking what the hell you think you're doing."

And as her dark eyes gazed into his, the helpless, vulnerable teenager was gone, too. In her place . . .

Kosta shook his head. "No. No, I . . ."

"So what now?"

That *was* a good question. "Why are they after you?" he asked.

She shrugged, her eyes never leaving his face. "I overstayed my welcome."

"Stowed away, you mean."

She shrugged again.

I could do it, Kosta told himself. *I could march her straight back inside and hand her over to those police at the doors.* It would be the right thing to do—after all, her little joytrip had cost the spaceline a lot of money. And it would serve her right for using him to walk her out straight under security's nose.

But turning her in would mean drawing official attention to himself.

Slowly, almost reluctantly, he let go of her arm. "Get out of here," he muttered. "Just . . . *go.*"

She stood there for another moment, and he thought he could see some surprise in that expressionless face. Then, without a word, she turned and disappeared into the flow of people heading toward the row of line cars.

Kosta shook his head, a grudging admiration beginning to seep in through the resentment as he made his way back to where he'd dropped his travel bag. Yes, she'd used him, all right. She'd used him neatly and blatantly and probably without a single scrap of shame to any of it.

But talk about brazening it out . . .

CHAPTER 7

"Welcome, sir," the gentle female voice of the line car said as Kosta got in and collapsed into the soft contour seat. "Where would you like to go?"

"The Angelmass Studies Institute in Shikari City," he growled, pulling the door closed with a muttered curse. "I suppose you'll need an address."

"That won't be necessary, sir," the line car said, pulling smoothly away from the curb. "Angelmass Studies Institute; One Hundred U San Avenue, Shikari City. Estimated time to arrival, forty-six minutes."

"Fine," Kosta grunted. "Let's get moving."

He glared out the window as the car maneuvered its way through the traffic, splitting his attention between the dull fatigue ache in his arms and his slow seethe at that fiasco the locals euphemistically called a spaceport baggage collection center. It had been possibly the worst example of inept design he'd ever seen—overcrowded, slow, with luggage carts nowhere to be seen. All of it far below the level of standards he was used to. He'd wound up having to manhandle all three of his cases out to the line cars on his own.

And the worst thing is they probably think they're doing just fine, he grumbled to himself. *Well, just wait—when the Pax gets here, we'll show you how to build a proper spaceport.*

Not to mention how a city should be maintained. The area he was passing through . . .

"Where are we?" he called, reaching into his inner coat pocket for the packet of maps the Pax had left for him at the Lorelei drop.

"Moving north on Kori Street, in the city of Magasca," the line car answered. "Approaching the intersection of Kori Street and Enamm Street."

Kosta nodded, locating it. From the layout of the two cities and their surrounding communities he'd already come to the conclusion that Magasca and Shikari City had been built at different times; from the view out his window, it was apparent that Magasca, at least, had been here for a considerable number of years.

Vaguely, he wondered how long a city had to be in existence before it created slums like this.

———

The aging streets and buildings of Magasca gave way—rather abruptly, it seemed—to the cleaner and fresher cityscape of Shikari City. And exactly forty-six minutes after leaving the spaceport they were there.

It was, Kosta had to admit, an impressive sight. Rising up out of the landscaped lawn surrounding it, the Angelmass Studies Institute looked for all the world like some modern architect's vision of a squat, towerless castle. Only four stories high, but spread out enough to qualify as rambling, it was all glass and brick and that marble-like stone he'd seen so much of at the spaceport.

The line car took him up a curving, tree-lined drive and stopped at what was obviously the main entrance. "How much?" Kosta asked, stuffing his maps back into his coat pocket and opening the door.

"Fourteen ruya twenty. Do you wish me to call a luggage cart?"

The question was a surprise; Kosta hadn't realized the Empyreals had the capability for that kind of double-linear communication linkage. "No," he told the car as he fed the appropriate bills into the cash slot and accepted his change in return. Going around back, he popped the cargo hatch and pulled his cases out onto the pavement. And wondered with a flush if he'd lugged them all around the spaceport for nothing.

The Institute's entrance lobby was fully as impressive as the building's exterior: an archway two stories high, done up with a lot more of the marble-like stone. In the center, seated behind a circular reception desk of the same material, was a dark young woman who watched him approach with a slightly quizzical look on her face.

"May I help you, sir?" she asked as Kosta set his cases down with a multiple thump in front of the desk.

"I hope so," Kosta said. "My name's Jereko Kosta, here on a temporary study program from Clarkston University, Cairngorm, on Balmoral. My credentials should have been sent a week ago."

"Let me check," she nodded, tapping keys on her desk. "Mr. Kosta . . . yes, it looks like you're all set. Will you still be wanting a room here at the Institute?"

"If there's one available, yes."

"We're holding one for you," she said, looking back up at him. "You'll be in room 433, on the top floor. If you'll put your luggage on the cart, I'll have it sent up."

Kosta looked down in surprise; he hadn't heard the luggage cart arrive. "Thank you," he said, reaching down for the first two cases. "These things don't take long to get heavy."

"I don't doubt it," the receptionist agreed. "There's a note here, too, that you're to check in with Director Podolak as soon as possible."

"Sure," Kosta said, forcing his voice to remain casual as he laid his travel bag carefully on top of the others. No need to panic; if the director had seen through his forged credentials they'd never have let him get this far. "I can go now, unless there's some reason I need to stop by my room first."

"No, the cart can get there fine on its own." She touched a button and a set of guidelights came on, leading up a wide stairway that led off the lobby to the right. "The director's office is right at the top of the stairs on the second floor; I'll let her know you're on your way."

"Thank you."

"You're welcome. I hope you find your stay here productive." She half rose from her seat to look down at the luggage cart. "Cart: room 433."

Obediently, it rolled around the desk and trundled off toward a bank of elevators just visible off to the left. Kosta watched it go; then, taking a careful breath, he turned the opposite way and started up the stairway.

The ID on the door was a surprise. From the decor downstairs and the obvious prestige involved with the place, he would have expected its director to have been given something fancy and eye-catching. A holo at the very least; more likely a projection or aureol or something they didn't even have in the Pax. Instead, he found a simple brass nameplate with the words *Dr. Laurn Podolak, Director* engraved on it.

The door itself wasn't any better: simple wood, with a knob and hinges instead of a sliding mechanism. Wondering uneasily if this was some kind of joke played on newcomers, he knocked tentatively on the panel.

"Come in," a voice said almost in his ear. At least they had an external speaker system. Twisting the knob, he pushed the door open.

Given the simplicity of the door, he should have been prepared for the woman smiling at him from behind the large wooden desk. He wasn't. Young middle-aged, perhaps, she was dressed in a neat but simple dress, her shortish hair completely unadorned by the sort of clips and frostsprays virtually all the upper-class women on the *Xirrus* had worn. Even her necklace, her one visible concession to style, would have looked distinctly shabby next to the ones he'd seen aboard ship.

Abruptly, he realized that he was staring . . . and that she was watching him do so with a slightly amused expression on her face. "I'm Jereko Kosta," he managed.

"Yes, Rose said you were on your way up," the woman said, rising and holding out her hand, palm upward. "I'm Laurn Podolak."

"I'm honored to meet you," Kosta said, stepping forward to lightly touch her palm with his bunched fingertips. He'd had nightmares during training about this particular honorific, terrified that he would forget himself and go instead into a normal Pax-style handshake. It had been a great relief to discover that the initiator's posture made such a slip almost impossible.

"It's a privilege to have you here," Podolak said, lowering her hand and gesturing to the chair facing her desk. "Your credentials were most impressive," she added as they both sat down.

"Thank you," Kosta said, wondering with a twinge of uneasiness exactly how glowing the Pax background on him had been. "It's a privilege to be allowed to study here."

She arched an eyebrow, that amused expression back on her face. "Even if the director isn't exactly what you were expecting?"

His initial impulse was to deny it. But there was a distinctly knowing look in her eyes. "I'm sorry, Doctor. I didn't mean any disrespect. I just thought—I mean, it's just that you're not—" He waved a hand helplessly.

"As upper-class as someone in my position ought to be?" she suggested mildly.

He winced. "Something like that, yes," he admitted.

The amused expression vanished. "There's still so much we don't know about the angels, Mr. Kosta," she said, her tone suddenly very serious. "So much we *need* to know if we're going to use them properly." She leaned forward and gestured to her left, to a full-wall status board Kosta hadn't noticed before. "*That* is where our money goes. To research, and study, and analysis. To people like you, on the cutting edge of the work. Not people like me, who merely organize it."

Kosta looked at her, a cold shiver running up his back. It was the same highly committed, grimly earnest expression he'd seen so often on the men who'd trained him for this mission. Men who'd spoken over and over again of the need to free the people of the Empyrean from their alien domination.

Their domination by the same angels Director Podolak was determined to flood the Empyrean with. "I understand," he heard himself say.

"Good." Podolak straightened up again, that almost religious intensity disappearing into a wry smile as she did so. "Sorry if I sounded a little high-flown there, but after you've gone through the same explanation roughly twice a week it starts to sound like any other speech. However, as long as we're on the subject of money—" She glanced down at the display on her desk. "Your last communication said you'd be bringing a total of twenty thousand ruya with you and setting up a local draw line. Is that still correct?"

"Yes," Kosta said cautiously. "Is that unacceptable?"

"Oh, it's acceptable enough," Podolak said, reaching into a drawer and pulling out a thin packet. "It's just not going to get you very far. Ergo, this." She handed the packet across the desk.

Frowning, Kosta took it. *Application for Empyreal Government Fund Assistance,* the cover said. "Fund assistance?" he asked stupidly.

"Of course," Podolak said. "I'm sure I don't have to tell you how expensive this kind of research can get. If Clarkston can't afford to give you more than twenty thousand, you're going to need to scare up more money from *somewhere.* Let me know if you have any trouble with either the forms or the High Senate funding rep in Magasca."

"Yes. Thank you." Kosta slipped the application into his coat pocket, a faint haze of unreality fogging his vision. Not only were they welcoming a Pax spy into their midst with open arms, they were offering to get him government funding for his mission on top of it. Telthorst and the other Adjutors were going to be ecstatic.

"It's why I'm here." Podolak glanced at her watch and stood up. "I was about to head down to the visiting researcher wing. If you'd like, I can show you to your new office."

It had taken Kosta six years, at three different universities, to earn his tridoctorum degree. Six years in which he'd met and dealt with a fair sampling of department heads, administrators, and other academic bureaucrats. Most, in his admittedly biased opinion, had run the foreshortened gamut from totally oblivious of student work to vaguely aware of it. A few—a very few—had managed to be moderately interested in it.

Dr. Laurn Podolak left every last one of them in the dust.

He'd expected her to simply walk him down the hallway to his office, nodding to or perhaps chatting a moment with those they happened to pass. Instead, she proceeded to take him on a complete and methodical tour of every single office and lab on his floor.

She knew everyone's name. She knew enough about everyone's project or study to make comments, offer suggestions, ask worthwhile questions, and give encouragement. Introducing Kosta around, she rattled off home cities and family details as if these were all longtime personal friends instead of the temporary academic visitors they actually were.

Somewhere far in the back of his mind Kosta had wondered how Podolak, without any of the visible trappings of authority, could possibly maintain the proper tone of the respect and discipline among her subordinates. By the time they reached the end of the hallway, he realized she'd found a far more effective motivator than mere respect.

"That's just about it," Podolak commented, pausing beside the last door— this one, unlike the others, a heavy-looking sliding type. "What do you think?"

"I'm impressed," Kosta answered, and meant it. "Not just by the facilities, either." He nodded back down the hallway. "These people are more like an in-coming batch of grad students than any visiting scientists I've ever known."

"There's a wonderful camaraderie here," Podolak agreed. "Part of that is the people themselves, of course. Not surprisingly, angel research tends to at-tract the highly idealistic. And of course, there's the angel effect itself."

"Of course," Kosta repeated, his lips suddenly gone stiff. The angel effect. A dangerous, alien influence . . . and here he was, as near the dead-crack-center of that influence as he could possibly be.

They'd talked a great deal, back on Scintara, of how the angels were sap-ping the will and altering the minds of the Empyrean's leaders. Somehow, no one had ever gotten around to answering the question of how Kosta was sup-posed to avoid that influence himself.

Podolak had turned to the door, pressing her right palm against the red-rimmed touch plate set into its center. "You'll need to go downstairs later and get your print entered into the computer," she told him. The touch plate rim changed to green, and with a puff of released air pressure the door slid open. "Until then, you'll have to get your officemate or someone else to let you in."

"What's in here?" Kosta asked, though the tightness in his stomach told him he probably already knew.

She cocked an eyebrow at him. "Your angel, of course. Come; let me show you."

She stepped inside. Taking a deep breath, Kosta followed.

The furnishings were similar to those of the other labs Podolak had shown him, though the room itself was much larger than any of them had been. The arrangement of the equipment, however, was strikingly different. Instead of being set out in standard rows, the worktables and stations here were arrayed in concentric circles around a chest-high cylindrical pillar rising up from the floor in the center of the room. A handful of people were scattered around the lab, hunched over notebooks or computers or complex-looking electronic breadboards.

"Doesn't look like anyone's in the middle of anything delicate," Podolak said quietly, glancing around. "Come on."

She led the way to the central pillar, and as they approached Kosta could see what appeared to be a small crystalline dome set in the center of its flat up-per surface. Stepping up to it, Podolak turned; and with an expression that was chillingly reminiscent of a proud mother showing off her child, she gestured to the little crystalline dome. "There it is."

It was rather unspectacular, really: a barely visible speck, even with the magnification given it by its encasing dome. "So that's an angel," Kosta heard himself say.

"That's an angel," Podolak confirmed. "And if you're like every other visitor who comes through the Institute, you're probably wondering if you can touch it. Feel free."

Not an order . . . but Kosta could feel the official weight behind the suggestion. She wanted him to reach out to it; to move into range of whatever this alien influence was . . .

"But you don't have to if you don't want to," Podolak added softly. "It's not a requirement."

Kosta gritted his teeth, cold hard reality forcing its way through his hesitation. More than likely, he would be spending his next few months literally surrounded by these things . . . and there would be no better time than right now to try and detect their influence. Bracing himself, trying to watch every facet of his mind at once, he reached his hand gingerly toward the crystalline dome and touched it.

Nothing. No wrenching of emotions, major or minor. No sense of alien thought or presence or influence. No overwhelming urge to confess that he was a spy.

Nothing at all.

He drew his hand back and let it drop to his side, feeling a strange mixture of relief and disappointment. Beside him, Podolak nodded. "Yes, that's the usual reaction. The angel effect isn't nearly as dramatic as most people think."

He looked her straight in the eye. "Is that what this object lesson was for? To eliminate any residual nervousness?"

A small smile twitched at the corners of her mouth. "As a matter of fact, yes, that's one of the reasons we try to bring newcomers into contact with an angel as soon as possible. We don't want to be too obvious about it, of course—people don't like to admit to fears they intellectually believe are unreasonable. That's why we like to include it in the general orientation. You understand psychology."

"A little. Mostly, I understand nervousness."

"But there are a few who do sense something right away," Podolak went on, her forehead wrinkling slightly. "Did you feel anything? Anything at all?"

Kosta reached out and touched the crystalline dome again, then took his hand away. Nothing. "No," he told her. "Nothing at all."

"Yes," she murmured. "Well . . . as I said, that *is* the usual reaction."

"Sorry to disappoint you." Kosta looked at the crystalline dome. "Question, though: which is the *real* angel? The subnuclear particle in the center that everyone calls the angel, or the particle plus the shell of positively charged ions it surrounds itself with?"

He watched Podolak's face, holding his breath. One of his instructors had suggested that question as a way to quickly establish himself as a visionary, independent thinker, the sort who might be able to get away with ignoring facts about the angels that every genuine Empyreal would already know. But if the question, instead of sounding original, merely came across as sounding stupid . . .

"An interesting question," Podolak said, her expression thoughtful. "The quick and obvious answer is that it's just the central particle; but quick and obvious doesn't necessarily equal correct. Offhand, I can't remember if anyone's ever tried to study the significance of the outer ion shell before. Beyond the simple physical explanation that a particle with a negative charge in the quadrillions has no choice but to pull a lot of positive ions over to it, of course. Might well be worth taking a look at." She cocked her head slightly. "You interested in volunteering?"

Carefully, Kosta exhaled. "I'd like to do a database search, anyway," he told her. "If it turns out no one else has done any work that direction, I might like to give it a shot."

"Sounds good," Podolak nodded. "Let's go back to your office and I'll give you a list of the database access codes."

CHAPTER 8

The man was young and thin and rather sloppy looking, his clothes smelling of oil, his lower lip twisted in a permanent smirk. But there was nothing lazy or funny about his voice. "Forget it, kid," he growled. "I got Rafe and I got me, and that's all the crew we need around here."

"And what about when you have to do some emergency maintenance?" Chandris countered, fighting to keep her voice calm and reasonable. "Not here, but while you're out in space. Who runs the ship while you and Rafe are busy fixing it?"

The smirk seemed to get bigger. "You, I suppose?"

"Why not?" Chandris demanded. "I'm an expert navigator and pilot, and I also know my way around an engine room. I could fly this thing out to Angelmass and back by myself if I had to."

"No, you couldn't," the man shook his head. "Want to know why?" He leaned forward, to smirk directly in her face. "Because you aren't ever gonna *be* aboard this ship."

With a snort, he straightened up again and reached down for the box he'd been carrying. "So get lost, huh? We're busy."

Turning, he headed back toward the mass of metal that towered over him, all but filling the large open-air service yard. Chandris watched him go, hoping desperately that, even now, he might reconsider.

Midway down the side of the ship, he disappeared up the long fold-out stairway that led inside. He'd never even looked back.

Blinking back tears, Chandris turned and trudged back to the wire fence and the gate with the faded sign *Hova's Skyarcher* above it. Across the street, visible between the ships parked on that side, the sun was touching the distant hills. She'd spent the entire day here, going from one huntership owner to the next, trying to find one who would be willing to take her on.

None of them had been especially polite. Most had been rude, or sarcastic, or even angry.

All had said no.

For a long minute she just stood there, leaning against the gate, too weary and drained to move. The clink of metal and the hums and growls of machinery came from all around her as huntership crews worked to get ready for the next morning's launches. All that studying aboard the *Xirrus*—all that time she'd spent reading and memorizing and struggling to understand. And then getting caught on top of it all, and having to chop and hop without a single nurking thing but the clothes she had on.

All of it for nothing.

A motion across the street caught her eye: a middle-aged man, rather overweight from what she could see of his profile, coming stiffly down the stairway of the huntership housed behind the fence over there. Carrying a small handled box in one hand, he disappeared toward the far end of the ship.

For a moment Chandris hesitated. It would end like the others, she knew; but it was the last huntership on this side of the launch area and the only one she hadn't yet tried her luck at. Might as well make a clean sweep of it.

The gate was unlocked, its overhead sign proclaiming the ship beyond to be the *Gazelle*. Chandris let herself in and headed back toward the stairway, studying the ship towering over her as she walked alongside it. In slightly worse shape than the average, she decided, at least as far as the exterior was concerned. A smooth circular indentation in the hull caught her eye, and she stepped over for a closer look. A handful of small flat lenses and fine-mesh gratings were grouped within it, their sparkle and cleanliness in marked contrast to the pitted and faded hull itself.

"It's a sensor cluster."

Chandris turned toward the voice. The overweight man was standing at the foot of the stairway, watching her. "Yes, I know," she told him, sifting quickly through her memory for the pictures of such things that she'd seen in the *Xirrus*'s files. "Half-spectrum and ion analysis."

He smiled. Not a smirk, but a simple, friendly smile. "Right as rain. You must be the little girl who's been driving everyone in the Yard frippy today looking for a job."

"I'm hardly a little girl," Chandris snapped, suddenly tired of having to take this dribble from every jerk on Seraph. "And if you just came over to tell me you don't need any help, don't bother."

She spun around and stomped off toward the gate, eyes blurry with sudden tears of frustration and fatigue. To hell with it. To hell with all of them. She should have known better than to try something this puff-headed in the first place. She might as well head back to the city where she could steal the price of a meal and find a place to sleep. Tomorrow she'd hit the streets, try and hook up with one of the local scorers—

"So tell me what sort of help you're offering."

She stopped. "What?" she called warily over her shoulder.

"You want a job, right?" he said. "So come inside and tell us what you can do."

Slowly, Chandris turned around to face him, half afraid this was just the setup for a parting twist of the knife. But there was nothing but calm curiosity in the fat man's face.

"Well, come on," he waved, starting up the stairs with the same stiff gait she'd noticed earlier. "It's not getting any warmer out here, in case you hadn't noticed. You like tea?"

Chandris took a deep breath, her fatigue vanishing like nothing. To have found *here*, of all places, a real, genuine, open-faced soft touch. Sometimes she couldn't believe her own luck. "Thank you," she said, walking quickly back toward the stairway. "I'd love a cup of tea."

The tea was hot and rich and strong, with a sprinkle of sadras spice and probably some cinnamon mixed into it. A solid, working person's drink; simple and hospitable, with no pretensions or apologies attached. Exactly the sort of tea, Chandris thought as she sipped, that she would expect soft-touch types to offer a stranger.

Not that it wasn't welcome. It was indeed not getting any warmer outside, and Chandris hadn't realized how cold she'd actually been until she began to warm up. Holding the mug to her lips, she inhaled the steam rising from it, suppressing a shiver as she did so.

Or at least she thought she'd suppressed it. "Still cold, child?" the plump woman sitting across the table from her said, reaching for the teapot. "—Ach!" she added, pushing back her chair to get up.

The overweight man in the chair beside her was quicker. "I'll get it," he said, heaving himself to his feet. He plucked the empty teapot from her hand and stepped toward the simmering samovar on the counter. "A sprinkle and a half of sadras, right?" he asked over his shoulder.

The woman gave Chandris a knowing look. "You can see how often *he* makes the tea around here," she said.

"Unfair," the other protested, turning around and throwing her a hurt look. "How can you *say* things like that? Why, I just made some—let's see—yes; it was just two years ago. On a Sunday, as I recall."

The woman rolled her eyes skyward. "I hope you like lots of sadras in your tea," she warned Chandris.

Chandris nodded silently, watched as the man bustled with cheerful clumsiness with the teapot, and wondered what in the world she'd walked in on.

Their names were Hanan and Ornina Daviee. Not husband and wife, as she'd first assumed, but brother and sister—the only such team, according to Hanan, among the two hundred–odd hunterships currently in business. The family resemblance was very strong, once she knew to look for it: both were of medium height, both overweight—Hanan more so than his sister—with long faces and intense brown eyes. Ornina's dark hair was shot through with gray; Hanan's hair had nearly disappeared entirely.

And Hanan was crippled.

Neither of them had said anything about it, but it wasn't like it was a secret they could keep. Every time Hanan stretched out his hand for something Chandris caught a glimpse of the thin exobrace running alongside his arm, and the ones running down his legs were almost that visible as they stretched the material of his coveralls.

And if she concentrated, she could hear the faint whine of tiny motors, starting and then stopping in time with his movements. Gazing down into her mug, listening to the motors but determined not to stare, she wondered uneasily what had happened to him.

Abruptly, right in front of her nose, the teapot spout appeared, jolting her out of her thoughts. Snapping her head up, she found Hanan looking down at her, an impish twinkle in his eyes. "More tea?" he asked innocently.

"Thank you," Chandris said, giving him a stern no-nonsense look as he poured. He smiled pleasantly in return, set the teapot down on the table, and maneuvered himself back into his chair.

Ornina hadn't missed any of it. "You have to excuse Hanan his little games, Chandris," she said, giving her brother the same kind of look Chandris had just tried, with about equal success. "Or at least learn to live with them. Arrested childhood, you know." She picked up the teapot, added some to Hanan's mug and then to her own. "Now, then. Hanan said you were looking for a job."

"That's right," Chandris nodded, shifting mental gears. The cold little girl routine had been an easy one to slip into, but that wasn't the role she was supposed to be playing here. "I've just graduated college, with degrees in astrogation, piloting, and spaceship functions. I wanted to get some small-craft experience, and thought this would be my best opportunity."

"I take it no one else agrees?" Hanan suggested.

Chandris grimaced. "I wouldn't know. No one else let me get even that far."

"Can't say I'm surprised," he said. "Huntership crews tend to be an ingrown lot. Not much given to strangers."

"Though there are exceptions, of course," Ornina said. "Where did you go to school?"

"Ahanne University on Lorelei," Chandris said. "My records were supposed to be here already, but I checked this morning and they hadn't yet arrived."

Hanan snorted gently. "Not surprised about *that*, either," he rumbled.

"There are only four regular skeeters a day between here and Lorelei, and Gabriel business probably takes up two and a half of 'em. Welcome to the real world."

"We'll take editorial comments on the state of the Empyrean later," Ornina told him. "Tell me about Sibastii regulators, Chandris."

Sibastii regulators . . . "They're a type of voltage regulator used in sensor-to-autonav interfaces," she quoted from the *Xirrus*'s lessons. "Usually used in areas where there's a high ion density." Dimly, she wondered what all that meant.

Ornina nodded. "A samsara switch?"

"A high-stroid device for automatically switching between several different computers, sensors, or navigational pylons."

"Anspala stabilizers?"

"They're used to keep the edges of a hyperspace catapult field from shifting."

"Twitteries?" Hanan asked.

Chandris looked at him, stomach tensing. *Twitteries?* "Uh . . ."

"Try to ignore him, child," Ornina said, giving her brother a warning look. "He just talks to keep his jaw in shape for eating."

"'Twittery' is a perfectly good word," Hanan insisted, that innocent look on his face again. "Not *my* fault if the schools don't teach these youngsters anything."

Ornina gave him another look, this one half strained patience and half resignation, with a touch of what-am-I-going-to-do-with-you thrown in. Judging from the way her face settled into the deep lines there, Chandris decided, she probably used that expression a lot. "A twittery, Chandris," she said, "is an old and slightly vulgar slang term for a Kelsey's Splitter."

"Oh," Chandris said, relaxing again. "That's a high-speed ion analyzer."

Ornina raised her eyebrows questioningly at Hanan, who shrugged. "Well, you've certainly got the book learning down cold," he said, eyeing Chandris thoughtfully. "I suppose you know what the next question has to be."

She didn't, exactly; but she could take a pretty good guess. "Whether I've had any experience?"

"That's the one," he nodded. "Have you?"

"Not really," Chandris admitted, watching their faces carefully. This was where she was going to find out just how good a puff-talker she really was. "I've done a lot of simulator work, of course, but only a very little real flying. Mostly in—" a quick search of her memory— "Khalkha T-7s."

"*Khalkhas?*" Hanan gave a puff of contempt. "You mean there's someone out there still using those fossils?"

"Ours was in pretty good shape," Chandris improvised. "They also used it to teach the maintenance classes."

"I'm sure it gave you lots of practice there," he grunted.

Ornina gave him another of her patient looks. "If the editorial department will kindly shut up . . . ? Thank you." She looked back at Chandris. "I'm sure you realize that a huntership like the *Gazelle* isn't very much like a Khalkha. What makes you think you could handle it?"

"I'm sure I couldn't, at least not at first," Chandris said, keeping her voice quiet and honest and professional. They were going for it—they were actually going for it. "But I know a great deal about ships and their operation in general. And though I don't want to seem immodest, I'd be willing to bet that I can learn everything I'll need to know about hunterships faster than anyone you've ever met."

An instant later she knew she'd pushed it too far. Hanan's eyebrows went up, and even Ornina seemed taken aback. They looked at each other, communicating in some private code of expressions and tiny movements that Chandris couldn't even begin to read, and she gritted her teeth in silent rage at her stupidity. *Nurk it all,* she thought, the bitterness she'd been feeling earlier flooding back in through the warmth of the tea in her stomach.

The warmth and, unfortunately, the caffeine as well. Already she was starting to tremble as stimulant hit a stomach that hadn't had anything put in it since breakfast. She looked down at her hands, folded together on the table, cursing the weakness and false hope that had dragged her in here in the first place. Now she'd blown it, and she had exactly two options left: to wait until her hands had calmed down enough to score a track, or just forget about eating until morning.

"How much?" Hanan asked suddenly.

She looked up at him, frowning. "How much what?"

"How much do you bet?" he said.

It took a moment for Chandris to remember what the hell it was he was referring to. Then it connected. "I don't understand," she said carefully, looking back and forth between them. "Are you saying . . . I'm in?"

"We can't promise we'll take you on permanently," Ornina warned. "Or even for more than a single trip, for that matter. However—" she glanced at Hanan, looked quickly away "—a huntership can always use an extra hand or two aboard. We'll give you a try."

Hanan levered himself to his feet. "Let me show you to your cabin," he said, stepping to the door. "Dinner will be in about half an hour. In the meantime, you can start reading through the *Gazelle*'s spec manuals."

"She'd do better to go get her things from wherever she's stored them,"

Ornina pointed out. "You won't have time to do that in the morning, Chandris—we're scheduled for a six o'clock lift."

"Good point," Hanan grunted. "You need a hand carrying anything?"

"At the moment, I don't need any hands at all." Chandris gave her lip a rueful twist. "Unfortunately, my luggage has been, in the words of the spaceline, 'temporarily misplaced.'"

"Lost down the same rabbit hole as your college records, no doubt," Hanan said, shaking his head. "Probably having a nice little chat together. Like I said, welcome to the real world."

"I'm sure it's not really *lost,*" Chandris told him. It wasn't, either, though she doubted she'd be going back aboard the *Xirrus* to retrieve it anytime soon. "But they said they probably couldn't track it down before tomorrow."

"Well, never mind," Ornina said, her eyes traveling up and down the white dress Chandris had escaped the spaceport in, a dress now streaked with dust and dirt. "Whatever you had probably wouldn't have been very practical for space, anyway. After dinner we'll go to the outfitters and get you some proper coveralls."

"That would be wonderful." Chandris hesitated. "I really want to thank you—both of you," she added, looking at Hanan, "for giving me this chance. I won't let you down."

"I'm sure you won't," Ornina said softly. "Better go with Hanan, now. You've got a lot of reading to do before we lift in the morning."

"All right." Chandris turned to Hanan, still waiting in the doorway, and smiled. She'd done it; she'd actually *done* it. "I'm ready."

And as he led the way down the narrow, metal-walled corridor, she smiled again. This time to herself.

CHAPTER 9

The database codes were simple enough to learn, the system itself considerably less so. It took Kosta over an hour to bend his Pax-oriented computer habits enough to use the Empyreal system without mis-keying every second command.

It took him the rest of the day to sort through the index of files on angels and Angelmass. Not the files themselves, just the index.

The sun was disappearing behind the squat buildings of Shikari City when he finally pushed his chair back from his desk, shoulders aching with fatigue and another, far different, tension. The database stretched back nearly thirty years: fifty years after Seraph's colonization, and a hundred fifty since the first group of breakaway colonists had arrived at Uhuru. Back then, Angelmass had been nothing more than a violently radiating quantum black hole, with the angels themselves little more than exotic curiosities for quantum theorists to argue about. It had only been in the past twenty years that all that had changed.

Which meant it had taken less than twenty years for the researchers from five underpopulated planets to amass all *this*.

Kosta had seen research projects tackled with single-minded intensity before. But this bordered on obsession.

He looked out the window at the buildings silhouetted against the brilliantly colored sky, a chill running up his back. No; this didn't border on anything. It *was* an obsession.

There was no other explanation. The Institute, the vast rows of huntership and their support facilities to the northeast, the whole of Shikari City— the Empyreals had poured incredible amounts of time and effort and money into this angel thing. Were still pouring time and effort and money into it.

As all the while, unnoticed under their feet, the city of Magasca lay rotting.

He shivered again. He hadn't believed—perhaps hadn't wanted to believe—that the angels were really the threat the Pax claimed they were. Now, for the first time, he did. Slowly but surely, the angels were indeed taking over the Empyrean. The political leaders were already under angel influence; now, he saw, so were the Empyrean's best scientists and researchers.

In fact, it was entirely possible that he was already too late to stop it.

It was a horrifying thought. But all the signs were there. Every Pax official he'd met during the course of his training had been grimly, deadly serious about stopping the spread of this alien influence. They'd emphasized the need to rescue the Empyreals and bring them under Pax protection; and they'd made it abundantly clear the Pax would do whatever it took to achieve that end. It was a message the Empyrean's leaders could hardly have failed to understand.

And yet, there'd been nothing but the most basic identity check at the Seraph spaceport. No check of any sort at the Institute itself. Director Podolak, head of the supposedly most important project in the Empyrean, had cheerfully welcomed him into the center of that project without so much as a single question about his qualifications or background or expertise.

His instructors had told him the Empyreals refused to understand the threat posed by the angels. Now, Kosta saw, they were equally blind to the threat posed by the Pax itself.

It didn't make sense . . . unless the alien influence was stronger than anyone realized. Unless everyone in the Empyrean had already been affected. Had already been turned into an unconcerned, passive, happyface robot.

For a long minute Kosta stared out his window at the sunset, turning that thought over and over in his mind as the flat, scaly clouds slowly changed from brilliant fire-red to light pink to dark gray. But—*No,* he told himself firmly. If that conniving little stowaway back at the spaceport had been a passive happyface robot, then Kosta was a frog.

The people of the Empyrean could still be saved. It was up to him to do it.

Hunching his shoulders back in one final stretch, he returned to his desk, arching his fingers over the keyboard. He was still gazing at the display, considering his next move, when the door abruptly swung open and a young man strode into the room, his nose buried in a sheaf of papers balanced on one hand.

"Hello," Kosta said.

The other looked up in surprise. "Oh. Hello," he nodded. "Sorry—I wasn't expecting company."

"Well, I'm not exactly *company,*" Kosta told him cautiously, wondering how the other was going to take this invasion of his hitherto private office. "More the officemate type, actually. I've just been moved in."

The other broke into a grin. "No kidding? That's great. I've been asking the director for months for some company." Stepping to Kosta's desk, he stuck his hand across it. "Yaezon Gyasi."

"Uh—Jereko Kosta," Kosta replied, staring at the outstretched hand for a split second before recovering and reaching out to touch the other's fingertips. He'd expected that, as the newcomer here, the proper gesture would be the fingertips-to-palm respect thing he'd done with Director Podolak; but Gyasi had instead initiated the greeting used between equals. Either Kosta still didn't grasp all the nuances of Empyreal culture or Gyasi was just a naturally friendly person. "I'm honored to meet you."

"As am I," Gyasi said. Stepping over to his own cluttered desk, he dropped his sheaf of papers onto a pile of similar ones and swiveled his chair around to face Kosta. "So. Welcome to Seraph and the Angelmass Studies Institute, and all that. Where are you from?"

"Palitaine, on Lorelei," Kosta said, reeling off his cover story with practiced ease. "Originally. I've spent the past few years doing graduate studies on Balmoral."

"Whereabouts?"

"Clarkston University in Cairngorm," Kosta said, mentally crossing his fingers. If Gyasi—or anyone else at the Institute, for that matter—had ever been to Clarkston themselves, there could be trouble. "You've probably never even heard of it," he added.

"Oh, no, I've heard of it," Gyasi nodded. "Never met anyone who went there, but it's supposed to be a pretty good school. Nicely landscaped, too, I hear."

"It is that," Kosta agreed, relaxing again. This part was easy—he'd spent a couple of days on Lorelei researching both Clarkston and Cairngorm, and probably knew them better than anyone on Seraph who hadn't actually lived there. "Sort of like the Institute's grounds here, though on a larger scale."

Gyasi nodded. "I'm from Uhuru, myself. Rungwe, to be exact—it's a few hundred kilometers west of Tshombe." Rolling his chair toward Kosta's desk, he craned his neck to look at the computer display, still showing the end of the file listing. "I see you've been getting your feet wet. Impressive, isn't it?"

"Very," Kosta nodded. "One might say overwhelming."

Gyasi chuckled. "One might, indeed. You want overwhelming, though, just wait until you get a close look at Angelmass itself. The next survey flight's going out in a couple of days. You coming along?"

"Probably depends on whether I've gotten more funding by then."

"Ah." Gyasi gave him a knowing look. "Yes, we get a lot of that around here. The High Senate's funding tends to palpitate a lot. You know the routine: small but loud group starts screaming about the government pouring extra money into angel research when they're already paying Gabriel's ridiculous prices for the things."

Kosta shrugged, thinking about the slums of Magasca. "Not necessarily an unreasonable argument," he said. "Especially with the Pax out there breathing down our necks."

Gyasi waved a hand in a gesture of scorn. "The Pax is no big deal. There's no way they can conquer us, and they're too madly in love with money and profit to destroy us."

"Unless they see us as a threat," Kosta pointed out, annoyed in spite of himself at having the Pax so casually dismissed. "My understanding is that they consider the angels to be alien intelligences in the process of invasion."

Gyasi snorted gently. "I know people in Rungwe who think that, too. A pity, particularly when there are so many more interesting theories to choose from." He cocked an eyebrow. "You *were* told, weren't you, that we're not supposed to discuss angel theories with people outside the Institute?"

"Not specifically, no," Kosta said, wounded pride vanishing in a surge of interest. Angel *theories,* plural?

"Well, consider yourself told," Gyasi said. "That goes for any other findings, too. You can write them up on the Institute's own net, but nothing gets released outside without prior approval."

"I understand." That was more like it. Maybe the Empyreals had some understanding of security after all.

"Good," Gyasi said. "It's no big deal, really, but after the Flizh embarrassment it's been standard policy to hash things out in private before we let the public in on the party."

"I understand." Kosta took a deep breath, phrasing his next question carefully—

"So what specifically are you going to be working on?" Gyasi asked.

"Uh . . ." With an effort, Kosta shifted gears. "First thing will be a lit search. I've more or less volunteered to see if anyone's ever proved that it's the central particle alone that constitutes an angel, as opposed to the particle plus its accumulated matter shell."

Gyasi frowned. "The angel's the central particle, of course. What does the ion shell have to do with it?"

Kosta shrugged. "Maybe nothing. Maybe a great deal. Either way, I'd like to find out for sure."

Gyasi peered at him. "You're not trying to revive Chandkari's old theory, are you? I thought that died its final death five years ago."

"I'm just looking for the truth," Kosta said, feeling a sheen of sweat breaking out on his forehead and wishing he knew who Chandkari was. It had probably been somewhere in the list he'd just waded through. "I'd like to keep an open mind while I do it."

"Yeah." Gyasi shrugged. "Well. An open mind is a nice thing to have, but don't forget that certain kinds of junk make it fill up real fast."

"Sure," Kosta agreed. "I just have a hard time believing that a single subatomic particle could create the kind of ethical effect angels are supposed to have."

"A lot of us do," Gyasi nodded. "That's what makes Dr. Qhahenlo's *Acchaa* theory so attractive. It fits the data, makes real, verifiable predictions, and practically *requires* that the angels be single particles." He jabbed a finger at Kosta. "Mark my words: in three years—four at the outside—the physicists will be scrambling to see how the *Acchaa* theory fits into Reynold's Unified."

"That'll be worth seeing, all right," Kosta agreed, allowing himself to feel a bit patronizing. In the Pax, the Grand Unified Theory had been modified and tacked onto so many times that it wasn't even called by Reynold's name any more. "Do I have to wait until then to hear what this *Acchaa* theory's all about?"

Gyasi grinned. "No. You're a member of the club now." The grin faded into a slight frown. "You don't mean you've never heard *anything* about the *Acchaa* theory, do you? I mean—" he waved a hand, encompassing either the room or the whole Institute— "you're *here*. Right?"

Kosta shrugged, thinking furiously. "Like I said, I wanted to come to Seraph with an open mind," he improvised. "Anyway, I figured half the theories I could have read about back on Balmoral would have been thrown out the window by the time I got here."

"Point," Gyasi conceded. "We *are* talking about Balmoral, after all."

"Cute," Kosta growled, remembering this time to stick to his role.

Gyasi grinned. "Sorry. Elitist condescension dies hard, you know."

The grin vanished, his expression becoming serious. "You see, the thing is that the angels can't be just another subatomic particle. If they were, they couldn't possibly be stable, not with that kind of mass and charge. That's why the *Acchaa* theory works so well; according to it, they're actually *quanta*—basic building blocks, just like photons and electrons. And quanta, by definition, have to be stable. You see?"

"I do know a little something about quantum theory, thank you," Kosta said, perhaps a little too dryly. "Balmoral isn't *that* far behind the times. So what exactly are they supposed to be quanta of?"

Gyasi seemed to brace himself. "They're quanta," he said, "of what mankind has always called *good*."

For a long minute Kosta just stared at him, the word ricocheting around his brain like an angry grasshopper trying to escape from a jar. "This is a joke," he heard himself say. "Right? It's a joke you play on newcomers."

Gyasi shook his head. "It's no joke, my friend." He gestured to Kosta's display. "Look it up yourself if you like—there are enough papers on the *Acchaa* theory to require two separate listings."

Kosta's brain was still spinning. "That's crazy," he told Gyasi. "Good and evil, aren't something you can quantize."

"Why not?" Gyasi asked.

"Why *not*?" Kosta clamped his teeth tightly together. "Come *on*, Gyasi. Good and evil don't exist in a vacuum—they're the results of things people do."

Gyasi held his hands out, palms upward. "Light is the result of hydrogen molecules fusing in the center of a star," he pointed out. "Or of someone flicking a switch. That doesn't mean that light isn't quantized."

"That's a fallacious argument," Kosta insisted. "You're talking about two entirely separate things."

"How so?"

"Well . . ." Kosta floundered a moment. "Well, for one thing, photons of light are the same everywhere. There's no such universal standard for defining good and evil. It's all culturally based."

"Interesting argument," Gyasi nodded. "Does that mean, then, that there aren't *any* common definitions of good and evil among human societies?"

Kosta eyed him, sensing a trap. "You tell me," he challenged. "You're obviously the expert."

"Oh, hardly," Gyasi shook his head. "But like everyone else here I've given it a lot of thought over the past few years. And if I haven't got all the answers, I *have* come up with some interesting questions."

"Such as?"

"Such as how good people can continue to exist in a culture that most outside observers would label as evil. And not just exist, sometimes, but actually turn the whole direction of the culture around."

"Big deal," Kosta growled. "Evil people can do that too."

Gyasi nodded. "Exactly. The reverse of the same coin. Then there are a whole group of questions that I guess would fall into a 'folk medicine' sort of category. You know—little bits of advice that people pass along generational lines; things they accept as true even if they don't understand the mechanism involved. The standard mothers' warning against getting into bad company, for instance, or the idea that you can change a person's character if you put in the time and effort and love to do it. Or even the question of whether there's some deeper physical significance to the fact that good is so often equated with light, which is itself quantized."

Kosta blinked. "Huh?"

Gyasi grinned. "Never mind. I just tossed that one in to see if you were still paying attention."

"Trust me," Kosta assured him. "But this still doesn't make any sense. You've got the whole thing backwards."

"Do I?" Gyasi asked, serious again. "Well, then, try looking at it this way: what's the difference—the *observational* difference, I mean—between a person doing something bad and therefore creating evil; and the evil influencing the person to then go and do something bad?"

Kosta stared at him, searching for a quick and glib answer. He couldn't find one. "It's still backwards," he finally said.

"There are parts of it that bother me, too," Gyasi admitted. "The concept of free will, for one thing, which I'm not quite ready to give up on. But I can't give up on *Acchaa,* either." He gestured around him. "Because the angels work."

Kosta dropped his eyes to his display. "Documented?" he asked. "I mean, *really* documented?"

"We've got data from five hundred thirty-eight High Senators who were in office both before and after the law requiring them to wear angels," Gyasi said. "Over a third of them had occasionally or frequently skated to the edge of ethical and legal behavior. Influence peddling, abuse of power, financial irregularities—you know the list. Now, twenty years later, that sort of thing just doesn't happen. Some of them took years to change; but they did change."

"Maybe it was peer pressure," Kosta suggested, uncomfortably aware that he was grasping at straws. "Or better public awareness of their activities that caused them to back off."

"The people who did the studies didn't think so," Gyasi said. "The reports are there—go ahead and look them up."

Kosta looked up from the display, shook his head. *Quanta of good . . .* "Sorry, but I still don't buy it."

Gyasi shrugged. "You're welcome to try and prove the theory wrong," he said equably. "That's what science is all about. Personally, I had enough philosophical struggles before the angels and *Acchaa* came along. I wouldn't especially mind if this particular complication got eliminated."

He leaned forward, an odd expression on his face. "But while you and your open mind are trying to find another explanation, take a little time to consider the possibilities if this really *is* true. The chances we'll have to finally get at the root cause of evil and injustice in the universe."

"What do you mean?" Kosta asked, easing back in his chair. The other's sudden intensity was unnerving.

"Suppose we can find a way to create the same effect without having to have angels physically on hand, for instance," Gyasi said earnestly. "That's one of the things my group's working on: trying to isolate the physical mechanism that the angels use to alter brain chemistry or neural structure. Dr. Shivaprasad's group, downstairs in Basic Research, is trying to devise a way of detecting the presence of natural angels in people; Dr. MaecDavz and *his* group are doing the same thing from another direction, trying to see if angels can leave residual field effects of themselves in physical objects. Think of what that might mean for the interpretation of history or current events."

Abruptly, he broke off. "Sorry," he apologized, looking a little sheepish. "I sometimes lie in bed at night having imaginary arguments with the people out there who'd try to shut us down as blasphemers if they knew what we were doing and thinking here. Sometimes those arguments leak out a little."

"That's all right," Kosta assured him. "I gather you think it would be a waste of time for me to try and split the ion shells off the angels."

"*I* think so, yes," the other said with a shrug. "But I'm hardly the last word on how the universe operates. If Director Podolak gives you the go-ahead, I'd say go ahead." He glanced at his watch and stood up, giving his chair a shove back toward his own desk. "As for me, I've got a tissue sample waiting in the bio lab. See you later."

"Right," Kosta said as the other pulled open the door. "Enjoy yourself."

Gyasi flashed a grin and was gone, closing the door behind him.

Kosta stared at the closed door, a shiver running up his back. Searching for the mechanism, Gyasi had said, that the angels use to alter brain chemistry and neural structure.

To alter brain chemistry and neural structure . . .

The words seemed to hang there in the silence like some strange and unpleasant smell. Once again, it was back: the whole disturbing question of how Kosta himself was going to avoid being affected by the angels.

Once again, he had no answer.

CHAPTER 10

With a jerk, Chandris woke to find herself moving.

For a second she lay there in the dark, panic bubbling in her throat as she tried furiously to break through the fog of sleep and confusion. The unfamiliar bed beneath her jolted to the side; and as it did so, the disorientation cleared.

The *Gazelle,* and the Daviees . . . and Angelmass.

Twisting around on the narrow cot that took up half the tiny cabin's floor space, she fumbled in the dark for the light switch. The ceiling went on, a low night-level glow that didn't burn her eyes as she swung her legs out of bed and planted her feet on the icy metal floor. A six o'clock lift, Ornina had said; but the clock built into the computer desk read only four thirty-five. Either Ornina had gotten her wires crossed, or something was wrong.

The *Gazelle* jerked again. Gritting her teeth, Chandris reached for her new coverall jumpsuit and started pulling it on.

The narrow corridors were silent and night-level dim as she made her way along them toward the front of the ship, occasionally bumping into walls as the *Gazelle* continued its rocking movement. Amid the occasional creaking of metal she could hear a faint whine, nothing at all like the dull background roar that had been a constant part of life aboard the *Xirrus.*

Her original goal had been the forward control cabin, but she was barely halfway there when she began to hear traces of what sounded like music over the whine. Following the sound, she came upon an open door spilling light into the corridor. Moving as stealthily as she could on the unstable floor, she eased up to the door and looked inside.

"Well, good morning," Ornina said, looking up from a mess of disassembled electronics spread out on a lab table in front of her and throwing Chandris a smile. "What are you doing—just a second," she interrupted herself, turning toward the expensive-looking sound system in the corner. "Music command: volume down two," she ordered.

The music obediently went softer. "One of our few luxuries," Ornina confessed, looking back at Chandris. "But we both love music, and it's so nice to be able to fiddle with it when both hands are full. Don't just stand there—come on in. What in the world are you doing up this early?"

"I thought something was wrong," Chandris told her, feeling a little foolish as she stepped into the room. "We weren't supposed to leave until six, were we?"

"To leave Seraph, yes," Ornina nodded. "But we can hardly launch from our service port, now, can we?"

"No, of course not," Chandris agreed, annoyed that she hadn't figured that out on her own. "I guess I just assumed you meant we'd leave the service port at six or so."

Ornina shook her head, turning back to the equipment spread out in front of her. "No 'or so' about it," she said, picking up a tiny block and peering closely at it. "When Shikari launch control gives you a slot, you'd better be on the launch strip at that time and not a minute later. Otherwise, you go to the end of the roster and maybe don't even get off that day. Ach."

Shaking her head, she handed Chandris the block. "Be a dear and tell me what the number on this strytram is, will you?"

"Uh . . ." Chandris frowned at the faded gray printing, wondering uneasily if she was supposed to know what a strytram was. "It looks like CR 57743. Or maybe CR 57748—the last one's not all there."

"It's a 48," Ornina nodded, taking it back. "It was the 77 I wasn't sure of. Thank you."

"You're welcome." Chandris looked around at the other pieces. "What's all this from, anyway?"

"A Senamaec high-end sampler," Ornina identified it. "Our backup, fortunately, or we'd be in trouble. I don't suppose you've ever worked on one before?"

"Afraid not," Chandris said, forcing her voice to remain casual. The *Xirrus*'s files had never mentioned Senamaec high-end samplers. Belatedly, she was starting to realize that those files hadn't been nearly as complete as she'd thought. "Where's Mr. Daviee?" she asked, to change the subject.

"Hanan, please," Ornina chided her gently. "And I'm Ornina. There's not nearly enough room on a huntership for unnecessary formalities. Besides, it makes us feel older than either of us likes."

"Sorry," Chandris murmured.

"That's all right. To answer your question, he's still in bed. Hopefully still asleep, too—he'll be handling the actual lift, and that's not a job for someone low on sleep." She glanced up at Chandris. "You were up pretty late last night, too, weren't you."

"I was trying to get through all the spec manuals," Chandris told her. "There are a lot of things about the *Gazelle* that I'm not used to."

"Hunterships are a unique breed of fish," Ornina agreed. "Have to be. You send an ordinary ship into the Angelmass region and you'd fry everything inside it to a crisp. Electromagnetic radiation, particle fluxes, magnetic twist fields—the works. But of course you know all that."

"Of course," Chandris murmured, a chill running up her back. Somehow, in all her studying, she'd never run across anything on Angelmass itself. If it was as dangerous as it sounded, she'd better correct that omission, and fast. "Well, unless you need me, I guess I'll go get some breakfast," she told Ornina, starting back toward the door.

"Go ahead," Ornina said. "But when you're finished, I'd appreciate it if you'd come back and give me a hand here. I want to get this put back together before Hanan wakes up."

Chandris clenched her teeth. "Sure," she said. "I'll be right back."

So much for more study time, she groused to herself as she swayed her way back down the jostling corridors. But still, that was more annoying than dangerous. After all, the Daviees had been doing this angel collecting thing for eleven years now. Surely they knew what they were doing.

No matter how bad Angelmass was, she could certainly handle a single trip out there. And a single trip was all she was going to need.

More from curiosity than any other reason, Chandris watched the control cabin chrono as she sat waiting; and at exactly 6:00:02 the *Gazelle* lifted.

It felt pretty much the way the shuttle launch to the *Xirrus* had felt, back when she'd first left Uhuru: a mostly smooth sense of movement along the thick concrete strip and up into the sky, with a steady roar of engines coming from behind.

But back then she'd been in a passenger cabin, without the monitors and displays and the running conversation between Hanan, Ornina, and the controllers . . . and it was quickly clear that a space ship launch was more interesting than it felt.

The sound of the engines wasn't just a single roar, for one thing. It was a mixture of several different roars, each coming from a different engine, with only the combination remaining steady. The sky was anything but empty, either: there must have been a hundred other vehicles flying around the area, all of them looking much too close for comfort.

"We're coming up on the launch dish, Chandris," Ornina announced from her seat. "Pelvic camera, if you want to watch."

Chandris shifted her eyes to the display showing the underside of the ship. There it was, or so she assumed, moving into view as the *Gazelle* flew over the landscape. It was almost fragile looking, shaped like a giant dinner plate . . . and looked like it was about to explode.

It really did. From a hundred places around the edge sparks were spitting, and she could see that the dish's surface was shimmering with a haze of light. Beneath the haze, the whole nurking thing seemed to be coming apart—

And then, without warning, it was gone. Along with the whole city.

Chandris blinked, eyes flicking between the displays . . . and gradually it dawned on her that the city was gone because the *Gazelle* was suddenly way off the ground.

Way off the ground.

"First launch dish lift?"

Chandris turned to find Ornina looking back at her. "Not really," she said, wondering uneasily whether it *should* be her first. There hadn't been a word about launch dishes in the material she'd read aboard the *Xirrus,* either. Was it something specific to hunterships? "First one where I've had a chance to watch what was happening, though," she added, hoping that would cover all the edges.

Apparently it did. "Pretty spectacular, isn't it?" Hanan commented. "Especially when the dish looks like it's about to come apart. I've never yet gotten a clear answer from a tech on what exactly causes that illusion."

"You want to double-check our vector, Chandris?" Ornina asked. "We should be on an orbital intercept for the catapult."

"Sure," Chandris nodded, swiveling the comp arm into position in front of her and getting her mind back on business. This part, at least, she'd studied like crazy. The *Gazelle*'s course vector . . . there it was. To calculate the orbital intercept all she had to do was to call up the proper display and superimpose the lines . . . "Looks good," she reported. "Maybe just a little on the short side."

"Short side, right," Hanan said. The roar of the engines deepened for a moment, then slackened off again. "No surprise there—Lift Two's always tended to kick a little short," he commented. "Maybe someday they'll get around to fixing it."

"Not till Lift Four's on line, though," Ornina said. "What was ETA on the catapult, Chandris?"

Chandris glanced across her display, located the proper number. "About fifteen minutes," she said.

"Good." She cocked her head a little to the side. "We'll be all right here now if you'd like to go back to your room and catch up on your sleep. Even after we hit Central it'll be another couple of hours before we're close enough to start looking for angels."

Chandris hesitated. She *was* tired—that was for sure. But she was supposed to be an expert at this stuff; and wherever she went next it would undoubtedly help her puff-talk if she knew what a catapulting looked and felt like. Most people, after all, weren't so gullible as to believe every lame thing she said. "Thanks," she told Ornina. "But I'd rather stay."

The catapult didn't have nearly the same class of light show as the launch dish had had. All Chandris could see as they approached, in fact, were five widely spaced clusters of multicolored lights, all of them flickering crazily, that seemed to match with the catapult pole markings on the navigation display. Hanan maneuvered the *Gazelle* into the middle of the lights, signaled someone that they were ready, and listened as the radio gave him a short, five-number countdown. An almost-felt jerk; and in an instant the flashing lights on the display had changed to—

Chandris's whole body lurched in a sudden spasm of shock. "Nurk!" she gasped.

"What?" Ornina snapped.

For a horrible second Chandris couldn't even speak; her body stiff with horror, her eyes frozen on the *thing* centered on the display. It was a spider—a huge, monstrous, impossible *spider.* In the distance she could see the massive hourglass-shaped body glistening evilly in an eerie light. Its spindly rear legs were almost invisible as they trailed out behind it; but the front legs, stretched out to grab the *Gazelle*—

"Welcome to Angelmass Central," Hanan said, his voice sounding distant alongside the pounding in her ears. "Often called the ugliest space station ever built. I take it from your reaction that you agree?"

With a supreme effort Chandris tore her eyes away from the horror on the display. "What?" she managed.

His eyebrows raised, just a bit. "It's a space station," he said gently.

For another minute she just looked at him, the words slowly registering through the fear. Then, steeling herself, she looked back at the display.

The spider was gone. In its place was, indeed, a space station.

The two halves of the hourglass body were two squat cylinders with tapering ends, their central sections rotating slowly to create an artificial gravity. Connecting them was a slender section that looked like a double choker composed of large pearls, pearls painted the bright orange of emergency escape pods.

She took a deep breath, exhaled it through quivering lips. "Sorry," she muttered, her face hot with shame. "I thought I saw . . . something else."

"At a guess, I'd say a giant spider," Hanan said.

Chandris took another deep breath. It seemed to help a little. "That's it," she nodded, forcing her mind and voice back into the proper role. "I'm sorry. I've never been very fond of spiders."

"Join the club," Ornina said. "There are some days I still get a chill myself when I see the place."

The *Gazelle* had pulled away from the outstretched spider legs now, enough so that the slowly flashing lights on the ends of each could be seen. "Those are the poles for the net, then?" Chandris asked tentatively.

"Right," Ornina said. "The other end of the station is the catapult for getting us back to Seraph."

"And the spider-leg connectors are there to tether both of them to the operations center and power plant in the middle," Hanan added. "Can't leave them floating free like you can in a normal planetary orbit—the particle wind from Angelmass would have the whole thing disassembled before you knew it, and then we'd all have to go back to Seraph the long way. Twenty light-minutes may not be all that much in the galactic scheme of things, but it would make for a very long ride home."

"True," Chandris murmured, searching her memory. A light-minute?—right, the distance light traveled in sixty seconds. At three hundred thousand kilometers a second . . .

Surreptitiously, she tapped at the calculator on her board. Three hundred thousand times sixty times twenty . . . three hundred sixty million kilometers.

She stared at the number, a chill running through her. The Barrio had extended maybe two kilometers at its widest; the whole of New Mexico City had stretched only thirty. Only once before in her life had she ever been further from home than she could walk if she had to, and even then it had only been a hundred-kilometer plane flight to Ankh.

Three hundred sixty million kilometers. For the first time, it was beginning to sink in just how different this world was she'd puff-talked her way into.

"I'll get some spin going," Ornina said. "Course vector check, Chandris?"

"Right away," Chandris said, shaking off the strangely depressing sense of not belonging. She keyed her comp arm, glanced at the main display—

And looked back again. Centered in the display, all alone in pitch blackness, was the brightest star she'd ever seen.

Angelmass.

"Impressive, isn't it?" Hanan said.

Chandris started; she hadn't realized she'd so obviously been staring at it. "Very," she agreed. "I didn't expect it to be so bright."

"It's a lot brighter than that," Ornina told her soberly. "At this distance it would blind you in a second if the sunscreens didn't automatically crank the gain down to tolerable levels. On Seraph you can sometimes see it in the daytime. Pretty impressive, especially for something that's only a few atoms' widths across."

Chandris frowned. Angelmass was that tiny? Somehow, she'd had the vague idea that black holes were huge things, big masses of nothingness that could eat up the whole centers of galaxies, or suck in stuff from hundreds of kilometers away.

Were those just a different kind of black hole? Or was Angelmass something totally unique?

Beside her, the display board suddenly beeped. "What was that?" she asked, starting.

"High-energy gamma ray, probably," Hanan told her. "The ones at the high end of the spectrum can punch right through the hull, and of course they're not bothered by the magnetic deflectors."

"What did it do?" Chandris asked, eying the display warily. It seemed all right now.

"Probably kicked a false signal through one of the optical switches," Hanan shrugged. "Nothing serious. After a while you get used to the equipment pinging and flickering and burping at odd times."

"There's no need to be worried," Ornina added. "Remember that these hunterships were designed to handle all the radiation and heat out there. The only real dangers are from those high-energy gammas and the occasional antiparticle that might get through the magnetic fields."

Chandris blinked. "Antiparticles?" she asked.

"From Angelmass's Hawking radiation," Hanan explained. "The tidal forces at the edge of a black hole this small are strong enough to create particle/antiparticle pairs. Like proton and anti-proton, or electron and positron. Anyway, sometimes one of the particles escapes while the other falls back in. That's what's called Hawking radiation; and in fact it's where almost all of the particle flux out here comes from."

"Everything except some radiation from gravitational infalling," Ornina said. "And the angels, of course. No one's quite sure where they come from."

Chandris gritted her teeth. "Of course," she agreed, knowing even as she said it how stupid she sounded. She was supposed to *know* this stuff. Instead, she was totally lost.

And she'd nurking well better correct that, and fast. This track was far from solid . . . and if it popped, there was nowhere to run. "Speaking of angels," she said, "you said we wouldn't start hunting for them for another hour?"

"Oh, we'll fire up the detectors in about half an hour," Hanan said. "But we're not likely to get anything for awhile after that. An angel picks up a coating of positive ions really fast, and you have to be pretty close in to spot 'em before that happens."

Chandris nodded. "In that case, maybe I'll go back to my cabin for awhile. Unless you need me, of course."

"No, go ahead," Ornina said. "Anyway, it may be days before we spot an angel—you might as well start learning now how to pace yourself."

"Thank you," Chandris said, unstrapping and getting gingerly to her feet. "I'll be back in half an hour."

"No hurry," Ornina called after her.

Chandris stepped to the door, slid it open . . . and paused, looking back into the control cabin as an odd thought struck her. If the radiations from Angelmass could affect the *Gazelle*'s electronic gear, could they also affect Hanan's exobrace system? And if so, what would it do to him?

Impatiently, she shook the thought aside. Considering what she was planning, the state of Hanan's health was hardly something she needed to be concerned with.

Stepping through the door, she closed it behind her and headed back toward her room. With any luck at all, the *Gazelle*'s computer would have a fair amount of information on Angelmass. She had just half an hour to learn it all.

CHAPTER 11

They followed the herald and the Speaker into the room; and as the herald stepped to the front, Forsythe let his eyes sweep around the intricately carved walls and vaulted ceiling. It was just as he remembered it: the Common Chamber of the High Senate, rich with grandeur and history and a sense of power.

For Forsythe, though, it was much more than any of those. It was like coming home.

He took a deep breath, the delicate scent of leather and brass and exotic wood triggering a kaleidoscope of bittersweet memories. Watching from the gallery above during session as his father spoke to the assemblage. Curling up in one of the huge leather chairs late in the evening, or wandering around looking at the carvings on the walls, waiting for his father to finish a conversation and take him home. The first time that, as one of his father's assistants, he had had to come right into the middle of session to deliver some last-minute papers, feeling proud and scared and horribly conspicuous all at the same time.

Standing there, helpless, as his father quietly but firmly handed in his resignation.

Lowering his eyes, Forsythe focused on the men and women sitting in the tiered seats beneath the dome of the ceiling. At the glitter of the angel pendants hanging around each of those high and mighty necks . . .

The herald pounded his ceremonial staff on the stone floor, the thud echoing through the chamber and quieting the last murmurs of conversation from the tiers. "The High Senate of the Empyrean is now in session," he intoned. "Let all rise and prepare their hearts and minds for service to the people of the Five Worlds."

There was a general shuffle of cloth on leather as the High Senators obediently rose to their feet. Stepping past the herald, the Speaker walked over to stand beside his own high-backed chair, and for a minute the room was silent. Then, at an unseen signal, the herald pounded his staff again. "May God grant wisdom, compassion, and courage to all who serve," he said. Pounding the staff a third time, he turned and went to his small archway at the back of the room.

The Speaker sat down, the chair creaking slightly with his weight. "Greetings to you all," he said gravely as the rest took their seats in turn. "I welcome you to the thirty-second session of the Empyreal High Senate; I trust you all came back ready to work." He glanced down at the desk display on his left. "Our first order of business this morning will be to welcome three newly elected members into our midst: Karym Daryani of Uhuru, replacing the late Bharat Jain; Arkin Forsythe of Lorelei, replacing the retiring Gabre Kassaie; and Vladmr Grosdova of Sadhai, replacing the late Raimon Sabatyat."

Two deaths and a retirement. It was, Forsythe reflected darkly, a perfect example of how the angels had corrupted the system. In his father's day politics had finally been hammered into a genuinely even-handed struggle, with a competent challenger having a real chance of unseating a less able incumbent. Now, only eighteen years later, the ancient patterns of entrenched imperial power systems had already reemerged.

The experts lauded it, of course, as they lauded everything having to do with angels. The theory was that the angel presence had given the people a new confidence in their leaders' ethical standards, which had in turn allowed them to safely focus more of their attention on the value of experience in choosing those same leaders.

No one seemed interested in the question of whether even ethical politicians could get too comfortable or complacent in their jobs . . . as comfortable and complacent as many of those same experts were in their own positions. Perhaps that was why the question never occurred to them.

"The new High Senators," the Speaker continued, "will now come forward, to swear their oath before the rest of the assemblage and to receive in return their badge of trust."

Or, in plain language, their angel pendants. Forsythe took a deep breath as, flanked by the other two, he stepped up to the Speaker's podium. Off to the side, near the section of the semicircular table where he would soon be taking his place, he could see Ronyon and Pirbazari standing ready.

"Karym Daryani; step forward," the Speaker said. Daryani did so, touching the other's palm in respect. "You have been chosen by the people of the Mbundu District of Uhuru to serve them as High Senator. Will you accept the responsibilities such service will demand of you?"

"I will," Daryani nodded, his voice holding just the right mixture of humility and confidence.

Forsythe turned his head slowly as the Speaker went through the rest of the ritual, just far enough to see Ronyon out of the corner of his eye. The big man stood unnaturally straight, his lips making small movements as if chewing on a piece of gristle, his eyes darting constantly around the room as if looking for an escape hatch. *Don't fall apart on me now,* Forsythe mentally urged him. *Fall apart later, if you want. But not now.*

". . . and so, in the name of the High Senate, I present you with your badge of service to the Empyrean," the Speaker was saying. "Wear it always, both as a symbol of your authority and as a commitment to the people."

The herald had returned during that last, carrying a small wooden box. Now, he lifted the hinged lid; and with a delicacy that bordered on the reverent, the Speaker reached in and withdrew an angel pendant. The crystal sparkled brilliantly in the light as he lowered the chain over Daryani's inclined head and settled it comfortably around his neck. "I welcome you, High Senator Daryani," he said.

There was a short burst of polite applause. Daryani touched the Speaker's palm again, then turned and climbed the steps to his new seat.

The Speaker turned to Forsythe. "Arkin Forsythe," he intoned. "Step forward."

Forsythe had never had much patience with official ceremonies, but over the years he had learned to put up with them. This one, at least, had the virtue of being short. They went through the routine: the Speaker asking the rote questions, Forsythe giving the rote answers; a straight duplicate of Daryani's swearing in.

Until the herald started forward with his wooden box.

"And so, in the name of the High Senate, I present you with the badge of service to the Empyrean."

"A word, if I may, sir," Forsythe said.

The Speaker stopped, his eyes narrowing. Perhaps he was remembering the elder Forsythe's refusal to wear an angel. "You may speak," he said, a note of caution in his voice.

Forsythe let him worry for another second. "I will, of course, accept the badge of service," he said. "And will wear it with the humility and honor it deserves. I ask, though, that as a further symbol of my commitment to the Empyreal people—" he glanced to his side— "that two of the common people—my aides—be permitted the honor of placing it around my neck."

He watched as a whole series of emotions flashed across the Speaker's face: relief that Forsythe was not, in fact, going to make a scene; annoyance that he was so cavalierly being asked to change his routine without prior notification; and finally, the equally annoyed recognition that, while he might have the technical right to refuse, to do so would leave him looking petty and stiff-necked in front of his colleagues. "Your request is unorthodox," he rumbled. "But with the High Senate's permission I will grant it." He looked over at Pirbazari and Ronyon. "Step forward."

Pirbazari nudged Ronyon, and together they walked toward the others—Ronyon, Forsythe noted uneasily, looking even more agitated than he had a minute ago. The Speaker nodded, first to the herald, and then to them. "Proceed."

Pirbazari nodded back and turned to the herald, taking the angel pendant out of the box. He held it up for a moment; then, with appropriate dignity, handed it to Ronyon. Gingerly, the big man took it, holding it as if it were something hot. He looked at Forsythe, licked his lips once, and stepped over to him—

And in a sudden flurry of fumbling fingers dropped it on the floor.

He was down on his knees before anyone in the chamber even got out a gasp, his big hands scrabbling across the floor and finally getting a grip on it. With a jerky motion he climbed back to his feet, chain and crystal clutched in a tangle in his hand, his whole body shaking and a wild look of fear plastered across his face. Forsythe gave him a reassuring smile and bowed his head slightly; still trembling, Ronyon untangled the chain and eased it carefully over Forsythe's head. Straightening up, Forsythe smiled again as Ronyon backed up hastily to stand beside Pirbazari.

The pendant felt strangely heavy, pressing against his breastbone and tugging at the back of his neck. Dimly, Forsythe wondered how long it would take him to get used to it.

"Thank you both," the Speaker said, nodding gravely to Ronyon and Pirbazari. He looked back at Forsythe, his expression more wry than angry at the momentary fiasco. "And now," he said, "I welcome you, High Senator Forsythe."

"Thank you, sir," Forsythe murmured over the applause. Touching the Speaker's palm, he stepped over to Pirbazari and Ronyon; and, with them beside him, headed to his new place at the table.

And wondered if the whisper of guilt nagging at him over what he'd just done was coming from the angel.

". . . and this is your private office," the young page said, opening the door and stepping aside to let Forsythe enter.

"I see," Forsythe nodded, craning his head to peer inside. As with the rest of the complex—the outer screening office, the central work area with its rows of desks, and the ring of private offices around the central room's edge—the bulk of the furniture and equipment was already in place, leaving only some personal items and a few boxes of records to be dealt with. "My communications system is operational?" he asked the page.

"Yes, sir, as of yesterday evening," the other answered. "Full computer and archives access, too."

"Good." Forsythe glanced at Pirbazari and Ronyon, standing a few paces back. Took a second look at the expression on Ronyon's face . . . "That will be all for now," he told the page. "Thank you."

"You're welcome, High Senator," the other said. "I'm on call to you any-time you need me." Ducking his head in a well-practiced gesture of respect, he headed across the common room and left.

Forsythe caught Pirbazari's eye. "I want you to get on the net, Zar," he told the other. "Get a dump of the last skeeter report from Lorelei and give it a quick sift—I want to know what's been happening out there."

"Yes, sir." Turning with his usual military precision, Pirbazari strode off to his office.

Forsythe cocked an eyebrow toward Ronyon. *Come on in,* he signed to the other. *I'd like to talk to you.*

He ushered Ronyon into his new office, closing the door behind them, and led the big man to the chair facing his desk. The other dropped into it, his posture that of a man trying to burrow his way backwards into the furniture.

Forsythe went around the desk and sat down. *I just wanted to tell you,* he signed, *that you did very well this morning.*

Thank you, Ronyon signed, his fingers showing the same lack of enthusiasm as his face.

You seem unhappy, Forsythe pointed out. *Do you want to talk about it?*

Ronyon lowered his eyes to the floor. *That wasn't a good thing I did,* he signed slowly, his eyes avoiding Forsythe's.

Of course it was, Forsythe insisted, leaning slightly over the desk so that his signing would be visible in Ronyon's peripheral vision. *What could be wrong with it?*

Ronyon looked up again, his face screwed up in anguish and confusion. *It was just like telling a lie.*

Forsythe pursed his lips. *We've been through this, Ronyon,* he reminded the other. *Remember? This is a very special, very precious gift that we've been given, and it's our job to protect it. You understand that, don't you?*

Ronyon dropped his gaze to the floor again. *I guess so.*

Well, then, Forsythe continued, *what better way to keep it safe than to hide it from people who might want to steal it?*

Ronyon shrugged, a hunching movement that reminded Forsythe of a turtle hiding under the edge of its shell. *I don't know,* he signed at last. *I just know it feels just like I do when I tell a lie.*

I know, Forsythe soothed. *But think about what I told you, all right? If you do, I'm sure you'll realize this is the best way to keep our angel safe.*

Okay. Ronyon swiped at his nose. *Okay. I guess I should give it back to you now?*

He dug the angel pendant out of his pocket and started to get up. *Just put it down there,* Forsythe signed quickly. *Underneath the cushion in that chair will do.*

Ronyon looked at him, eyebrows raised in astonishment. *It's the last place,* Forsythe added, *that a thief would think to look for something as valuable as an angel. Right?*

I don't know, Ronyon said, his face still puzzled. But he dutifully stuffed the pendant down the side of the cushion, poking several times before the entire length of chain disappeared.

Thank you. Forsythe eyed him. *There's still something bothering you.*

Ronyon hunched another shrug. *People are going to think I'm clumsy.*

Forsythe hid a smile. That wonderfully simple mind of Ronyon's—straightforward, uncalculating, concerned only with the surface effects of human interaction. Probably incapable of grasping the idea, even if Forsythe had wanted to try and explain it, that it was often a tactical advantage to be underestimated. *Some of them might,* he conceded. *But not the people whose opinions really matter. People like Mr. Pirbazari, for example, will just think you were nervous. They know things like that just happen sometimes. No one remembers them for long. Really.*

Ronyon swallowed. *I guess.*

Then let's put it behind us and get to work, Forsythe told him, putting some executive firmness into his face and fingers. *There's supposed to be a studio somewhere around here for my use. I want you to go find it and see what it's like. Okay?*

Okay. Ronyon levered himself out of the chair, already looking happier. *I'll go find out everything. Should I tell Mr. Mils, then?*

That's a good idea, Forsythe agreed. *And then you can come and tell me, too.*

Okay.

Forsythe watched him hurry out of the office, marveling at how easy it was to cheer up the big man. A little praise, a little job, and all worries were as good as forgotten.

He looked down at the chair Ronyon had been sitting in, and his smile faded.

He'd done it. In plain view of the entire High Senate he'd switched a real angel pendant for a masterfully constructed fake one. And, for good measure, he had worn the fake in public long enough for everyone to be absolutely convinced he was properly under its influence.

The charade had gotten off to an excellent start. Now all he had to do was make sure it didn't come crashing down around his ears.

Which meant, for starters, that he was going to have to find a better hiding place for the real pendant than under a chair cushion. Far enough away from him, but at the same time not *too* far. There were stories of people who could sense the presence of angels from as far as two meters away, and he couldn't risk having one of them sitting there wondering what had gone wrong with his personal radar.

But there would be time for all that later. The important goal, that he stay uncontaminated, had been achieved.

There was a tap at the door. "Come," Forsythe called.

Pirbazari poked his head into the office. "You have time for a quick item from the skeeter?"

Forsythe waved him in. "Let me guess. Another intrusion by the Pax."

"Yes, sir," Pirbazari said grimly, crossing the room and handing Forsythe a cyl. "From the configuration, looks like another mid-sized warship."

"Any shooting?" Forsythe asked, plugging the cyl into his reader.

"Not this time," Pirbazari said. "Of course, it was only in the net for about forty seconds before they 'pulted it out."

"Forty seconds is plenty of time to shoot if they'd wanted to."

"Agreed," Pirbazari nodded. "Which implies they didn't want to."

The record of the encounter came up on the screen, and Forsythe took a minute to watch it. The Pax ship came in, moved around a little as if trying to get out of the focus, then disappeared as it was catapulted out of the system.

Exactly the same thing that had happened to the last Pax ship. And the one before that. "That makes, what, three ships in two weeks?" he asked, backing up to the best view of the Pax ship and freezing the image.

"Right," Pirbazari said. "Counting that big monstrosity, the *Komitadji*."

Forsythe glared at the display. "One ship might just be harassment. But not three. What do you suppose they're up to?"

"I'm not sure." Pirbazari leaned over the desk to tap at Forsythe's keyboard. "But this may be significant: the ships all went to different nets."

Forsythe frowned at the display. "Coincidence?" he asked, though he was pretty sure what the answer would be.

"I doubt it, sir," Pirbazari shook his head. "You have to come from a particular direction to be caught by a particular net. That, or wait until the one you want has moved around in its orbit."

Forsythe rubbed his fingers gently on his desktop. Pirbazari was right, of course . . . and to hit each of three different quadrants from as far away as the Pax would take careful selection of catapult launch sites indeed. "They're looking for something," he said. "But what?"

"Wreckage from the *Komitadji*, maybe?" Pirbazari suggested. "You'll remember EmDef had to do a fast recalibration on that one. Could be they did it too fast and wound up sending the thing through a star after all."

"We can always hope," Forsythe grunted. "But in that case, shouldn't a single reconnoiter have been enough to show the ship wasn't destroyed at Lorelei? *And* shouldn't the follow-up ship have been sent to the same net?"

"There's another possibility." Pirbazari hesitated. "It could be they're mapping out the system. Defenses, belt mining and refinery centers, comm focal points. Maybe even Lorelei itself; we really don't know how good their optics are."

Forsythe stared up at him, a cold knot settling into his stomach. "You realize what you're saying."

Pirbazari met his gaze steadily. "Yes, sir. Pre-invasion reconnaissance."

Forsythe looked back at the display. "And they've even turned our own net system against us," he said. "Using it to get maximum coverage with minimum effort. Clever bastards."

Pirbazari nodded. "Anyway, I thought it might help you to have this before the joint Resource/Commerce meeting this afternoon."

"Yes. Thank you." Forsythe glanced at his watch. "Do me a favor, will you? Pull up the report we wrote and integrate this new material into it. You have a copy?"

"Yes, sir," Pirbazari said. "Incidentally, I also checked on the media coverage of the ceremony this morning as you asked."

"My father's name come up?"

"Inevitably," the other said dryly. "But they didn't play on him nearly as much as they could have. The general consensus these days seems to be that his resignation was a reasonable and legitimate act of conscience."

Forsythe snorted. "Generous of them to allow him his ethics," he said scornfully. "Maybe they've forgotten that was even possible before the angels came along."

"Sure couldn't prove it by some of them," Pirbazari agreed. "Mostly, though, they left your father alone and focused on your own record and prospects in the High Senate."

Forsythe nodded. "I hope they didn't dump too much on Ronyon for dropping the angel."

"Not a bit," Pirbazari said with a smile. "In fact, I don't think more than two or three of them even mentioned it. Whatever anyone things of you or your politics, everybody likes Ronyon."

"He's an eminently likable person," Forsythe said. So there went the last potential snag with this whole thing. If the media had been even slightly suspicious, they might picked at it until it came unraveled.

But as Pirbazari said, everyone liked Ronyon.

"At least we're done with the pomp and ceremony," he went on. "Let's get that report ready."

"Right," Pirbazari said, moving toward the door. "Maybe it'll be enough to finally get some action."

"Let's hope so," Forsythe said as the other pulled open the door. *Because if it doesn't,* he added darkly to himself, *they may not get another chance. Not before there are Pax troops on Lorelei.*

". . . so the bottom line here," High Senator Bjani of Uhuru said, slouching back in his chair and stabbing a pair of fingers at the graphs he'd put up on the central display, "is that the decision to move most of the hyperspace nets further out in their respective systems has played more havoc with shipping than we originally thought it would. So much so that if they don't get some sort of relief the smallest companies are likely to go under within the next few months." He sent a questioning look around the table. "Suggestions?"

Forsythe looked around the table, too, carefully keeping his mouth shut. As the newest member of the Resource Development Committee it really wasn't his place to respond first, particularly not in a joint meeting with fifteen other High Senators present. But from the graphs the Commerce people had drawn up it was clear that the proper approach would be to strike a deal between the shippers and the various mining interests.

And the psychological leverage, he knew from long experience, would go to whoever first offered the suggestion. He threw a glance at old Mleru Jossarian beside him, hoping the senior Lorelei representative here would be fast enough to jump on it before anyone else did.

He wasn't. "It seems pretty obvious," Schmid of Balmoral spoke up. "If those graphs are right, the bulk of the problem lies in the cost of mineral shipments, principally those from the Lorelei asteroid mines. Perhaps the gentlemen from Lorelei could offer some help."

"I'm sure we can," Jossarian nodded sagely. "A modest adjustment of profit margins via the tax structure should take care of it. I can have the proper papers drawn up and sent to the entire High Senate for vote by tomorrow morning. Then all it'll take—"

Forsythe's tongue unfroze. "Just a minute," he said.

The entire table looked at him. "You have something, Mr. Forsythe?" Jossarian asked mildly.

Forsythe stared at him, tongue threatening to freeze up again. Couldn't Jossarian *see* it? "Sir, we can't just give away Lorelei's profits," he told the other, keeping his voice low. "Certainly not without getting something in ex-change. The majority of the shipping companies are headquartered here on Uhuru—we need a solid commitment, in print, from Mr. Bjani and his people before—"

"Please." Jossarian patted Forsythe's hand, giving him an indulgent smile. "Excuse us," he said to the rest of the table. "You'll have to forgive my colleague; he's new to how we do things here. As I said, I should be able to get a vote on this by tomorrow afternoon and the orders sent to Lorelei by the next day." He looked at Bjani. "Will a fifteen percent reduction be acceptable?"

"It should," the other said, tapping keys on his board. The curves on the display flattened noticeably. "Very acceptable indeed," he nodded. "It will, of course, put a strain on your mining licensees, particularly the smaller companies. My numbers indicate a five percent reduction in equipment transport fees by our licensed shipping companies should be adequate compensation."

Jossarian was already busy with his own board. "Looks good," he said. "Though I'll need to run the numbers a bit more carefully to be sure."

Bjani nodded. "Certainly. Call me whenever you're done and we'll double-check them together."

Jossarian looked at Forsythe. "You see?" he said gently. "It all gets done. And in a much more civilized fashion."

"Indeed," Forsythe murmured. Yes, the High Senate was indeed civilized. Civilized and peaceful; and if this was a representative example of their work, highly productive besides.

And it chilled him straight to the bone.

Because it wasn't breeding or smiles or even efficiency that made a good politician. It was, instead, the absolute, single-minded goal of protecting and nurturing his constituents' interests.

And you never protected those interests by giving something away for free. Never.

It didn't matter that Bjani had turned around and granted the Lorelei miners a *quid pro quo* out of the goodness of his heart. It didn't even matter that the proposed trade-off would probably benefit the Empyrean as a whole. What mattered was that Jossarian had been sent to Uhuru to do a job. And he hadn't done it.

Forsythe dropped his gaze from Jossarian's placid face to the sparkling crystal resting against his chest. Once, he knew, Jossarian had been one of the best politicians on Lorelei, a man his father had always talked about with respect and admiration.

But that was before the angels.

"Well," Bjani said, glancing at his display. "I believe that completes all the old business we had on line for this afternoon. Does anyone have any new business they'd care to bring up?"

Forsythe braced himself. "Yes, sir, I have," he said. "I'd like to draw the joint committee's attention to my report on the recent Pax incursions into the Lorelei system. As a Pax invasion would impact rather severely on both commerce and resources," he added quickly, to forestall the obvious objection, "I feel it's within the province of this assembly to at least discuss the matter."

There was a brief shuffle of what might have been discomfort around the table. Bjani remained unperturbed. "I've read your report, Mr. Forsythe," he acknowledged. "As well as your conclusions. Setting aside the question of whether this is, indeed, a proper forum for such a discussion, it seems to me that you're perhaps taking all of this a little too seriously."

Forsythe stared at him. "Too *seriously?* With all due respect, Mr. Bjani, I find it highly unlikely that the Pax is throwing all these ships at Lorelei just for the fun of it."

"'All these ships' is a relative term, Mr. Forsythe," Bjani said soothingly. "Three ships in two weeks hardly qualifies as an invasion fleet."

"They're not likely to just keep escalating numbers until they happen to have enough to do the job," Forsythe countered. "They're also not going to give up the services of three warships for several months unless they stand to gain something equally valuable from it. They're up to something . . . and in my opinion, that something can only be a pre-invasion reconnaissance."

"Your opinion, and that of former EmDef Commander Pirbazari as well, I note," Rodrez of Sadhai rumbled, his fingers playing across the scan buttons on his display. "I see he co-authored this report."

"He did," Forsythe said. "And I would hope that, given his experience and reputation, his views on military matters would carry even more weight with the High Senate than mine do."

"None of us means to belittle Commander Pirbazari's qualifications," Bjani said. "Nor yours, for that matter. It's simply that, in our opinion, you're both missing the point."

"That point being?"

"That the Pax can't take over the Empyrean," Bjani said, his voice quietly confident. "And that they know it."

Forsythe consciously unclenched his teeth. "Perhaps you've forgotten the first ship they sent in two weeks ago, the *Komitadji*," he said. "That ship could, in all probability, have taken Lorelei all by itself."

"And what happened to it?" Bjani shrugged. "It failed to make even a dent in the EmDef forces arrayed against it before being 'pulted."

"That's not victory," Forsythe said bluntly. "That's a holding action. Read your history, Mr. Bjani—no one has ever given up territorial ambitions just because it looked like it would take some time and effort to achieve them."

"I *have* read my history, Mr. Forsythe," Bjani said, a slight edge creeping into his voice. "And perhaps territory is indeed what the Pax once wanted. But not anymore. What they want now is profit."

"You've never dealt directly with the Pax," Jossarian murmured from beside Forsythe. "We have; and we understand them. They love money—love it so much, in fact, that their entire political structure is built on that basis. And the leaders are fully aware that to conquer the Empyrean will cost them far more than they stand to gain."

"Normal military tactics simply can't handle the existence of hyperspace nets," Hammura of Seraph put in. "We're like a pre-aircraft mountain nation with only a handful of roads leading in. Easy to defend, incredibly hard to attack."

"Certainly the Pax is up to something," Bjani said. "They're trying to rattle us, hoping we'll get nervous enough to negotiate away concessions they can't win by force." He locked eyes with Forsythe. "But they won't succeed, because we have a strength the Pax can never understand. Our unity. We have no cracks for them to drive wedges into; no factions and jealousies for them to split off and exploit. Unity in mind, and purpose, and heart."

"And all due to the angels," Forsythe muttered, the bitter taste of defeat in his mouth.

"Indeed," Bjani nodded, a small smile on his face. "This is a turning point in mankind's path, Mr. Forsythe. You've read history. Now watch it being made."

He looked around the table. "Now. Any other new business?"

It took until late that night; but by 11:30 Forsythe finally had his computer system set up to search all information nets and official channels for ongoing research work on angels and Angelmass.

Perhaps, he thought more than once during that long evening, the Pax propaganda was in fact true. Perhaps the angels really were robbing the Empyrean's leaders of their humanity. He didn't know. What he did know was that, for whatever reason, the members of the High Senate had lost the ability to fight for their people's best interests. Perhaps for their very survival.

And it was those same leaders who were determined to flood the Empyrean with even more angels.

Leaning back in his chair, Forsythe keyed for a test run-through of his new system. Somewhere out there, buried amid all the studies being done on the angels, there must be something that would give him a handle on stopping this quiet invasion.

He only hoped he could find it before it was too late.

CHAPTER 12

"The first thing you learn out here," Ornina said, stepping over to the table with the dinner trays, "is that for angel hunters patience isn't just a virtue. It's an absolute necessity."

"I'm starting to realize that," Chandris said, accepting her tray.

And then nearly dropping it as yet another horrible *crack*! snapped through the *Gazelle*, somewhere behind her head. Like the whole nurking ship was coming apart, over and over and over . . .

Crack! "*Nurk* it," she snarled, wincing at the bite she'd just taken out of her tongue. "Don't those ever stop?"

"Not as long as we're near Angelmass," Ornina said, stirring some sugar into her tea. "Just keep reminding yourself that they're completely harmless." She eyed Chandris over the top of her cup. "And be thankful you *are* hearing them," she said, her voice going dark. "The only time you don't hear gamma-ray sparks out here is when there's something's seriously wrong with your electronics."

"I'll keep that in mind," Chandris muttered, more sarcastically than she'd meant to be. There was another *crack*—

Settle down, *nurk it*, she snarled at herself, wondering what the hell was wrong with her. Less than half a day into this track and she was already ready to pop the cord on it.

Or, rather, *would* have been ready if there'd been any way to do it. Out here, millions of kilometers from Seraph or anywhere else, there weren't a lot of places to run.

Was that what was bothering her? The fact that there was nowhere to run?

"Sorry about the food quality," Ornina said.

Chandris snapped out of her thoughts, realized she'd been picking idly at the pasty food on her tray. "It's fine," she said, trying a mouthful.

"You're too generous," Ornina said dryly. "Unfortunately, the diet is another of those things you have to get used to out here. When you spot an angel there's never enough time to get meals or drinks stowed away before you kill ship's rotation and zip off after it. This cheap zero-gee stuff stays with the trays better than real food would—makes the cleanup afterward easier."

"I understand," Chandris said, taking another bite. It was still better than a lot of the meals she'd eaten in her lifetime. "How long before that happens? That we spot an angel, I mean?"

"A few days," Ornina said, digging into her own meal with an enthusiasm that belied her apology for it. Maybe she'd eaten worse in her lifetime, too. "Gabriel's pay scale presupposes that it'll take an average huntership four days out here to capture one."

Four days. Chandris felt her stomach tighten up at the thought. Eleven hours out here and already she was falling apart. And she was supposed to do three and a half more *days* of it? "What happens if you don't find one in that time?" she asked, though she had a pretty good idea what the answer was going to be.

She was right. "We stay until we do," Ornina said around a mouthful of food. "Sometimes you hit an angel the first hour out of the net; other times you don't find one for a week. It all evens out."

"I see," Chandris murmured. With a sigh, she scooped another mouthful of the paste onto her spoon—

And, abruptly, a wailing siren split the air.

Chandris's teeth spasmed down on the spoon, sending a jolt of pain through her jaw. "What—?"

"Acceleration alarm," Ornina snapped, already on her feet. She slapped the lid down on her cup and charged for the door. "Come on—we've got one."

The *Gazelle*'s rotation was gone by the time they reached the control cabin. "Strap in," Hanan barked over his shoulder as Chandris got a grip on her chair and jammed her butt ungracefully down into it. Ornina, with farther to go to her own seat, was already strapped in. "Here we go—"

The *Gazelle*'s engines roared, and Chandris had to struggle for a second to get the last strap fastened. Swinging her display over in front of her, she keyed for an echo of Ornina's board. "What do you want me to do?" she called over the engine noise.

"Get on the backup tracker," Ornina said, her voice taut. "I'll figure the vector—you double-check me."

"Right." Another gamma-ray *crack* flashed momentary white on Chandris's display; this time, she hardly noticed it. On the main display was what looked like a blizzard of white, with hundreds of computer-calculated spirals superimposed on top of it. And in the very center, its trace still being drawn . . .

"Got it," she muttered under her breath. The procedure, memorized from the *Gazelle*'s manuals, was clear enough in her mind. But her fingers were inexperienced, and she found herself fumbling at the keyboard. Sweating, she tried to keep up with Ornina.

Abruptly, the engines cut back, and Chandris's ribs were squeezed against the side of her seat as the *Gazelle* swung to the right. "Losing charge fast," Ornina said tightly. "Neutral in maybe fifteen seconds."

"Almost there," Hanan told her. "Chandris?"

"I'm on it," Chandris called back. An arrow had appeared at the growing end of the angel's spiral now, its direction constantly changing even as the spiral began to both fade and straighten out. A pseudo cloud-chamber effect, the manual had called this, with ultra-sensitive detectors utilizing Angelmass's own particle radiation as background; but Chandris didn't have to understand it to know what it meant. The angel was picking up lots of other particles, losing the electrical charge that made it detectable. If that happened before they could figure out its final direction, they would lose it.

"Scoop's ready," Hanan said. "Time?"

"Five seconds," Ornina told him. "Four, three, two, one—"

The trace, a straight line now, disappeared from Chandris's display.

"—neutral."

"Right," Hanan muttered. "Scooping now."

Chandris listened hard, but the only sound she could hear was the hum of the magnetic field generators and the *cracks* of gamma-ray sparks. "What happens if we don't get it on the first try?" she asked. "Is there any way to get a second shot at it?"

"Not usually," Ornina said, hunched tautly over her board. "Between the tidal forces, gravity, and the solar wind, most neutralized angels eventually end up falling back into Angelmass."

Beside her, Hanan straightened up. "Did we get it?" Chandris asked.

"Don't know," he said. "We scooped about a hundred meters along its last trajectory, but with all the other particles and radiation out there for it to have scattered off of there's no guarantee it was still there."

"We picked up just under four micrograms of material in the scoop," Ornina added, turning to face Chandris. "The analyzer is running through all of it now. If the angel's in there—"

She was interrupted by a sudden two-toned beep from her board. "There'll be a beep," Hanan finished for her as Ornina spun back around. "Something like that one." He smiled at Chandris, some of the lines in his face smoothing out as he did so. "We have it?"

"We have it," Ornina confirmed, undoing her straps. "If you want to come down with me, Chandris," she added as she floated free of the chair, "I'll show you how to extract it from the collection bin and stow it in a storage box for transport."

"Thanks, but I think I'll save that for next time," Chandris said, unfastening her own straps. "Someone ought to head back to the kitchen and clean up what's left of our dinner."

"You don't have to do that," Hanan told her.

"No," Ornina agreed, pausing at the control cabin door. "We can tackle that together later."

"I insist," Chandris said firmly. "I haven't been a lot of help to you so far. The least I can do is a little manual labor."

Ornina glanced at Hanan, shrugged. "Okay," she said. "See you later."

It would have been extremely useful, Chandris thought regretfully as she left the control cabin, to see the actual procedure used for storing these angels. But in this case it was a luxury she couldn't afford. Back on the *Xirrus* she'd always assumed she'd have at least a couple of days to worm through whatever security they had around the angel and score it. But with Seraph only a couple of hours away by catapult, her first and only chance was going to be right now.

She bypassed the kitchen, heading instead down the corridor to a small room the floorplans had identified as a machine shop. It took only a minute to find a multiscrewdriver and small wrench and slip them down her coveralls. However the angel box was set up, those two tools ought to be enough to get into it.

And if they weren't . . .

For a long moment she stared at the small cutting torch, a strange feeling in the pit of her stomach. She'd used a similar one once before, and knew it made a good weapon. But for some reason . . .

The sudden roar of the *Gazelle*'s engines startled her out of her thoughts. "Nurk," she muttered to herself, grabbing the torch and stuffing it into her coveralls with the other tools. There were, she knew, two ways to approach the angel collection section at the *Gazelle*'s underside. Acting on the assumption that Ornina would have taken the most direct route from the control cabin, Chandris went the other, longer way.

She approached cautiously, alert for sounds. But the entire section seemed to be deserted. A good sign; it implied that the storage procedure was a simple one.

Of course, if Ornina had headed to the kitchen afterwards instead of back to the control cabin . . . Impatiently, Chandris shook the thought out of her mind. In two hours it wouldn't matter in the slightest what the Daviees thought of her.

The collection bin was right where the floorplans had put it: a massive and oddly complicated looking thing built into one of the inner walls of the storeroom. Digging the tools out of her coveralls, she laid them on the floor and started looking for the best way in.

"It won't do you any good, you know."

Chandris spun around, the sudden movement in the *Gazelle*'s low gravity throwing her off balance and dropping her to one knee. Her hand lanced out blindly to snatch up the torch.

They were there: Hanan and Ornina both, standing just inside the door. "Stay back," Chandris ordered.

"All right," Hanan said calmly, showing her his empty hands. "Don't be afraid. We're not going to hurt you."

"I'm not afraid," Chandris gritted. "If anyone's going to get hurt, it's going to be you two."

Hanan nodded. "We understand." He gestured toward the box behind her. "Ornina's right, though. Taking the angel won't gain you anything."

"I'll worry about that, if you don't mind," Chandris said, stomach beginning to churn as she tried to figure out what the hell she was going to do now. Disassembling the angel box while trying to hold them both at bay would be well-nigh impossible.

The box, hell. How was she supposed to bring the damn ship back to Seraph by herself?

They were still just standing there. Still just watching her. "I don't want to hurt you," she told them, feeling sweat collecting on her forehead. "All I want is the angel."

"And what are you going to do with it?" Ornina asked.

Chandris glared at her. "Don't play stupid," she snarled. "I'm going to sell it, of course."

"To whom?"

Chandris opened her mouth . . . closed it again. "I'll find someone."

"No," Hanan shook his head. "There aren't any fences for stolen angels, Chandris. No fences, no black markets—no unofficial markets at all, for that matter. The only people who buy angels are the Gabriel Corporation; and even *they* don't give out real money for them. All we get is a credit line against goods and services, and it's good only on Seraph."

The torch in her hand seemed to be growing heavier; with an effort, Chandris kept it pointed at them. "Then I suppose I'll have to take your ship," she growled.

Hanan cocked an eyebrow. "Having never flown one before?" he asked pointedly.

"Who says I've never flown before?"

He sighed. "Come on, Chandris. We may come across as hopelessly naive, but we're not stupid. We're perfectly aware that you've been lying ever since you came aboard last night. If you'd really gone through a spaceship training course you'd have known far more about Angelmass and black holes in general than you do."

"And," Ornina added, "you wouldn't have arrived on Seraph as a stow-away."

An invisible cord seemed to knot itself around Chandris's throat. "What are you talking about?"

"We're talking about Chandris Lalasha," Ornina said. "Who boarded the spaceliner *Xirrus* at Uhuru and disappeared, and was subsequently identified as a female stowaway caught in the upper-class section, who escaped from custody at the Magasca spaceport."

"Leaving a whole bunch of security types looking like idiots," Hanan added with a grin.

Chandris felt cold all over. They knew. And if they'd called for help before coming down here . . . "When did you find out?"

"The news report came through yesterday afternoon," Ornina said gently. "It included several pictures."

For a long moment the only sounds in the room were the muffled roar of the engines and the thudding of Chandris's own heart. "You're lying," she managed at last. "You didn't know. You couldn't have."

"Why not?" Ornina asked.

"Because if you had you wouldn't have let me anywhere near your ship," Chandris retorted. "You'd have called the police and I'd be sitting in a cell."

Ornina shrugged. "Which is more or less why we didn't call them. Because you'd have wound up in a cell."

Chandris snorted. "Save your sympathy. I've been in cells before, plenty of them. They've never hurt me yet."

"Maybe." Ornina's eyes were steady on her. "But they don't seem to have helped you much, either."

Chandris looked back and forth between them, survival instincts battling with an inexplicable rush of personal pride. If the Daviees really *had* known who she was last night, then they were a lot softer than she'd first thought. She could switch back to the poor, helpless, victimized little girl role; play for sympathy—

The pride won out. "And I suppose you thought you could do better?" she snarled. "Well, do me a favor and don't bother. Even Barrio food goes down easier than charity."

For the first time Ornina's face hardened. "I suggest you lose that word right now, girl," she said tartly. "Charity means giving things away for free, and that is the absolute *last* thing you're going to find here. Flying and maintaining a huntership takes hard work, and lots of it. If you decide to stay you're jolly well going to pull your weight."

Chandris glared back at her . . . and then, abruptly, the words registered. The words, and the offer behind them. "What are you talking about?" she demanded uneasily.

"We're talking about offering you a job," Hanan said. "Unless, of course, you'd rather keep running."

Chandris stared at him, a creepy sensation crawling up her back. There was a trap here—there *had* to be. "Why?" she asked, stalling for time.

"Why not?" Hanan countered. "You're a fast learner, you have a terrific memory for details, and you're obviously willing to put a lot of effort into getting what you want."

Chandris threw a quick look over her shoulder, half expecting to see someone there sneaking up on her. But there was nothing but a blank wall. "You called someone," she accused them. "You've got a police ship or something coming alongside."

Ornina shook her head. "We haven't called anyone. No one knows about you but us." Her gaze dropped briefly to Chandris's hand. "So I guess you've got a decision to make."

Chandris looked down at the torch. There was a trap here. Somewhere. "What if I say no?"

"Well, it cuts down a bit on the number of possible choices," Hanan said. "All you'll have to decide then is whether to kill us and try to fly this tub yourself, or else let us fly you back to Seraph and start running again."

"And of course you *promise* not to turn me in," Chandris spat, even as her stomach gave an extra twist. That was the second time Hanan had specifically mentioned running. Did they know more about her than they were letting on? "I've heard *that* before, too."

Ornina seemed to pull herself up to her full height. "Well, then, maybe this will make the decision easier." Extending her hand, she started forward.

She got three steps before Chandris shook off the sheer unexpectedness of it. "Hold it!" she snapped, jerking the torch for emphasis. "Go back or I'll burn you. I mean it!"

Ornina didn't even break stride. "It's all right," she said, her voice soothing. "We're not going to hurt you. And you don't really want to hurt us."

"Stay there," Chandris ordered . . . but even to her own ears the words sounded more like a plea than a command. "Stay there or I'll kill you. I swear I'll kill you."

"You're not a killer," Ornina told her firmly. Reaching out, she took the torch from Chandris's suddenly nerveless fingers.

Chandris took a shuddering breath, an empty feeling twisting her stomach. So it was over . . . and now when it was too late, she saw the trap. Something in the room—gas or drug or hypnot—had drained her of her will and strength. All that talk had just been them stalling, just like she'd thought, until it could take effect. "So what happens now?" she asked bitterly. "You drop me off at the big spider, or do I get to be strapped to my bed all the way to Seraph?"

Hanan rolled his eyes theatrically. "Why," he asked the ceiling, "does this always have to be so complicated?" He lowered his gaze to Chandris. "I'd like to feel we're at least making some progress. Can we assume that you've scratched the option of killing us and stealing the *Gazelle?*"

"You're real funny," Chandris snarled.

"Thank you," Hanan said, tilting his head in a slight bow. "I'm also tired and extremely hungry. Could we please try and get this settled?"

Chandris stared at him. Looked at Ornina. Back at Hanan. "You mean it," she said, her voice sounding distant in her ears. "You really mean it."

"We really mean it," Hanan nodded.

Chandris shook her head. "You're crazy. Both of you. Completely crazy."

"Why?" Ornina asked. "Because we offer a job to someone who obviously needs one?"

"I've *got* a job," Chandris snapped, the unreality of it suddenly slapping her in the face. "I steal from people. And sometimes I even kill them."

Ornina raised her eyebrows and lifted the torch, just a little. "Well, I threaten to kill them, anyway," Chandris muttered.

"So call it a career change," Hanan suggested. "The one you're in hasn't got much of a future, you know."

Chandris felt herself teetering. It was almost too good to be true . . .

No. It *was* too good to be true. "Maybe there's not much future in scoring," she growled. "But at least I don't have to work with crazy people all day."

Hanan's face collapsed into a look of hurt innocence. "Crazy? Me?"

"Quiet, Hanan," Ornina told him. "What makes you think we're crazy?"

Chandris snorted. "Offering a job to someone who's just threatened to kill you springs to mind."

Hanan shook his head. "Ah, the egocentricity of youth." He fixed Chandris with a steady gaze. "You don't really think you're the first one to try this, do you?"

"What do you mean?"

"He means," Ornina said evenly, "that you're the sixth person to come aboard the *Gazelle* in the past four years hoping to steal an angel from us."

An hour earlier, Chandris would have laughed out loud at the very idea of these passive, bloated soft touches fending off five hungry thieves. Now, somehow, it didn't even occur to her to question the statement. "What happened to them?"

"Two accepted our offer," Ornina said. "They stayed a few months each before getting better jobs and moving on. The other three disappeared as soon as we returned them to Seraph."

"One of them did eventually get an honest job, though," Hanan offered. "We got a letter from him just two weeks ago."

"You see, that's the basic flaw in the whole idea of stealing angels," Ornina said. "Angels change you. I know there are people who don't believe that, people who think the angel program is some sort of massive con game Gabriel and the High Senate are running on the Empyrean. But they really *do* work." She indicated the torch in her hand. "You're living proof of that."

Chandris looked at the massive box behind her, a cold shiver running up her back. She'd been near the angel for barely ten minutes now . . .

Hanan might have been reading her mind. "No, no—they're fast, but not *that* fast," he assured her. "Takes several hours of close contact, we've found, before these ingrained criminal tendencies even start to fade away."

Chandris stared at him . . . and, suddenly, it clicked. "You have another angel aboard."

"I *told* you you were smart," Hanan said, nodding. "Yes, it's one we found about six years ago. The second in that particular trip, which almost never happens."

"Why didn't you turn it in?"

Hanan shrugged. "We almost did. We talked about taking a nice vacation somewhere, or upgrading some of our equipment. But then we thought about the trips where you spend two weeks at Angelmass and come home empty anyway, so we decided to hang onto it. As it happened—" He looked at Ornina, shrugged again. "We just sort of never needed to use it."

Chandris eyed him. "Besides which, if you sold it you couldn't afford to let drifters like me anywhere near your ship?"

Ornina smiled. "Anyone ever tell you you have a cynical streak, Chandris?" she asked.

"Anyone ever tell *you* that you're a pair of open-faced soft touches?" Chandris countered.

"Many times," Hanan nodded. "The other angel hunters, mostly. But, then, they thought I was crazy before, so it wasn't that much of a change."

"If you'd like," Ornina said, "you can wait until we get back to Seraph to make up your mind."

Chandris shook her head. "No," she said, taking a deep breath. "No, I'm ready now. If you'll really have me . . . I guess I'll stay. For a while, at least."

"Wonderful," Ornina smiled. A genuine smile, Chandris noted, without any of that smug charity-type condescension she hated so much.

"Wonderful, indeed," Hanan agreed. "So. Can I have my dinner now?"

"*Yes,* you can have your dinner," Ornina said with that exaggerated-patience look she did so well. "Just as soon as you confirm the autocourse and Chandris and I get the kitchen cleaned up." She looked at Chandris, cocked her head to the side. "Or would you prefer us to call you something else now?"

Chandris shook her head. "'Chandris' is fine. It's as close to a real name as I have anymore."

"Well, then, Chandris," Ornina said. "Like I said before, there's a lot of work involved in running a huntership. Let's get to it."

After all, Chandris told herself as she followed Ornina down the corridor toward the kitchen, it wasn't like she had anywhere else to go at the moment. She might just as well hide out here as to try and find something better.

And besides, if she left now she would never know just exactly what the hidden catch to this deal was. She really ought to hang around until the Daviees tried to spring it on her. Just for curiosity's sake.

CHAPTER 13

Across the darkened room, a door opened. "Commodore?" an all-too-familiar voice called.

Commodore Lleshi sighed. "Come in, Mr. Telthorst," he said.

"Thank you." The door slid shut, and the Adjutor's shadowy figure started across the floor, just visible against the stars turning slowly beneath them. "Quite a view," Telthorst commented. "What is this place, anyway?"

"Visual Command Operations Center," Lleshi told him, giving the room's official designation. Not that anyone aboard ship actually called it that, of course. Pompous official titles were reserved for use with equally pompous visiting dignitaries.

"Ah," Telthorst said, sliding a chair over next to Lleshi's and sitting down. "The military equivalent of an observation deck, I suppose. That spinning must be hard to get used to."

"Not really," Lleshi said, taking a sip of his tea. "Was there anything in particular you wanted?"

"As a matter of fact, there was," Telthorst said. "I understand a drop pod from Scintara came in this afternoon."

"It came into the system, yes," Lleshi told him. "It arrived on the far side, though, so all we've got is a remote data dump."

"Why haven't I received a copy?"

"The signal was rather messy," Lleshi said. "We got it decompressed, but then had to run it through a scrubber to clean out the extraneous noise. Too hard to read otherwise."

"How thoughtful of you to take such good care of my eyes," the Adjutor said dryly. "Dare I predict that this wonderfully clean copy won't be available until after you send the wiring crews out?"

Lleshi braced himself. Here it came. "I've already seen the unscrubbed version," he told Telthorst. "There are no orders concerning your request."

"No actual orders, no," Telthorst agreed. "But they *did* authorize you to accept my recommendation."

Lleshi glared at him, a waste of effort in the dark. "Who told you that?"

"It doesn't matter," Telthorst said, his voice hardening. "What matters is that we now have the go-ahead. And we're going to take it."

"My crew is working double shifts to get this damn catapult put together," Lleshi ground out. "Shifting orbit now would cost us a minimum of two days. We'd have to haul all the loose equipment inside and tether the framework to the ship."

"It would have taken only fifteen hours if you'd accepted my recommendation when I first made it," Telthorst pointed out icily. "And if you let the actual wiring get started before you move, it could take as much as a week. I would think a military man like yourself wouldn't need to have the hazards of procrastination pointed out to him."

"It's a waste of time," Lleshi growled. "Of time, fuel, and effort. What's the point of moving the catapult closer in to a planet that'll never be developed anyway?"

In the dark, he sensed Telthorst shake his head. With a condescending look on his face, no doubt. "You continue to assume, Commodore," the Adjutor said, his voice matching the imagined expression, "that colonization is the only practical use for a planet. I'm perfectly willing to concede that the place is probably too dark and chilly for most people's taste. Though I seem to remember the Niflheim colony surviving nearly fifteen years under even more rigorous conditions than these."

Lleshi felt his lip twist. Niflheim. "Oh, well, if you're going to define *that* as a profitable development—"

"They built an extractor, refinery, and linac tube before they gave up," Telthorst cut him off sharply. "The metal the Pax has taken off since then has more than made up for the cost of sending the colony there in the first place. Anyway, that's beside the point. The point is that the probe shows enough surface metals to more than make up for the cost of the time and fuel you're so concerned with."

"And how do you put a price tag on my crewers' effort?" Lleshi demanded. "Or on their morale, when I have to tell them to unravel some of the hard work they've done just so you can move the *Komitadji* around?"

"Morale is not my concern, Commodore," Telthorst snapped. "But money is. This is a monstrously huge ship, with a totally unreasonable slice of the military budget required to keep it flying. Like everything else in the universe, it's required to earn its keep."

"We're going to give you the Empyrean," Lleshi retorted. "Isn't that enough earnings for you?"

"It might be," Telthorst said. "*If* I was assured that we'd get the entire package in undamaged condition. But as you yourself have pointed out, there's no way to guarantee that."

Lleshi stared at the dark silhouette, an uncomfortable tightness in his throat. "Is *that* what this is all about? That Hellfire simulation we ran back at Lorelei?"

"That, and the various scorched-ground simulations you've run since then," Telthorst said. "And don't bother denying it. I may not be military, but I know how to keep track of what goes on around me."

"I don't deny it," Lleshi growled, the first stirrings of real anger swirling within him. "Our job, Mr. Telthorst, is to be prepared for anything that might conceivably happen in this operation. *Anything.* Including planetary burn-offs, if that should become necessary."

"It won't become necessary," Telthorst told him, his voice soft but positive. "Trust me on that one. I'll pull the *Komitadji* out and wait for another opportunity before I'll let you go in just to destroy."

"*You'll* pull us out?"

"Yes, Commodore. Ultimately, you and this ship are responsible to the Supreme Senate . . . and right now, as far as you're concerned, I *am* the Supreme Senate."

"I don't accept that," Lleshi said. "You may represent them, but you have no direct authority here. This is *my* ship, and *I* will give the orders aboard it."

He stopped, and as the reverberations died away the room filled with a brittle silence. "You know, Commodore, you worry me," Telthorst said at last. "You and your other military friends. You asked the Pax to pour money into Kosta and his superfluous little fact-finding trip, and you got it. You asked us to risk the *Komitadji* to deliver him, and you got that, too. You then asked us to risk three other major warships for the rest of the Lorelei survey, and you got *that.* Now you balk at taking a few extra days and a little extra effort to make future development of this system easier. And for no better reason than that I asked you to do so."

"The Empyrean is a danger to the Pax," Lleshi said stiffly. "You've said so yourself, on many occasions. Alien influenced or not, those people aren't stupid—surely they know by now that we're planning some kind of major operation against them. Every unnecessary hour we stay out here gives them that much more time to prepare."

"We're talking about a few extra days, Commodore," Telthorst reminded him. "Not a year, not a month: a few days. What difference can a few days possibly make?"

"Against an unknown enemy?" Lleshi countered. "A few *hours* can spell the difference between victory and defeat. Sometimes even less than that."

Telthorst snorted. "Don't be ridiculous. This ship is indestructible. The Empyreals haven't got anything that can stand up to it, and we both know it. Scare tactics like that went out with the old military warlords." In the darkness,

Lleshi had the sense that the other was eyeing him thoughtfully. "You know, Commodore, in some ways you remind me of those warlords. Perhaps this ship has gone to your head, given you the idea that you can do whatever you want without regard for costs or budgets. It's a mode of thinking the Pax has worked very hard to bring under control. I'd hate to see isolated instances of it crop up and have to be dealt with."

"I thought scare tactics were out of date," Lleshi said coldly. "And as to the *Komitadji,* we've always delivered exactly what's been asked of us. The Pax has been well repaid for what's been put into this ship. And you know it."

The room fell silent. Lleshi watched the stars rotate beneath them; the stars and, at one point in the *Komitadji's* slow spin, the dazzling array of lights that was the embryonic catapult.

When and how, he wondered, had the Adjutors risen to this kind of power and authority? Certainly no such power had been given to them, at least not at first. They'd started out merely as a corps of professional mediators, calling themselves Adjudicators, dealing with disputes between warlords as the Pax slowly and painfully pulled itself together after the Splinter Wars a century and a half ago.

What had happened between there and here? The history books said the Adjudicators had shortened their title and shifted to advising the Pax on financial matters. That was their entire official standing even now, in fact.

But those who actually dealt with them knew the truth. The Adjutors, far from being mere advisers, had become a shadow government, with the final word on how the Pax's money was spent.

How had that happened? Lazy Senators, who relied more and more on their advisers' analyses and never bothered to check the figures themselves, until they couldn't function without Adjutors at their sides? Greedy Senators, who saw a way to make extra money on the side if a friendly Adjutor could quietly shave a few thousand out of a budget and funnel the funds elsewhere? Stupid Senators, who took their responsibilities so casually that they delegated authority with the same thoughtless attitude as if ordering lunch?

Lleshi didn't know. He doubted anyone knew, except perhaps the Adjutors themselves.

And they weren't talking. It was the victors, the saying went, who wrote the history. And, just as importantly, who decided what not to write.

"I could force the issue," Telthorst said at last. "If I sent a kick pod note out tonight, addressed to certain parties in the Supreme Senate, you'd have new orders within the next twelve hours. But I'd rather not do it that way. For one thing, you'd hate me for it, and I do so dislike being hated."

"Too late," Lleshi murmured. "You're already an Adjutor."

Telthorst seemed to consider rising to the bait, apparently decided against it. "The point is that the *Komitadji is* going to be moved," he said instead. "You can give the order, or you can accept the order. Which will it be?"

For a long moment Lleshi was sorely tempted to call the other's bluff. There was no reason for Telthorst or any other Adjutor to be aboard the *Komitadji* in the first place, let alone trying to control matters outside his tunnel-visioned field of expertise. Surely Telthorst's alleged friends in the Supreme Senate were smart enough to know that.

But the hallways of the Supreme Senate were crawling with Adjutors. And if they gave Telthorst what they wanted instead of slapping him down . . .

Lleshi ground his teeth together, the bitter taste of defeat coating his tongue. He couldn't risk it. If Telthorst got official sanction for this, it would create a precedent that would haunt every ship and commander in the Pax until the heat-death of the universe. "I'll give you your near-orbit," he told Telthorst, putting what little remained of his dignity into his voice. "But not because I'm afraid of these so-called friends of yours. I'll give it to you as a personal favor. The first *and* last such favor."

"Thank you, Commodore," Telthorst said smoothly. He wasn't fooled by the fancy words, of course. But then, Lleshi hadn't really expected him to be. "I'll keep that in mind. So. Was there any news on how the Lorelei project is coming? Or do I have to find that out on my own, too?"

"It's running on schedule," Lleshi told him. "The last of the ships has gone in and vanished, presumably catapulted someplace to hell and gone. I'm guessing we'll have the coordinates and orbit for the last net within another week."

"Then all we'll have to do is cross our fingers," Telthorst said, a sour edge to his voice. "And hope the cocoon is doing what it's supposed to and not just sitting there with its thumb in its nose."

Lleshi smiled grimly in the darkness. Nice of Telthorst to bring up yet another instance where Lleshi and the military Spec Ops people had gotten their way. "No way to know," he reminded the other. "Any kind of progress reports from the cocoon would have drastically increased the chances of discovery. Even spike-pulsed transmissions can be detected if the other side is clever or lucky enough. I'm sure you wouldn't want such an expensive collection of hardware to fall into Empyreal hands."

"Yes, I remember the arguments," Telthorst said, his tone frosty. "I just don't relish the thought of spending another four months in the middle of nowhere if this doesn't work."

Lleshi shrugged. "That's easily solved. We'll simply drop you off at Scintara before the jump-off."

Telthorst snorted. "You're too kind, Commodore. No, I'll be along for the invasion. If for no other reason than to make sure you don't damage anything you don't have to."

Lleshi was saved the need to reply by a chirp from his intercom. "Bodini here, Commodore. You wanted to be informed when the final scrubbing was finished on that last drop pod."

"Thank you, Ensign," Lleshi said, getting to his feet. "I'm on my way." He moved toward the door—

"Commodore?"

Lleshi half turned back. "Yes?"

"Don't forget to enter the order for the *Komitadji*'s course change."

Lleshi took a deep breath. "I won't forget, Mr. Telthorst."

Not that, he promised silently as he strode from the room, *nor the rest of this conversation. Not a single word of it.*

CHAPTER 14

A thin trail of smoke curled its way up from the circuit board, tickling Chandris's nose and sparking bittersweet memories of an electronics assembly shop she'd once tried to score. "Like this?" she asked.

"Right," Ornina said from behind her. "Make sure you get a good connection, then use the vac to get rid of the excess before it hardens."

Chandris nodded, biting gently on her lip as she concentrated on the task. She knew how the technique was supposed to go—Ornina had just showed it to her—but it wasn't as easy as it had looked. The end of the vac caught on the edge of the board, hissing its annoyance at her fumbling—

"Take it easy," Ornina soothed. "It's one of those things your fingers have to learn on their own."

Biting down a little harder on her lip, Chandris tried again. This time she got it right. "That's it," Ornina said. "Now do the same thing with those other two and you're done."

"Okay." Chandris stretched her fingers out once and set to work. "It's actually kind of fun, once you get the hang of it."

"I've always thought so," Ornina agreed. "And it took *me* a good deal longer to get the hang of it, I can tell you. You're an amazingly quick learner."

"I've got a good memory," Chandris told her, easing the sealant wire against the proper component leg.

"It's more than just good," Ornina said. "You remember everything you read or see, don't you?"

Chandris shrugged. "Pretty much." She paused as a faint sound down the corridor caught her ear. "Someone's coming," she said, old reflexes tensing before she remembered she was supposed to be here.

"Probably Hanan." Ornina turned toward the door. "Hanan?—we're back here," she called.

"Hi ho," Hanan's voice came back, and a minute later he poked his head into the room. "Hello, Chandris," he said, smiling at her. "Ornina didn't waste any time putting you to work, I see."

"Everything go okay?" Ornina asked.

"Oh, sure," Hanan said, an almost-smile playing around his lips as he crossed the room toward the repeater console. "No problems."

Ornina glanced at Chandris, back at Hanan. Perhaps she'd seen the smile, too. "What sort of 'no problems'?" she asked suspiciously.

"Just a second," he said, keying the repeater and stepping aside. "I want you to take a look at this, Chandris. I've tapped into the vision control monitor from the main launch tower. See the ship there, the one just rolling onto the strip?"

"Yes," Chandris nodded. It was rather hard to miss: similar in design to the *Gazelle,* but considerably larger.

"Here's its responder profile," he continued, indicating a small display below the larger one. "If you're ever out at Angelmass and this thing comes along and tells you to veer off, you veer off. Right away, without argument. Understand?"

"Okay," Chandris said cautiously. "Why?"

"Because it's the Angelmass Studies Institute's very own survey ship," Hanan told her. "It goes out about once a month, packed to the clavicles with scientists and study gear, and it has absolute priority out there. Just something I thought you should know."

"Something else you should know," Ornina put in darkly, "is that Hanan never lies—he just changes the subject when he doesn't want to answer a question. What happened at Gabriel, Hanan?"

Hanan looked at her with that wide-eyed innocent expression of his. "Whatever can you mean, sister dear?"

Ornina's mouth twisted sideways. "I mean that they were supposed to have some new trainees starting up soon in receiving. Can I assume one of them was on duty this morning?"

Hanan looked at Chandris, the innocent expression turning slightly hurt. "I ask you, Chandris: did I say or do anything to deserve this?"

Ornina folded her arms across her chest. "Quit stalling and spit it out," she said, a glint in her eye. "What did you do?"

Hanan spread his hands. "I just asked her to fill out my metals credit form, that's all."

Ornina rolled her eyes skyward. "Hanan, what am I going to do with you?"

"What's a metals credit form?" Chandris asked, trying to read the atmosphere.

"It's a little official-looking paper Hanan likes to spring on new angel receivers," Ornina said. "It allegedly requires Gabriel to analyze the spacedust material coating our angel, calculate how much of each element is represented, and then credit the total value to our account."

Something icy ran up Chandris's spine. No. It couldn't be. Hanan Daviee, certified open-faced soft touch, scoring a track? "What happened?" she said between suddenly stiff lips.

"Nothing much," he said, pulling over a chair and sitting down. "I had her running with it for about ten minutes, but then Carlie Sills wandered in and blew the whistle."

"What did you do?" Chandris asked.

He shrugged. "I got my credit and left."

"But—" Chandris looked back and forth between them, totally lost now.

Ornina frowned at her for a moment. Then her face cleared. "Oh, I see. It wasn't any kind of con game, Chandris. Just a very low form of alleged humor called a practical joke."

Chandris blinked. "A practical joke?"

"Uh-huh," Hanan said. "Why, don't they have practical jokes where you grew up?"

"Oh, sure," she told him, hearing an edge of bitterness creep into her voice. "Tripping people or half-poisoning them or setting fires. Most of the time it ends up in a knife fight."

"Good Lord," Hanan breathed, looking shocked. "Those aren't practical jokes. That's just plain cruelty."

"Sending a new employee into a tizzy-fit isn't?" Ornina put in.

"Of course not," Hanan said indignantly. "It's an important object lesson." He looked at Chandris. "You see, Chandris, this trick only works if the victim is too proud to admit he doesn't know everything. Which is, when you think about it, the normal state of life in this universe. The minute he's willing to admit to some ignorance and asks a supervisor—hey, the game's over. It's a valuable lesson in humility."

"If you want to disagree with him, feel free," Ornina advised dryly. "I don't buy any of it, myself. That stunt, in particular, deserves to be retired."

"You're right," Hanan agreed blandly. "I'm going to have to come up with something else. Most of the other receivers are still willing to play along, but I think the supervisors are getting tired of it."

"I should think so," Ornina sniffed. "I never liked the ones that humiliate a single person, anyway."

"I'm not trying to humiliate anyone," Hanan insisted.

Ornina shrugged. "I'll bet it looks that way from the other side." She looked at Chandris. "Don't worry—he was much worse when he was younger. He's actually mellowed some with age."

"And I'm certainly not going to try pulling anything on *you*," Hanan added. "Not after that reference to knife fights."

"That's comforting," Chandris murmured, still a little uncertain about the whole thing.

"Anyway; back to work." Hanan looked at his watch. "I stopped by Serhanabi's on the way back, Ornina, and they're not going to be able to get those conduyner coils for us for at least a week. It turns out that there are a pair across town at Khohl Supply, but they can't deliver. If you can spare Chandris for an hour, she and I can go over and get them and I can start installing them this afternoon."

Something flashed across Ornina's face, too quickly for Chandris to decipher. "Sure," she said, her voice sounding a little odd. "I'm just showing her around the work areas." She glanced at Chandris. "But wouldn't it make more sense for you to stay here and start the prep work while she and I go to Khohl?"

"Not really," Hanan said, getting to his feet. "There's nothing I can do until we have the underwrap in hand. Besides, don't you still have some work to do on the Senamaec?"

The look flickered again. "Yes," Ornina said.

"That's settled, then." Hanan looked at Chandris. "Let's get out there before someone else beats us to them."

A vehicle that looked something like a sawed-off truck was sitting outside the gate. "TransTruck," Hanan identified it as he opened the door for her. "Like a line car, but privately owned by Gabriel instead of being public. Button number four on the inlock phone if you ever need to call one."

Chandris nodded absently, her mind still back on Ornina. She'd seen that same look two nights ago, when they were offering her a job.

"You all right?"

She came to, realized with a start that they were already out of the service yard area. "Sorry," she muttered, annoyed with herself for getting distracted. "I was just . . . wondering."

"About that little scene just before we left?"

She looked at him, a strange feeling curling her stomach. "Yes, actually."

"Don't worry about it," he assured her. "That had nothing to do with you. Ornina's just got this idea that I shouldn't be lifting heavy objects like conduyner coils, that's all."

Chandris looked over at him. At the ends of the exobraces sticking a couple of centimeters out of his shirt sleeves . . .

"It's a degenerative nerve disease," he told her. His voice was very matter-of-fact, but Chandris could see a tightness around his mouth. "Hit me, oh, twenty-one years ago and has been wearing out my arms and legs ever since. Not at all contagious, I might add."

"I wasn't worried," Chandris said.

"I know. Actually, it's more nuisance than anything else, and you can see for yourself that it's being dealt with. The exobrace system compensates for the muscular weakness and also reroutes most of the neural traffic to my hands and feet. Otherwise I wouldn't have much control or feeling there."

"Can't they do anything else? The doctors, I mean."

"Oh, there are probably some nerve implant things or some such. Waste of time and effort."

"And money?" she added without thinking.

He cocked an eyebrow. "For someone who didn't think she was worth hiring, you know, you're pretty sharp."

Chandris bristled. "Who said I didn't think—?"

She broke off as it suddenly hit her. "You just changed the subject, didn't you?"

He grinned. "Well, I tried." The grin faded, and he grew serious. "Gabriel treats its people more than fairly, Chandris, but this isn't something they can be expected to deal with. Unlike your stereotypical giant corporation, they run their operation right at the edge of break-even." He grinned again, briefly. "One of those wonderful balances you get when you work with angels. No matter how rare or valuable the things are, the people handling them don't line their own pockets at everyone else's expense."

"What about your extra angel?" Chandris asked. "Couldn't you sell that?"

He hesitated. Just a split second, but enough. "It wouldn't be worth enough."

"I thought Ornina said you never lie."

He threw her a sideways look. "You *are* sharp, aren't you? But that wasn't a lie, just a—well, a creative phrasing of the truth." He took a deep breath. "You see, Chandris, I'm the only family Ornina's got left. She's spent half her life taking care of me; first supporting me in school, then helping me adjust to my illness. Somehow, in all that, she never had the time or the money to have a family of her own."

And suddenly it clicked. "Is that why you invited me aboard the *Gazelle?*" Chandris demanded. "So she can pretend I'm her family?"

"Does that bother you?"

Chandris bit down on her lip. "I don't know," she had to admit.

"She's not really pretending, you know," he said. "At least not in the sense that she's deluding herself. But it gives her the chance to care for someone else. Someone who—well, never mind."

"Someone who desperately needs her?" Chandris finished for him, a slightly sour taste in her mouth.

"Don't be offended. If it helps any, you're in much better shape than most of the others have been. You at least had a marketable skill, even if it *was* just stealing."

Another piece clicked into place. "So that's why you need to keep the extra angel. Right? Because otherwise you might take someone aboard someday who'd knife you both in your sleep."

He shrugged. "Something like that. Though of course we do try to screen our guests a shade better than that."

"The angel helps you there, too, I suppose?"

"Actually, no," he shook his head. "Angels don't seem to do anything quite that active." He grinned lopsidedly. "To tell you the truth, what's helped most was all the practical jokes I used to pull when I was younger. You learn how to read people when you're trying to rig a thimble on them. Don't tell Ornina that, though."

"Yeah, well, if you ask me your practical jokes sound just like scoring a track," Chandris told him. "Except that no one locks you up when you get caught."

"Actually, all the best jokes are ones where no one would have grounds to lock you up anyway," Hanan said. "The kind where all you're doing is—oh, I don't know; putting a slight *tilt* on the universe. It's hard to explain."

"So show me."

He frowned at her. "What?"

"I said show me," Chandris repeated.

Hanan's lips puckered. "All right. All right, I will. Let's see . . ." He patted his pockets. "See what's in that storage compartment," he said, leaning over to study the floor.

Chandris popped open the indicated door beside her knee. "Nothing but a map," she reported. "Oh, and a couple of candy wrappers and a piece of string."

"Nothing useful on the floor," Hanan grunted. He straightened up, a far-away look in his eyes, and for a minute was silent. "Okay," he said abruptly. "Give me the string."

She dug it out from under the map. It was about thirty centimeters long, frayed at both ends, with splotches of a tarry-looking substance at various points along its length. "What are you going to do?" she asked, handing it over.

"You'll see." For a moment he worked at it with his fingers . . . "Blast," he muttered. "Here—can you make a little slipknot in it for me?"

"Sure," she said, taking it back and making the knot.

"Thanks. Now watch carefully."

Easing the loop over his right ear, he pulled it tight and then stuck the free end into the right corner of his mouth. "How do I look?" he asked.

"Ridiculous," Chandris told him. "What happens now?"

"The joke, of course." Hanan peered out the windshield. "That's Khohl Supply coming up now. Just play it cool and observe."

The TransTruck pulled to the curb and they got out. The front door opened as they approached and Hanan led the way inside. The young man at the counter, poring over a display screen, looked up. "Hello, sir," he smiled. His eyes flicked to the string, and for just a second the smile seemed to freeze in place. "Ah—what can I do for you?" he asked, his voice suddenly gone odd.

"I understand you have some Ahandir conduyner coils in stock," Hanan said. "I'd like to buy two of them."

"Ah—certainly," the clerk said, bobbing his head once. His eyes flicked to the string again, turned resolutely away. "Let me check."

He bent over the display again; out of his sight, Hanan gave Chandris a wink. "Yes, we have some," the clerk said, straightening again, his eyes flicking once again to the string. "You have a Gabriel credit line, I assume?"

"Yes," Hanan said, handing over a thin card. The other took it, dipped it briefly into the slot on his display— "I'm sorry. You said you wanted how many?"

"Two," Hanan repeated pleasantly.

"Right," the other mumbled, bending again to his task. Across the room, Chandris saw, three customers who'd been poring over various equipment displays were staring at Hanan, a fascination that was instantly submerged as Hanan sent a leisurely glance around the store. The clerk finished, straightened— "Ah—will you need help loading them?" he asked, eyes struggling again not to stare.

"No, thank you," Hanan told him, leaning over to touch his thumb to the confirmation plate. "My associate here and I can handle them."

"Okay. Uh . . ." Licking his lips, the other craned his neck to look over at the delivery rack running along the side of the store. "They should be out any minute, sir," he said, his voice starting to sound distinctly uncomfortable.

"Oh, that's all right," Hanan assured him. "We're not in any hurry." He looked over at the three customers, who had now moved closer together and were whispering earnestly among themselves. Again, his look was all it took to turn them swiftly back to more innocent activities. From the side came a ping—

"There they are," the clerk said, and there was no mistaking the relief in his voice. "If you need help—"

"Not at all," Hanan said, stepping over to the rack and motioning Chandris to follow. "As I said, my colleague and I can handle them."

"Yes, sir. Thank you, and—uh—please come, uh, come back here. Again."

"I certainly will," Hanan said. Picking up one of the packages, he led the way outside.

"Well?" he asked Chandris as the TransTruck pulled away from the curb. "What did you think?"

She shrugged. "I was right the first time. It's just like scoring a track."

"How so?"

"You play off human nature," she said. "People don't like to ask questions they think will make them look stupid. So they don't, and you wind up getting away with things you otherwise wouldn't."

"Huh," Hanan grunted thoughtfully. "I never really thought about it that way, but you're right." He looked over at her. "I guess we're not as different as either of us would have thought."

Chandris felt her lip twist. *Except that you'd never stoop to anything so rude as actually taking money away from people this way,* she added silently. *Scrubbed saints, both of you.*

And yet . . .

No, he didn't take any money. But he kept pulling these stunts. Even though they sometimes made people look foolish.

Even though Ornina clearly didn't like them.

The first wisps of uneasiness began to curl around her stomach. They'd seemed to work so well together, he and Ornina; friendly, with a sort of harmony in their activities. People who cared for each other.

Just like she and Trilling had been at the beginning.

She glanced surreptitiously at Hanan, now humming softly to himself as he gazed out at the passing cityscape, the knot in her stomach tightening. Was *that* the real reason they kept the extra angel around? Not for any stupid soft-touch thing about helping the poor unfortunate downtrodden, but because they couldn't live together without it?

A shiver ran up her back. All along she'd known there had to be something else lurking behind this deal. But this hadn't been what she'd had in mind. Fellow scorers she could handle, and maybe even score right back again. But psycho defectives . . .

She gritted her teeth. *All right, let's not go and pop any cords here, okay?* she growled at herself. After all, this was all pure guesswork. And hadn't Hanan just said that angels weren't active?

And *that* was the real problem, she realized suddenly. She knew next to nothing about these nurking angel things. And most of what she *did* know had come from the Daviees. What she needed was more information. "That Angelmass Studies Institute ship you showed me," she said. "Is it based with the rest of the hunterships?"

Hanan looked at her, mild surprise on his face. "Yes, it's got a service building at the southwest edge of the landing strip. Why?"

"I thought it might be nice to learn a little more about angels," she said. "Especially if I'm going to be helping you hunt them."

"Well, then, you don't want the ship but the Institute itself," Hanan advised her. "It's out in the eastern part of Shikari City, at One Hundred U San Avenue. There are public terminals on the first floor that should tell you everything you need to know. You want to go over today, after we drop off these coils?"

Chandris hesitated. As far as she was concerned, the sooner she tracked this down the better.

But in her mind's eye she saw Ornina, worried about whether or not Hanan could handle the coils by himself. "Thanks," she told Hanan. "I'd rather stick around and watch you put these coils in. I've still got a lot to learn about the *Gazelle*."

Hanan glanced at her, and she could tell what he was thinking: wanted by the police, she was skittish about going out alone in public. "Okay," he said. "Just let Ornina or me know when you want to go and we'll show you how to call a Gabriel line car."

"Thanks," she said again. Tomorrow, or maybe the next day, she told herself, she'd go.

And after that she would decide if she was ever coming back.

CHAPTER 15

"Jereko?" Gyasi's voice came from the open doorway.

Kosta looked up, being very careful not to move his head too quickly lest it fall off. "Mm?" he muttered, wondering vaguely if he looked as rotten as he felt.

If Gyasi's expression was anything to go by, he did. "I take it," Gyasi said, "that you haven't had much experience with zero-gee space travel."

There was room there for some kind of witty reply, but Kosta was too ill to bother. "I'd say that's a fair statement," he said instead.

"Uh-huh," Gyasi nodded. "Well, if it helps any, they'll probably be rotating the ship on the way back to the catapult. Unfortunately, they can't do that on the way in—it would foul up too many of the experiments." Gyasi looked at his watch, a frown creasing his forehead. "You know, that stuff you took should have taken effect long ago."

"Oh, it is," Kosta told him. "Starting to, anyway. I'm not feeling quite as queasy as I was."

"Ah. Good." Gyasi peered at him. "You must have a pretty exotic metabolism for it to have taken this long."

If you only knew how exotic, Kosta thought. But he *was* feeling better, and improving by the minute. "How long till we get to Angelmass?" he asked.

"Maybe twenty minutes," Gyasi said. "That's to the inner radiation region. We've been inside the outer field since we 'pulted."

"I know." It wasn't something Kosta could have missed; the gamma-ray clicks from the ship's electronics were pretty distinctive. Also just a little bit scary. "That base—Angelmass Central—it sits out here permanently?"

"Sure does," Gyasi nodded. "Has to, you see—hunterships come and go across the clock, and the net and catapult have to be running at all times."

"Is it manned?"

"Usually, though the people are mostly there to help in case of huntership emergencies. The station is automated enough that you could set it up to run pretty much by itself if you had to. You can also turn the major systems on and off from Seraph."

Kosta nodded, thinking about people sitting in the outer radiation field of a blazing quantum black hole for weeks or months on end. The shielding technology alone that that implied was incredible. No wonder the *Komitadji*'s lasers and plasma jets hadn't put a dent in those Lorelei defense ships. "The gamma-ray clicking must drive them nuts," he murmured.

Gyasi grinned. "You get used to it. Just like you do riding around in zero-gee. You look like you're feeling better."

"I am," Kosta confirmed, nodding. This time his head didn't even threaten to come off. "That stuff works fast when it finally gets around to it."

"Only the best for us folks at the Institute," Gyasi said. "You feel up to heading forward and checking out some of the gear?"

"Sure." Carefully, Kosta gave himself a push away from the restraint straps and drifted across the room. Gyasi caught his arm as he approached, deftly helping him through the door. "I never got a chance to ask if you had any experiments aboard," he said as they headed down the corridor.

Gyasi shook his head. "I don't personally, though the head of my team does. Most of what I'm working on can be done easier in the lab." He grinned, his face a little dreamy looking. "I just like to come out here and look at Angelmass."

"So to speak," Kosta murmured.

"Well, not *directly* at it of course," Gyasi agreed. "But even through fifteen filters it's still an impressive sight. Here we are."

They had arrived outside a door marked STARBOARD ANALYSIS ROOM. It slid open at a tap on the touch plate, and Gyasi led the way inside.

The view in here was impressive, too. The room was long and relatively narrow, its entire length taken up on both sides by displays and tangles of equipment. Perhaps thirty people floated around and through it all, making adjustments or taking notes or just watching. A murmur of quiet conversation competed with the hum of cooling fans and cryogenic pumps, all of it punctuated every few seconds by a gamma-ray click. "Did they leave anything at all behind in their labs?" he asked.

Beside him, Gyasi chuckled. "This is nothing. On some trips the place gets *really* crowded."

"Right," Kosta said dryly. A monstrous apparatus at the far end caught his eye: a huge spherical tank wrapped with cables and metal coils. "What's that thing?" he asked, indicating it.

"Ah, *that*," Gyasi said. "Dr. Ciardi's angel decay detector. One of the three permanent experiments aboard; and heaven only knows how they're going to get it out of the ship if and when they're done with—"

"Wait a second," Kosta interrupted him. "*Decay* detector?"

"Right," Gyasi nodded. "Dr. Ciardi's one of those who isn't ready to believe in the *Acchaa* theory—he still wants angels to be nothing more than highly metastable subatomic particles. If his theory is right, an angel should spontaneously decay into a particular group of other subatomic particles. That thing is busy looking for that specific particle-track signature."

"Wouldn't it be simpler to just take one into his lab and sit on it?"

"Oh, he's doing that, too," Gyasi said. "But that could take a while—his theory predicts a half-life in the fifty-thousand-year range. I've heard he tried to get hold of a whole bunch of angels to help speed things up, but Director Podolak turned him down."

"Academic censorship?"

"Simple arithmetic. The High Senate and most of the top EmDef people have angels now, along with all the planetary governors and senators and a lot of judges. But there are still lower-level politicians, leaders of industry—you know the list. Maybe in ten years or so Director Podolak will be able to take fifty or a hundred angels out of the pool for that kind of study. But not now."

Kosta nodded, feeling more hopeful than he had in days. If the plan was going to require another ten years to complete, then perhaps there was still time to save these people.

Provided he, Kosta, did his job.

And finding out more about this Ciardi's theory might be a good place to start. If he could help sow doubt as to what the angels really were—

"Mr. Gyasi?" a woman's voice called from the other end of the room. "Can you give me a hand?"

"Sure," Gyasi called back. He kicked off the wall, bouncing his hands against walls and ceiling to skillfully maneuver himself through the maze of other occupants. Kosta followed more slowly, wondering just how often Gyasi had taken this trip.

He arrived at the far end of the room to find Gyasi and a middle-aged woman poring over a maze of circuit cables. "Ah—Jereko," Gyasi said, glancing up. "Dr. Qhahenlo, this is my new officemate, Jereko Kosta. This is Dr. Rae Yanda Qhahenlo, my supervisor."

"Honored, Mr. Kosta," Qhahenlo said briefly, not bothering with the usual greeting routine. "You know anything about mid-range samplers?"

"A little," Kosta said cautiously, hovering over their shoulders. He knew a great deal about mid-range samplers, actually. But Pax samplers, not their Empyreal counterparts. Even if the designs turned out to be parallel, translating the terminology might be tricky. "What's the trouble?"

"Output signal is way too noisy," Qhahenlo grunted. "I thought it was the 'sponder, but replacing it didn't seem to help."

"Um." Kosta looked over the apparatus. "What's in all that tubing?"

"Siitalon," Qhahenlo said. "Cryogenic heat-pump fluid—keeps the detectors cool."

"Fluorine-based?"

Qhahenlo frowned at him. "I think so. Why?"

"Well, it looks like you've got one of the line connections right over the 'sponder feed," he pointed out. "If you've got a small leak there, you may be getting some fluorine adsorption onto the line. Maybe enough to cause your noise."

Gyasi blinked. "You're kidding. I've never heard of anything like that."

"Actually, I have," Qhahenlo said, already searching through her tool kit. "I'd completely forgotten it, though. Let's see . . ."

For a minute she worked in silence, tightening down the suspect connection with a zero-gee wrench and then molding extra sealant around it. "Okay, give it a try."

Gyasi busied himself with the control board. "Well, it looks a little better," he said doubtfully, studying the display. "Wait a minute; there it goes." He looked up. "Nice call, Jereko."

"Thanks," Kosta said, letting out a breath he hadn't realized he'd been holding. Somehow, it had been vitally important to him to be right on this. "Lucky guess."

"One of my own favorite investigative tools," Qhahenlo said dryly. "Thank you, Mr. Kosta." She eyed him thoughtfully. "You must be new to the Institute."

Kosta nodded. "Just got here a couple of days ago. Still finding my way around."

"Any of the other research teams press-gang you yet?"

"Uh . . ." Kosta glanced at Gyasi, found no cues there. "No. Should they have?"

She cocked an eyebrow. "If this is a sample of your skills, they certainly will. Good diagnosticians are in high demand."

Kosta glanced at Gyasi again. Was Qhahenlo trying to hire him? And if so, did he have any say in the matter? "I do have some projects of my own I'm working on," he said carefully.

She smiled. "Don't worry—I'm not talking about kidnapping you away from your other work," she assured him. "But I would like you to work with my team. Even just on a consulting basis, if that's all the time you can spare."

"Though as a matter of fact," Gyasi put in, "you'll probably wind up working with Dr. Qhahenlo sooner or later anyway. That ion shell project of yours could be useful when the V/E experiment is finished."

"What ion shell project is this?" Qhahenlo asked, looking interested.

"I'm trying to see whether it's possible to strip off an angel's collected ion shell," Kosta said, feeling awkward. It was a little unsettling to have someone of Qhahenlo's obvious status and experience listening so closely to what he had to say. "My original thought was to see whether the shell had anything to do with the angel effect, but Yaezon tells me it's probably a dead-end approach."

"Never underestimate dead-end approaches," Qhahenlo advised. "At worst, they often generate useful spin-offs; at best, they sometimes turn out to be not so dead-end as everyone expected."

"I'll remember that," Kosta said. "May I ask what this V/E experiment is?"

"Certainly—it's not a secret," Qhahenlo said. "The Variable Exposure experiment is a long-term test of angel stability."

"Not like Dr. Ciardi's, though," Gyasi put in. "This one's based on a variant on the *Acchaa* theory that Dr. Qhahenlo's come up with. Instead of the angel being a single quantum of good, you assume it's a bundle of many quanta, with the angel particle being a kind of threshold for creation rather than the absolute minimum size that a strict quantum would imply. When you do that, the angel effect can be explained as a slow decay of these constituent quanta into fields of good that directly affect people nearby. Saves you a whole bunch of the headaches the theorists are having trying to come up with a workable mechanism for the angel/personality interaction—"

He broke off suddenly, looking at Qhahenlo with a somewhat sheepish expression. "Sorry, Dr. Qhahenlo. I interrupted, didn't I?"

"Don't worry about it," Qhahenlo told him with an amused smile. "The general rule is that enthusiasm is worth two to three extra lab techs. Anyway, that's basically where we're starting from, Mr. Kosta. Since all angel theories allow both positive and negative solutions, it seems reasonable to assume that there can be fields of evil—or anti-good, if you prefer—that might be able to affect the rate of decay of the quanta bundles in a given angel."

"Which is where the Variable Exposure experiment comes in," Gyasi said.

"Right," Qhahenlo nodded. "What we've done is to take four newly captured angels and put them in radically different environments. The first is locked in a deep underground vault, some fifty meters from any human being; that one's our control. The second is in a special cell with a convicted serial murderer. The third is being worn by Director Podolak herself, replacing one she'd been wearing for the previous five years. And the fourth has been sewn into a special harness being worn by a one-month-old child."

Something icy ran up Kosta's back. "A one-month-old child?" he repeated carefully. "A baby?"

"That's the layman's term for them, yes," Gyasi said dryly. "He's the son of two Institute employees—they've got an apartment on the grounds."

"We plan to run the test for about a year," Qhahenlo said. "If angels do in fact absorb evil, then there should be detectable differences between the four. Though what those differences will be we're still not sure of."

"I see," Kosta said mechanically. A baby. They'd put an angel on a baby. An unknown but very real force . . . and they'd turned it loose on an innocent and helpless child.

"We'd of course appreciate any suggestions you might have along the way," Qhahenlo continued. "And Mr. Gyasi's right; finding a way to strip off the angels' ion shells could be very useful when it comes time to compare them."

With an effort, Kosta forced his mind away from the image of that baby. "Yes," he managed. "I'll see what I can do."

"Good." Qhahenlo looked at her watch. "We should be getting close to our target zone. Give me a hand, Mr. Gyasi, and let's get this thing going."

"Attention, all passengers," the cool voice came over the speakers. "De-rotation will begin in three minutes. Repeating: de-rotation will begin in three minutes."

Hunched head to head with Qhahenlo over a display, Gyasi looked up at Kosta. "You going to be okay?"

Kosta nodded. "I think I've got the hang of it now," he said.

Qhahenlo looked up, too, as if noticing Kosta for the first time. "Incidentally, Mr. Kosta, you really don't have to wait around here if you've got something else you want to do. Watching other people sift their data isn't the most thrilling way to spend an afternoon."

"Actually, I've already been around the ship a couple of times," Kosta told her. "Nobody else has anything more interesting to watch."

Qhahenlo blinked. "When did you do all that?"

"About forty minutes ago."

Qhahenlo's lips puckered. "Occasionally, you'll find I get too engrossed in my work to be a proper host. My apologies."

"That's all right," Kosta assured her.

Qhahenlo looked back at Gyasi. "Anyway. Let's see; we were about *here* . . ."

Their heads went back together, already lost in the data again. Kosta watched them, a wisp of worried contempt tugging at him. They were the archetypical crystal-tower scientists, all right, both of them. So completely wrapped up in their research that they didn't notice the rest of the universe. So single-mindedly confident in what they were doing that not even the slightest doubt ever crossed either of their minds.

So infatuated by the angels that they'd lost all sense of perspective.

They'd put an angel on a baby. How long would it be before they were putting angels on all the babies?

"Yaezon?" he asked suddenly. "What kind of numbers are we talking about to get the Empyrean properly fitted out with angels?"

Gyasi looked up again. "Well, we need angels for all politicians from regional level on up. Then there are the judges, corporate executives, EmDef officers, trade officials—"

"Yes, but what I want is the total number of angels we're talking about."

Gyasi frowned. "No idea. Doctor?"

"Not offhand," Qhahenlo said. Without looking up she waved at another terminal. "But all that should be listed under the Empyreal Angel Experiment heading."

The approaching-zero-gee alarm was beginning to sound as Kosta found the proper sublist; and the ship's rotation was nearly at a stop by the time he located the current status information.

It was worse than he'd expected. The original estimate had been that it would take forty years to achieve the target level of one angel per hundred Empyreals. Now, barely eighteen years later, updated projections were guessing that goal to be only seven more years away. More hunterships, better shielding and detection equipment, the breakthrough invention of the hyperspace net—there were pages and pages of graphs tracing how each new scientific and technological advance had brought the goal closer. Already over eighteen thousand angels had been collected, with that number growing at an ever increasing rate.

Kosta paused, staring at one of the graphs, a quiet alarm bell going off in the back of his mind. He'd studied great quantities of black hole theory during the astrophysics segment of his tridoctorum degree. But if that graph was correctly drawn . . .

Strapping himself into the chair, hardly noticing his weightlessness, he got to work.

He was still at it when the announcement came that the ship had landed.

"So. What did you think?"

Kosta looked up from his display, feeling a flicker of annoyance at the interruption. "Of what, Angelmass?"

"Of Dr. Qhahenlo," Gyasi said. "And our project."

"Oh." Kosta shrugged, turning his attention to the display again. "I don't know. Okay, I guess."

Peripherally, he saw Gyasi put down his stylus and scoot his chair over. "Okay, I give up," he said. "What in the world is so interesting?"

Kosta hesitated. He was sure now. But whether he ought to tell any of the Empyreals about this . . .

No. Of course he ought to. He was here to save them, after all. "This," he told Gyasi, swiveling the display around. "It's a graph of number of angels captured per huntership per unit time, shown in one-year slices. You can see that it's gone up in the past couple of years."

Gyasi glanced at it. "No big surprise," he said. "There have been some major advances in technology and sensor equipment—"

"I've factored those out," Kosta cut him off.

Gyasi stopped. "Oh." He looked at the graph again, more carefully this time. "Well, maybe it's due to the fact that Angelmass is getting smaller. You know—as a quantum black hole gets smaller, it gets hotter and radiates its mass away faster." He reached for the keyboard. "Let's see; a hotter effective temperature would shift the mean particle spectrum upwards, creating more angels—"

"I've factored that out, too," Kosta told him.

Gyasi frowned. "You sure?"

Kosta nodded. "It's a simpler calculation even than the technological advancements. Check it yourself if you want."

"I'll take your word for it." For a long minute Gyasi gazed at the display, lips moving soundlessly. "Interesting and a half," he admitted at last. "What do you think is causing it?"

Kosta shook his head. "I don't know. But it's for sure that *something* strange is going on out there. Something in the Hawking process that current theory doesn't cover."

"Angels don't come from Hawking radiation," Gyasi said absently, eyes still on the graph. "At least not directly."

Kosta frowned. "What do you mean? I thought all particle radiation from a quantum black hole was Hawking process."

"Not angels, apparently," Gyasi shrugged. "Classical Hawking process is a tidal-force creation of particle-antiparticle pairs at the event horizon, one of which escapes while the other falls into the black hole. Right? So if angels are Hawking process, we should see anti-angels too. Only we don't."

"Never?"

Gyasi shrugged again. "No one's ever found one."

Kosta rubbed his chin. "But if it's not Hawking process, then what's the mechanism?"

"The theorists over in the west wing have been trying to answer that one for twenty years," Gyasi said dryly. "So far nothing they've come up with has been solid enough to hold soup." He shook his head. "I wonder why no one's ever noticed this before."

Because you've all got terminal tunnel vision where angels are concerned. "Probably because no one's thought to look," Kosta said instead. "That's why you bring in people like me who don't know what the unspoken assumptions are."

"I guess," Gyasi conceded. "You ought to get this written up and onto the nets as soon as possible."

Kosta felt his stomach tighten. For a moment there he'd almost forgotten who and what he was. Now, all of that came rushing back like a splash of cold water.

He was a spy in enemy territory. And spies were not supposed to draw attention to themselves by publishing inflammatory academic papers. "Actually, I thought I'd do a little more work on it first," he said cautiously. "Make sure I'm not seeing things that aren't there."

"Bosh," Gyasi snorted. "What are you afraid of, looking silly? No one cares about that." He held up a hand. "Okay, okay, I know you're new here. Tell you what: if it'll make you feel any better, you can have three days to run all the numbers back and forth through the sand sifter. But after that, either you write it up or I will. Deal?"

Kosta hesitated. But he really didn't have a choice. And if it made the Empyreals even slightly more cautious about these angels of theirs, it would be worth the risk. "Deal."

"Good." Gyasi waved a hand imperiously at Kosta. "Well, don't just sit there—get to work. The entire Empyreal scientific community is waiting for this."

"Yeah," Kosta muttered. "I'm sure they can hardly wait."

"That's the spirit," Gyasi said. "Hey, relax—even if you're totally wrong, no one's going to hang you."

Kosta shivered. If he only knew.

CHAPTER 16

Ornina looked up from the circuit board, a slightly bemused expression on her face. "Stop me if you've heard this before, Chandris, but you are absolutely amazing. Are you sure you've never done this sort of work before?"

Chandris shook her head, feeling her cheeks warming under Ornina's praise. It was embarrassing to stand here and listen to the woman go on like this. Embarrassing, and pretty stupid besides.

But she had to admit that, down deep, it felt kind of nice. "Not before last week," she said. "You must be a good teacher."

"Fiddlies," Ornina said firmly. "It's sweet of you to say so, but fiddlies nonetheless." She twisted her head around to look across the room at Chandris's assembly table. "That was the last of them, too, wasn't it? Well, let's see; what else needs doing around here?"

Chandris cleared her throat. "Actually, I was wondering if maybe I could have a couple of hours off. I thought I might go into Shikari City for awhile."

"Why, certainly," Ornina said. "Hanan showed you how to call a line car, didn't he?"

"Yes, but I thought I'd just walk. I feel sometimes like I haven't been outside the *Gazelle* for more than ten minutes since I first got here."

"It *is* a hard life," Ornina agreed quietly. "If it helps any, we aren't always going to be quite this busy. It's just that the *Gazelle*'s going to have to have some major overhauling done soon, and we need to get a bit ahead of schedule before then. Time-wise and money-wise both."

"I understand," Chandris said. "I won't be gone long."

"Oh, well, don't worry about that. Though you probably ought to take a phone along—it's possible we might need to get in touch with you." Ornina's forehead creased in thought. "Not to put you off or anything . . . but should you be wandering the streets this soon after your, ah, trouble aboard the *Xirrus?*"

Chandris had wondered about that, too. But this whole angel question had been hanging over her head for more than a week, and she was tired of not knowing what she was up against. She needed more information than the *Gazelle*'s library could provide, and going out was the only way to get it. "I can't hide forever," she told Ornina, heading for the door to cut off further argument. "Don't worry, I've had a lot of practice at not being recognized. I'll be back in a couple of hours."

"Okay," Ornina called after her. "See you later. And don't forget the phone."

It was a brisk fifteen minute walk from the *Gazelle* to the edge of Shikari City proper, and another ten to the huge glass-and-stone monstrosity that the *Gazelle*'s maps had identified as the Angelmass Studies Institute. Circling until she found the front door, she went inside.

"Public access terminals? Right over there." The receptionist pointed past a large stairway to a long room containing rows of low-walled carrels, about half of them occupied. "You have a ship's sign-on, I presume?" the woman added, her eyes taking in Chandris's coveralls.

"Of course," Chandris told her automatically. She got two steps toward the room before it belatedly dawned on her that the lack of privacy in there would keep her from using any of her normal techniques to crack into the computer.

It was another two steps before it likewise dawned that, for a change, cracking wasn't going to be necessary. A quick phone call to Ornina for the *Gazelle*'s sign-on, and she was in business.

Only to realize, forty minutes later, that the whole trip had been for nothing.

"Can I help you?" the receptionist smiled.

"I hope so," Chandris said, smiling back through the best poor/lost/vulnerable expression in her repertoire. "I'm trying to locate some special information on angels, and I can't seem to find it in those files. Have I missed some special access or sign-on or something?"

"I doubt it," the woman said. "There really isn't all that much information available on angels that most people don't already know from the news and learning channels."

"I guess not," Chandris agreed. "But there must be *some* other files here somewhere. I mean, you people study angels all day, don't you?"

"Sometimes far into the night, too," the other woman said wryly. "The problem is that most of what's done here is still in the preliminary stage. They prefer to wait until they're sure about something before releasing it to the general public. Otherwise you get conflicting stories and retractions and general confusion all around."

"I understand," Chandris told her, letting a bit of pleading creep into her tone. "But I'm not just general public. I'm a crewer on a huntership. Isn't there—oh, I don't know; some kind of special procedure for us to get the information we need to do our jobs safely?"

The receptionist's forehead wrinkled in thought. She was on Chandris's side now—her body language showed that much. The question was whether there was anything she could do to help. Keeping quiet, Chandris waited, letting her work through it.

"There isn't any way to let you into the main computer files," the woman said at last. "However—" Her eyes flicked past Chandris's shoulder, her hand darting up to beckon someone over.

Chandris's muscles tensed, and she had to fight to keep from turning around to look. If the receptionist had recognized her—if that was a guard coming over—she'd have a better chance if she looked harmless and blissfully unaware that anything was going down. A fist-sized decorative crystal adorned the receptionist's desk; easing a few centimeters to her left brought Chandris within reach of it.

"—maybe one of our researchers can tell you what you need to know."

"That would be wonderful," Chandris said, keeping her voice steady and her eyes on the receptionist's face. It still might be a trap, but if it was the woman was a nurking good actress. Footsteps sounded behind her now; casually, she turned around—

And froze. The man approaching was not, as she'd feared, a guard.

It was worse.

It was the young man from the spaceport. The one she'd scored into getting her past the guards.

Nurk! she thought viciously, twisting way too quickly back toward the desk to try and hide her face. *Nurk, nurk,* damn, *nurk*! If he remembered her . . .

He did. The footsteps behind her faltered suddenly, then came to an abrupt stop. Chandris kept her eyes on the receptionist's face, waiting for her to realize there was something wrong—

"Mr. Kosta, this is a huntership crewer who's looking for some information about angels," the woman said. "I saw you heading upstairs and thought you might have a few minutes to talk with her."

There was just the slightest pause. "I see," the man said from behind her. No mistake; it was his voice. "Well . . . sure, why not? Miss—ah—?"

Chandris ground her teeth. "Chandris," she told him, turning around.

His eyes seemed to dig into her face, his expression stony but with an odd undercoating of nervousness to it. She met the gaze evenly; and he blinked first. "Right," he said, and turned away. "Come on."

He led the way across the entrance foyer toward what looked like a small lounge, his whole back a solid mass of tight muscles. Chandris followed, wondering why she *was* following him instead of going for a straight chop and hop.

Though if she did, chances were she wouldn't even make it outside the building.

They went into the lounge, Kosta heading back toward an unoccupied corner. "Have a seat," he grunted, pointing her to a chair as he eased himself down into the one facing it.

"Thank you." Chandris sat down, casually taking in her surroundings as she did so. The archway to the entrance foyer and one unmarked door nearby seemed to be the only exits, aside from several tall and probably unbreakable windows.

"So you're a huntership crewer today, are you?"

She focused on him. "As a matter of fact, I am," she said, annoyed despite herself at his tone. "Is that so hard to believe?"

He snorted. "Coming from you?" he asked pointedly.

Chandris unhooked the phone from her belt and held it out. "Huntership Service Yard Number S-33," she told him. "The ship's named the *Gazelle*; operators are Hanan and Ornina Daviee. Go ahead—call them. I'll wait."

Kosta's eyes flicked to the phone. "Maybe I should just call security instead."

She could take him, she knew. She could stand up—he would stand up, too—a short, quick jab in the stomach with the tapered top end of the phone— "Maybe you should," she said. "But you won't."

"What makes you so sure?"

She looked him straight in the eye. "Because if you didn't turn me in at the spaceport, you won't turn me in here."

He glared at her. But his tight throat muscles showed that she was right. "I'll answer your questions," he bit out. "But when you walk out that door I don't ever want to see you again. Is that clear?"

Chandris felt her lip twitch with contempt. A typical over-schooled cloud-head, the type who'd rather look the other way than get involved with anything sticky. "Perfectly," she told him. "Actually, all I want to know is whether angels can make people love each other."

His jaw dropped. "Make them do *what?*"

"Love each other. What, are you deaf?"

"What, are you stupid?" he shot back. "There are a dozen aphrodisiac perfumes on the market. Go use one of those."

With an effort, Chandris held her temper. She'd hit something in there, all right, something all his noise couldn't quite cover up. If she could just wheedle it out of him . . .

"You misunderstand," she said, putting her best imitation of quiet professional dignity into her face and voice. "Let me explain. As I mentioned, the owner/operators of the *Gazelle* are named Hanan and Ornina Daviee. Brother and sister, both in their forties, and they've apparently been working together for quite a few years. As you may or may not know, angel hunting is grueling work, the sort that tends to enhance personality differences between people. You understand?"

"Yes," Kosta nodded. He was falling for it, Chandris saw; slipping into a student/professor pattern in reaction to her newly adopted persona. He must not be all that long out of school for the pattern to have kicked in so quickly.

"All right," she continued, fine-tuning her act a bit. "Now, during the past few days I've noticed several strong personality differences between the two of them, differences I would consider strong enough to put a strain on their relationship. Yet they stay together, working for the most part in harmony. The obvious question arises as to whether their close work with angels has something to do with this continued partnership."

Kosta frowned slightly, his eyes not quite focused on anything. He really *had* fallen for it. "Have you been with them on any actual angel hunts yet?" he asked.

"Yes, two of them."

"Did they behave any differently before and after they had an angel aboard the ship?"

Chandris hesitated. She definitely didn't want to tell Kosta about the Daviees' hidden angel. "It's difficult to say," she said instead. "There are many other factors that come in at that point, unfortunately. The pre-capture tension, for example, which largely disappears once the angel's aboard." She shrugged. "That's why I came here. I thought the Institute might have done some studies on this phenomenon."

"No," Kosta said, shaking his head. "At least, nothing I'm aware of. I suppose it *could* fit in with the general framework of the *Acchaa* theory, though. That kind of love could be one of several factors making up this theoretical 'good' we're supposedly quantizing. I don't know, though."

Chandris nodded, wondering what the hell he was talking about. But his tone and body language were more than clear. "I take it you don't put much stock in the *Acchaa* theory?"

His lip twisted. "Hardly. The whole idea of good and evil coming in bite-sized chunks makes no sense at all. It throws free will all to hell, for one thing."

"So what's the alternative?"

He locked eyes with her. "That the angels are alien intelligences," he said bluntly. "Either separately or together, as part of some kind of hive mind. And that this plan to flood the Empyrean with them—a plan put together by people who already have angels hanging around their necks—is nothing less than an invasion."

"I see," Chandris said, startled by the sheer intensity of the outburst. She wouldn't have tagged him as the sort to feel strongly about anything. "What exactly does this *Acchaa* theory say, anyway?"

He stared at her . . . and, abruptly, he seemed to remember just who it was he was talking to. His face tightened up with the unmistakable look of someone who's just sent a secret rolling across the floor. "It says that good and evil come in tiny packages," he said, a note of resignation in his tone. Probably decided that trying to backpedal now would just make things worse. "Like light comes in packages called photons, and electric charge comes in multiples of the electron charge." He lifted his eyebrows slightly. "Is this over your head?"

"I know all about photons and electrons, thank you," she said coolly. Or at least she knew what the files on Angelmass had told her about them. "So how exactly do you hammer good and evil into little packages?"

"Ask the people who believe the theory," Kosta said. "I'm not even convinced anymore that this so-called angel effect really exists. Maybe it's nothing but hype and placebo. People believe so hard in the things that they go ahead and make themselves change."

Except that Chandris hadn't known the Daviees had hidden an angel near her. And she certainly hadn't wanted to do any changing. "No," she said. "They work, all right. I've seen it. But this package-of-good stuff is crazy."

"Hey, don't argue with *me*," Kosta growled. "It's not *my* theory."

"Oh, right," Chandris said dryly. "*Your* theory is that they're tiny little invaders, here to overthrow the Empyrean."

His face darkened. "You ever hear of viruses? You get a handful of the wrong kind in your body and they'll kill you where you stand. Size by itself doesn't define a threat."

"Yeah, but if you don't have size you'd better have numbers," Chandris countered. "Those viruses of yours aren't just a handful anymore when they kill you. Even I know that much."

"Do you, now?" Kosta said. "Then maybe you'd also be interested in knowing that the number of angels your hunterships are finding out there has been increasing."

Chandris frowned. "What do you mean?"

"Just what I said. There are more angels available for capture than there were even three years ago. More than can be explained by numbers of ships or better equipment."

"So maybe it's because Angelmass is getting smaller and spitting out more of everything. You ever think of that?"

She had the immense satisfaction of watching him trip over his own

tongue, a look of total flabbergastment flooding over his face. It made those te-
dious hours of wading through the *Gazelle*'s Angelmass files all worthwhile.
"Where did you learn about quantum black holes?" he asked at last.

"I read about them," she said sweetly. "What, you think you can't learn
things without going to some fancy school somewhere?"

He snorted. "Certainly not some of the things *you* probably know."

Chandris gave him a long, cool look. Then, deliberately, she got to her feet.
"Thank you for your time, Mr. Kosta," she said, icily polite. "And for your rich
expertise. If I ever have any more questions, I'll be sure and go somewhere
else." She turned to go—

"Just a minute."

She turned back. "Yes?"

His face was a mass of conflicting emotions. "I have to ask you," he said at
last. "When you ran me down at the spaceport you were wearing a fancy
dress—blue and silver, I think it was, with embroidery or something all over it.
But when you showed up later you were wearing just a plain white dress.
Where did you get it?"

She eyed him, automatically searching the question for a trap. Self-
incrimination, maybe? But, no, he already knew who she was. And anyway, he
didn't strike her as smart enough for even that much finesse. "I didn't get it,"
she told him. "I made it. Fancy dresses like that always have fancy linings to
match. All I had to do was cut the outer part of the dress away and do some
trimming and shortening. It's not hard if you know what you're doing."

"Mm," he said, nodding thoughtfully. "But don't the seams show?"

"You can turn it inside out," she said. "But you don't always have to. People usually see what they want to." She hesitated; but it was just too tempting
to pass up. "Like if you want to see alien invasions, for instance."

An instant later she was sorry she'd said it. His head twitched back, almost
as if he'd been slapped, and for just a second he looked like a school kid who'd
been laughed at by his friends.

But only for an instant. "There's an invasion coming, all right," he said
softly, his face turning to stone as he stood up. "One way or another."

He brushed past her and left the lounge, stomping his way across the foyer
toward the wide staircase. Chandris followed more slowly, and caught just a
glimpse of him at the top of the stairs before he disappeared from sight.

For a moment she stood there, watching the spot where he'd disappeared
and wondering just what the hell that had been about. A cloud-head and a
half, that was for sure. And reeked three ways from dead on this invasion stuff
on top of it. *You bet,* she promised him silently, *that I'll stay away from you.*

She'd had more than her fill of reeked cloud-heads back in the Barrio. The last thing she needed was to start hunting them down on Seraph, too.

She took a deep breath, exhaled him out of her mind. And speaking of hunting, she really ought to be getting back to the *Gazelle.*

Crossing the foyer, she headed for the exit.

Great, Kosta snarled to himself as he stomped down the corridor. *Just great. It's so rare to see someone get the chance to make seven different kinds of fool of himself in a single ten-minute slot. And especially rare to see him succeed so brilliantly at all of them. It's an absolute pleasure to watch you work, sir.*

He reached his office and slammed his way in. Gyasi's presence at that particular moment—his presence, and his inevitable questions—would have completed the whole thing to perfection. But the laughing fates had missed that one; the office was empty.

He flopped down into his chair, but bounded up a second later, far too agitated to sit still. Stepping over to the window, he stood glaring out, pounding the back of his right fist gently into his left palm.

It was her. It had to be. The woman was a jinx, pure and simple. A jinx with the knack of twisting the universe straight out from under him every time he got within ten meters of her. Woman, hell—she probably wasn't even out of her teens yet.

Below, on the walkway, a movement caught his eye. A dark-haired figure in a huntership-type jumpsuit.

Yeah, you'd better get out of here, he thought bitterly in her direction. *I ever see you again, I* will *call the police down on you.* A huntership crewer—sure she was. She was nothing more than a rotten little con artist; even he could see that. A con artist with a knack for twisting him around her finger . . .

He took a deep breath, let it out in a snort. It would be nice to believe that. But down deep, he knew the trouble wasn't with her at all.

The trouble was with him. His life the past few years had been immersed so thoroughly in academic surroundings and people that he'd completely forgotten how to deal with anyone who didn't fit into that neat little mold.

If he'd ever known how to do it at all.

He watched the girl cross the main entrance road below, a wave of self-disgust souring his stomach. He could kid himself all he wanted, but it wouldn't make a scrap of difference to the universe at large. The plain, simple, brutal truth was that he'd been a socially incompetent child, a socially incompetent adolescent, and was well on his way to becoming a full-fledged socially incompetent adult.

He couldn't even handle his own culture without freezing up or babbling like an idiot. And so, of course, he'd been selected for an undercover mission to a totally foreign culture.

Why?

He'd asked his instructors that question during those long weeks of his espionage training. Had asked it a dozen different times, in a dozen different ways. And yet, somehow, he'd never gotten a straight answer to it. At the time he'd been too busy to pay much attention to the evasion; now, remembering back, he could see more clearly the half answers and smooth subject changes that had always seemed to happen.

They'd manipulated him. Like that Chandris girl out there, they'd manipulated him. And had done it just as successfully as she had.

But you can deal with the academic types like Gyasi and Qhahenlo, the thought whispered in the back of his mind.

It was a valid enough point, in its way. Probably the one they'd used to talk him into this mission in the first place, though he didn't remember that conversation very clearly. He *did* remember they'd made a big deal about his tri-doctorum degree including neural physiology along with astrophysics and tech design, and there did seem to be a fair amount of neural data in the Institute's files.

But surely there were other people in the Pax with as much expertise and better social polish. If Chandris was at all representative of the average Empyreal, he was probably damned lucky he'd even made it to Seraph without being exposed for who and what he was.

Unless that was exactly what they'd wanted.

For a long minute he stared out the window, not seeing anything at all. Could that really be what all this was about? Not a research mission at all, but just some kind of throwaway decoy to cover up the *Komitadji*'s real operation?

Because if it was, his life wasn't worth the plastic his phony ID was printed on. He'd be caught—sure as anything he'd be caught. They'd have made sure of that.

Behind him, the door opened.

He jumped, twisting awkwardly in the air, hand clawing uselessly for the shocker buried out of reach in the bottom of his pocket. He came down, trying to land in the combat stance they'd taught him—

"Hi, Jereko," Gyasi said absently, barely glancing up from the printout balanced across his left forearm as he ambled into the room and over to his desk chair. "What's new?"

Kosta swallowed hard, knees trembling with relief and reaction. "Nothing much," he said, striving to sound casual.

He obviously didn't succeed. Midway through turning a page Gyasi looked up, a frown on his face. "You okay?"

"Sure," Kosta said. "Fine."

"Uh-*huh*." Gyasi peered at him. "Come on, what's wrong?"

"It's something personal," Kosta told him, hearing the edge in his voice. "I just need some time to think."

Gyasi frowned a little harder, but then shrugged. "Okay, sure. You need someone to talk to, I'm right here."

"Sure."

Gyasi threw him a quick smile and, for all practical purposes, disappeared back into his printout.

Kosta watched him for a moment. Then, with an effort, he made his way back to his own chair, feeling both relieved and more than a little foolish. Of *course* the Pax hadn't thrown him to the sharks—the whole idea was crazy. Aside from anything else, this mission must have cost a fantastic amount of money. And if there was one thing everyone knew about the Pax, it was that no one in government deliberately threw away fantastic amounts of money. Not with the Adjutors hovering like hungry vultures over everything they did.

No, what they must have been counting on was something far more subtle: namely, the non-suspicious attitude the angels seemed to create in their subjects. It was the same mindset that had allowed him to breeze through interplanetary Empyreal customs and into a sensitive facility without his credentials ever being challenged, and it would very likely allow him to gloss over any cultural blunders as well. At least, with anyone who mattered.

"Oh, by the way," Gyasi said, looking up again, "what's the status of that angel-production paper I keep nagging you about? Anything new?"

"The research is done," Kosta told him. "I'll be writing it up this afternoon."

Gyasi's eyebrows went up. "Great. I'd like to show a copy to Dr. Qhahenlo before you put it on the net, if I may."

"Sure."

After all, the reason he'd joined this mission in the first place had been to help free the Empyreals from alien domination. Risky though it might be to draw attention to himself, it might be the only way to shake up the general complacency around him. To try and get the people in charge to take a good, hard look at their most basic assumptions.

And as to the other part of his mission . . .

"Speaking of Dr. Qhahenlo," he said, "is that offer from her still open?"

"I'm sure it is. You looking to join the team?"

"I'd at least like to do some consulting," Kosta said. "You people know so much more than I do about angels, and there's a lot I still need to learn."

"Great," Gyasi smiled, getting to his feet. "Let's go talk to her."

Kosta stood up, too, forcing a smile of his own. And wondered uneasily why the deception seemed to hurt his stomach.

"Well, we're off," Ornina said, tucking the flat angel holding box solidly under her arm as she made yet another adjustment to her floppy-brimmed hat. A horrendous hat, to Chandris's way of thinking, but Ornina obviously liked it. "We should be back within four hours at the latest."

"Sooner than that if the couplers at Glazrene's are down to their usual standard of quality," Hanan added, twirling his credit-line card around in his fingers with obviously strained patience as he waited for his sister to finish her primping. "Still, hope springs eternal, or some such thing."

Chandris nodded silently, her eyes on the spinning card. It was a strangely fascinating routine, very much like the palm-and-switch techniques of the three card monte scorers she'd known in the Barrio. Someday she would have to ask Hanan where he'd learned how to do that.

"Well, come on, Hanan," Ornina said briskly. "Let's get this show on the road. Good-bye, Chandris; we'll see you later. Enjoy the silence."

They headed outside and down the outer stairway. Chandris stood there, listening . . . and a minute later heard the sound of the TransTruck driving off down the street.

And she was alone. Alone with the *Gazelle.* Alone with several million ruya worth of equipment.

Alone with the angel.

For several minutes she just wandered the aft part of the ship, listening as her footsteps punctuated the now familiar sounds of the *Gazelle* at rest. But only the quieter sounds: engines and pumps, generators and fans. There was none of the music Ornina always played while she worked; none of Hanan's alleged singing and distinctive, slightly clumping walk.

She was alone. In the silence.

With the angel.

The samovar in the galley was, as usual, simmering gently with one of Ornina's long repertoire of tea blends. Peppermint, this one, a drink Chandris had developed a particular taste for over the past four weeks. She helped herself to a cup, throwing in an extra stick of peppermint, and carried it carefully up to the control cabin. There, amid the quietly glowing displays and flickering status boards, she pulled the restraint straps away from her chair and sat down.

She hadn't promised them anything. Not a single solitary nurking thing.
For that matter, they'd never promised her anything, either. Not even full
employment. As far as anyone had said, she was still here only on a temporary
basis.

Not that she really wanted the job, of course. It wasn't her kind of life. Too
dull, too honest.

Too permanent.

Four weeks. She'd been with the *Gazelle* for four weeks now. Probably the
longest she'd stayed in one place for years. Certainly longer than she and
Trilling had ever stayed anywhere while they'd been together.

Trilling.

She sipped at her tea, but the peppermint had gone flat in her mouth. No,
she couldn't stay here, not even if she wanted to. Right now, somewhere out
there, Trilling was looking for her. The longer she stayed in one place, the
sooner he'd find her.

She didn't owe the Daviees anything. Not a single solitary nurking thing.
The four weeks of room and board she'd more than paid for with all the work
she'd done aboard the ship. And it would be doing them a favor, really: a
painful but solid lesson in how the real world operated.

Painful, maybe, for everyone. But that was life, wasn't it?

There were only a few places the angel could be hidden, she knew, assuming that the Daviees had wanted her to be near it for as long as possible during
that first trip out to Angelmass. The obvious place to start was her cabin; and
it was barely two minutes' work to discover that the Daviees were as unsubtle
in this as they were in everything else. The flat angel holding box was underneath the head of her bed, fastened snugly against the mattress by a wire mesh
frame.

It took another minute to cut the mesh away, and three more to find an innocuous grocery bag in the galley to carry the box in. Then, changing back to
the white makeshift dress she'd worn when she first arrived on Seraph, she left
the ship.

For the last time.

Pedestrian traffic was light as she walked past the service yards and the
rows of dusty ships behind their wire fences. That was normal, she knew—
huntership crewers, when they left their yards at all, were usually in too big a
hurry to walk anywhere that a line car or TransTruck would take them. It made
Chandris more than a little conspicuous, but there wasn't much she could do
about it. Witnesses' memories were vague; line car records weren't.

Still, she breathed a sigh of relief when she finally cleared the edge of the
yards and headed into Shikari City proper. It was still a good couple of kilo-

meters to the Gabriel receiving office, but she was young and healthy and the exercise would do her good.

Besides which, she still had to figure out what the hell she was going to do once she got there.

It wasn't a trivial problem. She'd gone with Hanan on the last angel drop-off and knew the usual routine. But the usual routine wasn't going to do her a lot of good. Assuming that the Daviees hadn't been lying when they said angels couldn't be traded for cash—and she'd seen no evidence that they *had* lied about that—she was going to have to somehow get the angel dumped into a credit line that she could then convert to cash. That wasn't particularly difficult, but in the past she'd always had more prep time to work with. Now, she was going to have to make a chop and hop of it.

She felt her lip twist, a stab of self-recrimination twisting her stomach. No, she'd had the time, all right. Four weeks' worth of it. She just hadn't used it.

Which just made it that much clearer how much she needed to get away from this place. Sitting around being comfortable instead of watching for opportunities was a sure way to lose that hard edge.

And if there was one thing for sure, it was that Trilling hadn't lost *his* hard edge.

She forced her mind off depressing thoughts like Trilling and back to the problem at hand. What she really needed was a contact, someone here on Seraph who could help her get off the planet once she got the angel sold. Hopefully for a price she could afford; it was for sure she wasn't going to have time to charm or score anyone into doing it for free. No one but soft-touches like the Daviees did anything for free, at least not on purpose. But making contact with Seraph's criminal underground would take time.

And half a block later, like a gift from the god of thieves, the opportunity dropped straight into her lap.

It was a score in progress; the body language of the two participants showed that as clearly as if there'd been a sign hanging over them. One, dressed in shabby lower-class clothing, held something cupped in his hand as the other, upper-middle-class at the least, spoke into a phone. His face was still undecided, but Chandris could see from the way he stared into the other's cupped hand that he was already more than halfway gone. A little extra nudge on her part, and she would have her contact.

The targ hung up as she approached, slipping the phone back inside his coat with obvious uncertainty. The scorer said something Chandris didn't catch, pushing his cupped hand toward the other with just the right blend of reluctance and resolve. "But I really don't know if I should," the targ said, reaching a hesitant finger into the cupped hand.

"Look, like I told you before—" The scorer broke off, startled, as Chandris stepped up to them. "Hey, go away," he growled, snatching his hand back from her. "This is a private discussion."

But Chandris had already seen the glint of metal. "What have you got there, coins?" she asked, ignoring the order. "Let me see, huh?"

"I said go away—"

"Oh, let her see them," the targ interrupted. "He found them right over there in an envelope," he continued as the scorer reluctantly opened his hand again. "With a phone number on it. I just called, and the woman there said she'd lost them. She'll pay five hundred ruya to get them back."

"That's a lot of money," Chandris commented, stirring the coins around with her finger. Most of them were normal Empyreal currency, but there were a few that she didn't recognize. "You get her address?"

"Oh, sure—real fancy neighborhood in Magasca." He jerked a thumb at the scorer. "The problem is that he doesn't want to go there."

"Me, in a fancy neighborhood?" the scorer chimed in, looking plaintively at Chandris. "Come on. I wouldn't fit in there. Someone'd call the police before I even got to the door."

"And I told you that no one would accuse you of stealing them," the targ said, starting to sound a little annoyed. "She told me herself she lost them."

"All I want is for him to take them there," the scorer said, still to Chandris. "*He'd* be okay up there, now, wouldn't he?" He looked at the targ, almost sadly. "Fit right in with the rich people."

"But it's your money," the targ insisted. "Five hundred ruya. I can't take that."

"So just give me part of it," the scorer said. "I'll sell 'em to you right now." Again, he pushed his hand toward the targ. "I'll take whatever you want to give me."

The targ looked helplessly at Chandris, back at the scorer. "But I don't have that kind of money with me."

"I'll take whatever you can give me," the scorer said again, more plaintively this time.

"But—"

"May I see them?" Chandris put in. Before the scorer could react, she plucked the coins out of his hand, sorting the unfamiliar ones out for a close look. It was a variant on the old antique ring score she'd pulled a number of times: the scorer would get whatever he could, leaving the targ with a phony address and a fist full of worthless coins.

Which he obviously thought were worth a five-hundred-ruya reward. If she went ahead and confirmed their value, she would have her contact with the scorer clinched. Her contact, and the doorway she needed to get out of here.

"Okay, look," the targ said suddenly, reaching for his wallet. "I've got—I don't know; maybe sixty ruya on me. If that's really all you want I'll go ahead and take them. But I'd be glad—really—to just go out to Magasca with you so that you can get the whole thing." He reached into his wallet and began counting through the bills.

Maybe it was the offer to escort the scorer to Magasca to claim his reward that did it. Or maybe it was the earnest expression on his face as he pulled out the money, an expression that somehow reminded her of Ornina hunched over a circuit board.

But whatever it was, something deep inside Chandris suddenly snapped.

"I'd save my money, if I were you," she spoke up, dumping the coins into the hand that had been outstretched to take the targ's money. "These things aren't worth anything."

The targ blinked. "What?"

"I said they aren't worth anything," she repeated, watching the scorer out of the corner of her eye. At the moment he looked as if he'd been hit in the face with a brick, but the shock wouldn't last long. And with his cord popped he might decide to flip this over into a straight robbery. "I know what I'm talking about," she added. "My father used to collect coins."

"But the woman said she'd pay five hundred ruya to get them back," the targ protested, still not ready to believe it. "She said she'd put an ad on the nets to get them back."

"Ads with her phone number on them?"

The targ looked at the scorer, back at Chandris. "I suppose so," he said. "She didn't say."

"Probably someone's idea of a stupid joke," Chandris shrugged. "They read the ad, got a half-ruya's worth of coins together, and dropped it with her number on the envelope." She let her gaze sweep the area. "In fact, he might be watching right now to see what happens."

"Lousy thing to do," the targ growled, looking around as he stuffed his money back into his wallet. "Getting that woman's hopes up for nothing. I suppose I ought to call her back and explain."

Except that the hook would be long gone from whatever phone she'd been using. And if the targ tumbled now, the scorer would be in for it. "I wouldn't bother," Chandris said off-handedly as the targ put his wallet away and reached for his phone. "It'll teach her not to put phone numbers on the net instead of a netsign where she'd know who was at the other end."

"But—"

"And anyway," the scorer chimed in, "you call back now and tell her they're not worth nothing and she might think you're just trying to steal them."

The targ grimaced. "You may be right," he said at last, reluctantly. "Probably are." With a sigh, he dropped his hand empty to his side. "So much for that."

"They're probably still worth a couple of ruya at a coin shop," Chandris told the scorer helpfully. "Or else you could just keep them as a souvenir."

"Thanks," the other murmured, lip twitching in a wry smile. A smile solely for the targ's benefit. "Thanks for your help. A lot."

"You're welcome," she said. For a long moment she held his gaze, warning him with her eyes. Then, turning her back, she continued on her way.

Heading nowhere.

She knew it right away, down deep. But she walked another block before finally admitting it to herself. She'd had the chance to lock in with the Seraph underground, or at least one small corner of it. Had had the chance to get off this nurking planet, to be rid of the Daviees and their nurking huntership and their nurking middle-class naivete.

And she'd blown it. She'd deliberately blown it.

And the most frightening part was that she didn't know why.

The only alcohol she could find on the *Gazelle* was four small bottles of cooking sherry stuck way back in one of the galley bins. It tasted terrible, especially chased by peppermint tea. But she managed.

She had finished three of the bottles and was working on the fourth when the Daviees finally returned.

"Well—home at last," she growled when they poked their heads in the galley door. "Have a good little shopping trip?"

"We got what we needed, yes," Ornina said cautiously, her eyes taking in the empty bottles. "I see you've been having a little party. Any particular occasion?"

"I'm drinking to stupidity," Chandris told her. "Yours."

Their reactions were a great disappointment. She'd been hoping for anger or hurt, or at least surprise. But all she got was that maddening patience of theirs.

And, of course, jokes. "A wide ranging subject, that," Hanan said, clumping into the room to sit down across the table from her. "Our stupidity has been toasted from here to the south edge of Magasca. Toasted by experts, too, I might add. You're not going to set any records with four bottles of cooking sherry."

"Is that your answer to everything?" Chandris snapped. "Jokes?"

Hanan shrugged, his eyes hardening just a little. "What's *your* answer? Getting drunk?"

Chandris glared at him, trying hard to hate the man. But up his shirt sleeves she could see the glint of his exobraces . . .

She looked at Ornina. Maybe she'd be able to hate *her*. "You want to know why you're stupid? Do you? Well, I'll tell you why. You left me here alone. Here. With your ship. Alone."

"We trust you," Ornina said quietly.

"Well, you shouldn't," Chandris flared. "What kind of fools are you, anyway? You know what I am—I'm a *thief*, damn it." Abruptly, she ducked down to haul the angel holding box up off the floor. "You see this?" she demanded, banging it down on the table. "You see it? It's your stupid nurking angel, that's what it is."

"I see it," Ornina said. "I also see that it's still here."

"No thanks to you," Chandris bit out. "You leave the damn thing just *sitting* there, the first damn place a thief would look. You don't have any alarms or trippers or—nurk it all, I had it out of the ship and halfway to the damn Gabriel office."

Ornina nodded. "And then you brought it back."

"Only so I could tell you what I thought of you before I left." Chandris got to her feet, grabbing for the table as her head suddenly went foggy. "Let me alone!" she snapped, jerking back as Hanan reached out a hand. "I don't need your help—I don't need *anybody's* help." She started around the table, cursing as she banged her knee on the edge of the chair.

"Where are you going?" Ornina asked.

"Where do you think I'm going?" Chandris retorted. "Thanks for everything. Don't bother writing me a reference."

Ornina raised her eyebrows slightly. "The mood you're in, I don't suppose you care, but out here in the real world it's considered proper etiquette to give at least a week's notice before quitting a job."

"Funny woman," Chandris snarled. "Leave the jokes to Hanan—he does a better job with them."

"I'm not joking," Ornina said, taking a short step sideways to block the doorway. "If you really want to leave, of course you're free to go. But I want to hear it from you first."

Chandris stared at her. Was she actually saying . . . ? "Are you people completely crazy? I just tried to steal your angel."

"But you didn't," Ornina pointed out. "That's the important part."

"No, it isn't," Chandris shot back. "Maybe I just figured I couldn't sell it. Next time I'll know enough to take something else. I'm a *thief*, damn it."

"No," Hanan said from behind her. "You're a cat."

She spun around, almost losing her balance again. "What?"

"You're a cat," he repeated. "Ever see a cat kill a mouse? A pet cat, I mean, not a wild one."

She frowned at him, the sheer unexpectedness of it sidetracking her anger. It was the setup to a joke, probably, and she wasn't in any mood to listen to Hanan's jokes. But he looked so serious . . .

What the hell. "I saw a cat take out a small rat once," she told him. "There were a lot more rats than mice in the Barrio."

He nodded. "So he killed it. Did he eat it?"

She had to think back. "No. He stalked it and killed it, but then he just walked away."

"That's because he wasn't hungry," Hanan said. "Cats behave like that. A hungry cat will locate some prey, stalk it, capture it, kill it, and eat it. If he's not really hungry enough to eat, he'll still stalk and capture and maybe even kill. But if he's not hungry at all—" he waggled a finger at her for emphasis— "he'll still stalk and capture, but then let it go without hurting it."

She eyed him. Even with three and a half bottles of sherry inside her it was obvious where he was going with this. "And that's supposed to be why I brought it back?"

Hanan shrugged. "It's an interesting system," he said, as if she hadn't spoken. "Hunting and stalking take up a lot of time. If the cat starts the routine before he's really hungry, chances are that by the time he *is* hungry he'll have caught himself some dinner."

Chandris gritted her teeth, feeling her resolve slipping away. "I'm not a cat."

"No," Ornina agreed softly. "You're a little girl. And I'd say you've been hungry a long time."

Her vision was beginning to swim; angrily, Chandris clenched her throat against the tears. She would not cry. No matter what, she would not cry. "I can't stay here," she said harshly. "There's a man looking for me. A crazy man, getting crazier all the time. If he finds me here, he'll kill all of us."

Hanan and Ornina looked at each other, communicating in that wordless way of theirs. Chandris held her breath, wondering what they would decide. Wondering what she hoped they'd decide.

"Considering the circumstances," Hanan said suddenly, "I'd say we've got a case here of a subconscious being smarter than the person it's attached to."

Chandris blinked. "What does that mean?"

"I thought that was obvious," he said, still straight-faced but with that twinkle back in his eye. "You wanted to steal our angel and run; but your subconscious knew you'd be safer if you stayed here with us."

"Your friend will expect you to keep running," Ornina added. "Or else to hide out with other thieves and con artists." She raised her eyebrows. "Admit it: this is the absolute last place in the Empyrean he would ever think to look."

"You mean . . . ?" She swallowed, unable to finish the question.

"We mean," Hanan said, "that since we can always use a little extra intelligence around here—" he paused dramatically— "your subconscious is hereby invited to stay aboard." He shrugged. "And it can bring the rest of you along if it wants to."

"You're too generous." Chandris's voice broke on the last word, and once again she had to fight back the tears.

"I'm like that," he said with a flippant wave of his hand. But the flippancy was an act—she could see that in his eyes. A feeble attempt to shunt away some of the emotion charging the room.

"Are you going to stay?" Ornina asked.

Chandris took a deep breath. "I suppose I have to," she said, trying to match Hanan's tone. "Without me here, sooner or later someone's going to steal this ship right out from under you."

"Great," Hanan said cheerfully. "Just what I've always wanted: our very own guardian angel."

Ornina threw him that look of hers. "Hanan—"

"So, that's settled," he said, ignoring the warning. "Now. Can we eat?"

Ornina rolled her eyes. "Of course. You feel up to helping, Chandris, or would you rather go lie down for a bit?"

"I can help," Chandris said. Grabbing the table for stability, she headed for the pantry.

There would, she knew, be a lot of stuff to sort out later, after the haze of the sherry wore off. Things about the decision she'd just made, and how she felt about it. But for now, there was one thing that stood out clearly.

For the first time in her life, she actually felt safe.

The cocoon had been drifting through Lorelei system for over a month. Gathering data on the net fields, integrating it, correlating it, storing it, hypothesizing about it.

And now, at last, it was ready.

The vast computer system understood the net fields. They were, as its programmers had suspected, a straightforward if imaginative inversion of basic hyperspace catapult theory.

And with the theory understood, the technology involved was a fairly trivial extrapolation. Deep within the false asteroid, the fabricators came to life.

Quietly, stealthily, they began to build.

CHAPTER 18

The report flowing across the display came to an end. Not, to Forsythe's mind, a particularly satisfying end. "And that," he said, looking up, "is six weeks worth of work?"

Pirbazari held out his hands. "I'm sorry, sir; I know it's not very impressive. But all this stuff has to go through as extra mining equipment, and there are only so many boring lasers and orbit-shift explosives you can order at once. Not without raising some eyebrows."

"I know." Forsythe hissed between clenched teeth. "The problem is that time isn't exactly on our side here."

"We're doing the best we can, sir."

"I know that, too," Forsythe assured him, managing an encouraging smile. He'd learned long ago that it was counterproductive to take out his frustrations on people who weren't responsible for creating them. "What about the Ardanalle tracking systems?"

"There we *do* have some good news," Pirbazari said, reaching over the desk to tap keys on Forsythe's board. "It turns out that almost fifty percent of Lorelei's mining ships are running with outmoded trackers. We've gotten an order through for a whole bunch of Arda 601's, and they'll be upgrading the mining ships as they bring in loads."

"Good," Forsythe nodded. "How much modification will it take to give them target acquisition capabilities?"

"None, really—that's why I specified 601's. Of course, the miners themselves will have to be taught how to use them." Pirbazari hesitated. "I'm sure you realize, though, that if the *Komitadji* gets in through the net blockade, this whole exercise becomes academic. We could arm every ship in Lorelei system—miners, transports, *and* liners—and together they still wouldn't have a chance against it."

"Would you rather we just sit back and do nothing?" Forsythe countered. "At least we might be able to slow them down a little when they come." He shook his head, feeling the frustration rising again. "We need a weapon, Zar. Something new; something that could get through the defenses of a ship like that."

Pirbazari shrugged, looking strangely uncomfortable. "In theory, we've

got one," he said. "All you have to do is find a way to get a catapult to make un-
netted throws of less than half a light-day."

Forsythe smiled wryly. "Right. And if wishes were horses, we'd be up to
our chins in fertilizer."

Pirbazari didn't smile back. "True. It *is* theoretically possible, though."

"A lot of things are theoretically possible," Forsythe murmured, drum-
ming his fingers on the desk as he studied the other's face. "You want to tell me
what's bothering you?"

Pirbazari's cheek twitched, a sign of discomfort Forsythe didn't see very
often in the man. "Since you ask . . . I feel a little strange operating behind the
High Senate's back this way."

"We've cut through governmental bureaucracy before," Forsythe reminded him, choosing his words carefully. It was obvious where the other was
going with this, and those doubts had to be quashed right here and now. "Always with the best interests of the people in mind. And if I'm not mistaken,
subsequent events have always vindicated our actions."

"I know that, sir," Pirbazari said. "But this time—" He waved a hand
toward Forsythe.

Or rather, toward the pendant glittering around Forsythe's neck. "This
time I'm wearing an angel," Forsythe finished for him. "And you're uncomfortable because I'm talking war and no one else in the High Senate is. That
more or less cover it?"

"More or less, sir, yes."

"Fine," Forsythe nodded. "So let's examine it. First of all, is there anything
financially unethical in what we're doing? Are we stealing or otherwise misap-
propriating Empyreal funds to arm Lorelei's miners?"

Pirbazari thought about it. "No, sir, not really," he said at last. "All this stuff
is legitimate mining equipment, after all. None of it would go to waste even if
the Pax dropped off the edge of the universe tomorrow."

"Right. Are we ourselves profiting financially from any of this?"

Pirbazari quirked a smile. "Hardly."

"Are we profiting politically, then?" Forsythe persisted. "Am I likely to
make a great name for myself this way?"

"Well . . ." Pirbazari's eyebrows came together. "I suppose it's *possible*. The
man who was prepared when no one else was and all that. But you're just as
likely to look paranoid and even a little silly if nothing happens, so it's really
not that good a gamble."

Forsythe spread his hands. "So in other words this doesn't gain me anything at all," he concluded. "So where's the ethical problem?"

Pirbazari pursed his lips. "The ethical problem is that we're lying to the High Senate," he said bluntly. "A lie of omission, perhaps, but a lie just the same."

Forsythe gazed at him, a chill running up his back. *Oh, no,* he thought. *Not Pirbazari too.* "We're not lying to them, Zar," he said. Quietly, soothingly, as if talking to an upset child. "I've tried to tell them that the Empyrean's in danger. You *know* how I've tried to tell them that. But it's something none of them wants to hear. And you know as well as I do that if someone doesn't want to hear something you can't force them to listen to it."

"Don't patronize me, sir," Pirbazari said, an edge to his voice. "Just because I'm concerned about ethical matters doesn't imply I've lost the capacity for rational thought."

"Sorry," Forsythe apologized, mind racing. Somehow, he needed to deflect this line of questioning. "For a minute there I slipped into Ronyon mode," he added. "The way he insists on thinking about the universe in straight black/white, good/bad terms."

The tactic worked. Pirbazari seemed to straighten up, a slightly defensive expression flicking across his face. "I didn't mean to imply I thought *that,* sir."

"Oh, I know you didn't," Forsythe assured him. "It was just the way you said it, I guess." He locked gazes with the other. "I know it looks a little odd, Zar, but you're just going to have to trust me on this. Trust that I really do have the best interests of the Empyreal people at heart."

"I know you do, sir," Pirbazari said.

"And," Forsythe added, tapping his chest, "I *am,* after all, the one wearing the angel."

Pirbazari's face relaxed. Just a little, but enough. "There's that," he conceded. "Well. Unless there's something else, I'd better get back to my desk. I have a call in to Ardanalle about some 501's they're trying to dump. Not quite as good as the 601's; but if we could get them aboard some of the ore transports it would give them remote spotter capability."

"Good idea," Forsythe nodded. "Keep me informed."

"Yes, sir." Pirbazari glanced at his watch. "Don't forget you have a committee meeting in half an hour."

"Yes, thanks, I remember," Forsythe smiled. "Talk to you later."

He held the smile until Pirbazari had closed the door behind him. Then he leaned back in his chair and said a word he'd had to teach himself never to say in public.

It was backfiring. All of it. The work, the planning, even the expense of having his office remodeled to careful specifications—all of it would be for nothing if his staff came under the influence of the damned angel. Even if he himself remained free, because a High Senator without an able staff was a sound mind trapped in a crippled body.

One of the many things he'd learned from his father.

All right, don't panic, he told himself firmly. If the problem was all the other angels around here, there wasn't much of anything he could do about it. But if it was *his* angel that was at fault . . .

He frowned up at the decorative chandelier hanging over and just in front of the formal guest chair. Yes—that had to be it. The reason for having the chandelier put up in that particular place had been to keep the angel close to any visitors; but obviously it was also too close to the less formal desk-corner chairs that Pirbazari and the others used when they came in for private conversations.

Which meant that all he needed to do was find someplace else to stash the thing when his aides came to call.

Reaching down, he pulled open his lower left-hand desk drawer. It came easily; the flat safe he'd had installed there was heavy, but the motor assist more than compensated for the extra weight. He worked the combination lock and opened it, letting the lid swing smoothly up to lean back against the edge of the desk, then opened the carved wooden jewelry box sitting inside among the papers and cyls. Picking up his call stick, he went over to the door, making sure to give the chandelier a wide berth. He keyed the stick for code transmission and tapped four buttons.

The motors in the safe, installed by people who knew what they were doing, were totally silent. The motorized track system inside the false ceiling, installed by him, wasn't quite that good. But it was good enough. At the door, five meters away, he could just barely hear the hum, and only because he knew what to listen for. Mentally, he traced the track's movement: from the chandelier's hollow center up into the gap behind the decorative false ceiling, diagonally through the gap above the desk to the movable tile directly above the open safe . . .

The tile swung open, and in a glitter of gold and crystal the angel pendant appeared. It dropped leisurely toward the open safe on its telescoping memory plastic tendril, disappearing inside with a soft metallic *chink*. A second coded signal sent the tendril retracting back into its hiding place; a third closed the safe and the drawer.

Stuffing the call stick into a pocket, Forsythe went over to the guest chair and climbed up on it, balancing awkwardly with one foot on the seat cushion and the other on one of the arms. The ceiling tiles weren't fastened down but were simply resting on their framework; pushing one of them up, he stuck his head up and took a look.

One look was all he needed. The straight-line path between chandelier and desk had been the easiest for him to set up, but there was plenty of room up there for him to add a second track to the system. That one would allow him to send the angel pendant all the way to the side of the room, well away from his aides when they were in the office.

But he'd have to do that later, after everyone else had gone home. Right now he had a meeting to go to, and one chore to take care of before he left. Ducking down, he dropped the tile back into place and got down off the chair, pulling it back to its normal position beneath the chandelier. With his call stick he signalled for Ronyon, then crossed the room to the main computer access system he'd had set up in the corner and punched up a section of the daily report.

He was sitting there, pretending to be engrossed in an analysis of commerce projections for northern Sadhai, when Ronyon arrived. *You wanted me, Mr. Forsythe?* the big man signed.

Yes, Ronyon, Forsythe signed back. *I have a meeting to go to soon. Would you mind coming with me?*

Ronyon's face lit up, as if he hadn't done this countless times in the past six weeks. *Sure, Mr. Forsythe,* he signed eagerly. *You want me to get the angel?*

Yes, please.

He watched as Ronyon went over to the desk, a not quite comfortable feeling in the pit of his stomach. It was one thing to run rings around Pirbazari and his new-formed if still nebulous conscience. It was something else entirely to continue pulling this charade on Ronyon.

And the really troublesome part was that he didn't really know why it bothered him the way it did.

He took a deep breath. *It doesn't matter,* he told himself firmly. Ronyon's feelings, that child's trust and loyalty of his—in the vast scheme of things all of that was expendable. All that ultimately mattered was Forsythe's duties to the people of Lorelei and the rest of the Empyrean. And if it took lying to Ronyon or anyone else to fulfill those duties, it was a small price to pay.

But the feelings refused to go away.

At the desk Ronyon had the drawer open and was twiddling the combination lock. *Do you want me to carry it again?* he asked, signing one-handed.

Forsythe waited until the safe was open and Ronyon was looking at him before replying. *I think that would be best,* he signed. *It's still the best way to assure that a thief who tried to steal it wouldn't get hold of the real thing.*

Okay, Ronyon signed cheerfully, carefully scooping the angel pendant out of its box. For a moment he held it cupped in his hand, clearly delighted by the play of light off the crystal. Then, as carefully as he handled everything else of

Forsythe's, he put it into his side coat pocket. *Okay,* he signed. *Are we going to go now?*

As eager to please as ever, Forsythe thought with a twinge. Totally unquestioning as to why his boss would want to continue this strange behavior.

Yes, Ronyon, Forsythe signed, getting to his feet. All of it, he reminded himself, was expendable.

Ronyon closed the lid of the safe and slid the drawer closed. *All safe and sound, Mr. Forsythe,* he signed cheerfully. *What should I do now?*

Forsythe glanced at his watch. Cheerful at seven o'clock at night, and that after sitting in on nearly five hours of meetings and discussions whose content he probably wouldn't have understood even if he'd been able to hear it. The man was unbelievable. *You might as well go on home,* he told the other. *I just have a few things to do here, then I'll be leaving too.*

Ronyon's face fell a bit. His eyes flicked around the room, as they often did when he was thinking hard. *Can I call to the dining room for them to bring you some dinner?*

Bone-weary, Forsythe still had to smile. So eager to please . . . *Thanks, but no,* he signed. A thought struck him— *But I'd appreciate it if you'd get me some tea from the samovar before you go.*

Ronyon's face lit up again. *Sure, Mr. Forsythe,* he signed, and all but dashed from the office.

Forsythe shook his head in wonderment and turned back to the computer access display. It was rather like having a bipedal trained dog, he thought as he keyed for his private angel-data file. A trained dog who could bring coffee and make cookies—

The thought froze halfway. On the screen, with red stars all along its edge, was the abstract of a newly-filed paper . . .

An extensive theoretical and statistical analysis of the Angelmass emissions indicates that the rate of angel production has increased over the past five years. A significant portion of this increase cannot be explained by the general changes in Hawking radiation brought about by the gradual mass-evaporation of the black hole itself . . .

Forsythe skipped to the bottom of the abstract. Jereko Kosta, the tag identified the writer. Visiting researcher, Angelmass Studies Institute, Seraph.

Unobtrusively, a steaming cup of tea and a small pot appeared at his elbow. *Thank you,* he signed, looking up at Ronyon. *Go on home now. I'll see you in the morning.*

Ronyon ducked his head in an abbreviated bow. *Okay, Mr. Forsythe. Good-bye.*

He left. Taking a sip of tea, Forsythe turned back to the display and called up Kosta's article. He'd replenished the cup twice from the pot, and once from the outer office samovar, by the time he finished.

He leaned back in his chair, sipping at the cold dregs, and stared at the screen. "Damn," he said quietly.

It was about as bad as a mathematically top-heavy paper could possibly be. Because if angel emission wasn't explainable by current theory, there were only two possibilities. Either the current theory was lacking, or else the angels were not a totally natural emission of a black hole.

Forsythe hissed softly between his teeth. Few of the other High Senators, he knew, would even read the paper, let alone understand its implications.

But some would. He knew which ones . . . and he knew what their first thought would be. If angels weren't simply a natural product of a quantum black hole, there must be some other mechanism involved. A mechanism that might not require a nearby black hole to operate.

A mechanism that might possibly be laboratory reproducible.

Setting his cup down, Forsythe keyed for a bio on the paper's author. It was remarkably short, saying only that Kosta had joined the Institute six weeks earlier after graduating from Clarkston University in Cairngorm, Balmoral. With no mention of honors or other publications, it was probable that he was just some newly graduated kid who'd happened to luck onto something no one else had noticed yet.

But if he was, in fact, truly smart enough to isolate the angel-producing mechanism . . .

Forsythe keyed back to the last page of the paper. Kosta's current funding was coming from a foundation on Lorelei, one whose name Forsythe couldn't recall ever having heard before. Clearly a small foundation, though; attached to the paper was a cross-indexed request from Kosta for Empyreal government funds to continue his work.

For a long minute he thought about it. Then, hunching forward, he keyed for his orders file.

Fifteen minutes later, it was done. Kosta's paper had been shifted from the daily report listing to an obscure science file where chances were good that no one in the High Senate would ever notice it. The request for Empyreal funding had been located, brought forward in the considerations file, and denied. And the next skeeter to Seraph would include an official order to the Angelmass Studies Institute that Kosta's current credit line be indefinitely suspended.

For just a moment he hesitated over the latter, finger poised over the "send" key. If his imagined worst-case scenario was wrong—if this Kosta really *wasn't* smart enough to be a genuine threat—then cutting him loose like this was going to be pretty hard on the kid.

But if he *was* . . .

Steeling himself, Forsythe jabbed the button. He couldn't risk it. If Kosta's work led to a way to create artificial angels, it would create a flood that the Empyrean would be buried under. And if it cost Kosta his career . . . well, Kosta was expendable, too.

Unless . . .

Forsythe grinned tightly to himself and called up a different file. With luck, he might be able to have it both ways.

MEMO TO PIRBAZARI: GET ME A BACKGROUND CHECK ON JEREKO KOSTA, CURRENTLY AT THE ANGELMASS STUDIES INSTITUTE. EMPHASIS ON SCHOLASTIC AND SCIENTIFIC ABILITY; STRONG EMPHASIS ON PROBLEM-SOLVING CAPABILITIES. REPORT ASAP.

With a satisfied grunt he cleared the screen and stood up, wincing at the complaints from his muscles and joints, but with the latest twinge from his conscience gone. If Kosta was merely one-time lucky, he'd have his credit line back in a week or two, no worse for the experience and with a nice horror story of bureaucratic stupidity to pass around at late-night chat sessions.

And if he was indeed a genius, with no funding he'd have to go back to being a genius on Balmoral or somewhere else equally harmless. Under the circumstances, it was as fair a deal as Kosta was likely to get. Fairer than some would have given him.

Fairer, perhaps, than Forsythe himself would have given him six weeks ago.

He looked at his watch. It was late, and he was tired, but there was still one more thing he had to do before he could go home. It shouldn't take more than another hour to rig up a second track path above his ceiling.

And anyway, being tired was part of a High Senator's job. Another of the many things he'd learned from his father.

CHAPTER 19

Kosta read the printout twice, a cold knot settling into his stomach. "I don't understand," he said.

"I don't understand either," Director Podolak confessed. "All I can suggest is that someone on Uhuru scrambled up somewhere. Confused you with someone else, perhaps."

Kosta grimaced. Or else they *hadn't* confused him with someone else. Perhaps someone on Uhuru had unraveled the fragile paper credit line reaching back to the Pax computer setup on Lorelei.

Calm down, he ordered himself firmly. If Empyreal security had gotten that far, they'd hardly tip their hand by simply shutting off his funding. "That must be it," he agreed aloud with Podolak. "So what do we do while we wait for them to unscramble it?"

Podolak pursed her lips. "That's the problem," she said. "Not only has your personal credit line been frozen, but there's also an attached order forbidding any use of Empyreal funds in your behalf. And since all the credit lines I have available to me are government funds . . ."

The knot in Kosta's stomach, which had slowly been loosening, began to tighten again. "Are you saying," he said carefully, "that I'm effectively bankrupt?"

"It's not quite as bad as that," Podolak assured him. "Your room and board here at the Institute have already been covered for the next two and a half weeks, so at least you won't have to worry about starving. And as long as we don't need the space for anyone else, I don't see why you can't continue to use your office."

"But no computer time, I suppose."

"I'm afraid not," Podolak shook her head. "Or access to any of the labs, either."

Kosta looked down at the paper in his hand, steeling himself. "Or the Institute ship?"

"Or the Institute ship," she agreed. "I'm sorry; I know you were scheduled to go up tomorrow."

"It wasn't going to be a joyride," he told her, the words coming out harsher than he'd intended. It was a blatant breach of manners, but Podolak didn't seem to notice. "I have an experiment aboard. A very important experiment."

"It's going to have to come off," Podolak said quietly. Her eyes, Kosta could see, were hurting; but her voice was firm. "Space aboard the ship is paid for out of your credit line."

Kosta squeezed the paper hard between thumb and fingers, trying hard to choke down his frustration. It had taken him over a month to design and build a detector to sample these particular segments of Angelmass's emission spectrum, segments carefully chosen to give him some sort of handle on what was happening out there. There *had* to be a way to get it aboard. "What if I can get someone else to pay for the space?" he asked Podolak. "I've been consulting with Dr. Qhahenlo—maybe she can put the thing on her credit line, and get Gyasi or someone to operate it. Would that be acceptable?"

"Under some circumstances, yes," Podolak nodded. "Unfortunately, in this case Dr. Qhahenlo's own credit line comes from Sadhai, and she would need special permission in advance to run your experiment for you. She told me her backers will almost certainly grant it; but since it would take a minimum of twenty-four hours to get the request there and back by skeeter, you'd still wind up missing this flight."

"You already talked to her about it?"

"Her, and a few others. I hoped I could have a solution for you before I told you about the problem. I'm sorry."

Kosta exhaled silently. "Thanks for trying."

"Part of my job." She gave him half a smile. "I know it's frustrating, but try to remember that it's not the end of the world. I've already got a message on the next skeeter to Uhuru asking for a clarification. Chances are all you're looking at here is a three- or four-day vacation."

"But no matter what, I'll still miss the flight out to Angelmass."

"I know," Podolak agreed sympathetically. "And I know how much of a disappointment it'll be to have to wait another month for the next trip. But it's only a month, after all. In the universal scheme of things, that's not so much."

Standing there, looking at the sympathy and sincerity in her face, Kosta's mouth suddenly went dry. "I appreciate your time and effort, Director Podolak," he managed, folding the paper and slipping it into his pocket. "Thank you. I'll—I guess I'll figure out something to do."

"I'm sure you will," Podolak said as he turned toward the door. "And if you need any help or advice, feel free to come to me."

It probably hadn't been a very polite exit, Kosta realized as he headed down the stairway. But to stand there and hear her say that a month, more or less, shouldn't really matter . . .

Unbidden, that first close-up look he'd had of the *Komitadji* rose before his eyes. If Podolak only knew how much difference the next month could make.

It was a beautiful day outside; brilliant sunshine in a clear blue sky, with wispy easterly breezes bringing hints of something spicy. Some exotic native plant, most likely. The laughing fates, making counterpoint for his internal frustration. Jamming his hands into his pockets, Kosta picked a direction at random and started across the delicately landscaped Institute grounds.

And tried to think.

There were, at the bottom, really only two options. He could stay here and wait for the bureaucrats to unsnarl the mess they'd gotten him into. Or he could leave, going into hiding on Seraph or else buying passage back to Lorelei and waiting there for Commodore Lleshi to make his move. The latter option would stretch his emergency cash supply to the breaking point, but once back in contact with the Pax setup on Lorelei he might be able to get more.

But to run now would be to admit that he'd failed.

He glared at the ground at his feet. No; that was not an option. Period. He would rather be caught now by the Empyreals than go back and face that I-knew-it smirk of Telthorst's. And that left him only one option: to stay here, cultivate patience, and wait for next month's Angelmass trip.

Assuming, of course, that Lleshi didn't make his move before then.

He swore under his breath. Everywhere he turned, it seemed, he was running face first into no-win situations. One way or another, the laughing fates were determined to make him a loser on this one.

A glint in the sky caught his eye. A huntership, gliding in for a landing on the huge field to the north. Squinting against the sunlight, he could pick out half a dozen other points of light on similar approach paths.

Hunterships . . .

For a long moment he thought about it. It was a ridiculously long shot . . . but on the other hand, he had absolutely nothing to lose.

And maybe—just maybe—the laughing fates had missed one.

"Now this," Hanan said, pulling a lumpy metal stick out of his toolbox, "is what's known as a universal wrench. It can fit any bolt or nut you're likely to find outside an engine room, bend in seven different ways to get back into cubbyholes impossible for the human hand, and apply the kind of torque that had hitherto only been available if you knew a gorilla with a mechanic's certificate." He turned it over, sending glints of sunlight into Chandris's eyes. "You can also stir paint with it, and it holds up remarkably well against being thrown across a room in frustration."

Chandris nodded, squinting against the reflections. Having learned everything there was to know about the inside of the *Gazelle,* at least according to
Ornina, she'd been promoted to learning about the outside with Hanan. It
was, in her opinion, a dubious honor at best. "How come they put stuff in
places where people's hands won't go?" she asked.

"Because the designers don't have to work on the things themselves,"
Hanan grunted, bending the wrench at three of its joints and lifting it to the
open access hatch above them. "Allow me to demonstrate."

"Excuse me?" a voice called from the direction of the service yard gate.
Chandris craned her neck to look over Hanan's shoulder—

And froze. "Oh, nurk," she hissed.

"What?" Hanan asked, turning around to look. "Hello," he called to the
visitor before she could answer. "Come on in."

"Thank you," the other called. He opened the gate, somewhat gingerly,
and started toward them.

Chandris found her voice. "Get rid of him," she murmured to Hanan. "I
mean it. He's trouble."

Hanan had just enough time to throw her a puzzled look; and then he was
there.

"Hello," the young man said, his eyes flicking to Chandris and then
quickly away. "My name's Jereko Kosta. Are you Hanan Daviee?"

"That's right," Hanan nodded. "This is Chandris, one of my associates."

"Yes," Kosta said, his eyes reluctantly meeting Chandris's again. "We've
met."

"Ah," Hanan nodded pleasantly. If he noticed the tension in the air, he
didn't show it. "What can I do for you, Mr. Kosta?"

"I'd like to talk to you about possibly going along on your next trip out to
Angelmass," Kosta said. "I have a radiation detection experiment that I very
much need to get out there—"

"Institute ship broken?" Chandris put in coolly.

"Well, no—"

"You're still *with* the Institute, aren't you?"

"Well—"

"Chandris." Hanan put a restraining hand on her arm. "At the very least he
deserves a hearing. Please continue, Mr. Kosta."

She could see Kosta brace himself. "The fact of the matter," he said, the
words coming out in a rush, "is that some bureaucratic mistake has gotten my
credit line frozen, and without an active credit line they won't let me aboard
the Institute ship. It'll be another month before the next trip, and if I have to
wait that long—"

Hanan silenced him with an upraised hand. "How much space will this experiment of yours take up?"

"Not too much," Kosta said, a note of cautious hope creeping into his voice. "About like so," he added, slicing off about a cubic meter of air with his hands. "I can't pay very much now, but as soon as my credit's been unfrozen—"

"No problem," Hanan cut him off. "We'll be lifting tomorrow afternoon at two; you can sleep aboard tonight if you need a bed. Will you need any help getting your equipment over here?"

Kosta blinked. Probably, Chandris thought sourly, he'd expected to have to do more persuading. "Ah, actually, I could—" He glanced at Chandris, suddenly seemed to realize who Hanan would likely volunteer to go help him. "No, I can handle it myself," he amended. "And I've still got a room at the Institute."

"Good," Hanan said. "Then you'd better hop on back there and start getting everything together. We may be out there for a week, so pack accordingly."

Kosta seemed a little taken aback. "A week?"

"We're going there to hunt angels," Hanan reminded him. "No way to guarantee how long till we find one."

"No, of course not." Kosta threw Chandris another glance. "I understand. I just didn't realize I'd be imposing on you that long."

"If you can stand our company, I'm sure we can stand yours," Hanan said, solemnly straight-faced. "Now if you'll excuse us, we have work to do here."

"Oh. Right." Kosta hesitated. "I'd better go get my equipment, I guess. And thank you."

He turned and left, carefully closing the gate behind him. "Seems pleasant enough," Hanan commented as they watched him hurry down the dusty street. "A little awkward, but pleasant enough." He looked at Chandris. "This isn't the one chasing you, is it?"

"Hardly," Chandris growled. "He came in on the *Xirrus,* that's all. Oh, and I talked to him awhile back when I went to the Institute to find out what they knew about angels."

"I gather you don't like him."

"I don't know him well enough to not like him," Chandris retorted. "The point is that I don't trust him."

Hanan waited, the question implicit in his face. "I saw him at the spaceport," Chandris sighed. "Right after we got off the *Xirrus.* I—well, I sort of scored him into walking me out past the guards. They were looking for a single woman, you know, and I figured a twosome would get past them easier. Anyway, we got outside and clear before it popped and he recognized me."

"And off he went, screaming for the police at the top of his lungs?"

Chandris shook her head. "That's just it: he didn't. He just stood there like a sfudd and watched me get into a line car. And he didn't turn me in at the Institute, either."

"Interesting," Hanan murmured. "You think maybe he was just giving you the benefit of the doubt?"

Chandris snorted. "What doubt? He *saw* me under arrest. Hell, I practically ran him down on my chop and hop."

"Um." Hanan rubbed thoughtfully at his cheek with the business end of the wrench, leaving a black smudge behind. "Well . . . I suppose he could just be the type who hates to get involved with anything messy."

"Or maybe he's already involved in something messy and doesn't want to draw attention to himself," Chandris countered. "There's something wrong about him, Hanan. I've scored academic types before, and there's something about him that doesn't fit the pattern."

"Because he showed you mercy?" Hanan asked, raising his eyebrows slightly.

"That's different," Chandris insisted. "You and Ornina were trying to reform me."

"Different question, then," Hanan said. "Do you think he's dangerous?"

"He's trouble. Isn't that enough?"

"You should know better than that," Hanan said, quietly reproving. "But is he dangerous?"

Chandris took a deep breath, trying to sort out her thoughts from her feelings. "If you mean is he going to knife us in our sleep . . . no, I don't think so."

Hanan shrugged. "Well, then, I don't really see how we can refuse him. Do you?"

Chandris looked him straight in the eye—"No," she murmured. "I guess not."

"Good," Hanan said cheerfully. "Then that's settled." He raised the wrench, made a small adjustment. "Now: watch closely and I'll show you how this is done."

"Right," Chandris said, putting on her best submissive student persona and trying hard not to let her clenched teeth sound through her voice. So that was how it was going to be. She'd called it, and she'd been right. The Daviees, heavily under the influence of their angel, were apparently incapable of protecting their ship anymore.

So okay. She would just have to do it for them.

Watching Hanan work, listening to his running monologue and making suitable noises where required, she began to plan out her strategy.

". . . and this, obviously, is the control cabin," Ornina said, ushering Kosta in.

"Hello again," Hanan greeted him, barely looking up from his final pre-flight check.

Chandris, helping from her own board, didn't look up at all. But she made sure to keep Kosta visible in the corner of her eye. "Everything all right below?" Hanan added.

"Yes, thanks," Kosta said. "The package is secure and—"

"He was talking to Ornina," Chandris told him, giving him an exaggeratedly patient look.

She had the minor satisfaction of seeing him blush. "Sorry," he muttered.

"That's all right," Hanan assured him cheerfully. "You know how it is. Big ship and all, makes for mass confusion all around. Ornina?"

"Everything's fine," she said, showing Kosta to one of the two normally unused seats off to the side. "You'll have to excuse my brother's warped sense of humor, Jereko; he was dropped on his head when he was a baby and hasn't been the same since."

"Except for the two o'clock feedings," Hanan offered. "I still rather like those. Donuts, especially, or sometimes sausage. But I can't seem to get Ornina to—"

"Ha*nan*—"

"Anyway, better strap down," he added blandly. "We're tenth in line to launch. Five minutes, the way they're running today."

It took just over half that time for Ornina to show Kosta how to work his seat's restraint system and then to strap in herself. "So, Jereko," Hanan said when everyone was finally settled. "How long have you been with the Institute?"

"Just a few weeks," Kosta told him. "Actually, I'm not exactly *with* the Institute; I'm just a visiting researcher."

"Visiting from where?" Ornina asked.

"Clarkston University," Kosta said. "Cairngorm, on Balmoral."

"Never been to Balmoral," Hanan said. "Pretty rocky place, I understand. So tell us about angels."

The sudden shift in subject seemed to catch Kosta off guard. "What do you mean?"

"Angels," Hanan repeated, waving a hand airily. "Weird little particle things everyone's crazy to get their hands on."

"Yes, I know what they are," Kosta said, his voice sounding cautious. Trying to get a feel for Hanan, Chandris decided, and not doing too well. Though from what she'd seen of Kosta that was probably about normal for him.

"Good," Hanan said. "Then you can tell us what they—oops; wait a minute. Here we go."

Keeping half an eye on Kosta, Chandris gave her board one last check. The *Gazelle* lifted into the air, flew out over the launch dish—

"Friz!" The word that exploded from Kosta's mouth was half bark, half hiss. And on his face . . .

"I take it, Jereko," Hanan said without turning around, "that you've never watched a launch dish operate."

Kosta's eyes jerked away from the display to the back of Hanan's head . . . and for a single instant all the normal defenses were gone.

And in his face Chandris saw complete confusion.

The moment passed. "As a matter of fact, I haven't," he said with a fair imitation of calm. "It's . . . rather spectacular."

"You get used to it," Hanan shrugged, ramping up the *Gazelle*'s drive and making a slight adjustment to the ship's vector. "You were about to tell us about angels."

"I was?" Kosta glanced at Chandris, his expression suddenly wary. Maybe remembering how easily she'd drawn him out on the subject back at the Institute. "I doubt I could tell you anything you don't already know—"

"Tell them about the *Acchaa* theory," Chandris said.

Kosta looked visual knives at her. She held his gaze, reminding him with lifted eyebrows that she could tell them about it herself.

For a wonder, he got the message. "*Acchaa* is one of the theories currently in vogue at the Institute," he growled. "Basically, it says that angels are quantized chunks of good."

"Of what?" Ornina asked, frowning.

"Of good," Kosta repeated. "You know: the stuff behind ethics and justice." He looked pointedly at Chandris. "And honesty."

"Doesn't work," Hanan shook his head decisively. "The theory, I mean."

Back when she'd talked to him at the Institute, Chandris remembered, Kosta had seemed to have his own doubts about it. But the challenge in Hanan's tone was apparently too much for him. "I don't think it's all *that* obvious," he said, bristling a bit.

"Sure it is," Hanan said. "I suppose the idea is that all the quantum black holes that have evaporated since the Big Bang have scattered these angels around the universe like cosmic rays?"

"That's one possibility," Kosta said. He seemed surprised that Hanan had picked up on the idea so quickly. "Another is that the Big Bang itself created the bulk of them."

"Okay," Hanan said. "Either way, we wind up with a fairly even distribution. Right?"

"Right," Kosta said cautiously.

"Fine. So. I presume you're also assuming that the angels that landed on Earth were the cause of all that was good and fair and noble throughout human history."

"Not necessarily all of it," Kosta said. "Individual human beings may be able to add to or subtract from their effect, too. That's how, historically, an overall pattern of good and evil can fluctuate within an area or group."

"You have a mechanism for that?"

"Not yet," Kosta said. "But there's at least one theory about field effects that might allow for humans to affect the angels."

"What about the biochemistry of the angel/personality interaction?"

Kosta pursed his lips. "They're working on that, too."

Hanan nodded. "So we agree there's still a lot to learn. So let me ask you a question. When mankind invented the hyperspace catapult and moved out onto new planets, was there any noticeable change in their behavior?"

He paused, but Kosta didn't reply. "Because there *should* have been, you know," Hanan added, twisting half around in his chair to look at the other. "Fresh worlds—lots of untouched primordial angels lying around—"

"Yes, I understand the question," Kosta said, his forehead wrinkled in thought. In slightly worried thought, if Chandris was reading him right. "I'm afraid I don't know enough history to answer that."

"Well, I do," Hanan said.

And for the first time since she'd met him Chandris heard a trace of genuine bitterness in his voice. "The answer is a loud, flat *no*," he said. "The people who arrived on Uhuru spouted all kinds of pious pronouncements about peace and freedom and equality when they landed. But less than thirty years later they were already on the way back to the class separation and elitist power structure they'd originally turned their backs on."

"Maybe the old patterns were too hard to break," Kosta suggested slowly.

"In which case they should be too strong to break now," Hanan said, a note of decisiveness in his voice. "But they are breaking. Slowly and from the top down, maybe; but they *are* breaking." He shook his head. "Eventually, Jereko, you people at the Institute are going to have to accept the fact that Angelmass is unique."

"I'm sorry, but I don't see how that can be," Kosta disagreed. "Black holes have the most limited set of parameters of anything in the known universe: mass, spin, charge, and one or two others that are still being debated. I don't see how any combination of those could give rise to angels."

"Ah." Hanan lifted a finger. "But that assumes the angels are a purely natural phenomenon. What if, instead, they're a form of life?"

Kosta seemed to shrink into himself, just a little. "You mean like a wormhole alien invasion?" he asked warily.

"Not at all," Hanan shook his head. "You know anything about hyperspace catapult theory?"

Kosta took the abrupt change in subject better this time. "I know a little."

"Okay. Suppose you threw a ship across space via catapult and its vector passed through a quantum black hole like Angelmass. What would happen?"

"No one knows," Kosta said. "The equations break down at too steep a gravity gradient."

"Exactly." Hanan turned from his board again to look Kosta square in the eye. "And I think that's just what happened. Sometime in the past, a ship—human or alien—tried to go through Angelmass. And in the process left one or more lifeforms trapped at the event horizon."

He paused, and Chandris waited for the inevitable grin and punchline. But Hanan's expression remained serious, and after a long moment Kosta spoke. "If this is supposed to be better than the *Acchaa* theory," he said, "it isn't. How are these fragments of a nonphysical lifeforce supposed to have been changed into solid particles, for starters?"

The endburn alert pinged. "I'd guess it's a piggyback sort of arrangement," Hanan said, turning back to his board. "The lifeforce attaching itself to the angel for some reason. Or possibly the angel forms around it, the way a raindrop coalesces around a dust particle." He tapped a few keys and the dull roar of the *Gazelle*'s drive faded to a whisper.

And suddenly Kosta didn't look so good. "Trouble?" Chandris asked him.

"I'll be fine," the other said between clenched teeth. "These anti-nausea drugs always seem to take their time with me, that's all."

"Some tea might help," Ornina offered. "Chandris or I could get you some, if you'd like to try it."

"No, thanks," Kosta said. "It should clear up in a few minutes."

"Or we could put a little spin on the ship," Ornina continued, looking at Hanan. "Not too much; we'll be hitting the catapult in half an hour. But it would give your inner ear some sense of direction."

"Thanks, but that shouldn't be necessary," Kosta said, fumbling his restraints off. "If you don't mind, though, I think I'll go to my room for awhile."

"Sure, go ahead," Ornina nodded.

Carefully, Kosta maneuvered out of his chair, looked once at the main display. "I'll be back before we reach the catapult."

"Don't worry about it," Ornina assured him. "It's not like there's anything you have to do during the operation."

"Okay." Gingerly, Kosta propelled himself across the control cabin to the door.

Carefully avoiding Chandris's eyes the whole way.

Given that there was no particular hurry, Kosta took his time; and he was therefore less than halfway to the crackerbox he'd been given as a cabin when he noticed the trajectory of his floating passage was taking a distinct drift toward one side of the corridors. The Daviees, ignoring his protests, had gone ahead and started the *Gazelle* rotating.

Typical, he thought, feeling his lip twist as he oriented himself upright against the sense of weight. Less than an hour into this trip, and already his hosts were showing themselves to be the sort of compulsive do-gooders who insist on showering you with favors whether you want them or not. He'd known a few people like that back home, and he'd never been able to stand being near any of them for more than fifteen minutes at a time. The laughing fates only knew whether a week here would drive him crazy.

Still, he had to admit that having a solid deck under his feet *did* make his stomach feel better. Between that and the drug he'd taken before coming aboard, he was more or less recovered by the time he reached his cabin.

Recovered enough, in fact, that for the first time in several minutes he was able to concentrate on the air around him instead of on his own digestive tract.

He paused, still out in the corridor, taking deep breaths and trying to chase down the memory of where he'd come across that particular aroma before. Somewhere during his brief training, perhaps? Or at the university?

Abruptly, it clicked: Tech Design 300-something. Sliding open his cabin door, he stepped inside and poked at the intercom switch. "Hanan?" he called.

"Right here," Hanan's voice came. "You feeling any better?"

"I'm fine, thanks," Kosta told him. "But your air system isn't. I think one of the scrubbers is starting to go."

"Thought that was what I smelled," Hanan grunted. "Number three, probably—it's been giving us trouble lately. I'll take a look once we've catapulted."

"Why don't I go look at it now?" Kosta offered. "I haven't got anything better to do at the moment."

He expected to be turned down flat. Compulsive do-gooders, in his experience, were never as good at accepting help as they were at doling it out. But— "Sure," Hanan said. "There's a tool kit in the forward mechanical room. Turn on your cabin display and I'll spot both that and the scrubbers on a schematic for you."

The schematic wasn't nearly as clear as Hanan obviously thought, but the *Gazelle* was a small ship and it didn't take Kosta more than a few minutes to get the tools and locate the failing scrubber. Pulling off the front, he took a look inside.

The worlds of the Empyrean had been out of touch with the mainstream of Pax technology for nearly two hundred years, a fact Kosta had had driven home time and again as he worked with the equipment at the Institute. There was, however, only so much anyone could do with a device as simple and basic as an atmosphere scrubber.

As opposed to something exotic like, say, a launch dish.

An unpleasant shiver ran up his back. The launch dish. The Empyreals' hyperspace net had been bad enough, but at least there he'd had a vague sense of how an inspired twisting of catapult equations might possibly give rise to such a thing. The launch dish, on the other hand, might just as well be magic.

Magic his Pax military instructors had never mentioned. Magic that Commodore Lleshi and the *Komitadji* might not be aware even existed.

But then, theories aside, the angels themselves might as well be magic, too. Angels.

For a long minute Kosta stared into the humming scrubber, his mind back in the control cabin with Hanan and his strange angel theory. Strange . . . and yet, the more Kosta thought about it, the harder it was to simply dismiss out of hand.

Because he had a point. History had never been one of Kosta's main interests, but he knew enough to recognize that the pattern Hanan had described had been repeated over and over again on the Pax's other colony worlds. There had indeed been no blooming of culture or tolerance or friendship as humanity moved out among the stars. In fact, as often as not, the exact opposite took place.

"You waiting to see if it's going to fix itself?"

Kosta spun around, the sudden movement in the low gravity skidding him around on the deck. It was Chandris, of course, leaning negligently against the door jamb three meters away.

"You startled me," Kosta told her reproachfully, grabbing the edge of the scrubber to get his balance back. At least he'd tried to sound reproachful, but the words came out sounding merely nervous. "I didn't know you were there."

"You weren't supposed to," she said bluntly. "You going to fix it or not?"

Biting back a retort, Kosta broke open the tool kit. "You always go around sneaking up on people?" he asked over his shoulder as he got to work.

"You always sit around gazing soulfully into machinery?" she countered.

"I was thinking about what Hanan said about the angels," Kosta said. "Especially that bit about Angelmass hosting an alien lifeform. Does he really believe all that?"

"Why don't you ask *him?*"

So much for trying to be civil. "I *can* do this myself, you know," he growled. "There's no need for you to stick around. Unless you don't trust me to do it right."

"*Me,* not trust *you?*" she said, her voice fairly dripping with sarcasm. "A known thief and stowaway, not trusting the fine upstanding scientist-citizen who stood by and let her get away from the police? What a ridiculous idea."

Kosta braced himself. There it was, the question he'd known she would eventually ask. "I didn't want to get involved," he said, trying for a combination of embarrassment and sincerity and mentally crossing his fingers. "I was new to Seraph, and I was afraid blowing the whistle on you would get me embroiled in something messy. For all I knew, walking out with you might have been seen as accessory after the fact."

He risked a glance over his shoulder to try to gauge her expression. He might as well have saved himself the effort; her face was an unreadable mask. "What about later, at the Institute?" she demanded.

"It was a little late to start making noise then," he said, turning back to the computer. "I'd already let you go once. The safest thing to do was answer your questions and get you out of there before anyone recognized you."

"Especially while you were with me?"

"That, too."

"Uh-huh. So, of course, when you needed transport to Angelmass, the *Gazelle* was the first ship you thought of."

Kosta swallowed a curse. "Not that it's any of your business, but the *Gazelle* was the fifteenth huntership I tried. Most of them wouldn't even hear me out before giving me the toss." He hesitated; but she deserved this. "I figured that any people soft-headed enough to hire you might be willing to give me a ride."

"You're too kind," she said calmly. "Tell me about Balmoral."

He blinked. "What?"

"Balmoral," she repeated. "The place where you grew up, remember?"

"I didn't grow up on Balmoral," Kosta corrected, feeling a thin layer of sweat squeezing out from his neck pores. If she was going to start quizzing him on his fictitious background . . . "I grew up in a small town called Palitaine on Lorelei. I just went to college on Balmoral."

"Ah," she said. She didn't seem at all bothered by her mistake. If it had, in fact, been a mistake. "So tell me about college on Balmoral."

"What do you want to know?"

"Everything," she said . . . and there was no mistaking the hard edge to her voice. "The landscape, the climate, the university, the people you met there. Everything."

And if I make a mistake . . . Taking a deep breath, Kosta gathered his thoughts and plunged in.

It took him nearly twenty minutes to fix the scrubber, talking almost non-stop the whole time. Chandris occasionally interrupted with questions, but for the most part she just stood there and listened. And, no doubt, kept a sharp eye on his repair work.

He was putting the cover back on, and trying to describe mountain peaks he'd only seen in pictures, when relief finally came. "Chandris?" Ornina's voice called over the intercom. "We're going to be hitting the catapult in a few minutes. Do you want to come up and give me a hand?"

"I'll be there in a minute," Chandris told her. "I'm just watching Kosta finish up here."

"Okay. Thanks, Jereko—you've saved Hanan a messy job."

"No problem," Kosta called.

The intercom clicked off. "I guess I'll see you later," Chandris said, turning toward the door.

"Leaving me here all alone?" he asked pointedly. "I must have passed the test."

Slowly, deliberately, she turned back. "You already called it, Kosta," she said. "I don't trust you. There's too much about you that doesn't fit. You're too smart—too well educated, anyway—to be an ordinary scorer. But you're not a typical blank-tower science-type, either."

His first instinct was to deny it. But looking into those eyes . . . "All I want from you and the Daviees is transport to Angelmass," he told her quietly. "Nothing more."

For a long moment she gazed at him, her face still giving away nothing. "We'll see," she said at last. She turned back to the door. Hesitated. "You were right, by the way," she said over her shoulder. "I checked the *Gazelle*'s records last night. For the past six months it's taken an average of just over three days to capture each angel, even though Gabriel's pay scale still figures on an average of four."

It took a second for Kosta to catch on to what she was talking about. "Interesting," he murmured. "Could some of that be more advanced equipment?"

She shook her head, her back still toward him. "They haven't gotten anything really new in over a year. Actually, it's worse—a lot of their old stuff is overdue for replacement. I just thought you'd like to know." She glided through the door and was gone.

Kosta stared after her, an unpleasant shiver running up his back. So it wasn't just his imagination coupled with some kind of rogue statistical construct. Angelmass really *was* emitting more angels.

A week ago he would have been quietly excited by the confirmation. Now, with Hanan's theories echoing in the back of his mind . . .

"Friz," he growled, annoyed with himself. He was a scientist, and so far this was a purely scientific problem. The implications, if any, would be up to other people to worry about.

Dropping lightly to his knees in the decreasing gravity, he began collecting his tools together. And tried to shake off the vague fears.

CHAPTER 21

The rotational gravity had all but vanished by the time Chandris reached the control cabin. To her mild surprise she found that Ornina was alone, seated in Hanan's usual chair at the main command board. "Where's Hanan?" she asked, glancing around as she maneuvered herself toward her chair.

"No—up here, please," Ornina told her, indicating her own usual backup command seat. "We got a red light on one of the maneuvering-jet fuel pumps; Hanan's gone back to take a look."

Chandris nodded grimly. Just one more sign of how fast the *Gazelle* was falling apart. "Do we have any spares?" she asked.

Ornina looked at her in mock surprise. "You mean you haven't gotten around to memorizing our inventory list yet?"

"I've been busy," Chandris said with her best imitation of wounded pride. "I'm only down to the M's—haven't reached 'pump' yet."

Ornina smiled. "Actually, we do have a spare aboard if we need it. Whether he could actually get it mounted before we reach Angelmass is another question entirely."

Chandris pursed her lips. "Well, if it comes to that, Kosta could probably be pressed into service."

"Capable?"

She shrugged. "He knows his way around a wrench, anyway."

The intercom pinged. "Ornina?" Hanan's voice came. "Can you shut down power on the AA-57-C circuit for me? I need to get back into the coupling area and would just as soon not get singed."

"Right," Ornina said, punching in a command. "Okay; it shows clear."

"You need any help with that, Hanan?" Chandris asked. "I could come down and—"

"No, I'm fine," he assured her. "It's fixable; just going to take a bit more time than I thought. Speaking of time, why haven't we hit the catapult yet?"

"It'll be another few minutes," Ornina told him. "They're having some trouble with one of the supply ships going through to Central, and it's got things backed up."

"Typical," Hanan sniffed. "Well, keep me informed."

"And let me know if you want any help," Chandris added.

"I won't, but thanks." The intercom clicked off. Chandris turned to Ornina—

And paused. On her face . . . "You all right?" Chandris asked.

Ornina turned to look at her, the lines trying to smooth out as she did so. "I'm fine," she said.

A cold knot settled into Chandris's stomach. "Something's wrong with Hanan, isn't it?" she asked. "Is he getting worse?"

Ornina shook her head tiredly. "He has no choice but to get worse," she said. "It's a degenerative disease. Degenerative diseases by definition get worse."

"Then he shouldn't be down there alone," Chandris said, reaching for her restraint release.

"No, don't go," Ornina said, shaking her head. "You can't help him. Not any more. You're too much like family now."

Chandris stared at her. "I don't understand."

"Neither do I, really," Ornina said quietly. The lines of pain were back in her face now. As if, having said this much, there was no longer any point in try-ing to hide them. "He's funny that way, Chandris. It's pretty easy for him to ac-cept help from strangers and acquaintances, but very hard to accept it from family and close friends. Pride, or some strange form of denial, I don't know which."

Chandris thought back to when she'd first come aboard the *Gazelle;* com-pared Hanan's face and words then to how he'd looked and acted during her most recent lessons in ship's maintenance. Thought about the brief conversa-tion half an hour earlier, and Hanan cheerfully giving Kosta permission to fix the air scrubber. "That's why you don't sell your extra angel, isn't it?" she said slowly. "So you can make sure there's a steady stream of strangers like me who he can accept help from."

She locked eyes with the older woman. "Except that I'm not a stranger anymore."

"No, you're not," Ornina agreed. "You're far more valuable to us than a stranger would be."

"Right—except that I can't help you anymore," Chandris retorted, a frus-trated anger beginning to stir within her. "That's real valuable."

"You know the ship as well as the two of us put together," Ornina coun-tered, her eyes taking on a firmness and a frustrated anger of their own. "You're an extra pair of hands—an extra pair of *skilled* hands—and the way Hanan is going we're going to need those hands if we're going to keep the *Gazelle* flying."

"Oh, wonderful," Chandris shot back. "I keep the *Gazelle* flying, and in the process grind Hanan's pride into the dirt."

Ornina leveled a finger at her. "I want you to get one thing straight, young lady. You are not responsible for Hanan's quirks and flaws and bouts of false pride. *Yes,* it hurts him to have to be dependent on people. But that's reality, and denying it just makes things harder on himself and everyone else around him. Eventually, he's going to have to bite the stick and learn that, and he never will if people always cave in to him. Understand?"

"Yes," Chandris muttered.

"Good." Ornina took a deep breath, the momentary anger fading from her face. "And one more thing. Like it or not, Chandris, you were a godsend to us. We need you here. More than that, we *want* you here. In five years of taking in everyone from outcasts to thieves to fugitives we've never found anyone who clicked even remotely as well with us and the ship as you have."

A ripple of old fear twisted through Chandris's heart. "I can't stay here forever," she said. "I never said I would."

"I know." Ornina turned back to her board. But not before Chandris saw that her eyes were shiny wet. "You're free to leave anytime you want to, of course. I just wanted you to understand how we felt."

The board beeped. "Looks like the bottleneck's clearing up," she said. "We'd best get moving."

"Right," Chandris murmured, the word coming out with difficulty around the knot in her throat. Yes, she understood, all right. Understood that, for all the old fears and habits that still haunted her, she didn't want to leave the *Gazelle,* either. Understood that, for probably the first time in her life, she had found something that was worth fighting for.

She might not be a thief anymore. But she hadn't forgotten how to fight.

The almost-felt jerk came, and in a blink the Seraph catapult was replaced by the spidery arms of Angelmass Central's tethered net poles. "Approach vector?" Ornina asked, all business again.

"Vector logged in," Chandris confirmed crisply, matching the other woman's tone. "There seems to be a lot of traffic ahead, though. We might want to swing our approach a little wider than usual."

"Good idea," Ornina nodded, fingers playing across her keys. "Let's see . . . let's try this."

Chandris gave the projected course a quick study. "Looks good," she agreed. "Want me to implement, or confirm it with Central?"

"I'll call Central," Ornina said, reaching for the comm section of her board. "Go ahead and plug it in so we'll be ready when they give us clearance."

Chandris had just started keying in the new course when the door hissed open behind her. She turned, expecting to see Hanan—

"I see we've arrived," Kosta commented, drifting in.

"Quiet—we're working," Chandris growled, turning back to her board.

"Sorry," Kosta stage-whispered.

He headed over to his seat, busying himself with something. Chandris took her time, checking and rechecking the course and her inputting of it, with the desired result: Ornina finished her part of the task first. "All cleared," she told Chandris, switching off the comm. "Go ahead and execute. Hello, Jereko," she added, turning to Kosta. "Everything all right with your equipment?"

"Yes, thanks," he replied. "Better than all right, actually—I thought I was going to have to sit down there with it the whole time, but Hanan helped me tie the outputs into one of the *Gazelle*'s spare command lines so I can operate it from up here."

Chandris felt her lip twist. Kosta settling down in the control cabin. Terrific. "He's supposed to be working on a fuel pump down there," she told Kosta tartly. "Not fiddling around with your stuff."

"Hey, he insisted," Kosta shot back. "It's not my fault if he's the kind who likes to be helpful."

"He is that," Ornina murmured.

Chandris clenched her teeth; but they were both right. Much as she'd love to do so, she really couldn't blame Kosta for this one. "Well, next time make sure he's not already doing something, all right?" she growled.

"For whatever it's worth to you, there probably won't *be* a next time," he reminded her stiffly. "By the time we get back to Seraph my credit line ought to be untangled, and we can go our separate ways."

"Good," Chandris muttered. She glanced at Ornina; went back for a closer look. The older woman was gazing studiously at her displays, a slight but unmistakable smile playing around her lips. "What?" Chandris demanded.

"Nothing," Ornina said, the smile vanishing into the same sort of innocent look Hanan always used when he was about to close the trap on one of his jokes. "I must say, Jereko, that your work sounds fascinating. What exactly is this particular experiment supposed to do?"

"I'm going to be sampling several small bandwidths of Angelmass's radiation spectrum," Kosta told her. "Hopefully, it'll give me some clues as to why the angel emission has been increasing over the past few months."

"It's been increasing?" Ornina frowned.

"That's what my numbers tell me," Kosta said. "And yours, too, for that matter." He looked at Chandris. "Didn't Chandris tell you?"

Ornina looked at Chandris, too, eyebrows raised. "It didn't seem important," Chandris said with a shrug.

"Probably isn't," Ornina agreed. "Still, you can't always tell what's going to wind up being important down the line." She turned back to Kosta. "But enough shop talk. Tell us something about yourself, Jereko."

Kosta took a deep breath, and Chandris turned back to her board, permitting herself a tight smile. The same territory she'd just gone over with Kosta below, territory she now knew by heart. This could, she decided, be very interesting.

It was, too, though not in the way she'd expected. Kosta never contradicted any of what he'd told her, never slipped up on historical events or on the physical details of the places he said he'd lived. He was articulate enough, accurate enough, and apparently sincere enough for all of it to be true.

But it wasn't.

There was plenty of evidence she could point to, at least to someone who knew the drill. A few flowery phrases that sounded like they'd been pulled from a Balmoral Visitors' Guide; an occasional exact quote from their conversation below, something she knew from experience was exceedingly rare; an underlying preciseness in his voice that showed he was watching every single word he said. It was definitely puff-talk. Detailed and well rehearsed, but puff-talk just the same.

But at the same time, there was something missing, something that any scorer good enough to have worked up such an elaborate background ought to have had. A sense of daring, perhaps, or some of the oily arrogance that had been a part of all the really expert puff-talkers she'd known back in the Barrio. Kosta played more like an actor parroting someone else's lines.

Which made Kosta . . . what?

Chandris still didn't know. But she intended to find out.

And so she sat at her board, listening to every word he said and letting the *Gazelle* more or less fly itself toward Angelmass.

And with her full attention on Kosta, she completely missed the first subtle clue that something had gone terribly wrong.

". . . and so, rather to my amazement, the Institute accepted my application," Kosta concluded. "I didn't give them time to change their minds. I booked passage on a liner and—" he shrugged "—here I am."

"Here you are, indeed." Ornina shook her head—in wonderment, Kosta hoped, not disbelief. "That's quite a story, Jereko. I certainly hope you can get your finances straightened out quickly. It'd be a shame if such a promising career was derailed by something as trivial as a clerical error."

"I'm sure it will be," he assured her. He threw a glance at the back of Chandris's head, feeling some of his tension draining away. He'd poured a lot of hours into memorizing his cover story, but it had been time well spent. He'd gotten through it without making any errors, and with a certain degree of panache besides. Maybe he was finally starting to adapt to this spy stuff.

And just then, in the back of his mind, a quiet alarm went off.

He froze, searching frantically through what he'd just said. Had he, at the very end, made some kind of fatal blunder in his story?

And then he got it. The gamma-ray sparks—those damned noisy ubiquitous gamma-ray sparks—had stopped.

Which meant . . . what?

He was just opening his mouth to ask when an electronic scream split the air.

He jerked hard in his seat, pressing himself up against the restraints. Ornina spun back to her board, jabbing at it—

The wailing cut off as suddenly as it had begun. "—hell was *that?*" Chandris snapped in the ringing silence.

"Emergency call," Ornina said tightly. "Get on the tracker and locate the signal. I'll try to raise them."

Chandris was already busy at her board. "Got it . . . no. No, it's wavering."

"Must be heavy radiation out there," Ornina muttered, her hands dancing across her board. "Let's see if this helps. This is the *Gazelle,* calling distress ship; *Gazelle,* calling distress ship. Can you respond?"

There was a roar of static from the speaker, a roar punctuated by an incredible rapid-fire stutter of gamma-ray sparks. "*Gazelle,* this is *Hova's Skyarcher,*" a barely audible voice came through the noise. "We're caught in a radiation surge—losing control of everything. We need help."

"Chandris?" Ornina asked.

"I can't get a fix on them," Chandris said, her voice strained. "The radiation's messing up the calibration."

"You got anything even approximate?"

"Yes, but—"

"That'll do for now," Ornina cut her off. "*Hova's Skyarcher,* we're on our way. ETA, maybe ten minutes."

A sound that might have been a word, and then the static and signal were gone. "What did he say?" Kosta asked.

"He said 'hurry,'" Ornina said grimly. The *Gazelle's* engines, which had been idling softly, roared to full life. "Keep trying to get a fix on him, Chandris."

"I am." Chandris glanced over her shoulder. "Make yourself useful, Kosta—get on the intercom and get Hanan up here."

"Don't bother," Hanan said from the doorway even as Kosta moved to comply. "You can hear that siren all the way down at the pumps. What's going on?"

"Radiation surge," Ornina told him, getting out of her chair as Hanan slid into it. "It's got *Hova's Skyarcher.*"

"Damn," Hanan muttered, hands running over the board as Ornina and Chandris also played musical chairs, switching back to their usual seats. "Anyone else in range?"

"I don't know," Ornina said. "Not even sure anyone else heard the call—signals don't cut too well across radiation lines."

"Have you alerted Central yet?"

"Haven't had time. I'll do it now." Ornina busied herself with her board.

The *Gazelle* began to move, pressing Kosta back into his seat. "Can I do anything to help?" he asked.

"I don't think so," Hanan said over his shoulder. "Just sit tight."

Kosta squeezed his hands into fists. Wonderful. Another ship was getting roasted by radiation out there, and all he could do was sit tight. And not roasted slowly, either, if that chatter of gamma-ray sparks he'd heard had been any indication.

He stiffened. *Gamma-ray sparks?* Reaching to his board, he keyed for a real-time display from his detectors below.

Nothing.

For a long minute he stared at the result, not believing it. Even given that the package was selecting only a few narrow bandwidths, there still should be *something* coming in. He keyed for a more sensitive reading—

"Kosta!" Chandris snapped.

He jerked around. "What?"

"Get on the comm," she ordered. "Try and raise the *Skyarcher*—tell them we're on our way but can't get a solid fix on them. See if they can give us some location data."

"Right." Kosta turned back to his board. A minute later, he had them.

"*Gazelle,*" a voice called through the roar of static and gamma-ray stutter. "*Gazelle,* are you there?"

"We're here," Kosta called back. "Hang on, we're coming. Can you give us your location and velocity vectors?"

"We don't have them." Even through the noise, Kosta could hear the fear in that voice. "The whole damn ship is falling apart. You gotta help us."

"We're trying to get there," Kosta told him, an icy shiver running up his back. "Just hang on and try to relax—"

He broke off as something went *crack* behind him. For an instant he thought his ears were playing tricks on him, that the sound had come from the comm speaker. But it was followed by another, and another—

"Hanan!" he shouted over the roar of the engines and the increasingly noisy crackling. "We're getting into radiation."

"I know," Hanan called back. "No choice—it's our only intercept vector. Don't worry, the hull can handle—"

The rest of his statement was swallowed up in a sudden cloudburst of gamma-ray sparks.

And all hell broke loose.

Hanan screamed, a cry of pain that sent Kosta's teeth locking together. Ornina shouted something and grabbed for her restraints; Kosta got to Hanan first, without any clear memory of having left his seat. "What's wrong?" he shouted over the din, dimly aware that he was once again weightless—the *Gazelle,* clearly, was no longer under power.

"His exobraces," Ornina shouted back, trying to get her hand into Hanan's shirt. "They're misfiring—overloading the sensory nerves. Got to shut everything down."

Kosta swore, trying to remember everything he'd learned at the Institute about Empyreal electronics. There wasn't anything that even remotely touched on this sort of thing. Helplessly, holding Hanan's pain-curled arms as steady as he could, he watched as Ornina finally got to whatever cutoff switch she was trying for. The arms went limp, and Hanan gave a long, trembling sigh. "God," he muttered, the word just barely audible. "God, that hurt."

"You'll be all right," Ornina told him, her face tight. "Jereko, help me get him down to the medpack."

"Never mind me," Hanan insisted, trying to shrug their hands off. He succeeded only in flailing uselessly against Kosta's shoulder. "We've got to get the *Skyarcher* before it's too late."

"Stop that!" Ornina snapped, pushing his arm away from the restraint release. "You need help."

"So do Hova and Rafe—"

"They'll get it," Kosta cut him off, popping the strap on his side of Hanan's seat. "Ornina and Chandris can handle the ship while I get you below. Fair enough?"

A surge of pain came and went across Hanan's face. "All right," he gritted.

Kosta wedged a foot under the edge of the chair and took Hanan's arm, feeling the muscles trembling under his hand as he got the arm around his shoulders. "I'll need a few minutes at half a gee or less," he told Ornina, hauling Hanan bodily out of his seat and fighting hard against the fat man's inertia. "Can you do that?"

"Assuming we have any control at all, yes," she said grimly, wedging herself into Hanan's seat. "You know how to work a huntership medpack?"

"I do," Hanan said before Kosta could answer. "I'll be there with him, re-member?"

"Well, then, *get* there," she snapped, giving her brother one last look before turning back to her board.

Hanan turned slightly watery eyes to Kosta and gave him the ghost of a smile. "The hospital, officer, and step on it."

It took some effort, even at half a gee, to manhandle Hanan onto the med-pack table. But Kosta managed it, and under Hanan's guidance got it pro-grammed.

He had completed the procedure, and Hanan was starting to fall asleep, when the gamma-ray cloudburst abruptly dropped off to more or less normal levels again.

The intercom, when he tried it, was inoperable. He considered heading back to the control cabin to find out what was going on, but even though Hanan seemed all right he decided it wouldn't be a good idea to leave him alone.

And so he sat there, watching the glowing green lights on the medpack and listening to Hanan's steady breathing.

And tried to think.

Chandris was sitting in Hanan's usual seat when Kosta arrived in the control cabin. "How are we doing?" he asked her.

She turned to look at him, her eyes flat and dead. "We're going home," she said, turning back to her work. "How's Hanan?"

"He's all right," Kosta told her, moving forward to drop into the seat next to her. "Ornina says he's not in any danger."

"She probably told you, then."

"That the *Skyarcher* didn't make it?" He nodded. "Yes."

Chandris shook her head slowly. Disbelievingly. "It killed them. Burned all the electronics and optics out of their ship and just . . . killed them."

Kosta nodded again, looking at the display. At the stars and, just barely vis-ible now, the pattern of lights indicating the Angelmass Central space station. "We stopping at Central or going on to Seraph?"

"Probably the latter," Chandris said. "There's no need to stick around un-less either Hanan or the *Gazelle* need immediate attention. Central isn't set up for major long-term work."

"Yeah." Kosta looked at her. "That radiation surge. From the way Hanan and Ornina were talking, it sounded like this wasn't the first time it's hap-pened. You ever seen one before yourself?"

Chandris gave him a long, cool look. "Two men just died out there," she said, her voice even colder than her eyes. "Is it too much to ask for you to put your scientific curiosity into storage for a while?"

"I'm sorry," Kosta said quietly. "Did you know them well?"

"Hardly at all," she said, turning back to stare at her board. "I only talked to the owner once, back when I was trying to get a job. Before I found Hanan and Ornina." She shrugged, a slight movement of her shoulders. "He wasn't very nice to me. Sarcastic and pretty nasty." She snorted a sound that might have been a sort of laugh. "It's funny, you know. When I first came here I wouldn't have cared a two-ruya reek if a frag like that got himself sliced. Look at me now." She shook her head.

Kosta nodded, searching for something to say. "At least you tried. That has to count for something."

She looked at him again, a faint sheen of contempt in her eyes. "This isn't a university final, Kosta," she growled. "This is real life. There's no partial credit given for effort."

He winced at her tone. "That's not what I meant."

She sighed, the anger fading from her face. "I know."

For a few minutes they sat together in silence. Kosta was just wondering whether he ought to leave when Chandris stirred. "You were asking about the radiation surge."

"Yes," Kosta nodded. "I was wondering—"

"I remember the question," she cut him off. "I've heard stories of things like this happening, but I've never been this close to one before."

"Any idea what might have caused it?"

She shrugged. "You're the expert. You tell me."

"That's the problem," he said. "I can't. According to everything I know about black holes, what just happened should have been impossible."

She frowned at him. "What do you mean, impossible?"

"I'll show you. Come on back to my seat and I'll call up the data from my experiment."

"I can bring it up from here." She fiddled with her board, and a moment later a page of numbers appeared on one of the displays. "Okay, you've got access—that part of the board, there."

"Thank you." Kosta keyed in the plotting/extrapolation program, set it running. "Now, let's see just what this looks like . . ."

The numbers vanished, to be replaced by a fuzzy pink cone with an equally fuzzy dark blue line down its axis. Kosta gazed at it, a shiver running up his back. "I'll be damned," he murmured.

"What?" Chandris asked.

Kosta pointed, noting vaguely that his finger seemed to be shaking a bit.

"The blue line in the middle is the surge of radiation," he explained. "The pink cone is where there was no radiation at all."

Chandris looked at him. "*No* radiation?"

"None. At least, not in the frequencies my sensors were set for."

She looked back at the display. "But . . ."

"Yeah. I don't suppose you'd have any records of those other surges aboard, would you?"

"I don't know," Chandris said grimly, reaching for her board. "Let's find out."

CHAPTER 22

The baby was asleep, her eyes pinched shut against the gentle night-light in the room, a delicate pattern of veins crisscrossing her eyelids. Occasionally she stirred, waving her tiny hands around or making them into fists, and once made a series of sucking motions with her mouth.

Sitting in the semi-darkened room, sipping at a mug of cold tea, Kosta watched her sleep.

He'd been there perhaps twenty minutes when the door opened behind him. "Dr. Qha—? Oh, hi, Jereko," Gyasi interrupted himself cheerfully. "Aren't you supposed to be out at Angelmass or somewhere?"

"The trip ended early," Kosta told him. "If you're looking for Dr. Qhahenlo, she's down the hall in the lab."

"No rush. Who's that, baby Angelica?"

Kosta felt his lip twist. "That's her name, is it? I should have guessed."

There was a brief pause. "You all right?" Gyasi asked, his voice frowning.

"Not really." Kosta gestured at the screen with his mug, the movement sloshing a few drops over the rim and onto his fingers. "I don't understand this, Yaezon. What kind of people are you, that you blithely put an angel around the neck of a baby?"

"It's a bit of a gamble, sure," Gyasi agreed, coming over to stand beside Kosta's chair. "It was hardly done blithely, though. Or quickly, either—the argument and discussion lasted nearly a year, with just about the whole Institute getting in on it before it was over. Director Podolak and the others finally decided it was just something we had to do."

"For science."

Gyasi shrugged. "You could put it that way, I guess. Don't forget, though, that we didn't go in entirely cold. We had nearly two decades of experience with the High Senate and others to go on, not to mention a few years of lab studies before that. Even if we don't know exactly what the angels are, we know pretty well what they do."

"And what if you don't?" Kosta asked, turning away from the sleeping baby on the screen to look up at him. "Suppose they're not just quanta of good. Suppose there's more to them then that."

"Such as?"

"Such as motivations of their own," Kosta said. "Such as possibly even an intelligence of their own."

Gyasi blinked; and then his face cleared. "Ah," he said with a knowing nod. "That's right—you were aboard a huntership, weren't you? Let me guess: they pulled that old trapped-alien ghost story on you."

It was Kosta's turn to frown. "What do you mean, pulled it on me? You mean it was a joke?"

"Oh, it's no joke," Gyasi said. "It's just that that same theory, in one form or another, has been kicking around the huntership crews for years. No one really takes it seriously anymore."

Except maybe the Pax, Kosta reminded himself silently. "Why not?" he asked. "Do *you* know what would happen to a ship that tried catapulting through a black hole like Angelmass?"

"No, but that's not the point," Gyasi said. "The problem is that that theory doesn't do anything except push the real issue a step farther back. If the angels are one or more fragmented souls, why are they all uniformly good? Why don't we get demons mixed in with the angels?"

"Are you sure you haven't?" Kosta countered. "I mean, how would you test for something like that?"

"I don't know, actually," Gyasi admitted. "But the High Senate and the Institute seem to know how."

"Ah. Of course."

Gyasi raised his hands, palms upward. "At some point in life, Jereko, you have to accept the fact that you can't get by without occasionally trusting other people."

"Maybe," Kosta conceded grudgingly. "Doesn't mean I have to like it."

Behind them, the door opened again. "Mr. Kosta?"

"I'm here, Dr. Qhahenlo," Kosta said, squinting in the sudden brightness as he stood up.

"Watching Angelica, I see," Qhahenlo commented as she walked to her desk. "How's she doing tonight?"

"She's dreaming, I think," Kosta said, turning off the monitor and going over to the desk. "Did you find anything?"

Qhahenlo nodded. "Two things. First of all, the data you got from the *Gazelle* are perfectly correct: there have indeed been fourteen instances of unusual radiation pulses recorded over the past eighteen months. None of them anywhere near this strong, but definitely there."

"How strong are we talking about?" Gyasi asked.

"Extremely," Qhahenlo told him grimly. "The one Mr. Kosta recorded was strong enough to kill a huntership crew right through a sandwich-metal hull."

Gyasi gave a low whistle, turning to look at Kosta. "Not your crew, I hope."

"No," Kosta said, shivering with the memory. "But we were close enough that it could have been."

"Which brings me to the second point," Qhahenlo said, tapping keys. "We're still analyzing your data; but at the moment it looks as if that conical low-radiation zone is an artificial construct. Here's the picture we've come up with." She swiveled the display around for him to see.

Kosta frowned at it. The central fuzzy line of the main radiation pulse was still there, but the outer cone had been replaced by a strange, almost random-looking mottling. "That doesn't make sense," he objected. "The radiation data came out symmetric despite the fact that the *Gazelle*'s path curved all through that region."

"Which is obviously why your computer fitted a cone shape to it," Qhahenlo nodded. "This more sophisticated analysis was able to take into account the fact that your sampling was very limited in both space *and* time. It was also able to fit it closer to known black hole theory."

Kosta looked at her sharply. "What do you mean, fit it closer? Shouldn't you be taking the data on its own merits and seeing where it leads?"

"We did," she said. "But you have to understand that there wasn't all that much there, by the nature of your experiment's design and the incident itself. If we run it parallel to the theory, on the other hand, we can get a more likely explanation."

Kosta pursed his lips. It was, he had to admit, a fairly standard technique. Not much more, really, than a sophisticated version of curve-fitting. And under normal circumstances he would have seen nothing wrong with it.

But here, for some reason, he did. And didn't know why. "So what did the theory-fitting tell you?" he asked, fighting hard to stay open-minded.

Qhahenlo shrugged. "About as I expected," she said, tapping keys to bring up some numbers. "Best guess is that what we're seeing is a radiation self-focusing effect, probably triggered by a sudden influx of gravitational energy."

Kosta leaned over the desk, studying the figures. It did, indeed, seem straightforward enough: a significant mass, falling in toward Angelmass, would release gravitational potential energy as it fell, pushing some of the radiation streaming from the black hole over the threshold for self-focusing.

And yet . . . "Where are we assuming this triggering mass came from?" he asked. "Angelmass isn't big enough to get all that much gravitational energy from."

"True," Qhahenlo agreed. "And the self-focusing effect won't last all that long, either, so it gets a little tricky. We're assuming that the trigger is coming from the affected hunterships themselves—something dropped, or maybe something coming from the drive. We're looking into it."

"Mm." Kosta rubbed at his lower lip. "I don't know. That surge lasted an awfully long time."

"Oh, there's no doubt it pushes the edges of the theory," Qhahenlo nodded. "But I don't think it's going to take too much to fit it in. The tricky part will be to figure out what the trigger mechanism is and how to keep it from happening again."

"Is there enough data for that?" Gyasi asked.

"I don't know," Qhahenlo said. "Ideally, we'd like to have the exact configurations and operating procedures from each of the ships this has happened to. Try to find some common factor in the incidents. Whether we can get that or not I don't know, particularly with those that occurred more than a month or two ago. I presume we'll be studying the wreckage of the *Hova's Skyarcher*, too, once EmDef retrieves it. That should tell us something."

"And what happens until then?" Kosta demanded.

Both of them looked at him. "I'm not sure what you mean," Qhahenlo said.

And here's where it hits the blades, Kosta thought, bracing himself. "I mean I'd like to go ahead and publish this," he told her. "At least as a preliminary report. I think it's important that the huntership crews know what's happening out there."

A slight smile twitched at Qhahenlo's lip. "And you're worried the Gabriel Corporation may take exception to you stirring up trouble?"

"Why would they?" Gyasi put in before Kosta could answer. "You've found a problem no one else has noticed. They're more likely to thank you for pointing it out."

"Oh, of course," Kosta snorted. "Corporations always appreciate someone showing them up as incompetent or negligent."

Gyasi shook his head. "You're missing the point, Jereko. This is *Gabriel* we're talking about here. They can't act that way."

"Why not?" Kosta demanded. "Because they provide a vital service?"

"No," Qhahenlo said. "Because they deal with angels."

Kosta looked at her, feeling his arguments catch somewhere halfway down his throat. "But the corporate heads don't actually handle the angels themselves."

She nodded. "Yes, they do. Every single one of them, every single day. That was one of the first conditions the High Senate set up when Gabriel was created, precisely to make sure that the standard corporate fixation with bottom-line profits didn't take hold there. And it worked. Gabriel genuinely cares about the health and safety of its employees, including the huntership crews."

"Translation: go ahead and write it up," Gyasi murmured.

Kosta took a careful breath. "All right. I will. In fact, if you'll both excuse me, I'll get started right now. Thank you, Dr. Qhahenlo, for running the data for me."

"You're welcome," Qhahenlo said, nodding gravely. "We'll keep you up to date on what's happening."

"Thank you," Kosta said again, rounding the desk toward the door. "Hopefully, I'll have my credit line back in a couple of days and be able to keep track of it myself."

"I'm sure you will," Qhahenlo assured him.

I was sure, too, yesterday, Kosta reminded himself as he headed down the quiet corridor toward his office. But that was yesterday, and yesterday he didn't have information the Gabriel Corporation might not want people to hear. It would, he decided, be very interesting to see their reaction when they saw his paper.

And to see what, if anything, they did about it. To the hunterships, or to him.

CHAPTER 23

The wrench slipped and clanged against the edge of the access flange, narrowly missing Chandris's knuckles in the process. "Nurk," she gritted, lowering the tool and flexing her fingers. "It keeps coming off."

"That's because you're not setting the line-lock solidly enough against the connector," Hanan told her, his voice calm and soothing. "If it's tight enough, it won't slip."

"Well, *I* can't do it," Chandris growled, offering him the wrench. "If you can, you're a genius."

"Hardly," Hanan huffed. But it was a pleased sort of huff. "Let me show you."

Chandris stepped aside, maintaining her frustrated scowl as Hanan busied himself with the wrench. His hands, she could see, were still not a hundred percent steady; but she could also see that her modified little-miss-helpless routine was doing wonders for his morale. With any luck, he wouldn't catch on to what she was doing until his nervous system had gotten back in synch with the exobraces' electronics.

And when that happened, it would be time for her to leave.

"There," Hanan grunted, stepping back and gesturing with a slightly shaky hand at the wrench handle protruding from the access hatch. "Try it now."

"Thanks," Chandris said, getting a grip on the wrench and giving it a tug. This time it stayed on. "That's it, all right."

"Just one of those things you pick up with experience," Hanan said modestly. "You'll get it in time. That is, if you stay."

"Where else would I go?" she countered, keeping her eyes on her work.

She sensed Hanan shrug. "Back to running, I suppose. You were running when you first came here, if you remember."

With a final tug, Chandris got the connector loose. "I'm not much interested in running anymore, thank you," she told him, in a tone carefully designed to discourage further questioning.

It was a waste of good voice control. "You know, you never did give us any details about this crazy man you said you were running from," Hanan commented. "He must have been *really* crazy for you to have run all the way to Seraph to get away from him."

"He was," Chandris said briefly. "You have a spare grommet there?"

"Sure." He found one, handed it to her. "Tell me about him."

"Why?"

He sighed, just audibly. "So that maybe we can help you find a way to get clear of him. Before you leave us."

Chandris felt her throat tighten. "Who says I'm leaving?"

"Ornina. She was right, you know: we *do* need you here."

Chandris snorted. "That's the trouble with you two. You talk too much to each other."

"She talks and I listen, anyway," Hanan said, a hint of his usual flippancy peeking through. "I'm serious, though, about wanting you to stay. For starters, who else will play this helpless-maiden routine with me if you go?"

Chandris grimaced. So much for him not catching on. "Maybe that's why I want to leave," she growled. "Maybe I'm tired of playing games. Ever think of that?"

For a long minute he was silent. Chandris finished attaching the new connector, then set the wrench's line-lock on the next one and broke it loose. "We're all running from something, Chandris," he said at last, quietly. "Did Ornina ever tell you I wanted to be a surgeon?"

Chandris paused, the connector halfway off. "No," she said.

"It's an art, you know, surgery," Hanan said, his voice oddly distant. "One of the few real arts left. Maybe the only one where you can genuinely feel that you're doing some good for people."

Chandris heard the faint whine of his exobraces as he moved his arm. "How far had you gotten?" she asked.

"I was in my second year of college when our parents died," he told her. "Ornina had just finished basic, and insisted on going to work to help me pay my way. I was able to work some, too, but she was the one who kept us afloat. I let her do it because I knew that when I got into practice I could afford to send her to college, too. To pay her back for everything.

"I was six months from finishing when the disease showed up."

Chandris blinked away sudden moisture. "They couldn't do anything about it?"

"Well, that's the point, you see," Hanan said, his tone suddenly strange. "They could have."

She turned around to look at him, expecting to see anger in his eyes. But all that was there was sadness. "I don't understand," she said carefully.

He let out his breath in a gentle whoosh. "It could have been cured, Chandris," he said, gazing at his trembling hand. "Not just helped; *cured*. All it would have taken would have been some highly specialized neural surgery and six months of intensive treatment . . . and about two million ruya to pay for all of it."

Unbidden, a memory from the Barrio flicked into Chandris's mind: old Flavin, limping painfully along on an ankle that could easily have been replaced. "I'm sorry," was all she could think of to say.

Hanan's eyes came back from his hand and his memories, and he threw her a tight smile. "So was I," he said. "For a long time I was pretty bitter about it, I can tell you. I wasn't asking for charity, you know—I could almost certainly have paid all of it back over a lifetime of surgical work."

Chandris nodded, an old saying floating up from the depths of her memory. " 'The rich get richer,' " she quoted.

" 'And the poor get babies,' " Hanan finished.

"What?"

"My own version. Skip it." He cocked an eyebrow. "So. Your turn."

She felt her stomach tighten. "His name is Trilling Vail," she told him. "For two years he was—" she hesitated, groping for the right word.

"Your lover?" Hanan suggested delicately.

"Yes, that too. But he was a lot more." She shook her head. "You have to understand what the Black Barrio was like, Hanan. Poor people, lots of scorers and koshes—probably a lot like that part of Magasca near the spaceport."

"Sounds pretty grim."

"It wasn't fun. I started out as a trac—that's someone who plays decoy or distraction for a scorer—and worked my way up to where I was the one doing the scoring."

"All of this by yourself?"

"I was never really alone," Chandris said. "But there wasn't anyone who really cared about me, either. Mostly the people who kept me around did so because I was useful.

"And then, when I was fourteen, I met Trilling."

She turned back to the access panel, unwilling for Hanan to see her face. "He was real nice at first. He took care of me like no one else ever had. Taught me all sorts of tricks, got me involved with his friends, let me move in with him."

Bittersweet memories flashed past her eyes, making her throat hurt. "What can I say? He took care of me."

There was a brief pause. "What happened?" Hanan asked quietly. "Another woman?"

Chandris snorted. "Not Trilling," she said. "He always said he was a one-woman man. As far as I know he never tommed around while I was with him.

No, what happened was that he started acting . . . strange. I mean *really* strange. He'd try to score tracks he wasn't ready for, and then go crazy-mad when they popped. He'd get mad at me for no reason at all, or else drop into a black pit for days at a time. He'd disappear, too, at strange hours and blow up when I tried to ask where he'd been. And he started playing around with reeks a lot."

"Sounds like someone on the glide path to a mental breakdown," Hanan said. "Did you try to get him to talk to someone?"

"About twice a week. But he blew up every time I suggested it. Besides, there wasn't much of anyone left for him to talk to; most of his friends had chopped and hopped by that time. They said he was a crash waiting to happen and didn't want to be around when it did."

"Some friends," Hanan murmured.

"The Barrio was like that," Chandris told him. "No one ever did anything for anybody unless there was something in it for them."

"Well . . ." Hanan scratched his cheek. "Pardon me for pointing it out, but *you* stayed with Trilling. And it doesn't sound like you were getting much out of it."

Chandris felt her lip twist. "Don't try to make me look noble, Hanan. I wasn't. Even at his worst Trilling was the most security my life had ever had, and I didn't want to lose that. Or maybe just didn't want to admit that it was already lost. You lie to yourself a lot in a place like the Barrio."

"People lie to themselves a lot everywhere."

Chandris shrugged. "Anyway, it finally got to the point where I couldn't take it anymore. I decided I had to get out." A sudden, violent shiver ran up through her at the memory. "And then, like a complete fool, I went and told Trilling I was leaving."

Hanan took a step closer to her, his arm slipping around her shoulders. "Did he hurt you?" he asked gently.

Chandris shivered again, the memories flashing across her vision. "He never even touched me. All he did was stand there, staring at me with a crazy look in his eyes. And then he told me, in complete detail, what he would do to me if I ever even tried to leave him."

She shook her head. "I still don't know how I got away the way I did. I guess he didn't really believe I was serious."

For a long minute they stood there in silence. Chandris found herself leaning into Hanan's side, feeling the warmth and strength and security of his presence. In some ways it reminded her of how things had once been with Trilling; and yet, in other ways, it was an entirely new experience. There was no sexual content to the hug, none of the underlying current of predator ferocity that had seemed to saturate everything Trilling said or did. Hanan's touch was one of friendship; nothing more, nothing less. And it asked nothing more or less in return.

Which was only going to make it that much harder when she left.

She blinked back the tears from her eyes and straightened away from him. "I'm all right," she murmured. "Thanks."

Hanan dropped his hand away. "It's not always a blessing having a perfect memory, is it?"

"It's not a blessing at all," she said bitterly. "It's a tool that's been useful in scoring. Nothing more."

And speaking of tools . . . With a sigh, she reached for the wrench again—

And from the gate behind them came the sudden clink of the latch.

Trilling! Chandris jumped, banging her head on the underside of the *Gazelle*, feet scrambling for traction as she came down. She spun around, hand darting to the tool tray for something—anything—she could use as a weapon. Grabbing a long screwdriver more by luck than design, she twisted to try and get around Hanan's bulk—

It wasn't Trilling. It was Kosta, frozen like a startled animal halfway through the gate. "Uh . . . hello," he managed, eyes flicking to the screwdriver gripped in Chandris's hand and then back to her face. "Have I come at a bad time?"

"No, no," Hanan said cheerfully, his serious mood vanished without a trace. "That was nothing to do with you. I told a bad joke and Chandris was taking exception to it. Come in, come in."

Slowly, obviously not convinced, Kosta resumed his interrupted trip through the gate. "Because if it's a bad time—"

"No, really," Hanan waved him forward. "Chandris, put that screwdriver down. What brings you out this way, Jereko? You need another ride out to Angelmass?"

"I'm sure his credit line must be unsnarled by now," Chandris put in before Kosta could answer, tossing the screwdriver back into the tool tray in disgust. Kosta, anytime, was an annoyance. Right now, he was a flat-out intrusion.

She looked back up in time to see a muscle in Kosta's cheek twitch. "As it happens," he said, "it's not."

"Odd," Hanan frowned. "I thought it was just some sort of clerical error."

"So did I," Kosta agreed. "Apparently, it's something more complicated than that. What, exactly, I don't know. Director Podolak's still having trouble getting straight answers."

They probably caught on to whatever track you're trying to score, Chandris thought with sour satisfaction. Now if only Hanan would wish him well and send him on his way . . .

"Well, we'll be going up again in two days," Hanan offered. "If you want to come along, you're certainly welcome."

Kosta's eyes flicked to Chandris. "I somehow doubt the invitation is unanimous. Anyway, for now there's not much point in my going up. I want to look for the kind of conditions the theory says ought to precede these radiation surges, but until my credit line gets unfrozen I can't get any new equipment."

"Can't you do anything with your original experiment?" Hanan asked. "Modify it somehow?"

"That's what I'm trying," Kosta nodded. "So far it's going pretty slowly."

"Well, if you need any tools, you're welcome to use ours here," Hanan said. "Sorry that we can't offer you anything else, but hunterships tend to run on a tight budget."

"Oh, I understand," Kosta assured him. "And thank you for the offer. Actually, the main reason I came by was to see how you were doing." He glanced again at Chandris, his eyes a little hard this time. "For some reason, I've been having trouble getting hold of you by phone."

"Oh?" Hanan asked, throwing Chandris a speculative look.

"We've been having problems with the *Gazelle*'s phones," she told him evenly. "The system's been locking out some incoming calls. I've been working on it."

"Ah." Hanan held her gaze a moment longer, then turned back to Kosta. "Sorry about that. However, as you can see, I'm pretty well recovered. Certainly enough for Ornina to put me back to work. You mentioned a theory in the works about these radiation surges?"

The cheek muscle twitched again. "So they say. Dr. Qhahenlo thinks it's a self-focusing effect triggered by something falling into Angelmass from one of the hunterships. I'm not convinced, myself."

"I don't recall you liking the *Acchaa* theory much, either," Chandris put in. "Are there *any* theories you like?"

He glared at her. "Actually, I'm rather partial to the idea that the angels are a deliberate alien invasion," he said tartly. "Here to turn everyone in the Empyrean into something non-human."

"Unfortunately, we don't need alien help to become less than human," Hanan murmured, glancing at Chandris. "Matter of fact, Chandris and I were just discussing that."

Kosta looked back and forth between them, then shrugged. "Anyway, I wrote the whole thing up—results, comments, and everybody's theories as to what happened. We'll see what kind of response I get." He hesitated. "Incidentally, I also discussed your trapped-alien theory with a couple of people. They said that the idea's been around for quite a while."

"Old doesn't necessarily mean wrong," Hanan pointed out. "Did any of them actually refute it, or did they all just make the usual learnedly snide comments?"

"The latter, mostly," Kosta conceded. "One of them compared it to the ancient epicycle theory of planetary motion. Said it complicated matters without really explaining anything."

"You agree with that?"

"I don't know," Kosta admitted. "That's the other reason I came by, actually; I wondered if you'd be willing to discuss it some more with me. When you're not so busy, of course," he added hastily.

"I'm sure that would be fine," Chandris put in, letting a little acid drip off her tone. "Look us up in about six months. Eight, if we keep getting interrupted."

Kosta reddened. "I'm sorry," he said, taking a step back toward the gate. "I didn't mean to interrupt your work."

"Oh, don't mind Chandris," Hanan told him. "Though if you've got the time, we actually *could* use an extra pair of hands. You interested?"

"Uh—" Kosta looked at Chandris, a wary look on his face. "Well . . . sure. Sure, why not?"

"Good." Hanan stepped away from Chandris's side. "Why don't you give Chandris a hand with the connector replacements while I go inside and get the leak-checker warmed up."

Without waiting for a reply he ducked under the *Gazelle*'s hull and headed back toward the hatchway. Kosta looked at Chandris, seemed to brace himself. "Okay," he said, coming forward, his expression that of someone approaching a large dog. "What can I do to help?"

"Absolutely nothing," Chandris growled, turning her back on him. She reached into the access hatch and started unscrewing the loosened connector. "I mean that. You want to be helpful, go follow Hanan around. Better yet, go away."

She felt him come up behind her. "Look, I'm sorry you don't like me," he said. "I'm not exactly crazy about you, either, if you want to know the truth. But the fact of the matter is that Hanan and Ornina did me a big favor, and I'd like to try and pay them back a little. I don't know if you can understand that or not."

Chandris clenched her teeth hard enough to hurt . . . but under the circumstances there wasn't a single nurking thing she could say to that. "Give me one of those grommets," she ordered.

They worked in silence for a few minutes; Chandris doing the real work, Kosta handing her tools and parts as requested. She had just finished tightening the last connector when the phone hanging on the tool tray's handle trilled. "Chandris?" Hanan's voice called.

"Right here," she called back, giving each connector one last check. "I think we're ready to give it a test."

"Great," Hanan said. "Is Kosta still there?"

She resisted the temptation to say something sarcastic. "Yes," she said.

"Good." The click of a transfer—"Go ahead, Mr. Gyasi."

"Jereko?" an unfamiliar voice said.

Chandris felt Kosta start. "Yaezon?"

"Yeah," Gyasi said. "Finally. I've been looking all over for you—calling the *Gazelle* was a long shot. Listen, you've got to get back here right away."

"What's wrong?"

Something in the way he said those two words made Chandris twist her head around to look at him—

To find that it wasn't just in his voice. On his face was the rigid expression of someone not facing just a large dog, but a large dog with its teeth already bared.

"Nothing's wrong," Yaezon said, as if he hadn't noticed anything in Kosta's voice. Which he probably hadn't. "At least, not in the traditional sense of the word *wrong*. But you're going to want to see this."

Kosta threw a look at Chandris, his tongue swiping across his upper lip. "Sure. I'll be there as soon as I can."

"Good. Room 2205—Che Kruyrov's lab."

"Right."

There was the click as the secondary connection was terminated. "Jereko? Anything wrong?" Hanan's voice came back on the circuit.

"No, I'm sure there isn't," Kosta told him. But his face was still tight. "But I have to get back. I'm sorry."

"That's all right," Hanan assured him. "I'm sure we'll see you again."

"I hope so." He gave Chandris a nod. "See you," he said absently, and headed for the gate.

Chandris watched him go, an eerie feeling tingling along her back. It had happened again. Kosta had been acting like a relatively normal human being . . . and then suddenly, for no apparent reason, he'd gone all strange.

What the hell was the *matter* with the man?

She turned back to the access panel, frustrated anger swirling within her. Because the bottom line was that it didn't much matter what Kosta's problem was. If he was going to start hanging around the *Gazelle*—and Hanan had all but given him an engraved invitation to do so—then she had no choice but to stay, too. Whatever Kosta was up to, there was no way she was going to leave the Daviees to handle him alone.

And if he thought he could irritate her out of the way, he was in for a big disappointment. She'd been irritated by people far better at it than he was. He might as well get one of those aphrodisiac perfumes he'd once mentioned and try to charm her out of the way.

A frown went off at the back of her mind. *Aphrodisiac perfumes . . . ?*

"Chandris?" Hanan called from the phone. "You still there?"

With an effort, Chandris forced her thoughts back to the job at hand. "Sure," she said. "Ready at this end."

"Okay. Here we go."

The faint hiss of fluid through tubing came from the access hatch . . . and as she watched carefully for the telltale frosting of a leak, she swore.

Damn Kosta, anyway.

The blip traced across the screen; a nice simple horizontal line, nothing special. "Okay; got that?" Che Kruyrov asked.

"Got it," Kosta nodded.

"Okay." Kruyrov tapped a couple of keys. "Watch now."

The blip again began a horizontal line; but this time it seemed to hesitate halfway across the screen. Dipping suddenly, it tracked out what looked like half a parabola and then resumed its horizontal motion at a lower level. "There," Kruyrov said with a sort of grim satisfaction. "That look at all familiar?"

Kosta shook his head. "Not really. Should it?"

"Jees, where've you been burying your head?" Kruyrov snorted. "That's the response curve of a classical Lantryllyn logic circuit. You *have* heard of Lantryllyn logic circuits, haven't you?"

Kosta nodded, an unreal sort of numbness drifting across his mind. He'd heard of Lantryllyn logic circuits, all right. As recently as fifty years ago they'd been the basis of most of the Pax's SuperMaster computer systems, and at one time had been thought to be the breakthrough that would allow a genuinely sentient artificial intelligence.

And for the Lantryllyn response to be mimicked by—"And all you've got there is nine angels?" he asked, his voice sounding hollow in his ears.

"That's all," Kruyrov said, his voice sounding a little strange, too. "A three-by-three cubic lattice. And yes, that's all that's there, unless you want to count the lattice itself."

"Which is supposed to be electronically inert," Gyasi added.

"Theoretically," Kruyrov grunted. "But then, there's no theory that says angels can do this, either, so who knows?"

Kosta tried to unfog his mind. "When are you going to put this on the nets?" he asked.

Kruyrov's eyes widened. "Give me a chance, Jereko," he protested. "I only ran across the effect this morning, and even then it was ninety-eight percent accident. We haven't even gotten this thing off the ground yet."

"I realize that," Kosta said. "But it seems to me a preliminary report would—"

"Would kick up a firestorm," Gyasi put in. "Face it, Jereko, there are enough people even here at the Institute who are uncomfortable with the idea that angels are quanta of good. You try and tell them that they might be quanta of *intelligence,* too, and the reaction isn't going to be pretty."

"And it's wholly premature besides," Kruyrov said. "Fine; so a three-by-three cubic array can mimic one of the Lantryllyn reactions. What about a three-by-two? Or a four-by-four? Or a three-by-three with one missing? Or a spherical arrangement, or a cubic array with the angels farther apart, or—"

"Peace," Kosta interrupted, holding up a hand. "I concede the point."

"Good." Kruyrov's eyes bored into his. "I trust, too, that you're willing to concede more than that. The only reason you're here is that Yaezon said you'd be interested and then bullied me into showing it to you. You leak it before Dr. Frashni gives the okay and I'll wind up washing test tubes down in the bio section."

"I understand," Kosta told him. "Trust me: I know how to keep secrets."

"I hope so." Kruyrov's eyes strayed to the screen, his forehead furrowing with thought. "What do you think, though? Really?"

Kosta shook his head slowly. "I don't know," he admitted. "I can't get past the thought that maybe the angel hunters have been right all along."

"Yeah—that trapped-alien folk theory," Kruyrov nodded, lip twisting. "I used to think it was pretty simplistic. Now I'm not so sure."

"Yes, well, let's not go for the mystic long shots first," Gyasi warned. "There's no particular reason why angels can't be quanta of good and intelligence both, you know. Or maybe it's something subtle, like ethics and intelligence just being different aspects of the same thing."

Kruyrov whistled softly. "Boy, *there's* a concept. I think I'd rather believe in alien ghosts."

"Don't worry about it," Gyasi said dryly. "I'm an experimentalist, too. What do I know about theory?"

"I'm sure the theorists will find stranger things to come up with than even that," the other responded dryly. "Probably a dozen of them by lunchtime the day this hits the nets."

"If they're anything like the theorists I've known, that's a low estimate," Kosta agreed. "Is there anything I can do to help you and Dr. Frashni on this?"

"I'm sure you must have other—oh, that's right," Kruyrov interrupted himself, throwing a glance at Gyasi. "Yaezon told me you're at loose ends at the moment. Well—" He scratched thoughtfully at his chin. "Might be possible. I'd have to ask Dr. Frashni, of course."

"You've got a lot of work ahead of you," Kosta reminded him. "An extra pair of hands could speed things up."

"True," Kruyrov agreed. "On the other hand, Dr. Frashni might prefer to sacrifice speed for secrecy."

"But I already know about it," Kosta persisted. "And I do good work—Dr. Qhahenlo can vouch for that."

Gyasi cocked his head at Kosta. "You're pretty eager to get in on this. Any particular reason why?"

Kosta looked him square in the eye. "A couple of reasons, yes," he said evenly. "Both of them my own business."

"Ah," Gyasi said carefully. "Okay."

Kosta shifted his gaze back to Kruyrov. "I'm going back to my office—got a couple of test ideas I want to sketch out. Let me know what Dr. Frashni says, all right?"

"Okay," Kruyrov said, as carefully as Gyasi.

First rule of espionage: don't draw unnecessary attention to yourself. His instructors' warning echoed through Kosta's mind as he left the room. But at the moment he didn't much give a damn. Lulled by the casually friendly people here and all the idealistic talk of quantized good, he'd drifted a long way from the original thrust of his mission to the Empyrean.

But with Kruyrov's discovery, that drift was now over. Because if the angels were in fact some rudimentary form of intelligence, even if only in specially arranged formations, then there was indeed an alien invasion going on in the Empyrean. Benign, perhaps . . . but perhaps not.

The image of baby Angelica, sleeping peacefully in her crib, rose before his eyes. *The sins of the fathers,* the old, old proverb ran through his mind, *are visited upon the children.*

Muttering a curse under his breath, he hurried down the corridor toward his office. The hell with drawing attention to himself.

Forsythe read the report slowly and carefully, savoring every detail. There it was. At last, there it was: the ammunition he needed to finally shake up those infuriatingly complacent colleagues of his. Violent surges of radiation, damaging over a dozen ships and destroying one of them outright—it was absolutely custom-fitted for him.

He keyed back to the first page and the author's name. And with a wonderful touch of irony, it had even come from Jereko Kosta, the man whose work Forsythe had tried so hard to quash.

He keyed for the master operations file. That, at least, would be easy to fix. Freeing up Kosta's credit line shouldn't take more than a minute or two. It might even be a good idea to throw some extra funding in his direction, provided he could be trusted to stay with this line of research. A personal grant might help, or maybe even a personal visit—

Forsythe paused, his fingers resting lightly on the keys. There was a flashing star by Kosta's name, directing him to another file. He called it up, noting as he did so that it had just been attached the previous morning, and began to read.

He was still in the middle of the first page when he groped out his call stick and signalled for Pirbazari.

He had finished the report and was starting to reread the salient parts when the aide arrived. "Yes, High Senator?" he asked, closing the door behind him.

"This report on Jereko Kosta," Forsythe said. "Did you handle it personally?"

"Yes, sir," Pirbazari confirmed. "Interesting, isn't it?"

"If you define 'interesting' as making no sense, then it's absolutely fascinating," Forsythe growled. "How does a paper trail just disappear? Particularly a paper trail with this much money attached to it?"

"I don't know, sir," Pirbazari said. "At least not yet. We're going over the intermediate steps with a light-chopper, but so far nothing." He cocked an eyebrow. "But we *did* get something in this morning's Balmoral skeeter that might go a ways toward explaining it—I was just getting ready to flag it for you when you called me in. Clarkston University in Cairngorm claims they've never heard of anyone named Jereko Kosta. Not from Lorelei or anywhere else."

Forsythe stared at him, a cold knot forming in his stomach. "What?"

Pirbazari nodded grimly. "Yes, I remember seeing the transcript in his record, too. And presumably the Angelmass Institute wouldn't have let him in without seeing the original."

Forsythe looked down at the display, a strange taste in his mouth. "Or a very good forgery of it."

Pirbazari nodded. "Exactly. I'd say there's a good chance that our Mr.

Kosta has some kind of elaborate con game going. I did a check on the flight he took to Seraph aboard the *Xirrus*. There was also a teenage girl aboard, using the name Chandris Lalasha. She bought passage from Uhuru to Lorelei, but then gimmicked the ship's computer somehow and stayed aboard. A flag picked up the glitch, and they were finally able to track her down just before reaching Seraph. According to their investigation, she was a con artist working in and around New Mexico City."

"Has she fingered Kosta?"

"Not exactly," Pirbazari said dryly. "They landed her in custody, but as soon as they hit ground she kicked out a couple of guards and disappeared into the spaceport crowd. Far as I know, they still haven't caught her."

"You think she and Kosta are working together?"

Pirbazari shrugged. "It's the most reasonable explanation. It's hard to believe she could have escaped from the spaceport without an accomplice."

Forsythe nodded, feeling his lip twist. Kosta as a reputable scientist could give him the backing he needed to stop the flow of angels. Kosta as a con artist was worthless to him. "So what are they up to? What's the Angelmass Institute got that's worth stealing?"

"There you've got me," Pirbazari admitted. "The Institute's loaded to the ceiling with expensive equipment, but it's all highly specialized stuff. Resale value pretty near zero. Could be something to do with Institute funds, or maybe some kind of blackmail scheme."

Forsythe looked back at the display. *Perhaps a personal visit,* he'd just been thinking. "Let's go ask him."

Pirbazari's jaw dropped, just noticeably. "What?"

"Let's go ask him," Forsythe repeated. "Well, maybe not *ask* him, at least not directly. But let's find out what he and this teenager are up to."

"Well . . ." Pirbazari said slowly. "I suppose we *could.* Hardly qualifies as proper High Senate business, though."

"It concerns the angels, Zar," Forsythe reminded the other sternly. "The angels, the Institute—maybe Angelmass itself. That makes it High Senate business." He let his expression soften into a tight smile. "Besides which, a con artist used to dealing with police may not be nearly as adept at handling a High Senator. Or a former EmDef commander."

Pirbazari nodded, his expression that neutral one he seemed to be wearing more and more these days. "Yes, sir. With your permission, I'll go make the arrangements."

"Keep it small," Forsythe called as he headed for the door. "You, me, Ronyon, maybe one more, plus the crew. And keep it quiet, too. I don't want word of this leaking out."

Pirbazari paused at the door, and for a moment Forsythe thought he was going to insist on an explanation. But— "Yes, sir," was all he said.

The door closed behind him, and Forsythe swore gently under his breath. But Pirbazari and his neutral looks were the least of his worries at the moment. The key to stopping or at least slowing the flow of angels was—maybe—within his reach.

Kosta's data could prove vital to the Empyrean's survival. Even if Kosta himself wasn't.

Deep within the cocoon, the fabricators came to a halt. The task, at long last, was finished.

A tiny tunnel appeared in the side of the asteroid shell, similar to the one Kosta's ship had emerged from but much narrower. A chunk of rock rolled out, moving just quickly enough to drift slowly ahead of the cocoon. If the task force was on schedule, the next Pax ship would be coming into the nearby Empyreal net in six days, eighteen hours, and twenty-seven minutes. It would leave with the data-pulse satellite's message.

Shifting into low standby mode, the cocoon settled down to wait.

CHAPTER 24

"According to the receptionist's records," Pirbazari said, leaning over to peer through the line car's right-hand window, "Kosta headed out to the huntership fields early this morning. He took a bunch of equipment with him."

"Interesting," Forsythe said. Had Kosta somehow caught wind of this and rabbited? "How much equipment is there in a bunch?"

"Not much," Pirbazari said. "I don't think he's pulled the plug, if that's what you're wondering. She said he was just taking an experiment aboard one of the ships."

"The *Gazelle?*"

"That's the one," Pirbazari nodded. "Same ship he used before. Ten to one we'll find the *Xirrus*'s stowaway somewhere in the vicinity."

"I'd bet money on it," Forsythe agreed. "We have a number for the *Gazelle*'s yard?"

"Yes—S-33, south field. Owner/operators are a brother and sister named Hanan and Ornina Daviee. You want to head over and take a look?"

Forsythe looked over Pirbazari's shoulder at the Angelmass Institute looming behind him, his mind sifting the possibilities and options. "Yes," he said slowly. "But just Ronyon and me."

Pirbazari's expression hardened, just a little. "I strongly recommend against that, High Senator," he said. "We don't know what sort of people we're dealing with here. It could be dangerous."

"I don't think so," Forsythe soothed him. "Not yet, anyway. We know they're smart, and smart operators don't panic that easily. Besides, I may need you to move undercover later on, and it wouldn't do to let them know we're connected."

"The decision is of course yours," Pirbazari said grudgingly. "I still recommend against it."

"Recommendation noted." Forsythe nodded toward the Institute building. "Is Slavis going to have any trouble?"

"You mean in getting hold of Kosta's data?" Pirbazari shook his head. "No. High Senate staff IDs are quite persuasive."

"Good. You might as well go give him a hand. You didn't tell anyone I was here, did you?"

"No, sir. All we said was that we were members of your staff, here on a fact-finding mission. Which is all true, of course," he added, almost as an after-thought.

Forsythe suppressed a grimace. A few months ago Pirbazari wouldn't have had any qualms over a judicious lie or two in the line of duty. Clearly, despite Forsythe's best efforts, the angels were still having an effect on his people. "I'll see you later, then," he said, settling himself against the seat cushions. "Line car: huntership service yard S-33."

The vehicle pulled away from the curb; and as it did so Forsythe felt a diffident tap on his shoulder. *Yes?* he signed, turning to look at his companion.

Ronyon had a strangely puckered look on his face. *Is there danger?* he signed back.

Forsythe smiled. *Not really,* he assured the other. Seated to Forsythe's left, the big man had of course been able to lip-read only Pirbazari's half of the conversation. *We're just going to go and see some people. You have our angel?*

Ronyon nodded with his usual eagerness. *Right here,* he signed, patting one massive hand against his left-hand pocket.

Forsythe nodded and smiled again. *Good.* It was, not coincidentally, the pocket farthest from him. Among Ronyon's many endearing qualities was the ability to follow simple instructions to the letter.

With the emphasis on *simple* . . .

He threw Ronyon another look. Up till now the big man hadn't screwed up with any of this; but up till now he'd been in the more or less familiar setting of politics. This was different . . . and with a pair of con artists working the area, it would not be a good time for that first slip. *The people we're going to see are some of those who go out in little ships to look for angels,* he signed to Ronyon. *Because of that, there may be other people around who are looking for angels to steal. So I want you to be extra careful about keeping ours hidden away. Okay?*

Ronyon nodded, his expression solemnly eager. *I won't let anyone know.*

They were into the huntership yards now, row after row of dusty concrete rectangles, each blocked off from the street by a wire fence, many of them with a huntership resting on well-worn grooves in the middle. It was more than a little reminiscent of the condition the Iathrus Shipyards had been in before Forsythe rammed some reforms through the Lorelei Senate, and he made a mental note to check on just how much of the Gabriel Corporation's profits were going into basic maintenance.

Ronyon tapped him excitedly on the shoulder. *There it is,* he signed, pointing ahead. *S-thirty-three, right?*

Right, Forsythe agreed, settling himself into confrontation mode and trying to ignore his racing heartbeat. Smart operators, he reminded himself firmly, didn't panic easily.

There were two men standing outside the ship as the line car rolled to a halt: one balding and rather fat, the other much younger and looking like he was fresh out of university. Ronyon beside him, Forsythe stepped to the gate. "Excuse me," he called through the wire mesh.

Both men turned. "Hello there," the older man said, waving them forward. "Come on in."

Forsythe lifted the catch and swung the gate open. "Sorry to bother you," he said as he and Ronyon headed toward the ship. "I'm looking for a Jereko Kosta, and thought I might find him here."

Even at their distance Forsythe could see the flicker of surprise and wariness that crossed the younger man's face. "I'm Kosta," he said. "And you?"

Forsythe waited until he and Ronyon had reached the other two before answering. "I'm High Senator Arkin Forsythe of Lorelei," he said, watching Kosta closely.

The reaction was more or less what Forsythe had expected: another flicker of surprise and perhaps a shade more wariness, but nothing even approaching panic. "I see," Kosta said. "I'm honored to meet you, High Senator."

"And I you," Forsythe told him gravely. "I've been following your work very closely. There are parts of it I find extremely interesting." He looked at the older man. "You must be Hanan Daviee."

"Yes, sir," Daviee said, looking dazed but recovering quickly. "Very honored to meet you, High Senator."

Forsythe nodded to him and turned back to Kosta. "I had to come to Seraph for a few days, and thought that while I was here it might be enlightening for me to check on the progress of your work."

"At the moment, sir, I'm afraid things are going very slowly," Kosta said, his voice apologetic. "Somehow, my funding has been frozen, and until that's straightened out I can't use any of the Institute's facilities. Mr. Daviee has graciously allowed me to bring some sampling equipment aboard the *Gazelle;* otherwise, I'd be at a complete standstill."

"I see," Forsythe said. "Completely frozen, you say?"

"Yes, sir. Director Podolak's been trying to find the problem, but so far hasn't been able to."

"Perhaps I can look into it when I get back to Uhuru." Forsythe looked up at the ship looming over them. "You said you had some of your test gear aboard?"

"Yes, sir," Kosta nodded. "I could give you a tour of the setup, if you'd like."

"A very *brief* tour," Daviee interjected, looking a little pained. "Begging your pardon, High Senator, but we're scheduled to leave for Angelmass in less than an hour. The tow car will be attaching in twenty minutes—once we start rolling the regs require that the *Gazelle*'s hatches be sealed."

"Twenty minutes should be enough," Forsythe assured him. Ronyon was hovering in clearly nervous uncertainty at his shoulder; without glancing up, he signed the big man to follow him. "Lead the way, Mr. Kosta," he added aloud.

It had been many years since Forsythe had been aboard a working ship like the *Gazelle*. Enough years for him to have forgotten how small and cramped and unpleasant they were, particularly when compared to liners and official government transports. Gingerly, trying not to touch the walls any more than he had to, he followed Kosta through the maze. "I have to apologize for the mess, High Senator," Kosta said over his shoulder as he stepped over a section of half-disassembled machinery protruding into the corridor and started down a narrow stairway leading to the *Gazelle*'s lowest deck. "The Daviees have been working most of the night to try and get the ship ready to fly, and there are obviously still a few things to be done."

"I thought Gabriel was supposed to handle huntership maintenance," Forsythe said.

Kosta shrugged. "I don't know. You'd have to ask Hanan about that. Here we are."

He stopped in front of a small shiny box wedged into a space between two larger floor-to-ceiling equipment cabinets. A half dozen cables protruded from the top of the box, snaking their way to unknown destinations behind the cabinets. "This is the primary logic module of my experiment," Kosta said. "It takes data from a group of radiation sensors mounted on and just beneath the outer hull, does a fast analysis, and sends the results to a secondary module mounted in the *Gazelle*'s main computer room."

Forsythe nodded, eyes flicking across the six cables. Four of them were readily explainable: three standard data-transfer mesh ribbons and one low-voltage electronics power line. But the other two cables . . . "What exactly is this particular experiment supposed to accomplish?" he asked.

"I'm hoping it'll help me get a handle on these unexplained radiation surges," Kosta told him. "I'm still not comfortable with the self-focusing theory that's been suggested."

"Yes, I got that impression from your paper." Forsythe nodded at the box. "Tell me about it. In detail."

Kosta took him at his word, launching into a convoluted discussion of spectrum sampling, core-spiral generation, and real-time pattern analysis.

Forsythe was able to follow only about half of it; but that half was enough to show that the explanation wasn't simply built out of moonbeams and silk handkerchiefs. Whoever Kosta was—whatever this scheme was he was running here—he'd clearly done his homework.

"Interesting," Forsythe said when he'd finished. "And that's all this experiment's supposed to do?"

"Isn't that enough for one experiment?"

"I'm certain it is," Forsythe said, giving him a hard look. "I was curious about those two power lines coming out of your logic module." He gestured to the two cables that had caught his attention. "You're not going to tell me those are just more sensor lines, are you?"

The corner of Kosta's lip twitched. "No, they're part of something entirely different. A small test I'm piggybacking on top of the main sampling experiment."

"What kind of test?"

Kosta hesitated. "I'm sorry, High Senator, but I really can't talk about that. It keys off a discovery by another Institute member, something I promised to keep secret."

"Even from top government officials?" Forsythe demanded, adding a subtle note of threat to his tone.

"I'm sorry," Kosta repeated. "You can talk to Dr. Frashni directly—perhaps he'll be willing to tell you. But I can't."

"I see," Forsythe said, studying the younger man's face. Odd; he'd have thought a good con artist would try to avoid ducking questions he could just as easily invent answers to.

Unless he really *was* doing something for this Dr. Frashni. He made a mental note for Pirbazari to check it out.

Over the hum of machinery came the sound of approaching footsteps, and he turned to see Hanan Daviee come up behind Ronyon. "I'm sorry, High Senator," the fat man apologized, "but I wanted to let you know that the tow car is here."

"Thank you," Forsythe said, glancing at his watch. It had indeed been just about twenty minutes since he and Ronyon had come aboard. If there was one thing the Gabriel Corporation was famous for, it was punctual scheduling. "I'll get out of your way now. Good luck with your hunt."

"Thank you, High Senator," the other said. "If you'll come this way, I'll show you to the exit. Oh, and by the way, the reporters are starting to arrive."

Forsythe stopped in mid-stride. "Reporters? What are reporters doing here?"

Hanan blinked. "Why . . . I assumed you called them."

"No, I most certainly did not," Forsythe snarled, digging out his phone and punching in a number. This whole trip was supposed to be *secret,* damn it. If this leak was Pirbazari's fault—

Pirbazari answered on the second ring. "Yes?"

"It's Forsythe," Forsythe identified himself. "Why are there reporters gathering around the *Gazelle?*"

There was a second of stunned silence. "Reporters?"

"Yes, reporters. I thought I made it clear that my presence here was *not* to be mentioned to anyone."

"We haven't told anyone you were here, High Senator," Pirbazari insisted. "My only guess is that the Institute receptionist jumped to that conclusion on her own."

Who had alerted her superiors, who had alerted the media, who were now gathering like scavengers at a picnic hunting for crumbs. It fit, all right. Unfortunately. "Wonderful. What do you propose we do about it?"

"You'd better stay aboard the ship until they leave. Can you get this Daviee person to tell them you're not there?"

"Probably," Forsythe growled. "There's just one slight flaw in that plan: the *Gazelle*'s about to leave for Angelmass. I doubt they'd be interested in having us along while they go angel hunting. No, you're going to have to do something from there. And you're going to have to do it in the next three minutes."

Beside Ronyon, Hanan Daviee cleared his throat. "High Senator?" he murmured, raising a tentative hand.

Forsythe focused on him. "What?"

"If you'd rather not leave right now, you'd be welcome to join us," he said. "We have enough room aboard for both of you."

Forsythe stared at him, the automatic polite refusal catching midway up his throat. It was, on the face of it, a ridiculous suggestion.

But on the other hand, why not? The other High Senators talked a great deal about angels being the future of the Empyrean, but to the best of his knowledge not a single one of them had ever personally gone on an angel hunt. It was no more or less than basic research for a man in his position.

More to the immediate point, it would save him the trouble of facing a group of reporters and questions he didn't really want to answer right now. "Very well, Mr. Daviee," he said. "I accept your offer. Zar? Cancel the panic. I'm going to take a run out to Angelmass with the *Gazelle.*"

There was another silence from the phone, a longer one this time. "You're not serious, sir," Pirbazari said at last, his voice sounding sandbagged.

"Perfectly serious," Forsythe said. "Why not?"

"Why *not?* This isn't exactly your standard fact-finding trip, High Senator.

We're talking about Angelmass here. EM radiation, deadly particle fluxes, violent magnetic fields—"

"We're also talking about a huntership, Zar," Forsythe reminded him. "They're designed for that environment."

"You also haven't been checked out on huntership fundamentals, sir," Pirbazari said stiffly. "That's a basic safety rule. I'm sorry, but I cannot in any way endorse this course of action."

"Noted," Forsythe said. "Continue your work; I'll check in with you whenever I get back."

He closed down the phone and replaced it in its pocket. "Well," he said, nodding to Hanan. "Request permission to stay aboard, Captain. Or whatever the appropriate phrase is."

"Oh, we're not that formal here, High Senator," Hanan said, his face reddening a bit. "If you'll permit me to show you and your aide to your rooms—"

"Why don't I do that?" Kosta put in. "Then you can concentrate on getting the ship ready."

"That *would* be more convenient—if the High Senator doesn't mind, that is," Hanan added quickly, looking at Forsythe.

It was, for Forsythe, a familiar pattern: common man meets Important Personage and instantly starts walking on eggs. Fortunately, it was familiar enough for him to know how to handle it. "What the High Senator would like most," he told Hanan, putting a note of mild reproof in his voice, "is for you to relax. I don't want any special treatment or deference or to interfere with your work in any way. All right?"

"Ah . . . yes, sir," Hanan said. "I'll try."

"Good," Forsythe nodded. "It might help for you to pretend I'm just someone who's interested in angel hunting and came along to see what the business was like."

Hanan smiled wanly. "First thing I'd do is try to talk you out of it. Far too much work involved. Thank you, High Senator." His eyes flicked to Kosta. "We'll put them in cabins one and two. Get Chandris to help you change the bunks." With a nod, he turned and hurried down the corridor.

Forsythe felt a quiet chill run through him. Chandris. As in Chandris Lalasha, as in the *Xirrus*'s stowaway. He'd predicted to Pirbazari that she and Kosta were working together; now, it seemed, that prediction had been borne out.

She was aboard . . . and he was going to be spending several days cooped up on this ship with them.

He shook away the momentary twinge of uncertainty. These were con artists, after all. Con artists were almost never violent.

Ronyon was looking at him, uncertainties of his own puckering his face.

We're going to be staying aboard the ship for a few days, Forsythe signed to him.
*This is Mr. Kosta—he's going to take us to our rooms. The other man who was
here is named Mr. Daviee.*

Ronyon nodded, and Forsythe turned to Kosta. "Whenever you're ready."

"Right," Kosta said, his eyes lingering on Ronyon for just a second too
long.

Which meant he very much wanted to ask, but wasn't sure of how to do
so. "Ronyon is deaf," Forsythe said, saving him the trouble. "Also somewhat retarded. If you need to say anything to him that can't be communicated by simple gestures, you'll have to do it through me." Which wasn't entirely true, of
course. But there was no need for Kosta to know that.

"I understand," Kosta said. "Uh . . . if you'll follow me, the cabins are back
this way."

They retraced their steps back to the now-sealed hatchway and continued
a short way past it to one of several identical cross corridors. The first door
along it opened into a small but cozily furnished cabin. "This is normally Ornina's room," Kosta said as he ushered them in. "Hanan's is across the corridor.
Let me call Chandris and find out where fresh bedding is kept."

"All right," Forsythe said as Kosta stepped around him and went to the
bedside intercom. He wasn't really happy with the idea of throwing Hanan and
his sister out of their rooms; but this too was a reaction he'd run into before,
and he knew that they'd feel far more uncomfortable if he insisted on taking
less than the best accommodations they had to offer.

Kosta finished his conversation and looked up. "She'll be along in a few
minutes," he told Forsythe. "You can wait here, or else I can take you to the
control cabin and introduce you to Ornina."

"Let's do the control cabin," Forsythe decided. "After that, perhaps you'd
be good enough to pull up the specs for this ship and let me start learning my
way around."

"Certainly," Kosta said. "This way, please."

They had again passed the hatchway and turned inward toward the center
of the ship when, turning a corner, they came face to face with a young
woman, a stack of linens in her arms. "There you are," Kosta said, turning back
to Forsythe. "These are our guests: High Senator Forsythe and—ah—"

"His name is Ronyon," Forsythe supplied, giving the girl a quick once-
over. In her mid to late teens, he estimated, attractive enough in an immature
sort of way, her posture exuding confidence and control. Clearly, she belonged
here on the *Gazelle;* and for a brief moment he wondered if he'd jumped to the
wrong conclusion about who she was.

And then he took another, longer look at her face, with that neutral-polite expression, and those coldly calculating eyes. It was the measuring look of a professional politician . . . or a highly competent con artist.

No, there'd been no mistake. "And you, I take it," he added, "must be Chandris."

"Yes," the woman said, her gaze flicking once to Ronyon. "The *Gazelle* is honored by your presence. May I ask what brings a High Senator aboard our humble ship?"

"Circumstances, plus an interest in Mr. Kosta's work," Forsythe told her. "I'll try not to get in your way."

"I'm sure there'll be no problems," she said coolly. Her eyes dropped to the pendant around his neck, perhaps to reassure herself that he really *was* who he claimed to be. "If you'll excuse me, there are still several things that need my attention before we hit the launch strip."

"Of course," Forsythe nodded, stepping to the side of the corridor to let her pass. "If that's the bedding for our rooms, though, you can just give it to Ronyon. There's no need for you to take it there personally."

"All right." Stepping to Ronyon, she offered him the bedding.

The big man looked questioningly at Forsythe. *Take it back to our rooms,* Forsythe signed to him. *You remember the way?*

Sure, Ronyon signed, accepting the bundle and tucking it under one arm. *Should I wait there then?* he signed one-handed.

Might as well. I'll come back for you in a little while.

Chandris was still standing close to Ronyon, an odd look on her face. "He's deaf," Forsythe explained. "If you need to talk to him, you'll have to do so through me."

"I see," she said. "I'd better get back to work, then. Are you sure Ronyon can find his way back to your cabin alone?"

"He's got a good sense of direction," Forsythe assured her.

"Ah," she nodded. "Well, I'm going back that direction anyway."

"All right." Forsythe caught Ronyon's eye. *This is Chandris,* he signed. *She'll walk with you back to the rooms.*

Ronyon nodded, and together he and Chandris headed down the corridor. "And now, as I recall," Forsythe said, turning back to Kosta, "we were heading for the control cabin."

Kosta was staring down the corridor at the departing twosome. "Right," he said, bringing his attention back to Forsythe with obvious effort. "If you'll follow me, sir . . . ?"

And as they walked, Forsythe permitted himself a brief grimace. Kosta and

Chandris were up to something, all right. He could read it in their reactions to him as readily as he could read Ronyon's signing. All he had to do was to figure out exactly what it was.

And hope like fury that whatever it was wouldn't interfere with his plans to stop the flow of angels.

CHAPTER 25

Outside, the tow car took up the slack; and with a jerk, the *Gazelle* started rolling. Ronyon, still carrying the bedding, was caught off-guard by the sudden motion and staggered slightly, bumping into the corridor wall.

It was the opportunity Chandris had been waiting for. In an instant she was at his side, steadying his arm and pressing against him.

A couple of seconds were all she got before he was back on balance again and she had to pull away. But a couple of seconds were all she needed. Her senses had not, in fact, played her false during that conversation a minute ago with Kosta and High Senator Forsythe.

Ronyon was carrying an angel.

An angel. She repeated the word silently to herself, her thoughts spinning with old plans and fresh possibilities. *An angel.* Not the Daviees' spare, which she'd promised herself not to take, but a government angel. One of thousands. One that would probably never be missed.

All it would take, Hanan had told her, would be some highly specialized neural surgery and six months of intensive treatment . . . and two million ruya to pay for all of it.

I'm reformed, she reminded herself. But the words sounded hollow and meaningless. And anyway, she'd never said she was reformed. The only reason she hadn't stolen anything lately was that she hadn't happened across anything worth the effort.

Until now.

They reached Hanan's cabin and Ronyon went inside, smiling cheerfully at Chandris as he set the bundle of bedding on the desk. "You want me to do the beds?" Chandris asked before remembering he couldn't hear her. But even as she tried to think of how best to act out the question, Ronyon shook his head and tapped his own chest. Turning to the bunk, he began to strip it.

So he could read lips. Interesting that Forsythe had neglected to mention that fact. In fact, he'd strongly implied exactly the opposite, that Ronyon could only communicate through sign language.

For a long moment she stood in the doorway, gazing at Ronyon's broad back while he worked, the old juices starting to flow again as she considered how to make the approach. Picking his pocket would be the simplest if she knew where he was carrying it. But she didn't; and anyway, out here in the middle of nowhere she wouldn't exactly have the option of chop-hopping if he noticed the loss. The best way would be for him to give it to her, for whatever reason she could concoct. A man of his obvious limitations should be easy to score.

Ronyon finished the cot and turned back, seemingly surprised to see her still there. But he smiled again as he collected the other set of bedding. She smiled back, moving out of the doorway to let him pass. The smile faded as he crossed the corridor and went into Hanan's room. An easy score . . . except for one minor detail.

The track in this case was deaf.

Chandris bit at her lip, a swirl of uncertainty like she hadn't felt in years swishing through her stomach. She'd never scored a deaf person before; and up to now she'd never properly appreciated just how much of her talent was tied up in her voice. Her tone, her vocabulary, the texture of her phrasings— those were what made the tracks see someone who wasn't really there. Even more than basic disguise and body language, it was what had given her her edge through the years.

Only here, that edge was gone.

Across the room, the intercom pinged. "Chandris?" Ornina's voice called. "Where are you?"

She stepped to the desk and tapped the switch. "I'm in your room," she said. "Helping Ronyon get the bed changed."

"Ron—? Oh, right—the High Senator's aide," Ornina said. "I hadn't caught his name. I wanted to let you know we're almost to the launch strip."

Chandris grimaced. "I'll be right up."

The intercom clicked off. For a moment Chandris just stood there, staring some more at Ronyon's back and trying furiously to come up with a scheme she could run within the next sixty seconds. If she let this chance slip away . . .

She took a deep breath. *Relax,* she told herself firmly. *Don't push it. There'll be time enough later.*

She touched Ronyon on the shoulder. "I have to go to the control cabin," she said when he turned around, being careful to enunciate her words clearly. "Do you want to go with me so that you know the way?"

He looked down at the half-made bed, forehead wrinkled in thought, and shook his head. His hands began to trace out a pattern in the air in front of him—

"I don't understand that language," Chandris said, reaching out to gently stop his hands. "Maybe later you can teach me. Are you going to stay here?"

He nodded. "All right," Chandris said. "I'll see you later."

————

The roar of the *Gazelle*'s drive faded into a dull rumble, weight fading away with it. Kosta set his teeth carefully together, focused on the back of Hanan's head directly across from his jumpseat, and concentrated on not being sick.

"We're on course now for the Seraph catapult, High Senator," Hanan said, half turning. "It'll take about an hour to get there. I've started the *Gazelle* spinning—we should have enough for at least a little gravity in a couple of minutes."

"Thank you," Forsythe said. Kosta risked a look that direction, saw no trace of freefall sickness in the High Senator's face. As usual, Kosta seemed to be the only one having trouble. "How much of a wait will there be at the catapult?"

"Ideally, there shouldn't be any wait at all," Hanan said. "Turnaround is usually pretty much as we get there."

"Even with three launch dishes feeding one catapult?" Forsythe countered. "That sounds like a situation begging for a logjam."

"You're right, it does," Hanan agreed. "Oddly enough, though, that doesn't usually happen. For one thing, there's no problem with coordinate-setting; the catapult and Central's net are binary linked. As long as they're both functioning, you can't go anywhere else. Same thing coming home, too."

"What about mass settings?"

"The readings are taken by the launch dish," Hanan explained. "They're then transmitted directly to the catapult. That's usually the only time problems crop up, come to think of it: when ships get out of order and the mass settings are therefore scrambled."

"Interesting." Forsythe looked at the doorway. "I'd very much like to go over more of the operational details with you later, Mr. Daviee. But first, I should probably go and find Ronyon."

"Actually, I can just—no, I can't," Hanan interrupted himself. "He can't hear the intercom, can he?"

"No," Forsythe said. "I have a call stick, but that won't do any good unless he knows where I am."

"He was making the bed in Ornina's cabin when I left him," Chandris offered. "Shall I go get him?"

Forsythe shook his head. "Thank you, no."

"It's no trouble—"

"I said no," Forsythe repeated; and this time Kosta heard a slight edge in his voice. "It'll be better if I—"

He broke off as a sound Kosta had never heard came from Ornina's control board. "What was that?" he asked.

"EmDef ID," Ornina said, turning back to her board. "Someone with high priority is coming through . . . oh, God," she added, very quietly.

"What?" Kosta asked.

"It's *Hova's Skyarcher*," she said in the same quiet voice. "They're bringing it home."

"What, only now?" Forsythe frowned, leaning forward as if he would get a better look that way.

"It wasn't easy to retrieve," Hanan said. "Very close in to Angelmass. They had to send an autobooster in to push it out to where the towship could get it without frying the crew."

"Can we get a look?" Kosta asked.

"I'm trying," Hanan said. "They're pretty far away and going the opposite direction. Let's see . . ."

And suddenly, on all the displays, there it was.

Ornina inhaled sharply, and Kosta found himself feeling a little sicker than he already was. The *Hova's Skyarcher* was a wreck: its shape noticeably warped, its vaunted Empyreal sandwich-metal hull blackened and pitted. "It must have really gone deep to have taken that much damage," he heard himself say.

"Yes," Hanan agreed. He sounded a little sick, too. "Far deeper than it should have. The radiation surge must have scrambled all the control settings before it . . ." He trailed off.

Before it killed them, Kosta finished the thought silently. With an effort, he tore his gaze from the wrecked ship.

To find Forsythe watching him.

Briefly, he held the High Senator's gaze before turning away, wondering dimly what was going on behind that stolid face. But he wasn't especially concerned about it. For the moment, all his thoughts were tied up in the implications of what had happened to that ship out there.

"Getting out of range," Hanan murmured.

Kosta turned back to the displays. The dead hulk and the sleek EmDef ships towing it were becoming hazy as they pushed the limits of the *Gazelle*'s telescope and optical enhancement system. "They taking it to the Institute?" he asked.

"Probably to a decon center first," Hanan told him. "It's got to be blazing with secondary radiation—you saw the length of cable the tow ship was using."

Forsythe shifted in his seat. "Mr. Daviee, you said you normally only get logjam problems when the hunterships get out of order," he said. "Do you ever get logjams otherwise?"

"What do you mean?" Hanan asked.

"For the Institute's self-focusing theory to be right, hunterships have to occasionally drop bits of mass into Angelmass," Forsythe said. "If they drop things there, it follows that they should also sometimes drop things during other parts of the trip, too."

"Which could show up as recalibration problems when catapulting," Hanan said, nodding slowly. "Huh. I never thought of that. Jereko?"

"I don't know if anyone else has thought of it, either," Kosta said, glancing at Forsythe with newly heightened respect. In his admittedly limited experience, he'd never found government types to be exactly brimming with creative thought. Either Forsythe was an exception, or the Empyrean had found a way to attract a smarter class of people into public service than the Pax had.

Or else it had something to do with the fact that Empyreal politicians carried angels.

The others, he realized suddenly, were still waiting. "I don't know if the mathematics would work out, either," he added, forcing his mind back to the question. "It could be that the amount of mass necessary to start a self-focusing surge is still within catapult tolerances. Worth checking out, though."

"I've got a list here of all the catapult delays we've been involved in over the past year," Ornina spoke up.

"How do I get it?" Forsythe asked, fingers hovering over the control board in front of his seat.

"Allow me," Kosta said, unstrapping and stepping carefully in the low gravity to the High Senator's seat. He keyed for an echo of Ornina's screen, gave it a fast once-over. "I don't see anything obvious," he said.

"Me, neither," Hanan agreed. "Though that may not mean anything. One huntership for one year isn't much of a sample."

"Let's try anyway," Kosta suggested. "If you'll allow me, High Senator . . . ?"

"Certainly." Forsythe swiveled the panel around to where Kosta could more easily operate it.

The *Gazelle*'s computer library contained two different statistical packages. Kosta called them up for a quick look. "I don't think either of those can handle a sample this small," Hanan said, watching the echo of Kosta's work on his own display.

"No," Kosta agreed. "But I know of one that might be able to. Let's see if I can remember how it works."

It was a highly esoteric program he'd learned in his first year at the university, and he wound up with two false starts before he got it right. But finally it was ready. Feeding in Ornina's data, he set it running. "Interesting program," Forsythe said. "How long until it's done?"

"A couple of minutes," Kosta told him. "Speed is not its primary virtue." He let his eyes drift around the room, relaxing from the close-focus work of the display screen.

Chandris's seat was empty.

He glanced surreptitiously around the room, heart suddenly thudding in his ears. She was gone, all right. Sometime in the last few minutes, without anyone noticing, she'd just slipped away.

He opened his mouth to announce his discovery; bit down gently on his tongue instead. She'd probably just gone to find Ronyon, that was all. Or something equally innocent.

Except that Forsythe had already told her *not* to go after Ronyon. If she was up to something else . . .

The program beeped notice that it was done. Reaching to the board, Kosta keyed for the results.

He might as well not have bothered. "You're right," he said to Hanan as he dumped the screen. "One ship and one year just aren't enough."

"The catapult itself should have complete records, though," Ornina pointed out. "Perhaps you could ask them to send us a data copy, High Senator."

"I'm sure I could," Forsythe said. "However, as I told Mr. Daviee, I'm here on a strictly unofficial basis. I'd like to keep it that way."

"I see." Ornina looked at Hanan, and in her face Kosta could see that that bit of information had somehow missed getting passed to her. "I'm sorry. Ah—"

"The Institute should also have them," Kosta spoke up quickly. "When we get back I'll get Yaezon to look them up for me."

"There might be another way to get the information now, though," Hanan said, an odd tone to his voice as he tapped keys. "If they happen to have a new trainee or two on station at Control . . ."

He cleared his throat; and he was launching into a very official-sounding speech as Kosta quietly slipped out of the room.

He went first to Hanan's and Ornina's cabins, not from any real expectation of finding Chandris there but merely as a reasonable place to start his search. To his surprise, however, he heard the faint sound of running water as he approached. Someone inside Ornina's cabin was apparently taking a shower.

For a long moment he hesitated outside the door, a half dozen scenarios— some of them decidedly discomfiting—scrambling through his mind. But if Chandris was up to something underhanded, it was his duty to intervene. Bracing himself, he opened the door and went in.

No one was in the main living area, but there was a neat stack of clothes on the bed—Ronyon's, Kosta tentatively identified them. At the back of the room, through the open bathroom doorway, he could see back to the shower.

The shower door was only slightly translucent, but that was enough. The size and shape of the shadow showed that it was Ronyon in there. Alone.

Quickly, Kosta backed out into the corridor, cheeks hot with embarrassment and annoyance. The Chandris Effect, all right: give him half an hour with her and he'd make a fool of himself somehow. But at least she wasn't pulling some scam on Ronyon.

So where was she?

He looked up and down the corridor, wondering if there was any point in continuing the search. She'd probably left on some perfectly innocent ship's business, after all. For all he knew, Ornina or Hanan might even have openly sent her away while he was preoccupied with his statistics program.

Then, from down the corridor, he heard a faint grinding sound.

The sound came and went three more times before he located its source: the machine shop. Inside, hunched intently over a grinder, was Chandris.

"There you are," Kosta said, stepping inside. "What are you doing here?"

She didn't jump in her seat or spin around or do any of the other things people were supposed to do when they were caught doing something wrong. But it seemed to Kosta that she took a fraction of a second too long before turning her head to look at him. "What does it look like I'm doing?" she countered mildly. "I'm working."

"Now?" he asked, moving to her side and leaning over to look at the grinder. Held snugly in an electronics clamp was a small lens-shaped piece of crystal. "With the ship about to hit the catapult?"

"Why not?" she said with a shrug. "Hanan and Ornina can handle the ship without me. Anyway, it felt a little crowded up there."

"Uh-huh," he said, frowning down at the crystal. There was something about the size and shape that seemed familiar somehow . . .

"Don't you have some work of your own to do?" she interrupted his musings. "Calibrating your equipment or something?"

"No, everything's done," he said absently. He had seen something just like that crystal—he knew he had. Recently, too. If he could just chase down the memory . . .

"Okay, then, to hell with politeness," Chandris said. "Go away and let me work."

"Fine," Kosta said, straightening up. "You don't have to get huffy." He gave the crystal one last look—

And suddenly the mental picture he'd been searching for dropped neatly into place. High Senator Forsythe, outside the *Gazelle,* offering his hand for the respect gesture. And fastened to a chain around his neck, the delicate gold filigree and crystal of—

Kosta focused sharply on Chandris; and in her face he could see she knew he'd figured it out. "Okay," she growled. "So?"

"*So?*" Kosta hissed. "Are you crazy?"

"They need the money," she said. "They need it for the ship; they especially need it for Hanan. He's got a degenerative nerve disease, in case you haven't bothered to notice."

"That was unfair," Kosta said coldly. "I was the one who carried him down to the medpack, remember?"

She looked at him a moment . . . and for a wonder, nodded agreement. "You're right," she acknowledged. "It was a cheap shot."

"Yes, it was," Kosta nodded back, some of his anger draining away. "Look, I'm sorry about Hanan. I'd like to see him get fixed up, too. But this isn't the way to do it."

She gazed evenly up at him. "How are you going to stop me? Without getting me in trouble, that is?"

Kosta grimaced. So she thought that it was her he was trying to avoid getting into trouble. If she only knew. "I'll tell the Daviees," he said, turning back toward the door. "I'm sure they can find a way to keep you away from Forsythe's angel."

"Forsythe doesn't have the angel," Chandris called after him. "Ronyon does."

Kosta turned back. "What are you talking about?" he demanded. "Ronyon isn't wearing an angel."

"No, he's carrying it in his pocket," she said. "That's why I spilled machine oil on him and sent him to the shower. So I could find it and get a close look."

Kosta frowned at her. Could they be issuing angels even to High Senators' aides now? No—ridiculous. "They don't give angels to aides," he told Chandris. "Just to the High Senators themselves."

"Well, then, he's got Forsythe's angel," Chandris insisted. "Maybe *he* stole it."

"But Forsythe's wearing—"

"He's wearing a fake," Chandris said. She gestured to the unfinished crystal in the clamp. "Just like this one."

A cold chill ran up Kosta's back. A High Senator, with a fake angel? "There has to be a mistake," he said between suddenly stiff lips.

"Not a chance," Chandris said. "I know what an angel feels like up close."

Kosta thought back to his own first encounter with one of the Institute's angels. He hadn't felt a thing, and he'd really been trying to. "I didn't know angels felt like anything in particular," he said.

"Some people can't tell the flavors of different mushrooms apart either," Chandris said tartly. "I don't know how I can tell if an angel's there. I just can. The High Senator's wearing a fake. Period."

Kosta's gaze drifted away from her face, his mind spinning with sudden uncertainties. The underlying basis of this whole mission had been the Pax assertion that the Empyreal leadership was coming under the influence of alien intelligences. But if that wasn't true—if the High Senators were not, in fact, wearing angels—then that threat evaluation was way off target.

Unless Forsythe had engineered this deception on his own. In which case, he was blatantly defying Empyreal law, for some reason of his own. Having second thoughts about the angels, perhaps?

Either way, it was a situation worth following up on. Which meant, unfortunately, that he was again going to have to avoid rocking the boat. "I won't tell the Daviees about it," he said, knowing full well that Chandris was going to take this wrong. "Not now, anyway. But I'll be keeping an eye on Ronyon; and if you grab that angel, I *will* turn you in."

Turning his back on her, he left.

Chandris stared after him, her work on the crystal momentarily forgotten. It had happened again. Kosta had cracked her red-handed doing something illegal . . . and had just walked away rather than get involved.

But it wasn't just a dislike of getting involved, she saw now. It was more specific than that. It was an attempt to avoid situations where he would be drawing attention to himself.

Or more specifically, where he would be drawing *official* attention to himself.

Slowly, she turned back to her crystal. Kosta wasn't who he pretended to be—that much she'd concluded his first time aboard the *Gazelle*. But he wasn't a normal con artist, either.

So what was he?

She leaned back in her chair, frowning at the ceiling. There was something he'd said to her a long time ago, an off-handed comment that had sounded odd at the time but which she'd never gotten around to checking out for herself.

That strange comment about aphrodisiac perfumes.

Swiveling around, she reached for the machine room's computer terminal. But even as she did so, the intercom pinged. "Chandris?" Ornina's voice said. "Where are you?"

Chandris hesitated a split second, old ingrained reflexes whispering at her to come up with a quick and convincing lie. Suppressing the impulse, she tapped the switch. "Machine shop," she said.

"We'll be hitting the catapult in about three minutes," Ornina told her. If she wondered what Chandris could possibly be doing in the machine shop, it didn't show in her voice. "You want to come up?"

"Sure. I'll be right there."

"Thank you."

Chandris keyed off the intercom and set to work freeing her rough crystal from its clamp. She'd hoped to have the duplicate finished before they reached Angelmass and people started wandering around the ship again. But no problem. There would be plenty of time to get it done before the *Gazelle* got back to Seraph.

And if Kosta didn't like it, he could go jump.

She made it to the control room and into her seat with maybe twenty seconds to spare. Kosta was already there, sitting tight-lipped in Forsythe's earlier seat and doing his best to ignore her. The High Senator himself was nowhere to be seen. "Systems all okay?" she asked, keying back into her board.

"Running smooth as can be," Hanan said. "High Senator Forsythe left a couple of minutes ago to go find Ronyon."

"He's probably still in the shower," Chandris said. "I was showing him around the ship and accidentally squirted some machine oil on him."

Ornina frowned at her. "How in the world did you manage to do that?"

Chandris was saved the necessity of answering by the alert signal from the control board and the start of the catapult's five-second countdown. She ran her eyes over her board, confirmed that everything was ready; and with the usual not-quite jerk the spider-shape of Angelmass Central appeared in the center of her display.

Behind her, the door whispered open, and she turned to see Forsythe come in. "Everything all right back there, High Senator?" Hanan asked.

"Yes, thanks," Forsythe said. He glanced at Kosta, in his earlier seat, and for a moment Chandris wondered if he was going to demand it back. But instead he went over to one of the fold-down jumpseats. "I found Ronyon in his room," he added, strapping himself in. "He'd gotten some oil on himself and was showering it off."

He said it offhandedly, and the glance he threw at Chandris was equally casual. But for someone who'd been reading people as long as she had, it was more than enough.

Forsythe knew exactly who she was. Who she was, and what she was.

She turned back to her board, heart pounding in her ears. So it had happened, as she'd known someday it would. Lulled by the warmth and comfort of the Daviees, she'd let herself believe she could stay here forever.

Now, instead of just getting herself in trouble, she was going to drag them into it, as well.

"I hope he's almost finished," Hanan commented. "We'll have to drop the ship's rotation down to near zero soon."

"He's all finished," Forsythe said. "Just drying and getting dressed again. I let him borrow one of your shirts—I hope you don't mind."

"No trouble at all," Hanan assured him. "I guess I should have made it clear earlier that everything on the *Gazelle* is at your disposal."

"You made it perfectly clear," Forsythe said. "As I hoped *I* made clear that I don't want our presence here disrupting your normal working routine. Any progress yet, Mr. Kosta?"

"Yes, but it's mostly negative," Kosta said, studying something on his display. "There have been a few delays at the catapult due to huntership mass discrepancies, but all of them were traceable to errors at the launch dish. Nothing seems to be from material that fell off the ships along the way."

"Though that may not mean anything," Ornina pointed out. "As you said earlier, the catapult may have enough tolerance built into its programming."

"Agreed." Kosta shook his head. "The more I think about it, the less I like the whole theory. Angelmass just isn't massive enough to pull that much gravitational energy out of infalling paint chips or whatever."

Behind Chandris, the door slid open . . . and she turned just as Ronyon stumbled into the room, his fingers tracing agitated patterns in the air in front of him.

A look of absolute terror was on his face.

"What's wrong?" she demanded.

"He's frightened of something," Forsythe said, making quick finger gestures of his own. Ronyon replied—"I can't get any sense out of him," Forsythe said, starting to sound concerned. "He just keeps saying he's afraid."

"Is it the low gravity?" Ornina asked, starting to unstrap. A pair of gamma-ray *cracks* snapped through the room, making Chandris jump. "If he's never been in free-fall before—"

"He been in free-fall hundreds of times," Forsythe said shortly. He had a hand on Ronyon's shoulder now, his other hand still going through their complicated motions. "I don't understand this at all."

"Perhaps we should get him back to his cabin," Ornina suggested. She was at Ronyon's side now, holding his arm in a reassuring grip as she studied his face.

More hand motions, a violent shake of Ronyon's head—"He doesn't want to leave," Forsythe said. "Says he's afraid to be alone."

Chandris looked at Hanan. "Are there any sedatives in the medpack's drug dispenser?"

"There should be," he said, his eyes on Ronyon. "You know how to get the dispenser open?"

She nodded, reaching for her restraints. "Back in a minute."

It took her a little longer than she'd expected to get to the medpack, take the cover off the dispenser, locate the proper ampule, put everything back together again, and return to the control room. The others had gotten Ronyon strapped into Kosta's chair by the time she returned, but otherwise not much had changed. The big man still looked pretty miserable. "Thank you, Chandris," Ornina said, taking the sedative from her and reaching for Ronyon's arm.

He pulled the arm away from her, his eyes turning frantically to Forsythe. "It's all right," the High Senator told him, gesturing the words as well as saying them. "It's just something to help you relax a little."

Reluctantly, Ronyon put his arm back on the armrest. Ornina touched it with the ampule and gave him an encouraging smile. "You'll feel better in just a few minutes," she said. "High Senator Forsythe and I will stay right here with you until you do."

Ronyon nodded, already seeming to sag a little in the low gravity. Leaving the two of them to look after Ronyon, Chandris made her way forward and climbed into Ornina's seat. In the time since she'd gone to get the sedative, the gamma-ray sparks had worked their way up to a gentle but insistent rain, and she keyed her board for a location check.

The result came up. She looked at it, a frown starting to crease her forehead.

"It's accurate," Hanan said quietly from beside her.

She looked at the tight expression on his face, a creepy sensation working its way up through her. "You sure?" she asked, keeping her own voice low.

"I've run it three times in the past fifteen minutes," he told her. "No mistake."

Chandris turned back to her board, the creepy sensation getting stronger. If they were really still this far away from Angelmass . . . "The radiation's getting stronger," she murmured. She glanced back at Kosta, sitting in one of the jumpseats watching Forsythe and Ornina hovering around Ronyon. "Just like Kosta said."

"Yes," Hanan agreed. "I just hope the *Gazelle*'s hull can take the extra—"

He broke off, the last echo of his words vanishing into the silence.

Into the complete silence . . .

"Kosta?" Chandris snapped, twisting around to look at him.

"I know," Kosta said grimly, already out of his jumpseat and heading for Chandris's usual seat and control board. "The gamma sparks have stopped."

Chandris turned back to her display, stomach tightening as she keyed for radiation sensor readings. A memory flashed back: someone in the Barrio telling her a story about how a big wave had once swept in from the sea and wrecked a big part of Uhuru's main port city. And before the wave had come, the whole sea had pulled back from the shore, like it was getting itself ready to hit.

"Hanan, get on the radio," Kosta said. "Warn everyone there's a radiation surge coming."

"Right," Hanan said, reaching for the comm section of his board.

He never got there. Without warning, the eerie silence was shattered by a sudden violent burst of gamma-ray crackling.

The surge had hit . . . and the *Gazelle* was caught in the middle of it.

CHAPTER 26

Hanan screamed, a long, agonized wail almost inaudible above the violent sleet-storm of gamma-ray crackling that filled the control cabin. "What's happening?" Forsythe shouted over the din.

"Radiation surge!" Chandris shouted back. Ornina was at Hanan's side, fumbling under his shirt for the exobrace cutoff switches. Chandris reached for her restraints—

"Chandris, get us some rotation," Kosta called from behind her. "If you don't, the hull's going to get cooked."

Ornina found the switch, and Hanan collapsed trembling in his seat. "He's right, Chandris," Ornina shouted to her. "Do it."

Cursing under her breath, Chandris turned back and keyed in the command. The displays were unreadable through the multicolored snow that had suddenly appeared on them, and for a moment she wasn't sure whether or not the command had made it through. "You got it?" Kosta shouted.

"Hang on," she shouted back, trying to see through the snow on the displays. The numbers were still impossible to read, but she could feel her weight starting to increase. "Okay," she said. "Rotation's speeding up."

She turned back to Hanan. Ornina and Forsythe had gotten him out of his seat now and were supporting his weight between them. And the look on Ornina's face . . . "Ornina?"

Ornina turned a pale face to Chandris. "He's very bad," she said, her voice nearly lost in the gamma-ray noise. "We've got to get him to the medpack right away."

"I'll help you," Chandris said, popping her restraints.

"No," Forsythe said sharply. "We can handle him. You and Kosta get us out of here."

"But—"

"Don't argue!" the High Senator snapped. "You want to end up like that other ship?"

Chandris swallowed, the image of the burned and battered *Hova's Sky-archer* flashing through her mind. "We'll try. Kosta, get up here."

"Right." Kosta scrambled past the others and dropped into Hanan's seat. "What's working?"

"I'm guessing the major control lines are okay," Chandris told him, tog-gling through the *Gazelle's* sensor packs. "They've got a lot of redundancy and extra shielding. But I can't get anything out of the sensors."

"Burned out," Kosta grunted. "That, or the data lines are down."

"Must be the lines," Chandris agreed. "I don't get any response from the feedback register circuits, either."

"You don't need registers to fly the ship," Kosta pointed out impatiently. "If the control lines still work, fire up the engines and get us out of here."

"Yeah, well, there's just one problem," Chandris snarled. Her throat was beginning to hurt from the need to keep shouting over the gamma-ray noise. "I don't know where Angelmass is anymore."

"Is that a problem? We were heading more or less toward it. Just turn around and go."

"We could; except that with the registers gone I won't be able to tell when we've done a one-eighty." Or maybe it wasn't just the shouting that was hurt-ing her throat. Maybe it was plain, simple fear. "You said yourself that the *Hova's Skyarcher* must have gone in pretty deep."

For a long minute the only sound in the control room was the roar of the gamma-ray static. Chandris kept toggling through the sensor packs, searching for something—anything—that could still be read. But it was all uniform snow. "What about the ship's inertial nav equipment?" Kosta asked. "Does it have an external case display?"

Chandris had to search her memory of the *Gazelle's* spec manual. "It's got one, but you have to get the cover off to get to it. I don't think we've got enough time."

Out of the corner of her eye she saw Kosta suddenly hunch over Hanan's board. "Wait a minute," he called. "I've got an idea. Check your VK-5 display."

She keyed for it. It was the same pattern of colored snow that was on all the others. "So?"

"Keep watching. The static should increase and decrease, with about a half-minute period."

She glared at the display, wondering what game Kosta was playing. But he was right. It was tricky to see, but the cycle was definitely there. "Okay, it's there. So?"

"That's the feed from my experiment package," he told her. "It's tied into one of the command lines, so we can still get data from it."

And the highest intensity snow would be when the package was pointing at Angelmass . . . "Doesn't help," she shook her head. "Not enough. We could wind up running lateral to Angelmass instead of away from it."

"Hang on, I'm not done," Kosta said, clearly working this out as he talked. "Okay. We're already rotating around our centerline; so what we do now is put a slow dual-yaw rotation on the ship and watch the display. The sensor cluster I'm tied into is in the bow, and it's also recessed a little. That means the only time the snow pattern will be steady will be when we're pointing away from Angelmass. Right?"

Chandris thought about it. "It sounds like it could take awhile. I don't know if we've got that much time to spare."

"It's that or risk running us in closer," Kosta countered. "You have a better idea?"

"If I come up with one, I'll let you know," Chandris gritted, keying in a dual-yaw command. "All right, here we go. Keep watching."

She could sense the slight change in inner ear pressures as the *Gazelle* began its sluggish midpoint rotation. On her display the snow continued its barely detectable rise and fall. Distantly, she wondered if they really had a chance, or whether the radiation from Angelmass would burn out their control lines—and them—before they could figure out which direction was the safe one.

Wondered if Angelmass had already killed Hanan.

"I think it's starting to even out," Kosta called.

Chandris peered closely at the display, the stuttering lights hurting her eyes. Maybe; but with all that background gamma-ray sparking it was hard to tell. If there were just some way to block off some of the radiation coming through the hull . . .

Maybe there was. Reaching for her board, she keyed in a command. "Keep watching," she ordered Kosta.

For a single heartbeat nothing happened. Then, just for a few seconds, the snow on the displays faded a little. The pattern she'd been trying so hard to see was suddenly right there—

"That's it!" Kosta shouted. "We're there. *Go!*"

Chandris jabbed at her board; and the scream of the gamma-ray crackling was joined by the deeper roar of the drive. "You sure?" she shouted to Kosta.

"Positive," he called back. "I was able to get a halfway clear look at the numbers during that dip in the static. What did you do, anyway?"

"Dumped all our drinking water and half our fuel," she told him. "I thought it might block some of the gammas."

"Shouldn't have worked," Kosta said. "Not enough mass there to make a visible difference. Can't argue with success, though."

And on his last word, as abruptly as it had begun, the surge was over.

For a minute Chandris just looked at Kosta, her ears ringing with the sudden silence. A stray gamma-ray spark crackled, sounding almost friendly in comparison to what they'd just been through. "I didn't think we were going to make it," Kosta said at last.

"Me, neither," Chandris said, wondering vaguely at her willingness to admit such a thing in front of Kosta.

Kosta held her eyes a moment longer. Then, looking almost embarrassed, he turned back to his displays. "Did we take any damage?"

Chandris was turned halfway back to her own displays when it hit them simultaneously. "Hanan!" Chandris got the word out first.

Kosta was already poking uselessly at the intercom. "Not working," he said tightly. "Go—I'll watch things here."

"Right." Chandris popped her restraints and slid out of her chair—

And came to a sudden stop. Forsythe was at the door, a grim expression on his face. "You need to get on the radio right away," he told her, handing her a data cyl. "Call Central and tell them we've got an EmDef blue-three emergency—here are the authorization codes. They're to give you a priority catapult back to Seraph."

Chandris's heart skipped a beat. "Hanan?"

Forsythe nodded. "He's still alive, but not by much. Something to do with his exobraces—I'm not sure what. Ornina says it's critical that he get back to ground medical facilities as soon as possible."

Chandris spun around and climbed back to Kosta's seat. *Not Hanan,* she pleaded silently. *Please.* "The radio?" she breathed.

"Starting to come back," Kosta said, his voice as grim as Forsythe's as he took the cyl. "Go on. I'll make the call as soon as I can get through."

"All right." Taking a deep breath, unlocking suddenly stiff knees, she headed for the door.

"Blue-three," Forsythe reminded Kosta as Chandris came up to him. He looked down into her eyes, just for a second—"And if they give you any trouble, you put my name on it. Understand?"

He looked at Chandris again. "Come on. I'll take you to him."

The proximity alarm on the *Komitadji* trilled its warning. "Catapult remote: launch when ready," Commodore Lleshi ordered. The paraconducting underskin gave its usual stutter of protest; and abruptly, the stars vanished from the viewscreens.

After all these months in the middle of nowhere, the *Komitadji* was going home.

Lleshi gave his displays a quick check, but it was more from habit than anything else. The *Komitadji* had been ready for this flight for a long time.

"Breakout in five seconds," the helmsman announced. "Three, two, one—"

The stars came back. "Position check," Lleshi ordered.

"Position computed, Commodore," the navigator said a minute later. "We're just under three million kilometers from Scintara."

Lleshi nodded. Considering that they'd started nearly seven hundred light-years away with an essentially untested catapult, they were lucky to have gotten even this close. "Compute course for Scintara," he said. "Engage when ready. And get a comm laser on the planet; let them know we're here."

"They already know, Commodore," the comm officer spoke up. "Message coming in."

Lleshi keyed his board, and a moment later a familiar face appeared on his screen. "This is Captain Horvak aboard the Pax Warship *Balaniki*," he said. "Repeat: Captain Horvak calling Commodore Lleshi."

"We've acknowledged, Commodore," the comm officer said.

Lleshi nodded, mentally counting off the twenty seconds it would take for the signal to make the round trip. He'd reached twenty-one when Horvak's face changed. "Welcome back, Commodore," he said briskly. "You're the last to arrive—the rest of the task force has been assembled for nearly a week now. Everything seems to be go; we got a kick pod from the *Skean* two days ago with the cocoon's confirmation that it's built itself a hyperspace net. At least it thinks it has," he amended. "I suppose we won't find out for sure until we try to use it. Final green light came from the Supreme Council yesterday, along with the usual spate of last-minute amendments to the plan. Nothing major— I'll dump you a copy."

His lip twitched. "And the doomsday pods are here, sitting under heavy guard in far orbit. That's making us very popular with the people of Scintara.

"That's about it from this end, unless you have any questions. If you can give us your ETA and status report, we'll set up the operation count-down."

"Navigation?" Lleshi invited.

"ETA will be a little over thirty hours, sir," the navigator said. "Plus probably an hour for orbit insertion. We're too low on fuel to make more than a tenth-gee acceleration."

Lleshi glanced at the proposed course profile on his board. "How much can we cut that by having Scintara send out a fuel ship to rendezvous with us?"

Across the balcony, Telthorst stirred. "There's no need for that, Commodore," he said. "A few hours' savings isn't worth the effort of sending out a fuel ship."

Lleshi glared at him. First that power-play nonsense about moving their catapult halfway across the solar system, and now this. "You heard Captain Horvak," he said, keeping his voice as civil as he could. "The task force is waiting. *Has* been waiting, for a week."

"Then a few hours one way or the other isn't likely to make a great deal of difference to them," Telthorst countered coldly.

Lleshi turned away from that thin face, resisting the urge to push the exchange into a full-fledged argument. He should have expected Horvak's mention of the four doomsday pods to spark this kind of reaction from Telthorst. With two hundred kilograms of painstakingly created antimatter in each pod—an explosive yield theoretically in the gigaton range—they represented a huge expenditure of Pax money. But there was no way around it. The four hyperspace nets that sealed off all approaches to the Lorelei system had to be taken out if this attack was to accomplish anything at all.

And given the Empyreals' fancy sandwich-metal construction this was the only method that the experts had come up with that had a chance of doing that.

But Telthorst undoubtedly didn't see it that way. Until the assets of the Empyrean lay open before him, he would see nothing but how much this whole operation was costing.

He probably hadn't even gotten around to considering the danger the pods in their current positions represented to the people of Scintara. Except, perhaps, for how much an accidental detonation would cost to repair.

"Inform the *Balaniki* we'll be arriving at Scintara in approximately thirty hours," he instructed the comm officer quietly. "Mission refitting will begin at that time."

"Yes, sir," the comm officer said, and turned back to his board.

Lleshi leaned back in his seat. Someday, he told himself silently, the Adjutors would overreach themselves. They would push the rest of the Pax just that little bit too far and bring destruction down upon their own heads.

He could only hope that he would be there to see it.

CHAPTER 27

The Seraph catapult had called in the report while the *Gazelle* was on its way down, with the result that an ambulance was already waiting when Chandris set the ship down on the landing strip. An ambulance, and a dozen reporters.

"Uh-oh," Kosta muttered under his breath as he eyed the latter group.

"What?" Chandris growled as the ship rolled to a stop. She'd mentioned earlier that this was the first time she'd ever landed the *Gazelle* on her own; but if she'd found the prospect daunting, Kosta hadn't been able to see it in her face during the approach. Then, as now, her single-minded obsession with Hanan's condition had left no room for anything as trivial as nervousness.

"Those reporters," Kosta said. "The High Senator didn't want anyone knowing he was here."

"Nurk the High Senator," Chandris said shortly, releasing her restraints. "Stay here and watch things—I'm going to open the hatchway."

She all but ran to the door, nearly bowling Forsythe over as he·stepped into the control room. A muttered word that might have been an apology, and she was gone.

"How is Hanan?" Kosta asked.

"Not good," Forsythe said, walking over to Chandris's vacated seat and sitting down. He looked tired. "He doesn't seem to be in any immediate danger, though."

"Any idea what's wrong?"

"Some kind of neural feedback through his exobraces, I assume. Beyond that, I haven't a clue."

Kosta nodded soberly. "I know the feeling. Oh, your cyl's still there in the comm panel. Thank you."

"No problem," Forsythe said, pulling it out and dropping it into his pocket. "You have no idea what's causing these surges, do you?"

Kosta shook his head. "What happened out there is theoretically impossible. At least, by any theory I've ever heard." He threw Forsythe a sideways look. "And it's getting worse."

The High Senator was gazing at the hatchway display and the medics busily preparing their equipment. "You're saying the surges are getting stronger?"

"I meant the whole thing is getting worse theoretically," Kosta said, wondering if he should be telling Forsythe this. The numbers he'd pulled were still highly preliminary, particularly given that they'd been recorded in the middle of that surge.

But if they were right . . . "You remember when we saw the *Hova's Sky-archer* I said that it must have gone pretty deep toward Angelmass to have gotten that much radiation damage?"

Forsythe nodded. "Hanan agreed with you."

"Right," Kosta said. "I've pulled the records from the *Gazelle*'s inertial navigational system and compared them to the position data from Angelmass Central's beacons. There's a definite discrepancy between the two."

"So the inertial data is wrong."

"I wish it was that simple," Kosta said. "The problem is that during the surge the beacons show us moving closer to Angelmass while the inertial system shows us moving *away* from it. A drive misfire wouldn't have done that. Neither would the maneuvering jets or the solar wind."

"Which leaves what?"

"Only one thing I can think of. Gravity."

Forsythe frowned. "I don't follow."

"I'm not sure I do, either," Kosta admitted. "But it's the only scenario I've come up with that fits the data. The small test masses in the inertial nav system would respond much faster to a sudden increase in Angelmass's gravitational attraction than the *Gazelle* itself. And since the test mass movement would be inward, the system would interpret it as an acceleration *away* from Angelmass."

Forsythe gazed hard at him. "You realize what you're saying?"

Kosta nodded, meeting the other's eyes with an effort. "That the radiation surge was accompanied by a similar surge in gravitational attraction."

"Which I presume is theoretically impossible?"

Kosta nodded again. "Extremely so."

Forsythe held Kosta's eyes another moment, then turned back to the hatchway display. Chandris and Ornina were visible there, standing helplessly back out of the way as the medics got Hanan's stretcher into the ambulance. "Is there any way to get independent evidence?"

"I think so," Kosta said. "If Angelmass's gravitational field was somehow being polarized toward the *Gazelle,* then the other hunterships operating around it should have registered a drop in gravity at their positions. Not a big one—the *Gazelle* didn't get all that much of a boost. But again, it'll show up as a discrepancy between their inertial systems and the beacons. And it ought to be measurable."

"Can you get copies of those records?"

"Yes, but not for a while," Kosta said. "Most of the hunterships will be staying out for at least a couple more days, and the Institute won't get their record-ings until they return to Seraph."

Forsythe nodded slowly. "Perhaps Central can get them faster. They could contact the hunterships directly, pull copies of their data, and then laser it all back here."

"It won't hurt to ask, anyway," Kosta agreed.

"I'll see what the government center can do," Forsythe said. "You'll be at the Institute later?"

"Ah—yes," Kosta said, frowning. From the way the High Senator had talked earlier—for that matter, the whole reason he'd been aboard the *Gazelle* in the first place—

Forsythe might have been reading his mind. "There's no way I can keep my presence on Seraph a secret anymore," he told Kosta. "Aside from all this, I need to take Ronyon to the hospital and have him checked over."

Kosta felt a twinge of guilt. Preoccupied first with the *Gazelle* and then with Hanan, he'd completely forgotten Ronyon's near-collapse before all this had started. "Yes—Ronyon. How is he?"

"Resting in his cabin," Forsythe said. "He seems to have gotten over that panic attack, though that could just be the sedative Ornina gave him. I'll col-lect him and we'll get off."

Behind them, the door opened and Chandris walked in. "How is he?" Kosta asked her, glancing at the hatchway display in time to see the ambulance drive off.

"He's all right for now," she said tiredly. "Whether he's going to stay that way they don't know yet. I've got to get the ship off the strip and back to the yard."

"I'll get out of your way, then," Forsythe said, standing up. He glanced at the hatchway display, now showing free of reporters, and moved toward the door. "Mr. Kosta, I'll contact you at the Institute."

He left, the control room door sliding shut behind him. "What was that all about?" Chandris asked as she began shutting down the *Gazelle*'s systems.

"Something strange is happening with Angelmass," Kosta told her. "I don't think I should talk about it right now."

"Fine with me," Chandris said, her thoughts clearly elsewhere. "So you two are getting together later?"

Kosta opened his mouth . . . closed it again. It had been a perfectly casual question, asked in a perfectly casual way. But this was Chandris, and he was slowly learning that with Chandris you always had to look beneath the surface. And in this case, below the surface meant— "You still gunning for that angel?"

She turned to look at him, her eyes suddenly hard and cold and far older than they had any right to be. "Don't get in my way, Kosta," she said quietly. "I mean that."

"Stealing Forsythe's angel isn't going to solve anything," he said. "All it'll do is get you in trouble."

"Only if I get caught," she countered. "Anyway, why do *you* care if I get in trouble?"

"I don't know," he shot back. "Probably because you'll drag Hanan and Ornina down with you, and I don't want them getting hurt. That's not why I'm here."

For a long moment Chandris just looked at him, an unreadable expression on her face. "Look," she said at last. "They need money. Desperately. What do you expect me to do, just sit around and watch them go under?"

"Of course not," Kosta said. "But there has to be some other way to raise money than by stealing Forsythe's angel."

"How?" Chandris demanded. "Sell something? Look around you—they haven't got anything of value. Except—never mind."

"Except what?" Kosta asked.

Her lip twisted in obvious annoyance with herself. "They've got a second angel stashed away in the storage room," she said. "But don't tell them I told you—no one's supposed to know about it."

Kosta frowned. "They've got a second angel? Why haven't they sold it?"

Chandris shrugged. "Maybe it helps them stay on good terms with each other. I asked you once whether angels could do that kind of thing, remember?"

Back when they'd first run into each other at the Institute. "Yes," Kosta murmured, his thoughts racing. A spare angel . . . "How long have they had it?"

"A couple of years at least. Maybe more. Why?"

Kosta shook his head. "Just curious."

From somewhere forward of them came a dull thud. "That's the tow car connecting up," Chandris said, turning back to her board. "You've got about two minutes to get off if you don't want to ride all the way back to the Yard."

Kosta shook himself out of this thoughts. "Right," he said, getting to his feet. "I'll be in touch."

"I'll be at the hospital later if you need me," she told him distractedly, her attention back on her work.

"Okay."

He paused at the door and looked back at her. A spare angel. A spare angel, moreover, that had spent a good deal of time since its capture in the vicinity of Angelmass. "Say hello to Hanan and Ornina for me," he added to Chandris before ducking out into the corridor.

Because there was a good chance he wouldn't make it anywhere near the hospital himself tonight. A very good chance indeed.

The *Gazelle's* service yard was dark when Kosta returned that night, in marked contrast to several nearby yards whose outside lights were blazing brightly as huntership crews worked to prepare for early-morning launches. The *Gazelle* itself was sealed, but that was no problem: on that first trip out, Ornina had given him the combination for the exterior lock.

Inside, it was even darker than the yard outside, with only the dim night panels giving a ghostly glow to the corridors. For a long moment Kosta stood just inside the hatchway, listening for sounds of life. But there was nothing. Obviously, Chandris and the Daviees were still at the hospital.

Alone or not, though, his training had been very specific on the proper procedures involved in breaking and entering. Slipping his shocker from his pocket, he adjusted it for a wide field of fire and got it nestled inconspicuously across his right palm with his thumb resting on the firing stud. With the angel box he'd borrowed from the Institute in his other hand, he headed for the storage section at the bottom of the ship, wishing his heart wouldn't pound so loudly.

But the flowing adrenaline was all for nothing. He saw no one and heard nothing along the way, and he reached the storage room without incident. Here, as everywhere else, only the night panels were on, their faint light throwing dark fuzzy shadows everywhere. Lowering the angel box to the deck, he reached for the wall switch—

"Don't bother," Chandris said from his left.

—and even as he spun toward the voice a dazzling light flared to life in front of him.

He squeezed his eyes shut, automatically throwing his left arm up to protect his face from the glare. "Chandris?" he called. "Come on, it's me. Jereko."

"I know," she said, her voice icy. "I was expecting you. I figured telling you about the Daviees's spare angel this afternoon would flush you out."

Kosta winced. He'd done it again. The great Pax spy, making a thorough mess of it.

And, naturally, making a mess of it because of Chandris. "I'm not here to steal the angel," he said, trying to keep his voice steady. "I just need to borrow it overnight to run some tests."

"What, the Institute's run out of angels?" she countered sarcastically.

"Theirs aren't any good for this," Kosta told her. "I need one that's spent a lot of time near Angelmass."

"They've all done that. That's where they come from, remember?"

"That's not what I mean," Kosta insisted. "Look, can't we sit down and talk about this?"

"Stay where you are," she said sharply. "I've got a cutting torch, and I'm not afraid to use it. You give me trouble and I'll slice you in half."

Kosta frowned at the shadow behind the light. "What in the world has gotten into you, Chandris? Come on—you know me."

"Do I?" she demanded. "Or do I just know the role the Pax taught you to play for us?"

And there it was. The moment Kosta had been dreading ever since his ship and the cocoon had been blown out of the *Komitadji*'s cargo hold into Empyreal space. "It's not a role," he said, a part of him marveling at his own unexpected calm. After all the worrying and nightmares, the actual event had become anticlimactic. "I really am a researcher. They just sort of maneuvered me into this job."

"What's *that* supposed to mean?"

"It means they came by one day and hauled me out of school," Kosta told her. "Said they needed someone with my expertise to find out what the angels were and how they were affecting the people of the Empyrean. They said the angels were an alien invasion, and that if we didn't stop it both the Empyrean and the Pax would be taken over and destroyed. I guess they convinced me that I could keep that from happening." He shrugged uncomfortably. "Maybe I convinced myself."

"You still believe that?" Chandris asked. "The invasion part, I mean?"

"I don't know," Kosta admitted. "A week ago I would have said no. Now . . . I don't know." He gestured to the angel box beside him. "That's why I need to borrow the Daviees' angel."

"Is this test of yours important?"

"Very important. Possibly even critical."

"Then why don't you just shoot me and take it?"

Kosta felt his stomach curl up inside him. He'd completely forgotten about the shocker pressed against his right palm. "I didn't think you could see it from there," he said between suddenly stiff lips.

"I know what it looks like when someone's palming something," Chandris said. "You haven't answered my question."

Kosta swallowed, his heart suddenly pounding in his ears. She was right, he realized. At this range, with the shocker still set for wide field, a single shot would take out the light, the cutting torch, and Chandris herself.

A simple, casual tap on the firing stud, and he would be free. He could take the angel, run his tests, then escape back across the Empyrean to Lorelei. There he could hide; and when the *Komitadji* returned he would be able to face them all with the knowledge that he had succeeded beyond all their expectations. Even Telthorst would have to wipe that smirk off his face then.

He squinted past the light, to where Chandris waited silently with her torch. A torch she could have fired, but didn't . . . and belatedly it dawned on him that she was running a test of her own here. A test just as critical as the one he had planned for the Daviees' angel.

"I didn't come to the Empyrean to kill people, Chandris," he said quietly as he set the safety on the shocker. Dropping the weapon on the floor, he kicked it her direction. "I came here to help."

For another minute the room was quiet. Then, to Kosta's surprise, the light dazzling his eyes went out. "The light switch is beside the door," Chandris said.

Kosta found it and flicked it on. Behind the light stand she'd rigged up, Chandris was standing by the storage room wall. There was no sign of any cutting torch. "What's this test you want to run?" she asked.

Kosta glanced down. The shocker was still lying on the deck where he'd kicked it. "I want to measure the angel's mass," he said, looking up again. "I think it may help us figure out what's happening to Angelmass."

"You mean with these surges?"

"The surges, and a theoretically impossible shift in its gravitational field," Kosta said. "That's what I was talking to High Senator Forsythe about after we landed."

"You know what's going on?"

"I've got an idea," Kosta said grimly. "I hope I'm wrong."

For a long moment she studied him. Then, abruptly, she nodded. "All right. But you have to promise the angel won't be damaged."

"There's no danger of that," Kosta assured her. "None of the tests I want to run will hurt it."

"And I have to be with the angel at all times." Reaching down, Chandris picked up the shocker. "Here—put this away somewhere," she said, tossing it to Kosta.

He almost fumbled it in his surprise. "Don't you want to keep it?" he asked. "I mean, as a guarantee of my good behavior?"

She snorted. "Good behavior be nurked. If you think I'm going to risk getting caught with a Pax weapon on me, you're crazy." She brushed past him. "Come on—the angel's in a carrying case in my room. You've got three hours to do your tests."

CHAPTER 28

On the display screen Kosta's friend Gyasi straightened up from the big shiny box and busied himself for a moment with an inset keyboard. He watched it another moment, then turned and gave a thumbs-up signal to the monitor camera before walking out of its range. "Okay, he's got it running," Kosta said, half under his breath. "We'll know in a few minutes."

Chandris nodded, looking at the big box still centered on the screen, and the other equipment stacked on the table behind it. All that, just to measure the weight of a tiny little angel. "How much smaller than the other angels do you think it'll be?"

He sighed. "I don't know," he said. "According to everything we think we know about quantum theory it shouldn't have lost *any* mass. By definition, a quantum is as small as that particular package can be. Unless Dr. Qhahenlo's quantum bundle theory is right. But I've never really liked the mathematics she used to cook that one up."

"So who decided it had to be a quantum?"

"It's a subatomic particle with a mass in the quadrillions of AMUs," he said. "Nothing that big has any business being stable unless it simply can't break down into smaller pieces."

"So who decided it had to behave like everything else you've ever found?" she persisted. "And don't give me any of that 'if you were an expert you'd understand' crapsy."

"I wasn't going to," Kosta said. But he was staring hard at the display, his forehead furrowed with concentration. "I wish I knew, Chandris. But I don't. I'm not sure I know anything at all."

She thought about that, watching him out of the corner of her eye. "Your masters aren't going to be very happy with you, are they?" she commented at last.

He snorted in derision. But even as he did, the vague demons swirling across his face seemed to recede a little. "I'm beyond caring what they think of me," he said. "What gave me away, if you don't mind my asking?"

She snorted. "What *didn't* give you away? You might as well have hung a sign around your neck saying you didn't belong here. That background story you spun for Hanan and Ornina was part of it. Too good and too well-memorized for an amateur con man, but without the flair a professional would have put into it."

Kosta nodded. "I could tell there was something about it that bothered you. I guess my trainers didn't expect me to run into someone with your expertise."

"But it was that snide comment you made about aphrodisiacal perfumes that finally cracked me into you," Chandris went on. "I'd never heard of anything like that, but I didn't get around to checking up on it until tonight. Turns out they don't exist. At least, not in the Empyrean."

"Aphrodisiacal perfumes," Kosta said ruefully. "I don't even remember making that comment."

"You did. Trust me."

"Oh, I believe you," he said. "I'm not all that surprised I did, either. Too much information was the number-one fatal error on my trainers' list. Given the rest of my record, it was inevitable I'd trip over the most amateurish mistake in the book."

Chandris was still trying to come up with a response to that one that wouldn't sound too sarcastic when the door opened behind them and Gyasi came in. "Anything?" he asked, nodding toward the computer display.

"Not yet," Kosta told him, leaning forward and tapping a key. "Still working the baseline."

"This mass tracer's always been a little slow," Gyasi said as he slid into the chair beside Kosta. "While we wait, you might want to take a look at the package that just came in for you."

Kosta sat up straighter in his seat. "The huntership data from High Senator Forsythe?"

"I didn't see a name on it," Gyasi said. "Sending address was Angelmass Central, though. I wasn't sure if your files would be accessible, given your funding freeze, so I dumped it into one of mine. You want me to pull it up for you?"

"Please."

Gyasi swiveled a terminal over and keyed in a command. "So this is from a High Senator, huh? I swear, Jereko, you're getting more interesting stuff done since your funding froze than you ever did when things were purring along."

"You have no idea," Kosta said, hunching a little closer to the display. "Here it comes."

Chandris frowned at the screen. A fuzzy ball made up of short multicolored vector lines had appeared in the center, rotating slowly around its vertical axis. "I was right," Kosta said softly. "Damn. I was right."

"About what?" Chandris asked, a creepy sensation sending a shiver through her. Kosta's demons seemed to be contagious. "What is all that?"

"It's a global vector map of Angelmass's gravitational shifts during that last radiation surge," Kosta told her. "Those shifts go clear across the board."

"I don't believe this," Gyasi breathed, his voice sounding awestruck. "Look at that scale—those decreases are up to a tenth of a percent in places."

Chandris's mind flashed back to the conversation aboard the *Gazelle*. "Could it be something statistical?" she asked. "You said the *Gazelle* didn't give you enough data points."

"There are more than enough data points here," Kosta said. "It's not a mistake, either. Or a malfunction, or—"

"Hang on," Gyasi interrupted, tapping the screen. "What's this coming up?"

A narrow cone of brightly colored red was becoming visible as the vector map rotated, a red cone with a thin white line down its center.

And suddenly Chandris felt her stomach trying to turn inside out. "It's the same picture," she identified it, her voice sounding strange in her ears. "The one you got when you plotted out the surge that killed the *Skyarcher*. The same picture exactly."

"It's close, anyway," Gyasi said cautiously. "We'd have to run a curve comparison to be sure."

"Don't bother," Kosta told him. His voice, Chandris noticed distantly, was trembling slightly. "If Chandris says it's the same, it's the same. And there it is—there; that blue point that the white line's cutting through. That's where the *Gazelle* was."

Gyasi shook his head. "This is insane, Jereko," he insisted. "A black hole hasn't got any internal structure. None. What possible theoretical mechanism could exist to explain something like this?"

"Angelmass isn't a normal black hole," Kosta said. "Not anymore."

Chandris eyed him closely. There was a tension around his eyes, a graveyard look to his face. "What do you mean, not anymore?" she asked.

A muscle in Kosta's jaw twitched. "I've got a theory. But you're not going to like it."

"More than I don't like impossible gravity fluctuations?" Gyasi countered. "Come on, let's hear it."

Kosta hesitated, then shook his head. "Let's wait on the mass reading," he said. "This is crazy enough that . . . no, let's just wait."

"I hate waiting," Gyasi declared, getting to his feet. "I'm going to go check on the tracer."

He left the room. "So which way are you hoping it goes?" Chandris asked.

Kosta rubbed his eyes. "I'm a scientist, Chandris," he reminded her. "We're not supposed to hope data goes one way or the other."

"Yeah," she sniffed. "Right."

"Besides, I'm not even sure it matters anymore," he conceded. "Whether angels are standard quanta or Dr. Qhahenlo's quantum bundles, *something* weird has definitely happened to Angelmass."

He gestured toward the row of computer terminals on the long lab table beside them. "I wish I could get into the files and check some of the details of her theory. I know it predicts some mass loss here, but I don't know how much."

"Can't you do the calculation on your own?"

"This isn't like looking up the mass of a hydrogen atom or calculating a force vector," he said. "The mathematics involved are way too complicated to do by hand. And with my funds frozen, I don't have access to the computers."

Chandris looked at the terminals. "You want me to get you in?"

He threw her a startled look; suddenly seemed to remember who it was he was talking to. "You can do that?"

"Probably," she said, swiveling the closest terminal over into easy reach. "Want me to try?"

For a pair of heartbeats he stared at her hands as they hovered over the terminal, a battle going on behind his eyes. She waited . . . "No," he said quietly, reaching over to take one of her hands away from the keyboard. "We can't risk getting caught. Not now."

His hand was cold and rigid; and as she held it, Chandris found herself looking into his face. Into those foreign eyes, into the dark tension behind them.

Earlier, waiting in the darkness of the *Gazelle*'s angel storage room, she'd thought a lot about whether confronting a Pax spy alone was really a smart thing to do. He'd persuaded her to give him the benefit of the doubt for now, but she'd been ready to chop and hop the second he showed what he was really up to.

But now, suddenly, she realized her mental preparations had been unnecessary. Kosta had no sinister private plan, because Kosta was exactly what he claimed to be: a simple academic who'd been thrown into the deep end of the tiger pit. "Don't worry," she said. "I'm not going to turn you in."

He shook his head, his gaze drifting outward into space. "I'm not worried about myself, Chandris."

"Then what—?"

She broke off as, behind them, the door opened and Gyasi came back in. "Well?" Kosta demanded, letting go of Chandris's hand.

"It should be finished," Gyasi said, crossing toward them. "See if you can pull it up."

"Right," Kosta said, punching at the keyboard as Gyasi slid back into the seat beside him. The numbers came up . . .

Gyasi muttered something under his breath. "There it is," he murmured. "You were right again, Jereko."

"It lost mass?" Chandris asked, running her eye down the numbers and trying to make sense of them.

"Mass and charge both," Kosta told her, his voice tight. "Almost three percent each."

"And it lost them right through the outer mass coating," Gyasi added. "You know, if the angel's breaking down, the mass loss ought to show up as high-energy particles leaking through the shell. Let me go see if there's a radiation detector setup free."

"Don't bother," Kosta said. "This isn't any spontaneous breakdown. The damage has already been done."

"Yes," Chandris murmured, a sudden ache in her heart as she stared at the numbers. She'd tried so hard to convince herself that the angel's presence hadn't been what had kept Hanan and Ornina working so peaceably together all these years. Apparently, that had been nothing but wishful puff-think.

"Chandris?"

She started out of her thoughts. Kosta was frowning at her. "What?" she said, turning her face away from him.

"It's not the Daviees who did this to it," he said quietly.

Did I say it was? the defensive retort bubbled automatically up into her throat. To her vague surprise, it stayed there. "Then who did?" she asked instead. "You? Me?"

"No," Kosta said. "Angelmass."

She turned back, half expecting to see something on his face that would show he was making some stupid joke. But his expression was deadly serious. "What do you mean, Angelmass? What does Angelmass have to do with it?"

"It's the source of the angels," Kosta said. "Hawking radiation, remember? A particle-antiparticle pair are created at the event horizon. One falls in, the other escapes outward."

"But there aren't any anti-angels," Gyasi objected.

"Yes, there are," Kosta said. His voice was firm, and just as serious as his expression. "We just haven't found them yet. But they're there."

He waved toward the display. "That alone proves it, as far as I'm concerned. Dr. Qhahenlo's theory allows for both quantum bundles and field effects, remember? Angelmass has a *huge* field—the corrosion of the Daviees' angel shows that much. If that field isn't being generated by an equally huge mass of anti-angels inside the black hole, where's it coming from?"

"Maybe from the Daviees?" Gyasi suggested. "I don't know these people. Maybe they're—" He waved a hand helplessly.

"What, evil incarnate?" Kosta scoffed. "Come on, Yaezon. Anyway, there's an easy way to check. Remember that mass murderer you've got on the grounds with the angel in his cell? When was the last time that angel was checked?"

Gyasi made a face. "It's checked every six weeks," he conceded. "You're right; if there'd been any change the whole Institute would have heard about it. But if there *are* anti-angels, why hasn't anyone ever seen them?"

"I don't know for sure," Kosta admitted. "But try this. An angel has a huge negative charge, which means that as soon as it's created it starts pulling positively charged particles to it."

"Which is what creates the matter shell," Chandris put in.

"Right," Kosta nodded. "And the most common positive particles out there are the protons and helium nuclei from the solar wind, plus heavier particles from Angelmass itself."

Gyasi muttered something startled sounding. "Of course. Of *course.*"

"Of course what?" Chandris demanded, looking back and forth between them.

"Anti-angels would be positively charged," Gyasi told her, his voice the sour tone of someone who's just failed a child's brain-tweaker. "That means they would be pulling mostly electrons. And electrons, being a lot lighter than protons, will get yanked in to it that much faster."

"Which means an anti-angel could go neutral so fast that your average huntership would never even see it," Kosta concluded.

"So simple." Gyasi shook his head. "You said you had a theory about Angelmass. Did it have something to do with possible structure?"

"I don't know," Kosta said. "Maybe."

"Well, spit it out," Chandris said.

Kosta braced himself. "What would you say," he said, "if I told you I think Angelmass has become sentient?"

For a long minute the only sound in the room was the humming of the computer cooling fans. "I'd probably say you'd been working too hard," Gyasi said at last. "Jereko, it's a *black hole*. A fruitcake would have more chance of spontaneously developing sentience than it would."

"Would it?" Kosta countered. "You're forgetting Che and his nine angels."

"Easy," Gyasi warned, jerking his head urgently toward Chandris. "We're keeping that quiet, remember?"

"Keeping what quiet?" Chandris asked.

"Che Kruyrov found that a cubic array of nine angels mimics a Lantryllyn logic circuit," Kosta told her. "That was a system that people once thought could form the basis for a fully sentient computer."

Chandris blinked. "So now your quanta of good have become quanta of sentience?"

"We don't know what it means," Gyasi said, looking pained. "But I'm sure it *doesn't* mean you can make a jump from a single Lantryllyn circuit straight to a sentient black hole."

"It attacks hunterships," Kosta said flatly. "It's done it twice, firing dead-on at moving targets."

"Maybe more than twice," Chandris said, staring at the white line as the image on the screen continued its slow rotation. "You said there were other radiation surges before the one that hit the *Hova's Skyarcher*. Were they all pointed at hunterships?"

"I don't know," Kosta said grimly. "We'll have to check on that. *And* it's had to alter its internal structure and even its gravitational field to do so."

"A black hole hasn't *got* an internal structure," Gyasi snapped.

"Then it's altered its event-horizon environment," Kosta said. "*I* don't know what the hell it's doing, or how it's doing it. But you can't deny it *is* doing *something*."

Gyasi snorted. "Next you're going to try to tell me this has some bearing on the increase in angel production you calculated."

"As a matter or fact, I'm sure it does," Kosta said. "Hawking radiation is caused by strong tidal forces at the event horizon. A side effect of Angelmass's gravitational and radiation surges could well be an increase in the number of angels it turns out."

Gyasi exhaled loudly, looking back at the display showing the rotating vector field. Kosta stirred, as if preparing to speak; Chandris touched his arm warningly, and he subsided.

"So what do we do?" Gyasi asked at last. "We put something like this on the net and we're going to have a lot of scared people out there."

"Agreed," Kosta said. "I was thinking of telling Director Podolak and a couple of others. Dr. Qhahenlo, certainly, and probably Che and Dr. Frashni, too."

"What are you going to use for data?" Chandris asked.

Kosta frowned at her. "What do you mean? The angel, of course."

"The Daviees' angel?" she asked pointedly. "The one it's illegal for them to have?"

"Yes, the—" Kosta broke off. "Illegal?"

"I looked it up earlier, while I was waiting for you to show," Chandris told him. "Angel hunters are required by law to turn in any angel they find."

Gyasi waved a hand impatiently. "Sure, but in this case—"

"No," Chandris said flatly.

"She's right," Kosta seconded. "They've got enough trouble right now, with Hanan in the hospital and a half-wrecked ship." He looked at Chandris. "Anyway, I promised we'd put the angel back when we were done testing it."

"Then what do we do?" Gyasi asked.

"We dig up some independent data," Kosta said. "Let's start by seeing if we can find evidence of anti-angels."

He reached for the terminal; checked the motion with a muttered curse. "Yaezon, if you would?" he said. "Check for me when the last time was anyone went out looking for one."

"We've done a complete bio-chemical analysis on Mr. Ronyon," the white-jacketed doctor said, punching keys on the nurses' station computer. "There are still remnants of the stress-created chemicals, but we can't find anything that might have triggered the stress itself. We're still waiting on the results of the neural scan, but I'm not expecting to find anything." He paused, just noticeably. "Aside from the obvious malfunctions in a brain like his, of course."

"Then what caused it?" Forsythe asked.

"I'm afraid I don't know," the doctor conceded. "Though with someone with Mr. Ronyon's congenital problems, I imagine things like this just happen every now and again."

"No," Forsythe said icily. "They don't."

The doctor blinked as he looked into Forsythe's eyes. What he saw there made him shrink back a little. "My apologies, High Senator," he said hastily. "I didn't mean it that way."

"This was not something random caused by his physical or mental disabilities," Forsythe continued in the same tone of voice. "Something happened to him out there. I want to know what."

The doctor bobbed his head nervously. "Of course, High Senator, of course. We'll do all we can."

"I expect nothing less." The woman manning the nurses' station, Forsythe noted peripherally, was puttering around in the back of her alcove, striving to look invisible. "When can I see him?"

"Ah . . . not until morning, I'm afraid," the doctor said. "I mean, you could see him, but he won't be awake until then. The neural scans require the subject to be sedated—"

"I understand," Forsythe cut him off. "I'll see you in the morning."

The doctor gulped. "Certainly. Until morning, then."

He turned and hurried down the corridor toward Ronyon's room and the examination room beyond. Forsythe watched him go, thinking quietly contemptuous thoughts in his direction. He disappeared through the doorway, and Forsythe turned around—

"You were a little hard on him, weren't you?" Pirbazari commented quietly.

"I'm not going to stand here and let him push off what happened on vague he-was-born-that-way excuses," Forsythe said tartly, moving away from the nurses' station. "Nothing like that has ever happened to him before. I want an explanation."

"I wasn't there, so I can't comment on what happened," Pirbazari said diplomatically. "I would merely suggest that jumping down the doctor's throat isn't going to help."

"The fear of God can do wonders for someone's motivation," Forsythe growled.

"Or else freeze them up completely."

"You let me worry about that," Forsythe said shortly. "What's happening with the Angelmass gravitational data?"

"It's been collected, compiled, and sent on to Kosta," Pirbazari said, his voice going a little grimmer. "And I'm no expert, but it's obvious even to me that something weird is going on out there. I've got a copy if you want to take a look."

"Later," Forsythe said, blinking his eyes a few times to moisten them. "What about the other matter?"

Pirbazari glanced around, making sure no one was in hearing range. "Slavis went through the local police records for the past few months," he said in a quiet voice. "No reported con games involving anyone even close to their descriptions."

Forsythe stroked his lower lip. "Interesting," he murmured. "Especially on the girl's part."

"You think she's gone straight?"

"Do you?"

Pirbazari shrugged uncertainly. "She *has* been working around angels."

"Tigers don't change their stripes, Zar," Forsythe said firmly. "Once a con artist, always a con artist. If she hasn't pulled anything since arriving on Seraph, it just means she's got something long-term in the works."

"Teamed up with Kosta?"

"That's the logical assumption," Forsythe agreed. "The problem is, what could it be? Something involving the Institute? Then why didn't they cut and run when we froze Kosta's account? That should have been a dead giveaway that we were on to them."

"Maybe it has to do with that huntership," Pirbazari suggested. "The *Gazelle*."

Forsythe shook his head. "That makes even less sense than an Institute con. I was on that ship, and there's nothing aboard worth stealing. At least, nothing that would require more than a lock-breaker and a TransTruck to haul the stuff away."

He paused as a sudden thought struck him. Turning on his heel, he retraced his steps back to the nurses' station. "May I help you, High Senator?" the duty nurse asked as he approached.

"I'd like you to pull up the record for Hanan Daviee," he said. "He came in the same time as my aide Mr. Ronyon."

"Yes, we all saw it on the news," the nurse murmured, pressing keys on her board. "Terrible situation . . . here it is. He suffered severe damage to his exo-braces, with feedback damage to his own neural system. He's currently stable, but weak."

"Prognosis?"

The corners of her mouth tightened as she scanned the listing. "He'll need to have some reconstructive work done on his spinal cord," she said. "How much he'll be able to recover will depend on how much work they can do."

"What are the limiting factors?" Pirbazari asked from Forsythe's side.

Her mouth tightened a bit more. "To put it crassly, money," she told him. "The work involved is complex and expensive. Very simply, the more he can afford, the more of a recovery he can make."

"I thought Gabriel paid for work-related health problems," Pirbazari said.

"Some of them, yes," the nurse said. "The entire hospital stay will be taken care of, for instance. But his long-term neural problems are congenital, not work-related, and they aren't covered."

"Thank you," Forsythe said, taking Pirbazari's arm and turning away. "Interesting," he commented as they headed down the corridor again. "Maybe you were at least partially right, Zar. The tiger may not change his stripes, but he may occasionally roll over and purr."

Pirbazari shook his head. "You've lost me."

Forsythe nodded back toward the nurses' station. "Our friend Mr. Daviee needs large amounts of money for an operation. Our other friend, Chandris Lalasha, is a lady whose profession is to separate people from large amounts of money. Coincidence?"

Pirbazari frowned. "Are you suggesting the Daviees hired her to get money for them?"

"Or else she's taken them on as a charity case," Forsythe said. "Either way, she still bears watching."

"All right," Pirbazari said, not sounding entirely convinced. "You want me to put the police onto her?"

Forsythe pursed his lips. "Not yet," he said slowly. "She may have ways of keeping tabs on what the police are up to. Let's just watch her ourselves for a couple of days."

"Both of us?"

"Yes," Forsythe said. "I've got an inside connection with these people; you're an outsider none of them know. Between us, we should have them pretty well covered."

"You're going to stay here yourself, then?" Pirbazari asked. "There's a lot of work waiting for you on Uhuru."

"There's enough I can do here," Forsythe said. "Try to catch up on my reading, for one thing. I'll send Slavis back—he can sit in on any meetings and take notes for me."

"He can't cast votes for you."

"There's nothing important coming up for at least two weeks," Forsythe said firmly. "At any rate, Ronyon's not going to be able to travel for another day or two at the earliest, and I'm not leaving without him."

He glanced into a deserted lounge alcove as they passed it, looking at the darkness outside the far windows. "Besides," he added quietly, "whatever Lalasha and Kosta are up to, they didn't cause what happened at Angelmass. Something strange is going on out there. I'm not leaving until I find out what."

CHAPTER 29

The equipment list came up, scrolling down the screen; and beside Kosta, Gyasi gave a low whistle. "Holy scud, Jereko," he said. "It's going to take all *that?*"

"Looks like it," Kosta conceded, a sinking feeling in the pit of his stomach as he ran his eye down the list. A couple of the items there he could probably sneak out for a few days without anyone noticing. But not all of them. Not a chance.

"What's that, your equipment list?" Chandris asked, swiveling around from the terminal she'd been working on.

"That's it," Gyasi confirmed. "And it might explain why no one's ever seen an anti-angel before. Half this stuff didn't even exist the last time anyone went out hunting for one."

"And it might as well not exist now for all the good it's going to do us," Kosta added sourly. "We're never going to be able to collect all this."

"Anyone ever tell you you give up too easily?" Chandris chided, coming over and standing over him, leaning forward to peer at the display. "The big question is whether we can fit it all aboard the *Gazelle.*"

"Is the *Gazelle* going to be able to fly any time soon?" Kosta countered.

"The damage assessment's mostly done," she said. "The refit's going to take some serious work, but it's nothing a good maintenance crew can't handle."

"Sure, but how long will it take?"

"That one *is* a problem," Chandris said reluctantly. "Maintenance hasn't even got it scheduled yet; but from the size of their current work list my guess is they won't get to it for at least a month. Maybe more."

Kosta shivered. "We can't afford to wait that long," he said. "Someone else is bound to get killed before then."

"Then our other option is to contract it out," Chandris said. "Get a private firm in to do the work."

"Can you do that?" Gyasi asked. "I thought Gabriel handled all huntership maintenance."

"Officially, it does," Chandris said. "As a practical matter, no one's going to complain if we do it ourselves and save them the expense."

"And how high is that expense likely to be?" Kosta asked.

Chandris's mouth twitched. "High enough," she said.

"*How* high?"

"You let me worry about that." She waggled a finger at his equipment list. "You worry about how you're going to smuggle all this stuff out of here and aboard the *Gazelle.*"

Kosta frowned up at her, a sudden suspicion twisting his stomach. The High Senator's angel . . .

She caught the look and sent back one of her own. "I said let me worry about it," she repeated, her tone warning him to drop it.

Gyasi cleared his throat. "I think I'll go to the lab and see what equipment Dr. Qhahenlo's got on hand," he said. Getting up from his chair, he escaped from the room.

"You can't steal Forsythe's angel," Kosta growled, swiveling around so that he could face Chandris better.

"Why not?" Chandris retorted. "Is one angel worth more than however many people Angelmass will kill in the next two months?"

"Of course not," Kosta ground out. "But if you get caught, the whole thing blows up and they die anyway." He hesitated. "And then you'll be in trouble, too."

Her lip twisted sardonically. "I didn't think you cared."

Kosta's first impulse was to turn away from her, to back off the way he always did. But for once, and to his own mild surprise, he stood his ground. "Of course I care," he said quietly. "I also care about Hanan and Ornina. They've put themselves on the line for both of us. We can't let them down."

Chandris drew herself up. "We won't," she said firmly. "How soon can you get that stuff together?"

Kosta looked at the list again. "I don't know," he said. "A couple of days, maybe."

"All right," Chandris said. "Let's call it three days. I'll have the *Gazelle* ready to fly by then."

Kosta looked up at her again. "Be careful," he said.

"I will," she assured him. "Don't worry, I know what I'm doing."

She waved toward the door. "Come on, let's go get the angel. I need to get started, and you probably need to walk me out."

They were waiting outside the main entrance for the line car Kosta had called before Chandris spoke again. "Something else occurs to me," she said, her face invisible behind her blowing hair. "You said that the increased angel production might be accidental, a side effect of the radiation surges. You suppose it could also be deliberate?"

Kosta felt his throat tighten. "You mean as in Angelmass figuring out that the more angels it spits out, and the more anti-angels it absorbs, the smarter it gets?"

She hunched her shoulders. "So you thought of that, too. That's not a good sign."

"I know," Kosta agreed soberly. "Of course, it could just mean we're both wrong."

"It could also mean we're both right," she said. "We'd better get the *Gazelle* flying, and fast."

Kosta looked up at the stars blazing across the night sky overhead. "Yes," he said. "Let's."

The news report was a repeat, the third time today that this particular item had been shown. But Trilling Vail didn't mind. He watched it anyway, fingers resting on the cool glass of the display, keeping the sound turned down low so as not to wake the sleeping girl in the bed behind him. The camera zoomed in on the ambulance, and the stretcher the medics were rolling toward it.

And there she was, standing with her arm clutched around a fat old woman as the stretcher rolled past. There she was, just as beautiful and fragile and helpless as ever.

Chandris.

Trilling pressed his fingers harder against the glass, hungrily drinking in the sight of her. He'd tracked her here to Seraph just fine; but then the trail had unexpectedly died away. No one he'd talked to had admitted working with her, or seeing her, or even hearing of her, no matter how hard he pressed them. One of the koshes had finally admitted he knew where she was, but after he was dead Trilling had found out he'd been lying, just to get him to stop. He hated when people did that to him.

But none of that mattered anymore. She was *here*. Half a planet away from where he'd ended up, but that was nothing. She was here, and he was here, and as soon as he could get transport over to Magasca they would be together again. And then they could stay here, or go back to Uhuru, or do whatever they wanted. They would be together again. It would be just like old times.

The news report ended, and he switched off the set. Quietly, stealthily, he moved through the darkness of the room, listening to the slow breathing of the sleeping girl as he collected his belongings together. It didn't take long; there wasn't much there, and anyway he could score whatever he needed along the way. The cash was a different matter, and he took all of that he could find, making sure not to forget to check the pockets of the girl's jeans hanging lopsidedly on the chair at the foot of the bed.

Finally, he was ready. He doubted any transports would be heading toward Magasca at this time of night, but it was a bit of a walk to the depot anyway, and he was eager to get started. Soon he and Chandris would be together again.

He zipped up his bag and stepped to the side of the bed. The girl was an amazingly sound sleeper, he realized, or else just couldn't hold her reeks very well. They hadn't been together long; it had only been about two weeks since he'd waltzed her off the streets and started teaching her the tricks of the trade. With her bright face and winning voice she had a lot of potential, and more than once he'd thought she would be worth hanging onto until he found Chandris.

But now that was over, of course. Setting down his bag, he leaned over the girl and got his hands around her throat.

She *was* a sound sleeper. She never even woke up before she died.

Trilling picked up his bag again and stepped to the door, feeling a twinge of regret. But he'd had no choice. He was a one-woman man, and Chandris was a one-man woman, and now that he'd found her there could never again be anyone between them. He'd had no choice.

Opening the door, not looking back, he headed out into the night.

CHAPTER 30

"Scintara Catapult Control calling, Commodore," the comm officer reported. "They signal green."

"Acknowledged," Lleshi said. It was, he reflected, almost a straight reenactment of the situation they had been in a few months back. The same jump-off point, the same target, the same enemy.

Except that then the mission had been a quick penetration into enemy territory to drop off the false asteroid and, almost as an afterthought, to throw the young academic Jereko Kosta to the wolves.

This time, the *Komitadji* was going to war.

It was a difference that was heavily underscored by the four bright orange spheres ahead of him in the launch queue, each being shepherded gingerly by its tugs toward the undulating focal point of Scintara's catapult. The doomsday pods, each with multiple gigatons of explosive power hovering restlessly in the center of its magnetic bottle. "Target position check," he ordered.

The nav display flickered once and changed to a schematic of the Lorelei system, with each of the four Empyreal nets scattered throughout the asteroid belt represented by a flashing red point. The new Pax net flashed yellow, the machinery buried deep within the asteroid waiting patiently for the burst of light and radiation that would be its signal to activate.

For a moment Lleshi studied the flashing yellow light. Even after several months of drift, the newly created net was uncomfortably close to the net that Pod Three would be popping into the center of in a few minutes. If the doomsday blast was powerful enough to damage it, this whole operation would suddenly become extremely problematic. The Pax ships would still penetrate Lorelei system; but at that point there would be nothing to stop five systems' worth of EmDef forces from descending on them like a swarm of hornets. The *Komitadji*'s task force wasn't set up for that kind of defensive action.

"Getting a little nervous, Commodore Lleshi?" Telthorst asked from his station. "Not quite as sure of this grand strategy of yours anymore, are we?"

"Prepare to launch Pod One," Lleshi ordered, ignoring him.

Telthorst apparently wasn't in an ignorable mood. "I asked you a question, Commodore," Telthorst said. His voice was still quiet, but there was the potential below it for more volume, the threat of taking the argument off the privacy of the balcony and down onto the full command deck. "In my experience, men who are sure of what they're doing don't keep checking everything over and over."

"In my experience, men who don't are fools," Lleshi said shortly. "SeTO?"

"All green, Commodore," Campbell confirmed. "Ship and crew at full battle stations."

"Commodore—"

"Mr. Telthorst, we are preparing for battle," Lleshi told him. "Either be quiet, or be removed to your quarters."

With a glare that could have flash-cooked raw meat, Telthorst swiveled back to his status boards. "Fleet status?" Lleshi called.

"The *Balaniki* and *Macedonia* have formed up on our aft flanks," the fleet operations officer said. "Support vessels are standing by in formation. All ships report green."

Lleshi nodded. Standard textbook attack procedure was to send a wave of fighters, blast ships, and mine-sweepers into a system ahead of the main war vessels, both to soften up the first wave of resistance and to have full tactical sensor data ready to download to the fleet commander when the flagship finally made its appearance.

But this was the *Komitadji*, and the *Komitadji* didn't hide behind support ships. Once the doomsday pods had done their job, they would be the first ship through.

A warning note trilled: the first pod was touching the catapult's focal ellipsoid, its tugs backing away from it with orderly haste. "Pod One ready," Campbell announced.

Lleshi nodded. "Scintara catapult, launch Pod One."

The pod flickered and was gone. "Move Pod Two into position," Lleshi ordered, glancing at the chronometer. "Ninety seconds."

The men in the tugs were good. Less than seventy seconds after Pod One had disappeared, Pod Two had been nudged into the edge of the ellipsoid. Twenty seconds later, it followed its brother into the void. Three minutes after that, Pods Three and Four had likewise been sent on their way.

The first phase was over. It was time now to see if all the time and effort—and yes, all of Telthorst's precious money—had indeed bought the Pax the foothold it coveted in Empyreal space. "Move us in, helm," he ordered, alternating his attention between the chrono and the nav display. If Pod Three had blown on schedule, the primary and secondary blast and radiation waves should have now washed over the Pax asteroid. The sensors there would have noted the event . . .

On the display, the flashing yellow light flicked to green. "Net activated," Campbell announced.

Lleshi shifted his full attention back to the chrono. Theoretically it had activated, anyway. Whether it had actually done so they wouldn't know until they reached Lorelei space.

"Commodore, the net is green," Telthorst prompted.

"I heard, thank you," Lleshi said.

"The energy wave front has passed the net," Telthorst persisted, an edge starting to creep into his voice. "We don't want to give them time to pull themselves together."

"I'm aware of the tactical considerations," Lleshi said, continuing to watch the seconds tick past. The explosion's main wave front would indeed be well past the asteroid by now, but there would also be slower but still dangerous debris expanding outward behind that front. He gave it a few more seconds, then nodded toward the comm officer. "Scintara Catapult, launch when ready."

The stars disappeared.

Automatically, Lleshi counted down the seconds, muscles tight with tension. If the scheme hadn't worked, the *Komitadji* would soon be going on yet another trip to the edge of nowhere. The stars returned . . .

The scheme had worked. Instead of the distant triangular-pyramid array of Empyreal catapult ships they'd encountered their last time into this system, there was only the false asteroid concealing their own net floating off their starboard stern.

"Incoming!" Campbell snapped.

Lleshi shifted his eyes to the tactical as the collision alert warbled across the bridge. But it was not, as first reflexes had assumed, an attack by survivors of the doomsday pod. It was, instead, a scattering of asteroid fragments sweeping like retreating soldiers across the sky. Three of the shards, according to the tactical, were on a direct course for the *Komitadji*.

It was far too late for the big ship to maneuver to avoid them. Gripping the arms of his chair, Lleshi braced himself; and with a thundering crunch of metal, the pieces slammed into the hull, shattering to gravel with the impact.

"Damage report," he called, peering at the hull monitors as the debris ricocheted off into oblivion. He needn't have worried. The *Komitadji* was the ultimate warship, with the ultimate elephant's hide to match. Even a high-speed encounter with bits of flying asteroid seemed to have done little more than dent the outer hull. "And locate the nearest blastpoint," he added. "Scan for enemy ships or bases."

"Damage report, Commodore," the comm officer called. "Partial collapse of Number One hull at three points in sectors A-22 and A-31; no breech. Light impact damage to Number Two hull in the same sectors; no reduction in structural integrity. Number Three hull unaffected. Four sensor nodes are out of commission; minor concussion damage to various pieces of equipment in portside locations."

"Acknowledged," Lleshi said, looking at the back of Telthorst's head. "I see we didn't wait at Scintara quite long enough, after all."

Telthorst didn't reply, or even bother to turn around. "Still," Lleshi couldn't resist adding as he turned back to the business at hand, "it's good to know the designers of the *Komitadji*'s hull spent their money well."

"I have the blastpoint now, sir," the sensor officer called.

Lleshi had seen the computer-projected results of a doomsday pod explosion several times, most recently during the planning sessions for this invasion. But he had never seen the actual aftermath of the weapon until now.

On a planet, it would undoubtedly have been an awesome vision of destruction and carnage; a strategic hydrogen warhead multiplied by a thousand. Here, in the middle of an asteroid field, the results were more subtle but just as real.

And, in their own way, just as horrible.

For a thousand kilometers around where the Empyreal net had been, space was empty. Completely and totally empty. Every solid object within that sphere, be it asteroid, sandwich-metal-hulled combat ship, or fragile human body, had been disintegrated down to its component particles. Outside that zone, everything else seemed to be in motion, with small chunks of rock hurling outward and even large asteroids now carrying a vector component away from the point of the blast. Each of the asteroids the telescope screen was able to get a clear view of seemed partially shattered or half melted.

"Move us out of the net area," Lleshi ordered the helm, feeling oddly ill. "What about Lorelei's kick-pod catapults?"

"There was one with each net," Campbell said. He sounded as awed as Lleshi felt, though there was no indication of the disquiet the commodore himself was feeling. "There's also the one near Lorelei itself."

The tactical display shifted to a projected schematic of the planet Lorelei, showing the small catapult in high polar orbit around it. Simultaneously, one of the telescope displays lit up with a slightly fuzzy real-time view. "The light from the nearest pod explosion will reach Lorelei in about three minutes," Campbell went on. "That will be the first they'll know about our attack."

And the enemy's first act ought to be to put a quick alert message together and get a kick pod out to that catapult. "Run a confirmation on the catapult location," Lleshi ordered. On one of the aft displays, the *Balaniki* flickered into view as it was caught in the Pax net. "What about the main catapult?"

"It's orbiting ahead of Lorelei in the planet's leading Lagrange point,"

Campbell said. "A pretty good distance out; they won't be able to get a ship there very quickly."

Provided there weren't any ships already on the way. But there was nothing Lleshi could do about that. Besides, with the Pax net now the only door into Lorelei system, it wasn't nearly as critical that word of the invasion be delayed.

Still, the more time they had to consolidate their position, the better. Reaching over, he punched his direct feed to the *Balaniki*. "Captain Horvak?"

"Yes, sir," Horvak replied briskly. "Thunderhead is loaded and ready, awaiting your orders. If the Empyreals are still on the same schedule, their most recent kick pod went out half an hour ago."

Which meant that if they could knock out the kick-pod catapult, it would be another five and a half hours before the other four Empyreal systems would even begin to suspect anything was wrong.

If. "You've received our up-to-date sensor readings?"

"Received and calibrated in," Horvak said. "We're aligned and green."

"Good." Lleshi shifted his gaze to the display showing the *Balaniki*. "You may fire when ready."

"Yes, sir. Thunderhead: *fire.*"

There was nothing to see, really; only a half-imagined flicker of movement just before the circle of warning lights around the opening in the *Balaniki*'s nose went out. But the sensor display showed what human eyes were too slow to catch: the slender black missile that had been launched from the mass driver running the entire length of the *Balaniki*'s centerline, now hurling toward the distant planet. Lleshi looked back at the main display, silently counting down the seconds; and abruptly, the missile's solid-fuel core ignited, burning with incredible ferocity and adding to the missile's already blistering velocity at an acceleration that would have crushed a human crew.

It would take the *Komitadji* over two days to reach Lorelei from here. The remnants of the Thunderhead missile would make that same trip in just under an hour.

At which point, if the sensor data and computer calculations were correct, the warhead would fragment into a cloud of ultrafast hundred-gram particles and slam into Lorelei's kick-pod catapult, shattering it and cutting off the Empyreals' fastest method of contacting the outside universe.

On a Pax world, Lleshi knew, confusion and sheer bureaucratic inertia would delay the launch of an emergency kick pod at least that long. On an Empyreal world, under angel influence, there was no way to know if the Thunderhead would be in time.

Or, for that matter, whether the Thunderhead would even hit its target. If it had been misaimed, or if unexpected gravitational or solar wind forces deflected it even slightly off its proper course, those hundred-gram weights could conceivably slam full into the planet Lorelei itself at a significant fraction of the speed of light.

And if they did, the destruction the doomsday pod had caused out here among the small number of EmDef defenders would be multiplied a thousandfold among the people of that world.

Innocent people. People whose salvation from the angel threat was the purported reason for this military activity in the first place.

"We're wasting time, Commodore," Telthorst said impatiently.

Unfortunately, this time the little man was right. The Thunderhead missile and Lorelei were now in the hands of the laughing fates. Whether or not the alert went out on the kick-pod catapult, the *Komitadji*'s next task was the same: to capture and secure the main catapult running in orbit ahead of Lorelei.

Preferably before the Lorelei government got its act together and got a ship up there and out of the system. But to capture and hold it nonetheless. "Acceleration alert," he ordered. "Lay in a minimum-time course for Lorelei."

And as the acceleration warning sounded and the big ship began to move, he wondered vaguely what had happened to Kosta.

The hospital corridor was quiet, its lighting slightly muted to late-night levels, as Chandris slipped in through the stairwell door. More importantly for her purposes, the area also seemed to be deserted.

No, not completely. There was a more brightly lit alcove area just off the center of the corridor behind a wide window-shaped service opening, and as she eased the stairwell door closed behind her she heard the faint sound of shuffling feet and papers.

Still, as long as she stayed at this end of the hallway—and as long as none of the duty nurses poked their heads out through the service window—she ought to make it okay. Moving as quietly as she could, she headed down the corridor, hugging the wall and trying to look all directions at once. It was a job more suited to a kitty-lifter than a lowly con artist like herself, and she was beginning to sweat by the time she reached her target door. Easing it open, she slipped inside.

The room lights had been turned completely off, but there was enough of a glow from the indicators on the various medical monitors for her to make out the outline of the big man lying motionlessly beneath the blankets. She was halfway across the room, concentrating on not finding anything to bang her shins on, when she spotted the other figure sitting half propped up in a chair beside the bed, clearly asleep. Hesitating only a moment, she changed direction and circled the end of the bed to the chair. She reached out to the other's shoulder, wondering belatedly if this had been such a good idea after all, and gently squeezed. "Ornina?" she whispered.

The woman awoke with a start. "What—?"

"Shh, it's all right," Chandris hastened to assure her. "It's just me, Chandris."

Ornina sagged tiredly in her chair. "Oh, Chandris, you startled me," she said with a sigh. "Wait, let me get the light."

"No, don't," Chandris said. "I don't want to wake up Hanan."

"It's all right," Hanan said from the bed. "I'm already awake."

Chandris grimaced. "I'm sorry," she apologized as Ornina groped for the small light on the bedside table and flicked it on. The glow was dim, but Chandris still blinked a couple of times before her eyes adjusted. "I was trying to be quiet."

"And you succeeded admirably," Hanan said, his voice as cheerful as always. But his face in the faint light was drawn and seemed to Chandris to be deathly pale. "I just don't sleep well in hospitals, that's all. Probably the food."

"We missed you here earlier tonight," Ornina said. "Visiting hours—" She squinted at her watch. "Aren't they over yet?"

"Long over," Chandris admitted, feeling even more uncomfortable about this intrusion. "And I wouldn't have bothered you so late at night except— look, I need some advice."

"You've come to the right place," Hanan said, nodding toward the other guest chair against the back wall. He did not, Chandris noted uneasily, raise a hand to point to it, as he normally would have. Not a good sign. "Pull up a chair and tell us all about it."

Chandris took a deep breath. "The reason I wasn't here earlier—"

She broke off as, behind her across the room, the door swung stealthily open and a figure slipped inside. She spun around, automatically scrambling for a cover story to tell the nurse—

"Ah," Kosta said lamely, his face a study in awkward surprise. "Uh—"

"Is it a party?" Hanan said cheerfully into Kosta's discomfiture. "I love parties."

"What are you doing here?" Chandris demanded.

"I'm sorry," Kosta said, sounding thoroughly chagrined now. "I'll go."

"No, please," Ornina said, getting up from her chair. "Here; sit down."

"No, no," Kosta said hastily. "I'll go. I just thought . . ."

The pieces suddenly clicked. "You thought I came here for Ronyon's angel, didn't you?" Chandris accused. "You followed me from the Institute."

Even in the dim light she could see Kosta's face redden. "Do you blame me?" he countered. "You tell me to trust you; and then you head straight here to the hospital. What was I supposed to think?"

"Whoa, everyone," Hanan cut in. "Could we get a little annotation on this argument? For starters, what do you mean, Ronyon's angel? Don't you mean High Senator Forsythe's angel?"

"Forsythe isn't wearing an angel," Chandris told him. "Ronyon's got it. I was thinking that since everything about that was illegal anyway, one good crime deserved another."

"Or to put it another way, she was planning to steal it," Kosta said. "She's been planning it as far back as the *Gazelle*."

"Oh, Chandris," Ornina said. The sorrow and disappointment in her voice was like a twisted knife in Chandris's stomach. "Please. Don't."

"I just wanted to find a way for Hanan to get well," Chandris said, hearing an unaccustomed note of pleading in her voice. "He needs it more than ever now."

"I'll be all right," Hanan assured her. "Really I will. The Gabriel Corporation's picking up the bill for all this, and the doctors say the long-term prognosis is hopeful."

"I don't want hopeful," Chandris said, the taste of bitterness in her mouth. "I want you well."

"I know," Hanan said, smiling sadly. "And I appreciate it, Chandris, more than you can ever know. But this isn't the way to do it."

"Maybe not," Chandris muttered. She still wasn't ready to let this drop, but there was no point in discussing it any further now. "But in the meantime," she added, looking pointedly at Kosta, "there's been another development."

"You're engaged?" Hanan asked hopefully.

Chandris snorted. "Hardly," Kosta said. "Mr. and Mrs. Daviee—"

"Hanan and Ornina," Ornina corrected him mildly.

"Mr. and Mrs. Daviee," Kosta repeated stubbornly, "I must inform you that I am an agent of the Pax, sent here to study Angelmass and the angels."

"Really," Hanan said. "And she's right, by the way: it's Hanan and Ornina."

Kosta frowned at him. "Did you hear me?" he asked.

"Of course," Hanan said, lifting his eyebrows toward Ornina. "Pax spy, here to study Angelmass."

"That's what I heard, too," Ornina confirmed, nodding. "Have you found anything interesting?"

Kosta looked at Chandris, clearly completely confused now. "Don't look at me," she told him with a shrug. "These are the same people who knew I was running from the cops when they hired me. They don't rattle easy."

"We have a secret weapon against the rattles," Hanan said with a conspiratorial grin. Against the backdrop of his strained face, Chandris thought, the grin looked forced. "So tell us. What have you found out about these angels of ours?"

CHAPTER 31

They were four hours on their way toward Lorelei when the first sign of resistance appeared.

"They appear to be mining ships, Commodore," Chief Sensor Officer Dahlgren said, peering back and forth between his displays. "About thirty of them, moving in on individual intercept vectors. The nearest ones have started tracking us. Looks like they've got fairly low-grade target acquisition systems, possibly something adapted from a mining sensor package."

"Weaponry?" Lleshi asked.

"Minimal," the other said. "The best they've got are medium-focus lasers, again probably adapted from standard equipment, plus some probe rockets with small, primitive warheads."

"How primitive?"

Dahlgren shrugged. "They're non-nuclear, just a few kilograms of high explosive each. Frankly, sir, they look almost handmade."

Lleshi exchanged frowns with Campbell. "Did he say primitive or pathetic?" Campbell asked. "What in the worlds do they think they're doing?"

"Maybe trying to distract us," Telthorst put in. "Ever think of that?"

Lleshi lifted his eyebrows to Dahlgren. "Lieutenant?" he invited.

"No other craft showing, in either inner or outer scan range," Dahlgren said. "And we're coming to the edge of the main asteroid mass, which means they're running out of places to hide. I suppose they could have mines planted on some of the rocks we haven't passed yet, but if so they're going to be pretty low-yield."

"And still only HE?" Lleshi asked.

"No radiation readings to indicate nuclear."

"I don't like it," Telthorst growled. "They can't just be sacrificing men and mining ships this way. I strongly recommend we launch fighters and engage them at a safe distance from the *Komitadji*."

Again, Lleshi and Campbell exchanged glances, this time looks of mutually strained patience. "That won't be necessary, Mr. Telthorst," Lleshi said. "The *Komitadji*'s defenses are quite capable of dealing with this threat."

"Unless it's a feint."

"It's not a feint," Lleshi said, feeling his temper beginning to strain. "This is the tactics of desperation; nothing more. The Empyreals are throwing whatever they have at us in an attempt to slow us down until they can bring real warships into the system."

"They almost certainly don't realize there's still a net left in the system and that we control it," Campbell added. "They'll be counting on defense forces from the other four systems being able to sweep in on us. With that assumption, any delaying action will seem reasonable to them, no matter what the cost."

"At any rate, dropping and regathering fighters would take time I'm not willing to waste," Lleshi concluded.

"What's the hurry?" Telthorst asked. "As you say, there's nothing the Empyreals can do."

His eyes narrowed suspiciously. "Or could it have something to do with that liner that left Lorelei orbit an hour ago, just after the Thunderhead took out their kick-pod catapult?"

Lleshi had hoped Telthorst hadn't noticed that. "Yes, the liner is part of it," he confirmed, keeping his voice steady. "We naturally want to cut it off at the catapult before it escapes."

"Why?" Telthorst demanded. "At their current acceleration, it'll take them nearly as long to get there as it will us. Long before then the absence of scheduled kick pods will certainly have alerted the enemy to our presence here. What do we care if they leave with confirmation that the *Komitadji* is in Lorelei system?"

His eyebrows lifted. "Unless, of course, you have other plans for the liner. Or for the *Komitadji*."

The man was definitely smarter than he looked. "What other plans could we have?" Lleshi asked.

"None, I hope," Telthorst said darkly. "Because as I'm sure you're aware, your *orders* are to take and hold Lorelei system."

"My *orders* are to bring the worlds of the Empyrean under the authority and dominion of the Pax," Lleshi said, enunciating each word precisely. "My initial *strategic* instructions are to take and hold Lorelei system."

"To use as a bargaining chip to force open the rest of the Empyrean," Telthorst bit out. "That means you are to sit and hold and consolidate."

"The *Balaniki* group is already holding the net," Lleshi countered. "When the *Macedonia* group reaches Lorelei, they will hold the spacelanes around the planet. My orders make no mention of sitting."

"I see," Telthorst said, his voice deadly quiet. "So in other words, victory is as good as achieved. Congratulations. So what *are* your intentions?"

Lleshi looked him straight in the eye. "The Supreme Council refers to this campaign as a rescue mission," he said. "Our stated purpose is to save the people of the Empyrean from the ongoing invasion of angels."

"And?" Telthorst prompted.

"It therefore seems only right," Lleshi said, "that we push our attack into our true enemy's home territory.

"I am therefore taking the *Komitadji* to Angelmass."

Telthorst's face went rigid. "What?" he snarled. "If you think you can—"

He choked down the rest of the sentence. "That's an insane move," he said instead, his voice still tight but under control again. "You saw what happened on our first trip to Lorelei. The minute we show up in a Seraph net, they'll throw us straight out again."

"I know." Lleshi gestured to the display. "That's why I need that liner."

"Explain."

"You don't give the orders aboard this ship, Adjutor," Lleshi reminded him. "You'll see when we get there."

Telthorst glared at him with an expression that was pure hatred. "I *could* give the orders aboard this ship, *Commodore*," he said quietly. "I could declare you incompetent and take command. Despite your obvious contempt for the Adjutors, I *do* have the authority to do that."

"Perhaps," Lleshi said. "But only if you can persuade everyone else aboard to believe you. *And* can prove me incompetent."

For a long minute the only sound was the hum of soft conversation from the command deck below. On the balcony itself, no one spoke, and Lleshi had the odd impression they were all holding their breath. Perhaps they were. "In two days there will be no need for me to prove your incompetence," Telthorst said at last. "You'll have proved it for me."

"Perhaps," Lleshi said. "Until then, I am still commander of this ship."

Telthorst's eyes darted to the tactical display. "And what does the commander choose to do about those incoming enemy ships?"

"I've already told you," Lleshi said. "Commander Campbell?"

"Harpies locked onto incoming spacecraft," Campbell said briskly and, to Lleshi's ear, with a note of quiet relief in his voice.

"Fire Harpies," Lleshi said, his eyes still on Telthorst.

"Harpies firing, sir."

Ornina shook her head. "Who would have believed it?" she murmured.

"I'm not sure I believe it myself," Kosta admitted, searching her face and Hanan's for some clue as to what they were really thinking about all this.

As if he, with his eight whole weeks of secret agent training, would be able to decipher any such clues even if he did spot them. "But even if I'm misinterpreting the facts, the facts themselves are still there."

"I believe it," Hanan said, his pinched face thoughtful in the dim light. "So many other things suddenly make sense now."

"Like Ronyon's fear reaction when we hit the system," Chandris said. "Somehow, he was able to sense it in a way the rest of us couldn't."

"Yes; Ronyon," Hanan said. "Other things, too. Do you remember what Jaar Hova was like, Ornina, when he first started flying his huntership?"

"He was a nice man," Ornina said, nodding. "A bit gruff around the edges, but essentially a nice man."

"He wasn't very nice to me when I came looking for a job," Chandris murmured.

"No, he wasn't very nice at all there at the end," Hanan agreed. "So many of the others have gone sour, too. Or bitter, or just plain mean. I've always assumed it was the stress of an angel hunter's life that had gotten to them. Perhaps instead it was all that time spent close to Angelmass. Close to all that evil . . ." He shivered. "So what do we do about it?"

"The first step is to prove there actually are such things as anti-angels," Kosta told him. "Either to find a pseudo cloud chamber track or, even better, to actually capture one."

"What about the damage to our angel?" Hanan suggested. "Can't you use that as proof?"

"We're not using it," Chandris said.

"No, but—"

"We're not using it," Chandris repeated, her tone accepting no argument.

"She's right," Kosta seconded, mildly surprised that he was on her side on this one. From the quick look she shot him, she was apparently surprised, too. "Besides, all it proves is that *something* is happening out there. We still need an anti-angel to show what that something is."

"All right," Ornina said, a sudden decisiveness in her voice. "What do you need from us?"

"I can get the test equipment together," Kosta told her. "At least, I think so. What I need is a ship to take it out to Angelmass."

"That means the *Gazelle*," Chandris said. "So we need you to get repairs started on it as soon as you can."

Ornina pursed her lips. "I can try," she said doubtfully. "But Gabriel's repair schedule has always been something of a work of fiction."

"We don't need Gabriel," Chandris said. "You get a private repair firm on the job. I'll supply the money to pay for it."

Ornina looked at her. Shifted her eyes to Kosta; back again to Chandris. "May I ask how?"

"Legally," Chandris assured her. "That's all you need to know."

"Of course it'll be legally," Hanan said firmly. "We know that. All right, that's the rest of you. What about me?"

Ornina frowned. "What *about* you?"

"What's my job in this?" Hanan asked.

"I think lying there getting well should about cover it," Kosta said.

Hanan drew himself up, or at least drew himself up from the neck up. The rest of his body didn't seem to want to move. "Now see here, everyone," he stated with exaggerated dignity. "I am the captain of the *Gazelle;* and the captain does *not* simply lie around while his ship is on a mission."

Ornina drew herself up, too. "Hanan—"

"Compromise," Kosta put in quickly. "We've got at least a couple of days' work ahead on the ship before we can head out. If, Hanan—*if*—you're a good boy and you lie there and heal, we'll think about taking you with us when we go."

"That's better," Hanan said, blandly mollified. "Wise old ship's captain, you know. Fountain of knowledge and sage advice—"

"Or failing that, a little extra ballast," Ornina said with a sigh. "All right. I'll get a service contract written as soon as Shikari City opens for business."

· "And make it a rush job," Chandris told her. "As many men and crews as you need. I'll make sure we have enough to pay whatever they want."

"Chandris—"

"People are already dying out there, Ornina," Chandris said quietly. "We have to stop it. Whatever it takes."

Hanan cleared his throat. "All of us?" he asked. "Including you, Jereko?"

Kosta braced himself. He'd been waiting for this other shoe to drop ever since he'd revealed his true identity to them. "If you think it'll help, I'm willing to turn myself in."

Out of the corner of his eye, he saw Chandris jerk slightly. "Wait a minute," she objected. "You can't make him do that."

"Why not?" Hanan asked.

"Because—" She hesitated, just a fraction of a second. "It'll tie up the rest of us six weeks from Sunday, that's why. They'll be bound to investigate his link to the *Gazelle,* and we'll never get off the ground."

"Maybe if I turn myself in you won't have to," Kosta suggested. "If I can convince them of the danger, maybe they'll mount an official study. A full Institute investigation will find an anti-angel a lot faster than we could."

"*If* they believe you," Chandris countered. "Would *you* believe a self-confessed spy?"

"If he had the data, yes," Kosta said, wondering why she was arguing so hard on his behalf.

And then suddenly it hit him. "Look, I wouldn't have to call them right now," he added. "I could hold off a day or two. Plenty of time for you to get away."

The look on her face was like someone had just slapped her. "Is that what you think?" she asked quietly. "That I'm just worried about me?"

Kosta winced, feeling ashamed. Now, for the first time since realizing who and what she was, he suddenly saw her not as a con artist but as merely a young woman struggling to survive a battering life. "No, of course not," he managed. "I just thought . . ."

Helplessly, he looked at Hanan. "Come on, fountain of sage advice, I'm drowning here," he growled. "A little help?"

"Oh, I don't know," Hanan said thoughtfully. "It's quite instructive to watch the two of you. At any rate, I wasn't going to suggest you head straight over to the police. As Chandris rightly points out, it would at the very least bury us in official paperwork and paperwork shufflers. *But.*"

He lifted his eyebrows. "When this is all over and we have the proof we need, you *will* need to come clean. There's no way around that."

"I understand," Kosta said. "Do you want me to write you out a confession or something right now?"

"No," Hanan said. With a clear effort he turned his right arm over and opened his hand. "But you might give me your weapon."

Kosta blinked. "How did you know about that?" he asked, pulling the shocker out of his pocket and laying it across Hanan's palm.

"Because I'm a wise old ship's captain, of course," Hanan said with a straight face.

"Don't pay a bit of attention to him, Jereko," Ornina admonished, standing halfway up and peering uncertainly at the weapon. "He was just guessing. How dangerous is this thing?"

"The safety's on," Kosta assured her, showing them both the small switch. "And it's tuned to its lowest setting besides. Even if you managed to accidentally fire it, you'd only shock your target a little."

"Good." Hanan closed his hand on the shocker and yawned prodigiously. "So are we finished for the night?"

"As far as I'm concerned." Kosta looked at Chandris. "You have anything else?"

She shook her head. "And I have a busy day tomorrow. I'd better get back to the ship and get some sleep."

"Sleep fast," Ornina warned her. "Ship repair services open at six in the morning, and I hope to have someone at the *Gazelle* by seven. Did you happen to pull up a damage survey, by the way?"

Chandris nodded. "I can transmit it here to you if you want."

"Yes, please," Ornina said. "It'll save time in the morning if I can tell them what exactly they'll need to do." For a moment her eyes searched Chandris's face. "You know, we can probably scrape up the money from somewhere else."

"I said I'd take care of it," Chandris told her, standing up. "You just concentrate on getting the ship ready to fly."

"All right, dear," Ornina said, giving Chandris a small and clearly forced smile. "You take care, then." She looked up at Kosta. "You, too, Jereko."

"We will," Kosta promised her. "Come on, Chandris, let's get going."

"High Senator Forsythe?"

With a jerk, Forsythe started awake, the muscles in his neck screaming with the sudden movement. He was, he discovered with some embarrassment, sprawled across one of the couches in the fifth-floor hospital lounge where he'd apparently fallen asleep. "You startled me, Zar," he said reproachfully, blinking his eyes to clear them. The horizon outside the window, he noted, was starting to lighten with the coming of dawn. He'd been asleep for probably the past five hours or so.

"Sorry, sir," Pirbazari apologized. "Are you all right?"

"Sure." Forsythe said, frowning at the tightness of his aide's expression. "What's the matter? Ronyon?"

Pirbazari shook his head. "A level-one message just came in from Uhuru. Lorelei has gone silent."

Something got a grip on Forsythe's throat. "What do you mean, 'gone silent'?"

"It's been twelve hours since the last scheduled skeeter to anywhere," Pirbazari said. "That puts the last one six hours overdue."

And there were five skeeter-sized catapults in the system, any one of which could fire out the regular capsules if necessary. "Could the planetary catapult have gone down, and for some reason they couldn't get a transmission to any of the ones in the belts?"

"Not likely," Pirbazari said. "For starters, there are six different official transmission systems out to the asteroids, plus all the commercial and private channels the government can commandeer in a pinch. And SOP is to send *something* on schedule, even if it's just a notice that systems are temporary down."

Forsythe hissed under his breath. "Which means all five catapults have been knocked out."

"Looks that way," Pirbazari conceded. "And fast enough that no one had time to get out a warning."

"How fast would that be?" Forsythe asked, reaching to his throat and tightening his neck clasp back into place.

Pirbazari pursed his lips. "Not much more than an hour. Maybe an hour and a half, depending on how badly the situation caught them napping."

"'The situation'?" Forsythe bit out. "Is that the official EmDef term for a Pax invasion?"

"We don't know that it *was* an invasion, sir," Pirbazari warned. "Or that the Pax was involved. Jumping to conclusions isn't going to get us anywhere with EmDef Command."

"Oh, the Pax is involved, all right," Forsythe said grimly. "I don't know how they did it, but it was them. If EmDef Command hasn't figured that out, they all ought to be fired. What's anyone doing at the moment?"

"Uhuru sent a quick courier to Lorelei four hours ago to look things over," Pirbazari said. "As of my last check, it hadn't yet responded."

"And when it does, it'll report back to Uhuru anyway," Forsythe said, retrieving his jacket from a nearby chair and slipping it on. "Where's the local EmDef HQ?"

"Eastern end of the huntership yards," Pirbazari said, dropping into step beside Forsythe as the High Senator headed for the lounge door. "Far side of the launch dishes."

"Good," Forsythe said as he pushed open the door and hurried out into the quiet corridor, still with its night lighting in place. "I want a courier of our own sent to Lorelei right away, with a collapsed skeeter catapult aboard."

"You think that's a good idea?" Pirbazari asked carefully. "The only way for the Pax to have destroyed the skeeter catapults at all four nets would have been for them to have overwhelmed the defenses there. Those sectors will be crawling with Pax ships."

"True," Forsythe said. "But follow it through. If they've destroyed the defenses at the nets, there's a fair chance they also destroyed the nets themselves."

"Which would mean the whole system would be open to their incoming ships," Pirbazari pointed out.

"And to ours," Forsythe reminded him. "If we can put something small into the system, maybe at a good distance from anything the Pax would be interested in—"

"There's a fair chance it could sit there quietly and put together a skeeter catapult without being noticed," Pirbazari finished for him, the first hint of cautious hope tugging at his voice. "It might work. But what if there's still one net working?"

"Then we'll have lost a courier," Forsythe said. "Hardly worth counting after we've lost a whole system."

"I suppose not," Pirbazari murmured.

Forsythe threw a sideways look at him. "Something?"

"I was just wondering," Pirbazari said slowly. "All those mining ships we armed."

"What about them?"

"We gave them targeting systems," Pirbazari said. "But we never gave them any instruction about tactics or strategy. I hope they've organized themselves into some kind of guerrilla-style resistance among the asteroids instead of just throwing themselves uselessly at incoming Pax ships."

Forsythe grimaced. "Let's hope they were smart and not just brave," he said. "In the meantime, let's see if we can find out what's going on."

CHAPTER 32

The receptionist on the Stardust Metals executive floor was regally seated behind a desk the size of the *Gazelle*'s machine shop, working diligently at a petite little computer terminal as Chandris pulled open the heavy door and stepped from the hallway onto a wide expanse of light gray carpet. To the casual observer, she supposed, the receptionist would probably have appeared totally engrossed in her work, oblivious to the newcomer's approach.

But to Chandris's street-trained eye, it was clear the whole thing was an act. The receptionist was fully aware of the younger woman's presence; and from her body language Chandris could guess she was wondering who this intruder was.

Who, or what. Chandris still hadn't really nailed down the proper upperclass clothing styles, and she'd had even less to work with on Seraph than she'd had aboard the *Xirrus*. Dressed in the best outfit she'd been able to throw together, she probably still looked a mess.

But there was no time for anything better now. And besides, she wasn't going for the sophisticated seductress role now. This time she was going straight for an even more basic human motivation.

Greed.

She was three steps from the desk before the receptionist finally looked up. "Good morning," she said. Her voice was polite enough, but there was a slightly contemptuous edge to the look she sent up and down Chandris's outfit. "May I help you?"

"Yes," Chandris said, nodding toward the five doors set into the curved wall behind the receptionist. The upper-class voice and gestures, at least, she had down cold, and she could tell the receptionist was taken slightly aback by it. "Please tell Mr. Amberson Toomes that Chandris Adriessa is here to see him. We met on his last flight from Lorelei aboard the *Xirrus*."

For a second she thought the woman was going to refuse, or at least ask for some ID first. But the upper-class mannerisms had apparently triggered her standard business reflexes, and without a word she picked up the phone and touched a button. "A Miss Chandris Adriessa to see you, Mr. Toomes," she announced.

For a minute she listened in silence, her eyes occasionally flicking to

Chandris. Chandris returned her gaze with the best air of unconcern she could manage, mentally running through possible escape routes in case she had to chop and hop. If Toomes was calling the police . . .

The receptionist replaced the handset. "He'll see you now, Miss Adriessa," she said coolly. "Center door behind me."

"Thank you," Chandris said, circling the desk and heading for the indicated door. This didn't prove anything, either. Toomes could just be giving her a little more stall-rope while the police collected themselves and got over here.

The door opened as she reached it. Holding her head high, she stepped inside the room.

Toomes was standing beside a thickly padded chair in a contoured work area probably twice the size of the receptionist's, across a room that made the desk look relatively small by comparison. "Hello, Chandris," he said. "It's been awhile, hasn't it?"

"It's good to see you, Amberson," Chandris said, studying him as she walked toward the desk. He was exactly as she remembered him from the *Xirrus*, only not as drunk. There was the same easy charm, the same air of ego and self-absorption, the same predator's smile aimed in her direction.

Or perhaps not. All the surface cues were still there; but as she got closer she could see that underneath was an edge of caution or tension that was new since the last time they'd been together. Perhaps because they were here in his office, surrounded by people he worked with, instead of in the relative anonymity of a spaceliner?

Or was it because the last time he'd seen her she was being escorted under guard to a landing boat?

"So," he said, coming out from behind the desk as she approached, easing his way through the narrow aisle between the desk and the display table with its multiple status monitors. His timing was perfect; he arrived at the front of the desk just as she did. "What have you been doing with yourself?"

For a split second she wondered if he was expecting her to kiss him. But something warned her off. "Keeping busy," she told him, glancing over at the chairs and couches over by the right-hand wall.

He took the hint. "Let's get more comfortable, shall we?" he suggested, gesturing her toward a long couch that seemed to be upholstered entirely in white feathers. "Then you can tell me all about it."

A dozen thoughts raced through her mind on that long walk to the couch. Was he expecting what he thought he'd been getting aboard the *Xirrus?* Or was he just toying with her, playing the feline half of a game of cat and mouse while he waited for the police?

She reached the couch and sat down at one end. To her mild surprise, he didn't sit down beside her. "I trust you cleared up that little customs problem?" he suggested, choosing one of the chairs facing her.

It was an obvious invitation to lie. A little *too* obvious. "You know better than that," she chided him gently. "It wasn't anything to do with customs. I was a semi-stowaway."

" 'Semi?' "

"I had a ticket to Lorelei," she told him, watching his face carefully. There wasn't a single atom of surprise there that she could detect. Clearly, he'd already been over the official version of the whole incident. "Lower class section. I decided to continue on to Seraph."

"Why?"

In the old days, she would have had a sugar-story all set and ready to spin. "I was running," she said instead. "There was a man I needed to get away from. I didn't have the cash in hand to do it."

"*Did* you get away?"

"I think so," Chandris said, shivering involuntarily at the thought of Trilling Vail lurking in some shadow behind her. "This isn't the kind of place where he would look for me."

Toomes lifted his eyebrows. "I trust you don't mean that the way it sounds," he warned. "My office is hardly equipped for live-in occupation."

"This isn't the 'here' I was referring to," Chandris said. "I meant Shikari City in general."

"Ah," Toomes said. He sounded relieved, but his face didn't match the voice. "So. What do you want?"

So much for any chance he might still be feeling romantic toward her. "I came here to offer you a business deal," she said.

For the first time his expression twitched. "Really," he said. "What sort of deal?"

"You give me money; I give you information," Chandris said. "Information a businessman like yourself would find exceedingly useful."

He pursed his lips. "What exactly does this information concern?"

"It concerns Angelmass," she said. "That's all I can say for now."

"Really," he commented, leaning back and crossing his legs. "You surprise me, Chandris. A good business strategist never gives away anything for free."

"Perhaps I'm not a good strategist, then," Chandris said evenly.

Toomes smiled. "Having had you run me around the track a few times, I hardly think that likely."

Chandris inclined her head slightly in acknowledgment of the point. "In that case, I'll concede it would have been obvious anyway once you heard your side of the bargain."

"That sounds more like it," he agreed. "Go on."

"I fly with a huntership that's been badly damaged," she told him. "I need it repaired."

Toomes's smile abruptly hardened. "The *Gazelle?*"

"That's the one."

He was frowning openly at her now, and behind his eyes she could see the news stories of the incident replaying themselves. The damage to the *Gazelle,* the damage to Hanan—

And High Senator Arkin Forsythe standing with reluctant prominence amid the chaos.

"Well," he said at last. "Interesting, indeed. But I thought Gabriel handled huntership repairs."

"Gabriel works at bureaucratic speeds," Chandris said. "We need it fixed now."

"We?"

Chandris hesitated a fraction of a second. But Toomes wasn't going to give her what they needed without something more. "I'm working with a researcher at the Angelmass Studies Institute," she said. "His name's Jereko Kosta."

"Kosta," Toomes repeated, studying her carefully. "I'll be checking with him, of course."

Chandris gestured toward his desk. "Call him now, if you'd like. I'll wait."

For a half dozen seconds she was afraid he was going to take her up on the offer. No problem; except that if he called out of the fog like this, Kosta the naive spy was likely to tell him everything they knew or suspected about Angelmass. That would be a lot of something for nothing, and Toomes could well decide it was all he needed.

Too late, now, she wished she'd told Kosta what she was planning and prepped him a little. But he'd been so sure she was going to pull something illegal that she'd figured he deserved to stew in his own juices a little.

But Toomes merely shrugged. "Later will do," he said. "Bottom line: how much are these repairs going to cost?"

Chandris braced herself. The estimate from the service crew foreman had come in from Ornina just as Chandris arrived at the Stardust building. This was not going to be pretty. "A hundred eighty thousand ruya."

Toomes's eyebrows went up again, but at least he didn't laugh out loud. "That's a lot of money," he said. "What makes you think this information will be anywhere near that valuable?"

"It's worth considerably more than that," Chandris said. "I'm not exaggerating when I say that this has the potential to drastically affect the entire economy of Seraph system. Possibly the entire Empyrean."

"Really," Toomes said. "Something of such devastating import, and you're proposing we keep it to ourselves?"

"Of course not," Chandris said. "We couldn't bury this even if we wanted to. And we don't. All I'm proposing is that you get the report a day before anyone else does."

"Inside information," he said. "What you're suggesting skates very close to the edge of illegal activity."

"You're supplying a service to us," Chandris pointed out. "That makes you something of a partner. It seems to me you're entitled to have our data as soon as we collect it."

"And of course, everyone else would have to wait until we could draft a proper news release," he said. "Naturally, the wording on such things is very important. I'm guessing it could take as long as three days to get it done properly."

Chandris felt her heartbeat speed up. Toomes was going for it. He was bargaining with her, angling for more time to work whatever business or stock manipulation he might want to do with his inside information. "I don't know," she said, putting reluctance into her voice. "Kosta's writing skills are pretty good. I don't think it would take us more than a day."

"This isn't something you want to rush into," Toomes warned. "If you're right, this news will be a major topic of conversation across the entire Empyrean. The release itself could conceivably be quoted verbatim in history texts for generations to come. The wording will be incredibly important. It has to take three days."

"You're right about the historical significance, of course," Chandris conceded. "But even so, I can't see it taking more than two days at the absolute most."

For a long moment he gazed at her. "All right," he said at last. "Two days." He lifted a finger. "*Plus.*"

She frowned. There was an unpleasant glint in his eye. "Plus what?"

"I'll have a credit chit here for you at five-thirty tomorrow afternoon," Toomes said. "One hundred eighty thousand ruya. At that time—" He lifted his eyebrows. "You and I are going to do it."

Chandris felt her blood freeze. "It?"

"That's right," Toomes said. "You see, for all the time we spent together on the *Xirrus,* I somehow can't remember us actually doing anything *personal* together. It makes me wonder if we ever really did."

"You drank an awful lot on that trip," Chandris said between stiff lips. Oh, no. No. Not this.

"Yes, I did," he said. "I can't help wondering why."

"I wasn't ordering your drinks for you."

"No," he said. "But perhaps there was subtle encouragement." He waved a hand. "It doesn't matter. The point is, whatever did or didn't happen on the *Xirrus*, it's going to happen tomorrow afternoon."

He stood up. "The office staff leaves promptly at five," he said. "Be here at five-thirty if you want your money."

Chandris stood up, too. "I'll be here," she said, gazing at his face. It hadn't been a predator's smile she'd seen when she came in, she realized now. It had been the smile of injured pride seeing a chance to balance the books. "Good-bye, Amberson."

Stardust Metals' main clerical area was three floors below the executive floor, a warren of small offices and large, desk-filled spaces. It was crawling with busy people and filled with the kind of controlled chaos that seemed to go with every bureaucratic operation Chandris had ever seen.

In the midst of all that activity, it was inevitable that someone would leave a hand computer lying around unattended somewhere.

She found one in two minutes flat and retired to the privacy of the women's restroom with her prize. On the *Xirrus*, she'd had to fry her borrowed computer's ID register to keep it from spotting unauthorized usage. Here, she didn't need to be nearly that fancy. All she wanted this time was a few cozy minutes with Stardust's central computer.

The security protection on this system, she quickly discovered, was far looser than she'd had to cut through on the *Xirrus*. And for good reason: the particular hand computer she'd scored could only access the most basic of Stardust's housekeeping programs.

But that was all right. Basic housekeeping was exactly what she wanted. A simple work order, logged in for a specific time, and she was done. Poking around the menus, she spotted an unexpected bonus among the more routine areas and logged that in, too. Another brief dip into the clerical chaos to return the computer, and she was finished.

She waited until she was back on the lobby floor and had some quiet space around her before she called Ornina. "It's set," she told the older woman. "I'll have the money tomorrow afternoon."

"Good," Ornina said. Her voice sounded anything but relieved, though. "Chandris . . ."

"It's all right," Chandris said. "Really. A simple trade, all legal and ethical and aboveboard."

"And what exactly are we trading?"

"Nothing we can't do without," Chandris assured her.

"Mm," Ornina said. "Jereko is worried about you. Worried that you're going to, in his words, sell your soul for this."

Chandris sighed. "Not my soul, no," she said. "Trust me, Ornina. Please."

"You know I do, dear," Ornina said. "I just don't want you bearing more than your share of the burden for this."

"I'm heading back," Chandris said. "You have the repair crews going?"

"As Hanan would say, they're going at it like their pants are on fire," Ornina said. "With enough people, the foreman says they can be finished in three days. Two and a half if we get a miracle or two."

"That's why we're paying them the big money," Chandris reminded her. "Anything you want me to pick up on the way back?"

Ornina hesitated. Chandris could visualize her face, lined with age and care and worries. Some of those lines and worries for Chandris herself. "No, I don't think so," she said. "Unless you want to stop at the hospital and see how Hanan is doing."

"I could," Chandris said. "I was thinking instead that I'd take over for you at the *Gazelle* and let you go see him."

"That would be very nice," Ornina admitted. "If it won't be too much trouble."

"No trouble at all," Chandris said. "Go get ready. I'll be there as soon as I can."

"All right. Thank you, Chandris."

"Good-bye," Chandris said, and hung up. She keyed a call for a line car, then headed across the lobby and back out to the street.

She would take over for Ornina, all right. Ornina was a first-rate pilot and ship manager, and a sweet, kind woman besides. She didn't have the kind of finesse and sheer underhanded skullduggery necessary to get work crews to do their best and their fastest.

Chandris did. And miracles or not, the ship *would* be ready in two and a half days.

She'd stood by and watched as two men died out at Angelmass. No one else was going to die that way. Not if she could help it.

Trilling had been walking the streets of Shikari City for hours; and he was just about to give up for the morning when there she was.

His heart leaped, his throat tightening with excitement. She was dressed in some outlandish would-be upper-class outfit that made her look like a little girl playing dress-up, her hair tied up into the kind of fancy swirls and braids he'd always hated. But it was her, all right, standing there across the street halfway down the block. He would know her anywhere.

The one true love of his life, and he'd found her.

Peering down her side of the street, she didn't seem to have spotted him yet. Grinning like a friendly tiger, he started casually toward her. He would stay on this side of the street, he decided, waiting until he was directly across from her before crossing. That way, he would have a clear view of her face and her own excitement when she realized they were back together again.

She had missed him so very much. He could hardly wait to see her face.

He was halfway there when a line car pulled up to the curb beside her and stopped. Chandris got in, and the car pulled away again.

"No," Trilling breathed, staring in disbelief. To lose her again, here, now, just as they were about to get back together? "No!" he snarled, breaking into a run. A middle-aged pedestrian gaped at him; without a second thought, Trilling shoved him viciously out of his way, every gram of his concentration focused on the accelerating line car. He had to catch it. He *had* to.

But it was no use. He was too far away, and the line car's computer brain too stupid to recognize true love when it saw it. The vehicle picked up speed and vanished around a corner.

And she was gone.

Slowly, reluctantly, Trilling slowed down, trotting to a bitter halt. After all this time . . .

He looked across the street. That was the building Chandris had come out of. *Stardust Metals, Inc.,* the bronze plaque beside the door said. Some hoity corporation, probably, with more money than anyone had a right to have.

So what had Chandris been doing in there?

He smiled. No, he hadn't lost her again. Of course not. Far from it. The outfit she'd been wearing had to be for some track she was scoring in there. Unless the whole thing was finished and she was ready to hop, she'd be back.

And when she did, they'd be together again. They'd have the cash from this track to run away with, and they would never be apart again. That was probably what Chandris had in mind, in fact. To score a track right here and now so that she and Trilling could run away together.

She was always so thoughtful that way. It proved just how much she loved him.

He glanced around, then headed down the street toward a narrow alleyway where the corner of a trash bin was visible. No, she would be back. All he had to do was find someplace to settle down and wait.

And then they would be together again. Forever.

CHAPTER 33

"ETA to catapult, five minutes," Campbell announced. "Speed has eased up to twenty-one hundred. Looks like we've picked up a little gravitational acceleration."

"Acknowledged," Lleshi said, glancing over his own boards. Everything was ready; all systems showed green. For the past two days the *Komitadji* had been following a standard, minimum-time acc/dec course, driving at constant acceleration toward the distant catapult for the first half of the distance, then flipping over and decelerating at the same rate. Trying to beat the slower spaceliner to the catapult.

It had been a long, hard race, and it was coming down now to a laser-etched finish. But Lleshi had run the numbers, and the *Komitadji* was going to win.

"Commodore Lleshi!"

Lleshi bit down hard on the first words that sprang to mind. "Yes, Mr. Telthorst?"

"What in the name of the laughing fates is going on here?" the Adjutor snarled, bobbling to an awkward stop in the slight gravity of the *Komitadji*'s slow rotation. "We're supposed to be heading for that catapult out there."

"And we are," Lleshi said. "Our ETA is just under five minutes."

"Then why are we in free-flight?" Telthorst demanded. "Our speed relative to the catapult—" he squinted at Lleshi's board "—it's over two thousand kilometers per hour. We should be decelerating—should have been decelerating the whole way."

He jabbed an accusing finger toward the tactical display. "Now we're too close. We can't possibly decelerate the rest of our speed away fast enough."

"No, we can't," Lleshi agreed. "I didn't intend to."

"Really," Telthorst said frostily. "May I ask what exactly you *did* intend to do, then? Wave at the station as we shot past it?"

Lleshi gestured to the tactical display. "The spaceliner out there has a catapult ETA of nineteen minutes," he said. "A standard acc/dec run, if I had stayed with that, would have had us arriving nearly ten minutes behind it."

"The Empyreals already know we're here, Commodore," Telthorst bit out. "They sent a courier ship into the system, remember?"

"Two of them, actually," Lleshi corrected. "A second courier hit the net about eighteen hours ago, while you were sleeping."

Telthorst's eyes narrowed. "Why wasn't I told?"

"It wasn't necessary," Lleshi said. "As with the first, the *Balaniki* captured it without trouble. Captain Horvak has the crew aboard for questioning; if he'd learned anything he would have relayed it to me."

"And of course you would have relayed it to me?"

"Of course." Lleshi felt the corner of his lip twist. "Don't worry, this ship was also captured undamaged," he couldn't resist adding.

For a moment Telthorst just looked at him. "We'll ignore that for the moment, Commodore," he said at last. "You're supposed to keep me fully informed—*fully* informed—on all aspects of this operation. But we'll ignore that."

He jabbed again at the tactical display. "What we will *not* ignore is that this whole silly race has been a waste from the very first. A waste of time *and* fuel, neither of which we have to spare. It doesn't make a half-penny's worth of difference if that spaceliner gets away; and now it appears you aren't even going to get that half-penny's worth of profit out of it."

"On the contrary," Lleshi told him. "It could make a great deal of difference. And the spaceliner isn't going to get away."

"Really." Telthorst looked over at the main display, now showing the view aft toward the catapult they were racing toward. "Then you'd better plan to wave extra hard at it," he said. "Because in a few seconds you're going to have your first and last close-up look at it."

"I'm aware of the timing, thank you," Lleshi said. "SeTO?"

"Board is green, Commodore," Campbell said briskly. "Long tubes ready for launch."

"*Long* tubes?" Telthorst echoed, looking like he'd been hit in the face. "You're wasting Hellfire missiles on a *spaceliner?*"

"Hardly," Lleshi said, smiling tightly. "Hellfires aren't the only things on a warship that can be launched through the long tubes."

Telthorst's face was a twist of confusion. "What in hell's bank are you talking about?"

"Just watch," Lleshi advised. The timer clicked down to zero— "Fighters: launch."

From the cluster of tubes along the big ship's centerline came a faint rumbling growl, more felt than heard, as the mass-driver launching electromagnets activated. In his mind's eye Lleshi could see the wave of fighters riding that magnetic wave, accelerating through the *Komitadji*'s core at a punishing ten gravities. They reached speed and shot out the bow of the ship, traveling at twenty-one hundred kilometers per hour.

Or rather, they came from the tubes at twenty-one hundred relative to the

Komitadji. Since the *Komitadji* was traveling backwards at that same speed, the fighters emerged effectively stationary between the catapult and incoming spaceliner.

In perfect position to draw a line in the sand.

"Full deceleration," Lleshi ordered. "Fighter command?"

"Fighters moving to interdiction positions," the fighter commander called as the roar of the *Komitadji*'s engines began to rattle the command deck. "Giving challenge to the spaceliner."

"Catapult lasers responding," Campbell reported, a touch of contempt in his voice. "Looks like basic meteor defenses. Pitiful."

"They're still powerful enough to cause damage," Telthorst pointed out stiffly. "Those fighters are expensive, too."

"Instruct the fighters to stay clear as best they can," Lleshi ordered. Telthorst's precious money be damned; he simply didn't want to waste valuable pilots. "We'll have plenty of time to deal with the catapult defenses once we've finished decelerating and can get back to the station."

"And then?" Telthorst demanded, challenge in his voice.

Lleshi smiled. "Then perhaps I can make you that half-penny's worth of profit."

"We've shut down all the nets except the one here," General Akhmed said, tapping a spot on the tactical display. "That will give us only one entrypoint to defend. Our destroyers are arranged thusly—" he indicated the green triangles hovering protectively around each of the four catapult ships "—with support ships and fighters forming defensive screens. It's a standard three-layer defense, easily capable of holding long enough for the catapult ships to send any intruder packing."

"What about the Seraph and Central huntership nets?" Pirbazari asked.

"Binary linked to each other," Akhmed said. "They don't enter into the calculation."

Forsythe shook his head. "Not good enough," he said.

Akhmed's eyebrows lifted politely. "I beg your pardon, High Senator?"

"A standard containment approach may be good enough to deal with the occasional Pax military probe," Forsythe told him, gesturing toward the schematic. "But we're talking full-bore invasion here. The Pax may not be willing to play your game with them."

Pirbazari cleared his throat. "It's not a matter of playing games, sir," he said. "The nets are the only way into the system. If they can't get out of the net area before they're 'pulted away, that's that. They don't have a lot of say in it."

"Then how did they get into Lorelei system?" Forsythe retorted. "Because they *are* there, Zar. That courier we sent has been silent for over twenty hours. How long does it take to put together a collapsible skeeter catapult?"

Pirbazari's mouth tightened. "Ten hours," he conceded. "Twelve at the outside."

"Leaving them plenty of time to have looked around and written up a report," Forsythe said. "If they aren't talking, it's because someone has shut them up. You have any candidates in mind other than the Pax?"

"With all due respect, High Senator," Akhmed said politely, "what exactly is it you want us to do?"

"For a start, how about arming the hunterships?" Forsythe said, reaching over and pulling up another list. "They have the best shielding of anything in the Empyrean."

"They're designed for a high-radiation environment, sir, not combat," Pirbazari reminded him. "Pax lasers and plasma jets might not bother them, but I wouldn't bet on their chances against high explosives."

"Nonsense," Forsythe said firmly. "Explosives are nothing but high energy in a compact package. Anything that can survive Angelmass's energy output shouldn't have trouble with a few warheads. Put some weapons aboard and we'll have another layer of defense."

Akhmed and Pirbazari exchanged glances. "Sir . . ." Pirbazari said hesitantly.

"What?" Forsythe demanded, looking back and forth between them. "You don't like the idea of being prepared?"

"It's not that, sir," Pirbazari said. "It's just . . . I think we're both wondering if you might be overreacting a little."

Forsythe took a deep breath, a blistering retort dropping into place in his mind like a missile in its launch tube.

And then he took another look at the expression on Akhmed's face . . . and suddenly felt his blood freeze.

He'd forgotten he was supposed to be wearing an angel.

His retort and frustrated anger vanished together in a sudden flash of panic as his eyes dropped to the angel pendant around Akhmed's neck. It had been a bad slip. Possibly even a fatal slip. Angel-wearing politicians weren't supposed to be so quick to advocate violence, not even in self-defense. They were quiet and placid and confident, three qualities Forsythe was definitely not manifesting at the moment. If Akhmed suspected—if he demanded the High Senator turn over his own pendant for examination—then Forsythe was finished. It would mean scandal and removal, probably even prosecution.

And in the midst of it, the Pax would sweep into the Empyrean and destroy it. "What do you mean?" he asked between stiff lips.

"All I mean is that we know how the Pax sees things," Pirbazari said. "Everything is either profit or loss to them. Even if they somehow get past the defenders and the catapult ships, they're hardly going to lay waste to Seraph."

"That means that whatever happens, we've got time," Akhmed added. "Time for negotiation or political maneuvering." His eyes flicked down to Forsythe's angel pendant. "Or for combat, if it comes to that."

"I suppose," Forsythe murmured, watching the other closely. But if Akhmed had figured it out, it didn't show in his face. "I'll leave it in your hands, then, shall I?"

"I think that would be best, High Senator," Akhmed agreed, sounding relieved. Even for an EmDef general, apparently, going head to head with a High Senator was an unwelcome fight.

Which meant that perhaps Forsythe had overreacted after all. Not about the Pax invasion, certainly, but about the possibility of Akhmed realizing he wasn't wearing an angel. The state of mind created by the general's own angel might even be working in Forsythe's favor, making such suspicions unlikely.

Still, the momentary uncertainty had served a useful purpose. Even as he tried to single-handedly whip the Empyrean into battle readiness, Forsythe needed to remember there was a mask he had to wear. It was a lesson he would take care to remember.

"I'd best leave you to it, then," Forsythe said, stepping away from the display and offering Akhmed his hand. "Let me know immediately if there's any new information."

"I will, High Senator," Akhmed promised. "Don't worry, sir. We're a considerably harder nut to crack than the Pax might think."

I hope so, Forsythe said to himself as he and Pirbazari left the building. *I sincerely hope so.*

"Almost done," Gyasi announced, poking his head up over the box he was fastening. "You?"

"Just about," Kosta said, double-checking that all the foam padding was in place around the delicate spectrum sampler before putting the packing box lid in place. "I can't believe we were actually able to get all this stuff together."

"Shows what clean living will do," Gyasi said dryly, setting the top of his box carefully into place and working the sealing levers. "Okay. Finished."

He collapsed into a chair beside the stack of boxes, waving a hand vigorously at his face as if fanning himself to cool off. It was an unusual gesture for Gyasi, one Kosta had never seen him make before.

And because it was unusual enough to catch Kosta's full attention, he also spotted the other's subtle, almost furtive glance at his other wrist.

At his watch.

Kosta turned back to his own packing box, a sudden surge of uncertainty running through him. It could have been a totally innocent act, of course; Gyasi simply wondering how long they had been working, or how long it had been since lunch.

But it could also be as *un*innocent as a paranoiac's nightmares. Half of the stuff piled around them was in this room illegally, shamelessly borrowed or flat-out stolen from labs neither Kosta nor Gyasi had any business even being inside.

Gyasi hadn't objected to their private scavenger hunt. He'd been rather enthusiastic about it, actually, cheerfully and efficiently doing inventory searches to pinpoint the items on Kosta's list. So cheerfully and efficiently, in fact, that at times Kosta had thought he could even give Chandris's professional larceny some stiff competition.

Problem was, this was the same Yaezon Gyasi who'd also spent a lot of time around angels.

So was Gyasi waiting for someone? The police, or an Empyrean Defense Force anti-espionage force? Helping Kosta neatly wrap up the evidence for them?

Or was Kosta simply fighting against the pangs of conscience? He'd spent a fair amount of time around angels, too.

He got the top onto the box and sealed it into place. "Done," he said. "I guess we're ready to call a line truck and start moving it."

"Yeah," Gyasi said, making no move to leave his seat. "How are the repairs on the ship coming?"

"Better than expected," Kosta said, an unpleasant tingle starting to vibrate across his skin. Gyasi couldn't be that tired. He was waiting for something, all right. "Chandris has a gift for getting people to do what she wants."

"I can believe that," Gyasi said. "When is it supposed to be ready?"

"Sometime tomorrow," Kosta said. "She's supposed to pick up the credit chit this afternoon."

"You never told me how she'd pulled that one off."

"*She* never told me how she pulled it off," Kosta countered. "But Ornina checked up on this Stardust Metals group after Toomes called me. The business is legitimate, anyway, even if whatever Chandris has planned isn't. Come on, let's get this stuff out of here."

Gyasi's face twisted. "Well, actually . . ."

He didn't seem inclined to finish the sentence. As it turned out, he didn't have to.

Across the room the door swung open. Kosta turned toward it, his hand twitching reflexively toward his pocket before he remembered he'd surrendered his shocker to Hanan.

"Hello, Mr. Kosta," Director Podolak said, stepping into the room. "I see you've been busy."

"Director Podolak," Kosta said, the words coming out as a half sigh. It was worse than the police. Worse even than Empyreal security. Those he could have resisted, maybe even successfully.

But not Podolak. Not the woman who'd done so much to help him over the past few months. Not the woman who'd supported his work at every step along the way.

Not the woman who'd trusted him.

"I'm surprised we still have an Institute out there," Podolak commented wryly as she walked into the room, glancing at each stack of boxes as she passed it. Doing a mental inventory, no doubt; she probably knew exactly how many test tubes and marking pens each lab was supposed to have. "Looks to me like half of it is right here."

"I need it to run an experiment," Kosta said. To his mild surprise, his voice was clear, his tongue working without tangling over itself. A far cry from the fumbling, easily panicked amateur spy he'd been when he first landed in the Empyrean. "My credit line is still frozen. I didn't think we had time to waste jumping through bureaucratic hoops."

"I see." Podolak shifted her gaze to Gyasi. "Mr. Gyasi, would you excuse us a moment?"

Gyasi stood up without a word, flashing a single glance at Kosta as he stepped out the door and closed it behind him.

"This is very disappointing, Mr. Kosta," Podolak commented, sitting down in the chair Gyasi had just vacated. "I would have thought that by now you'd know you could come to me with problems like this."

"I know that," Kosta conceded, feeling a flush of shame. There was no anger in her voice or face that he could detect, but her quiet calmness had an undercurrent of hurt to it. "I didn't want you involved. It was my idea, my gamble. I didn't want anyone else in trouble if it didn't work out."

"What about Mr. Gyasi?"

Kosta lifted his hands. "I didn't want him, either, but he insisted. Anyway, he was already in on it."

"In on this theory of yours that Angelmass has become a focus of evil?"

Kosta grimaced. Gyasi would have told her everything, of course. "I know it sounds crazy," he admitted. "But I've already found indications that something in or near Angelmass has an eroding effect on angels."

"But no actual evidence?"

Kosta thought about the Daviees' angel, and his promise to keep its existence a secret. "Nothing I can use, no," he told her. "That's what all this equipment is for. To see if I can find and identify an anti-angel, the equivalent quanta of evil."

Podolak shook her head. "There is no quantum of evil," she said quietly. "Any more than the angels themselves are quanta of good."

Kosta frowned. "I thought the *Acchaa* theory was pretty well accepted around here."

"Acceptance doesn't equal truth," Podolak said. "I don't know what the angels are, or how exactly they affect the people they come in contact with. But the idea that they're little chunks of something as vague and undefinable as 'good' simply doesn't work."

"Why not?"

"Because they do not, in fact, force people to do the right thing," Podolak said. "Not always."

Kosta studied her. Podolak's eyes were steady on him, an odd layer of tension about the corners of her mouth. "What do you know," he asked carefully, "that the rest of us don't?"

Her lips tightened. "That in the past ten years, with the angel program well established, no fewer than seven High Senators have been caught in embezzlement, fraud, or influence-peddling."

Kosta felt his jaw drop. He'd been expecting her to trot out some esoteric data from the Institute's angel-control studies. "Are you serious?"

"In that same time," she added, "at least fifty other angel-wearers have also skated over the edge."

"And you managed to keep all this a secret?"

"The High Senate has been very good at covering up the problems," she said. "And for what it's worth, most of the people involved turned out to have serious mental or emotional instabilities they'd managed to hide up until then."

"Even so," Kosta protested. "Isn't this something the people ought to know about?"

"Yes, it is," she admitted. "And if it were up to me, they would."

"So who *is* it up to?" Kosta asked. "The High Senate?"

"Even most of the High Senators don't know," she said. "Only the top leaders, plus a few senior EmDef officers. Their view is that seven High Senators in ten years is hardly a terrible failure rate."

Kosta snorted. "More likely they just want to cover their tails after all these years of telling the people how safe the angels have made them."

"No, I don't think so," Podolak said. "The problem is that the angels *do* work, at least most of the time. They've made the High Senate run more smoothly and efficiently, as well as drastically lowering the crime rate."

"How drastically?"

"Substantially," Podolak said. "In the twenty years before the introduction of the angels, over two hundred High Senators were indicted, censured, or removed from office for illegal or unethical behavior."

"I guess that is significant," Kosta conceded.

"And the same pattern has translated over into EmDef and the local government sector of angel-wearers," Podolak said. "So you can see their point in not rocking the boat at this stage."

"But you don't agree."

Podolak sighed. "You're right, the angels have made the people feel safe. The problem is, they've made them feel *too* safe. The normal vigilance a population needs to maintain toward its elected officials has been dulled, if not completely eliminated. Even if the angels were perfect, that wouldn't be a healthy thing. As it is, it's more than a little dangerous for the society."

Kosta felt his throat tighten. "Not to mention the Pax. The whole reason they're breathing down our necks is that the High Senate has convinced them the angels are an irresistible alien force."

"Perhaps," Podolak said. "Still, if it wasn't that excuse it would be something else. The Pax just likes to conquer people."

Kosta looked around at his stacks of equipment boxes. "So what is it you want me to do?" he asked.

"The same thing that all good scientists want," Podolak said. "I want you to find the truth."

"And then?"

"Let the political and social chips fall where they have to," Podolak said, standing up. "Now. You and Mr. Gyasi need to get going, I expect. Unfortunately, neither of you can check out this much equipment at once."

She smiled faintly. "Which means I need to go to the gate with you. You'd better call for some luggage carts; you're going to need them."

CHAPTER 34

It was five-thirty precisely, and most of the Stardust Metals building had gone deathly quiet, as Chandris arrived at Amberson Toomes's office door and rapped against the panel. Toomes was clearly ready and waiting; the door slid open immediately. Squaring her shoulders, Chandris stepped inside.

He was waiting, all right. He was seated on the feather-upholstered couch, dressed in an elaborately embroidered ankle-length robe. Chandris couldn't tell whether he was wearing anything under the robe or not, but she rather expected she would soon be finding out.

"You're on time," he greeted her, his predator's smile back in place. "I like that."

He waved a call stick, and the door slid shut behind her. "I'm glad you approve," she said, walking toward him. There was a small clothing-style box on a corner of his desk; she pretended not to notice it. "You're all ready, I see."

"I am," he said. "But you're not. There's a box on my desk. Open it."

She changed direction to the desk. The box was smaller than it had looked from the door, she saw now. If it contained a robe like Toomes's, there wasn't going to be a lot of material to it.

She opened the box. No robe, but a full outfit nevertheless: bra, panties, leggings, and a short covering sarapi with bright red ribbon-ties. She was right about there not being much actual cloth involved, though.

"You want me to put this on, I suppose," she said, gazing down at the filmy material.

"If you would," Toomes said. As if she really had a choice.

"What about the money?" she asked.

Toomes gestured. "Pick up the outfit."

Chandris did so. The promised credit chit was lying at the bottom of the box. One hundred eighty thousand ruya, just as agreed.

"Leave it there for now," Toomes ordered, stretching ostentatiously and setting the call stick on the floor beside the couch. His robe opened slightly with the movement; he wasn't wearing anything else above the waist, anyway. "You can pick it up on your way out."

For a brief moment Chandris considered simply grabbing the chit and making a run for it. The money was there, and once she had it there was nothing Toomes could do to freeze or block the transaction.

But Toomes was surely smarter than that. The door was probably locked, with the call stick the only way to open it. There was nothing she could do but go through with this.

Or at least, part of the way through. "All right," she said.

"You can change in the bathroom back there," Toomes went on, pointing toward a door in the far side of the office. "Don't be too long."

A bathroom on the far side of the office, half a room away from the credit chit and a full room away from the call stick. "This is pretty," she said, dropping the filmy sarapi casually onto the desk beside the box. "But it won't be necessary."

"Why not?" Toomes asked. "I thought you wanted to be nice to me."

The word jarred oddly against Chandris's ear. Nice. *Nice.*

No. What Toomes wanted wasn't the definition of *nice.* Nice was what Hanan and Ornina had been to her when she'd come straggling along, cold and hungry, with nowhere to go. Nice was what they'd been to Jereko Kosta. Nice was what Forsythe was to his ever-cheerful handicapped aide, Ronyon.

Nice was even what Trilling had been to her, back in those early days.

Would Trilling have asked her to do something like this? Of course not. He'd taught her how to use her face and body, certainly; to distract men, or to weaken their resolve, or to pump them for information. But he would never have asked her to go all the way with anyone. Only with him had she ever had that kind of special closeness.

And now, after living with the Daviees and their angel all these months, she was even less interested in letting Toomes tom her. It was wrong for him to demand it—just plain wrong. He was already getting his money's worth; Kosta's information about Angelmass would be worth far more than a mere hundred eighty thousand ruya. Toomes was just being vindictive, or childish, or predatory.

And that made it just as wrong for Chandris to let him get away with it.

"Of course I want to be nice," she said, smiling seductively. "But I can do better than this on my own."

She started slowly across the office toward him, putting an exaggerated sway into her hips. "Let me try."

The predator smile was still there, but there was an edge of caution to it. But a man like Toomes would never admit to being worried that she could outsmart him. Not again, anyway. "Okay," he said, looking her up and down appraisingly. "I'm game. Let's see what you can do."

She took her time crossing the room, teasing down the sealing strip of her blouse as she went. She reached the couch and stopped an arm's length away from him, slipping the blouse fully open. The bra she had on underneath wasn't nearly as fancy as the one she'd left on the desk, but it should do for the purpose required. Toomes still looked a little uncertain, but it was clear he found this interesting enough to let her do it her way a little longer.

Hopefully, long enough. She didn't dare glance at the carved-rim wall chrono over his head. He would surely pick up on that, and she couldn't afford to let him get suspicious now. But she had a pretty good time sense, and she didn't think she would have to drag this out more than another two minutes.

Barring an agonizing stretched-out moment she'd once spent cowering in the shadows watching angry police charge past, it was probably the longest two minutes of her life. Toomes stared unblinkingly up at her as she eased off her clothing, occasionally licking his lips. His expression was that of a hungry tiger playing games with a lamb before moving in for the kill.

Chandris played it as slowly and sensuously as she could. She'd never done anything like this herself, but some girlfriends of Trilling's buddies had once had an impromptu competition at a party, and she had that slightly disgusting memory to draw on.

But even slow and sensuous, it was clear she was running out of time. Toomes's breathing had become short and erratic, his muscles visibly trembling as he watched the show. She could smell alcohol on his breath, which added another couple of turns to his coiled-spring tightness. The man was primed and ready for action, and it wouldn't be long before impatience and desire overwhelmed whatever limited self-control was left in that reek-fogged brain.

And when that happened . . .

When that happened, she would do whatever she had to. Whether it was right or wrong, whether it was utterly repulsive or merely horribly unpleasant, she would do whatever she had to. Hanan and Ornina were counting on her.

And people were dying out at Angelmass.

She had undressed to the waist, and was beginning to roll her panties slowly down over her hips, when the fire drill she'd programmed into the building's housekeeping system the day before finally went off.

"What's that?" she gasped, spinning around and nearly losing her balance as she accidentally stepped on one of her shoes. "Amberson—it's the police!"

"No, no," Toomes said, his voice almost unrecognizable. "It's just a fire drill. Some idiot must have reset the—"

"Fire?" Chandris gasped, jerking like she'd been shot. *"Fire?"*

"It's a drill," Toomes insisted. "Just a griffy little—wait!"

It was too late. Chandris had already scooped up her discarded blouse—and with it Toomes's call stick—and was running on bare feet toward the desk. "Wait!" Toomes shouted again, his voice accompanied by the squeak of embroidered cloth against feathers as he leaped up and charged after her. Chandris didn't even pause at the desk, simply snatching up the credit chit on the fly and making for the door.

"Hey—get back here," Toomes snarled, his voice suddenly ugly as the prospect of frustrated lust loomed before him. He was running now, trying to cut her off at the door.

But he was on bare feet, too, and was wearing a full-length robe, and Chandris was already up to speed. The sliding panel opened with gratifying promptness as she keyed the call stick at it, and she beat him to the doorway with three paces to spare. There was a brief tickling of air on her bare back as he swung a hand in an unsuccessful grab, and then she was out and racing across the reception room.

Toomes followed, alternately cursing and cajoling and pleading. Chandris was younger and lighter, but Toomes was in pretty good shape, and as she reached the door to the hallway she could tell he was still right behind her.

Behind her, and showing no signs of fading in the stretch. As far as he was concerned, he'd paid a lot of money for this chance, and he was not going to let it get away without a fight. And with a small maze of doors, hallways, and elevators lying between Chandris and the street, it seemed inevitable that he would eventually drag her back to the feather couch, by her hair if necessary.

The outer reception door, she remembered, swung outward. Lowering her shoulder, she slammed into it full tilt, getting it open but losing precious momentum in the process. Even as she stumbled out into the hallway, Toomes's hand raked down her back. With a squeal of triumph, he caught the back of her panties. "*Got* you, you little—"

The noun never came. An instant later he skidded to a startled and terrified halt, his fingers dropping their grip on Chandris's panties as if the cloth had suddenly caught fire.

Judging by the stunned expressions on their faces, the eight men and women standing on and under the scaffolding flanking both sides of the hallway were probably at least as startled to see Toomes as he was to see them. They stood there gaping, their sprayers and cans of paint hanging forgotten in their hands, as Toomes scrambled madly to get his robe closed over what was left of his dignity.

Chandris didn't bother with either the dignity or the embarrassment. Clutching the blouse haphazardly to her chest, she charged down the center of the gauntlet, still babbling about fires.

No one tried to stop her. No one, as far as she could tell, even moved, except maybe to follow her with their eyes, as she sprinted down the bank of elevators halfway down the hall. Across from the elevators was the stairway, and with a final gasp of relief, she vanished through the doorway and started down the stairs.

Two floors down, she emerged again and slipped into a nearby women's restroom. The spare clothing she had stashed there on her way into the building fifteen minutes earlier was undisturbed, and a few minutes later she was back on the stairs, dressed in a typical cleaning woman's outfit.

Instead of the earlier mad dash, she took this part of the trip a little easier. Caught red-handed in the act of assaulting a half-naked girl a third his age, Toomes wouldn't be in any shape to continue the chase any time soon.

Eventually, of course, it would occur to him to wonder who in the world had logged in an order for the executive-floor corridor to be painted that particular evening. Hopefully not before she was out of the building and beyond his reach.

Still, she couldn't help but feel a twinge of conscience as she got into the line car she'd called. *She* didn't consider what she'd just done to be cheating, but Hanan and Ornina might not see it the same way she did. Better, maybe, that she just keep the details to herself.

And of course, there was no way in hell and eggs that she was going to tell Kosta. No way at all.

Predictably, Kosta was waiting near the gate as the line car let her out. "How did it go?" he asked, his voice sounding more anxious than he probably intended it to.

"Better than expected," Chandris said, handing him the credit chit as she gave the *Gazelle* a quick once-over. None of the workers she'd left here earlier were in sight. "How are the repairs going?"

"Same way," he said, peering at the number on the chit and then tucking it carefully away in his pocket. "They've got an automated setup in the bow doing radiation-hardening on the new electronics, and another one in the engine room doing likewise. There's nothing they can do either place until that's finished, but the foreman says it should only take a couple more hours. They've all gone off to dinner until then."

"That's going to be a pleasantly long dinner," Chandris said, gesturing up at the gaping holes still scattered across the *Gazelle*'s hull where damaged plates had been. "What about out here? I told him I wanted the hull finished by tonight."

"It will be, mostly," Kosta assured her. "They've got all the old plates out and are fabricating the replacements back at their shop. He said they'll have them finished tonight and can start putting them on in the morning."

"They can start putting them on tonight," Chandris retorted. "What's this 'tomorrow' stuff—they've got spare work crews. Where's that foreman, off at dinner with the rest of them?"

"Actually . . ." Kosta hesitated. "I think Ornina told them they could knock off on the rest of the hull work until tomorrow. It's okay," he added hastily. "I can't get all my stuff wired up until tomorrow, anyway."

"I don't care if you can't get it wired until next week," Chandris growled. "I told him we wanted it as soon as possible. Tomorrow is *not* as soon as possible."

"I know," Kosta said. "But—"

He broke off, his eyes shifting to something over Chandris's shoulder. "Can I help you?"

Chandris turned around, expecting to see one of the workers.

And froze.

"Sure can," Trilling Vail said genially, smiling an insane smile as he walked toward them. "My name's Trilling. I've come for my girl."

CHAPTER 35

For that first brief second Kosta didn't get it. The name meant nothing, and the man's smile seemed pleasant enough.

And then, with a strange little whimper, Chandris backed hard into him . . . and suddenly, somehow he knew.

Chandris had been running since the first day he had seen her across that *Xirrus* dining room. And the smiling man coming toward them was the reason.

He caught Chandris's shoulders with his hands, steadying her as he slipped around her right side and slid himself between her and the other man. "I think you have the wrong ship," he said.

Trilling's lips didn't lose their smile. But suddenly, the lines around his eyes tightened and hardened.

And in the eyes themselves, Kosta could see an edge of madness.

"So you're the new one, huh?" Trilling commented quietly. He was still coming, his right hand stuck casually in his coat pocket. Did he have a weapon in there? Probably. Knife or gun; it didn't matter which. Trilling looked like the kind who would be at home with either one.

"He's not a new one, Trilling," Chandris spoke up. Her voice was strained and tight, but her initial shock seemed to have vanished.

"It's the kosh in the fancy building, then?"

"No, not him, either," Chandris said. "There isn't anyone new."

"Don't give me that grist!" Trilling snarled. "You walk in that place wearing one set of clothes and come out wearing another, and you're going to stand there and tell me he didn't tom you?"

"No, he didn't," Chandris said. "He really didn't, Trilling. He was just a touch. A targ. I had to dig in and soften him up. There isn't anyone new."

The madness in Trilling's eyes seemed to fade into an almost childlike happiness. "So there really *isn't* anyone?" he asked hopefully. "You mean it's just like it was? We're together again?"

With her shoulder pressed against his back, Kosta could feel Chandris's body tense up again. "What is it you want?" he put in before she could say anything.

Trilling looked at Kosta as if noticing him for the first time and not liking what he saw. "Are you deaf?" he demanded. "Or just stupid? Chandris is my girl. Always has been. Always will be."

"What if she—" Kosta stopped. *Doesn't want to go with you,* was how he'd planned to finish the question. But looking into Trilling's eyes, he suddenly realized that phrasing it that way might not be a good idea. "We need her here," he said instead. "There's an important scientific experiment we need her help with."

Trilling gave a snort, which shattered into dark laughter. "Now you think *I'm* stupid," he said between laughs.

The laughter vanished. "I don't like people who think I'm stupid," he said, his voice shaking with rage. "I'm not stupid."

"We know that, Trilling," Chandris soothed, her voice starting to tremble, too. "We don't think you're stupid."

"Because you'd have to think I was stupid to think I'd rent something that glassy," he said, glaring at each of them in turn.

"It's not glassy," Chandris insisted. "Jereko has to do an experiment, and I need to help fly the ship."

Trilling leveled a finger at her. "You?" he asked. "*You?* Fly *this?*"

"Yes," Chandris said. "I can. Really."

Trilling snorted again. "And I can eat rocks for breakfast," he said scornfully. "If you can fly this thing—"

"How much, Trilling?" Kosta cut in, suddenly aware of the weight of the credit chit in his pocket. A hundred eighty thousand ruya, free and clear.

Chandris must have been thinking the same thing. "No," she murmured urgently, clutching at his arm. "No. We can't."

"Quiet," Kosta murmured back, his full attention on Trilling. This was Chandris's life they were talking about. "I'm asking how much it would take, Trilling, for you to just turn around and walk away."

He had thought Trilling had been angry before. Now, he realized that that had just been a warmup. Trilling took another step toward them, his face reddening, the veins in his face bulging out like he was about to have a stroke. Chandris's fingers dug harder into Kosta's arm, and for a long moment he was sure he was about to die.

"Don't say that to me again," Trilling warned, his voice as cold as dry ice. "Don't you *ever* say that to me again. You hear me? Don't ever say it."

The anger abruptly cleared from his face, and he smiled almost tenderly at Chandris. "Chandris is a one-man woman," he said, "and I'm a one-woman man. We were meant for each other."

"All right, Trilling," Chandris said softly. "We can be together again, if that's what you really want."

"Okay, good," Trilling said, shrugging as if it was suddenly no big deal to him. "What about him?" he added, eyeing Kosta again.

"He has something we'll want to take with us," Chandris said. "There's no need to start out broke, is there?"

Trilling's eyes glistened. "He's got cash?"

"No, but something just as good," Chandris said, her voice low and persuasive. "Something we can sell for a lot of money. An angel."

Kosta felt his heart seize up inside him. So that was what she was angling for: to get Trilling into range of the Daviees' spare angel, hoping that its influence for good could change him.

Except that that wasn't what angels did.

Only Chandris didn't know that. "Chandris—"

"Quiet," Trilling said, dismissing him with a flick of a contemptuous glance. "These angel things are worth money, huh?"

"This whole ship was built just to look for them," Chandris told him, waving a hand at the bulk of the *Gazelle* looming over them. "We can go inside and get the angel, then we can leave. Just the two of us. Okay?"

Trilling looked at Kosta, and a slight smile touched his lips. "Sure," he said. "Whatever you say."

Kosta swallowed painfully. The other's face wasn't hard to read. They would leave, all right, but not until Trilling had taken care of all witnesses to the theft.

"Jereko?" Chandris asked tentatively.

For a heartbeat he was tempted to grab Chandris by the arm and make a run for it. But even if they managed to get away, Trilling might decide to come back and start poking around inside the *Gazelle*.

And Ornina was in there. Alone.

He took a deep breath. He'd been trained, however cursorily, in hand-to-hand combat. Inside, in closer quarters, he might have a better chance. "Okay," he said, gesturing back toward the hatchway. "Come on. I'll take you to the angel."

"Chandris can lead the way," Trilling said, pulling his hand out of his pocket for the first time. It was a knife, all right, with a short but wickedly serrated blade. "You stay back with me."

The ship was eerily quiet as Chandris led the way along the *Gazelle*'s corridors. Kosta walked behind her, with Trilling close behind him. Occasionally the tip of the knife brushed against Kosta's shirt, sending a shiver up his back.

They reached Chandris's cabin and she pulled the angel carrying case out from under her bed. "This is it," she said, offering it to Trilling.

"Open it," he ordered, staying where he was behind Kosta.

"Not here," Chandris said, shaking her head. "It's not safe. The angel is very small, and if we're not careful we could lose it."

For a long moment Trilling was silent. Kosta watched Chandris's eyes, wondering if there would even be enough time for her to warn him with her reaction when Trilling pulled the knife back to stab him. "Fine," Trilling said at last. "What about a storeroom? You got a storeroom or something here?"

Chandris's eyes flicked to Kosta, and he felt his throat tighten in reaction. That was where Trilling planned to do it. Somewhere a little less obvious than Chandris's cabin, someplace where it would presumably take longer for someone to stumble over a dead body.

For a moment he considered turning and having it out right here. But Trilling's knife blade wasn't pressed against his back at the moment, which meant he didn't know exactly where it was. For a faster, better trained martial artist that might not have been a problem. For Kosta, it was the difference between death and even a chance at life.

He would have to wait, and hope that a better opportunity presented itself.

They had made their way to the narrow stairway and were nearly down to the lower deck when they heard the soft singing.

"Hold it," Trilling hissed, wrapping a hand around Kosta's throat and freezing them both in place. "Who's that?"

"It's Ornina Daviee," Chandris whispered, half turning, a sudden new tension in her face. Clearly, she hadn't expected Ornina to be down here. "This is her ship."

Reluctantly, Kosta thought, Trilling let go of his throat. "Okay," he said, the knife pressure leaving Kosta's back again. "Let's go. Real careful, now."

Hunching her shoulders once, Chandris started forward again. With Trilling's breath hot on the back of his neck, Kosta followed.

Ornina was kneeling beside the angel collector bin when they entered the storeroom, a set of delicate adjustment tools laid out on the floor beside her. "Hello, Chandris," she said as they came in. "And Jereko. Oh—and who's your friend?"

"He's not exactly a friend," Kosta said, watching her face as Trilling moved a little to the side and the knife in his hand came into Ornina's view. The older woman's eyes flicked to the weapon but otherwise her expression didn't change. "His name's Trilling," Kosta continued. "He's here to take Chandris away with him."

"Ah," Ornina said calmly, looking back at Chandris. "And the angel, too, I see," she said, nodding at the carrying case under Chandris's arm. "Welcome to the *Gazelle*, Trilling. Can I get you a cup of tea?"

"Very funny," Trilling said, giving Kosta a shove that sent him stumbling into Chandris. "Not much of a storeroom."

"We don't usually have much that needs storing," Ornina said. "Mostly it's where the angels get collected. I was serious about the tea, you know. Or you could take the angel from Chandris and she could go up and make it."

Trilling snorted. "You *are* funny," he said. "Okay. You—Kosta—get over there with her."

"Trilling, you don't have to do this," Chandris said, her voice soft and pleading as Kosta moved over beside Ornina. "Please. I'll go with you if you'll just leave them alone."

Trilling turned those insane eyes on her. "Of course you'll go with me," he said, sounding surprised. "We were meant to be together."

"Trilling, please," Chandris repeated.

"Chandris, what's gotten into you?" Trilling demanded. "What are these targs to you, anyway?"

Kosta darted his eyes around the storeroom, searching for inspiration, his mind flashing back to the other night when Chandris had confronted him with a bright light in the face and the threat of a cutting torch behind it. If she'd actually had a torch, and if it was still in here . . .

But she hadn't, and it wasn't. Ornina's tools? Too small to serve as weapons. Loose pipes, then, or discarded storage crate lids? But there wasn't anything he could see that wasn't fastened down.

"Enough!" Trilling barked, snapping Kosta's attention back to the discussion. The argument, such as it was, was over.

And Chandris had lost.

"You don't want to watch, you can leave the room," Trilling went on, looking back at Kosta and lifting his knife. "This'll just take a second."

Beside him, Kosta felt Ornina's hand fumble for his. He took her hand, and she squeezed once. Not a grip of panic or even fear, but merely of comfort and friendship. And, perhaps, farewell.

And then she gently disengaged her hand from his. Leaving him free for whatever action he was preparing himself for.

A sudden flood of determination surged through him like a hot cup of Ornina's sadras tea. Ornina was counting on him for her life; Chandris was counting on him for her freedom from this man.

There was no way in hell he was going to fail them.

"All right," Chandris said, her voice humble and defeated. Her eyes flicked once to him as she stepped behind Trilling and headed for the door. Lifting his knife, his eyes glowing with expectation, Trilling started forward.

Kosta let his knees bend slightly into the combat stance he'd been taught and turned his torso slightly, presenting a smaller target to his opponent. His hands were still at his sides, but he could visualize bringing his left arm up to sweep Trilling's knife arm away to the side. With Trilling's torso open, he would throw the hardest kick he could at the other's knee, and follow it up with another kick to the abdomen . . .

And then, behind Trilling, Chandris turned silently on one foot and brought the angel carrying case down as hard as she could onto his head.

Trilling bellowed with rage, shaking his head once to clear it as he spun around toward his betrayer. A sweep of his left arm knocked the box from her hands and sent her staggering backwards. The knife flashed in his hand as he brought it back for a killing blow—

And with another bellow he sprawled off-balance as Kosta's kick landed in the back of his right knee.

He hit the deck hard and twisted catlike around onto his back. Kosta started to dive on top of him, broke away at the last second as he belatedly saw that Trilling still had hold of his knife.

Too little, too late. Even as he tried to veer off, Trilling slashed the weapon in a vicious upward arc across Kosta's chest. He felt the tug as his shirt was sliced through; and then his momentum and tangled feet got the better of him and he too toppled onto the deck.

Trilling was back on his feet in an instant. Chandris started toward him; half turning, he slashed the air once to keep her back, then turned back to Kosta, his face contorted into something inhuman. Kosta scrambled backwards crab-style, his eyes fixed on the knife, trying desperately to get far enough away from Trilling to be able to get back onto his feet.

But Trilling clearly had no intention of giving him that much breathing room. Baring his teeth, he kept coming, his knife held ready. From somewhere to Kosta's left came a soft buzz—

And suddenly Trilling jerked in place as if he'd stepped on a jellyfish. The enraged madman's expression softened into an odd sort of bewilderment, the knife dangling in a loosened grip.

"Again!" Kosta shouted, scrambling to his feet and shooting a glance to his left. Ornina was standing there, her eyes wide, Kosta's shocker gripped in her hand. "Hit him again!"

She squeezed the weapon. There was another buzz, and Trilling jerked again. "Again," Kosta ordered, gingerly trying to ease past the wavering knife. The shocker was still on its lowest setting, and that wasn't going to hold someone like Trilling very long. If Kosta could get to Ornina and dial a higher power—

And then, with a sort of gurgling moan, Trilling lunged at him.

If he'd been in full control of his muscles, Kosta would have died right there. But two jolts from the shocker, even at low power, had scrambled his nervous system just enough. Kosta jumped back, and the knife blade sliced through his left sleeve instead of burying itself into the center of his chest. Reflexively, he slapped at Trilling's knife arm with his right hand, and to his own vague surprise the knife went flying away to clatter off the pipes and conduits lining the bulkheads.

For a fraction of a second Kosta could see his own surprise mirrored in Trilling's face at the loss of his weapon. Then, with a slurred curse, Trilling lunged again.

Kosta tried to slap away the hands stretching out toward his throat. But Trilling was already shrugging off the effects of the shocker and the countermove failed. An instant later the hands reached their target, one grabbing him by the throat, the other closing around Kosta's left upper arm.

An agonizing wave of pain shot through the skin and muscle like a crack of lightning. He had just enough time to gasp once—

And then his back was slammed against the bulkhead hard enough to knock the wind out of him. The grip around his throat tightened, cutting off his air, and Trilling began to beat his head against the cold metal.

Kosta's vision began to waver, fog alternating with sparks of pain with each blow. He tried to bring up his knee into Trilling's groin, but his body seemed to have turned into soft cotton. He was vaguely aware of someone screaming something in the background, but he couldn't make out the words. He reached up to try to pull Trilling's hand off his throat, but there was no strength there, and he was barely even able to grab hold of the other's wrist.

And then, suddenly, the hammering of his head stopped. Even as he wondered whether the halt was real or simply the hallucination of a dying brain, the grip around his throat loosened and then was gone. His head began to clear, and he found himself sagging against the bulkhead, gasping for breath, his left arm throbbing with pain.

And then Chandris was at his side, gripping his right arm. "It's all right," she said, her breath coming in shaky gulps. "Just sit down, okay? Just sit down."

"I'm okay," he said, letting her help him down into a sitting position on the deck. The words hurt his throat to say.

"Here," Ornina said, appearing on his other side with a first-aid kit. "Chandris, can you start getting his shirt off?"

"Sure."

She began carefully pulling off his shirt. Kosta winced as a line of fire flashed across his chest, joining counterpoint with the agony in his left upper arm, and to his amazement he noticed for the first time that the shirt there was soaked with blood. Apparently, that first slash had been deeper than he'd realized. Odd that he hadn't felt any pain there until now.

It was only then, as he raised his eyes from the blood on his chest, that he saw Trilling.

The man was crumpled on the deck behind Chandris, unmoving. His right hand was wet with blood where he'd been squeezing Kosta's slashed arm.

Protruding from his back was the hilt of his own knife.

Kosta looked back at Chandris. Now, for the first time, he could see the tears running down her cheeks. "Chandris?" he asked softly.

"I had to," she said, her voice so low he almost couldn't hear it. "He was going to kill you. He was going to kill you both. There was nothing else I could do."

"I know," Kosta said, wincing as Ornina carefully rolled a bandage across the cut in his chest. "I'm—"

"No, don't," she cut him off, flashing a tortured glare at him through the moisture brimming in her eyes. "Don't."

She dropped her gaze away, half turning toward the body lying on the deck behind her. "He was my friend once," she said, her body jerking with silent, gasping sobs. "He was all I had. He cared for me, protected me."

She bowed her head and closed her eyes. "Loved me."

Kosta gazed at her profile, at the tears still flowing freely.

And for him, at least, there was no longer any doubt. Chandris could protect her friends, yet cry over what she had had to do. She could make sacrifices for a higher need, yet retain her pride and dignity. She could feel anger, and sadness, and regret, and love.

The Pax propaganda was wrong. The angels weren't turning the citizens of the Empyrean into something less than human. If anything, they were allowing people like Chandris to become more human than they'd ever been. More human than they'd ever dared to be.

Ornina had shifted now to bandaging his arm. Their eyes met, and he read the message there. Reaching over with his good arm, he took hold of Chandris's shoulders and gently pulled her close to him.

And as if that had been the breaking of the final barrier, she turned her face into his chest and sobbed like a child. Like the child that in many ways she still was.

Like the child, perhaps, that she had never been allowed to be.

CHAPTER 36

"I'm sorry, High Senator," the doctor said, peering down at his hand computer. "I'm afraid we still don't know what happened to Mr. Ronyon."

Forsythe looked over at Ronyon. The big man was studiously fastening his shoes, with the same intense concentration he brought to every technically challenging job. "But he *is* all right now?"

"As far as we can tell," the doctor said. "If you'd like to leave him with us for a few more days, we might be able to come up with something."

"You mean you might be able to dream up some new test that no one's ever thought of before?"

The doctor shrugged uncomfortably. "It does rather come down to that, yes," he conceded.

"Yes," Forsythe said. "I appreciate the offer, but I think we'll pass."

Ronyon finished his shoes and straightened up. *Can we go now?* he signed to Forsythe, his forehead wrinkled with nervous hope.

Yes, Forsythe assured him. It had been clear from their conversation earlier that afternoon that Ronyon was very unhappy here, lying in a strange bed and being periodically poked and prodded and frowned at by the small army of medical men and women who were continually carting him off to various examination rooms. There was no point in making him go through any more of that, particularly when they'd run out of ideas anyway.

And in truth, Forsythe was just as anxious to get the big man back at his side. The tension of not knowing what was happening at Lorelei was starting to affect him, making him moody and short-tempered. And everyone from Pirbazari to the temporary staff the Seraph government had insisted on assigning to him knew it. The sooner he had Ronyon's happy innocence around him again, the better.

"Best of fortune to you, then," the doctor said. "If he has any more attacks, please let me know at once. Good-bye, Mr. Ronyon."

Are we going home now? Ronyon signed as he and Forsythe headed down the hospital corridor toward the admissions desk where Pirbazari should be about finished with the release paperwork.

Not yet, Forsythe told him, struggling to keep his emotion from showing in his face. For all they knew, there might not even be a home left for them to go back to.

But of course Ronyon knew nothing about this. For the moment, it was best they keep it that way. *We're going to the Magasca Government Building,* he added. *We have some temporary office space there.*

Oh. Ronyon paused, his forehead wrinkling a little more. *Why aren't we going home?*

We can't leave yet, Forsythe said, studying Ronyon's face. To the casual observer, he seemed to have recovered fully from whatever had happened to him at Angelmass.

But Forsythe had known him a long time, and he could tell that there was still something lingering below the surface. There were new lines at the corners of Ronyon's eyes, and a thin film of solemnity lying across his expression like a nearly transparent veil.

Maybe that would disappear as the memory of the trip faded away. Forsythe hoped so. *There are still some things we need to do here.*

You mean like with Hanan and Ornina and Chandris? Ronyon asked. *Is Hanan all right?*

To his embarrassment, Forsythe realized suddenly that he hadn't even checked on Hanan Daviee since hearing that the pilot's condition had been stabilized. *I think so,* he signed. *If you'd like, we can check on him before we leave.*

Some of the new lines in Ronyon's face seemed to smooth out. *Can we?* he signed eagerly.

Forsythe smiled. *Of course,* he said. *I'm sure Hanan will be happy to see you—*

"High Senator?"

Forsythe looked up. Pirbazari was hurrying down the corridor toward him, his phone clutched in his hand.

Come on, Forsythe signed to Ronyon, picking up his own pace, his heart abruptly pounding in his ears. News from Lorelei at last?

They met in the middle. "I just got a call from EmDef," Pirbazari said, taking Forsythe's arm and pulling him off to the side of the corridor. "You're not going to believe this."

Forsythe braced himself. Here it came. "Lorelei's been taken?"

Pirbazari shook his head. "No. I mean, I don't know—there's still no word from there."

He waved his phone again. "It's Angelmass. The thing's moving."

Forsythe glanced at Ronyon. "What do you mean, moving? Moving where?"

"Into a lower orbit," Pirbazari said. "Dropping in toward the sun. Just a little so far, but the change is definitely there."

"What's causing it?"

"You got me," Pirbazari said. "In fact, you got all of us. No one at EmDef *or* the Institute has the faintest idea."

Forsythe frowned. "Zar, there aren't a lot of possibilities here," he said. "In order to change something's orbit, you have to apply force to it. Where's the force coming from?"

Pirbazari shrugged helplessly. "They've checked solar wind, magnetic anomalies, dust concentrations, even looked for stray dark masses that could be affecting it. So far, nothing."

Forsythe rubbed his chin, trying to visualize the configuration out there. An inward change in orbit, he remembered from college physics, meant an increase in orbital speed. And with Angelmass Central running in the same orbit ahead of it . . . "It's moving closer to the station," he murmured.

"Yes, but not very fast," Pirbazari said. "And Central is pretty heavily shielded. At the rate Angelmass is gaining, it'll be at least a couple of weeks before it even starts to pose a radiation hazard. And of course, if the orbit continues to sink, it may end up too low to bother the station by the time it passes anyway."

"I wouldn't want to bet on that," Forsythe said. "Especially since we don't know how or why it's sinking in the first place. Better have the station personnel prepare for evacuation, just in case. Do they have any ships there?"

"EmDef can have a transport to them in twenty minutes," Pirbazari said. "There's also a double ring of emergency escape pods set around the tube connecting the catapult and net sections of the station. They've got steerable drive nozzles with enough fuel for half an hour of steady burn time, plus two weeks' worth of life-support."

"Shielding?"

"Huntership-grade sandwich metal," Pirbazari assured him. "Actually, the pods are the main shielding for the connection tube."

"All right," Forsythe said. "Speaking of hunterships, what's being done with the ones that are out there?"

"They've been alerted," Pirbazari said.

"That's all?"

"Well . . ." Pirbazari floundered a moment. "The orbit's only changed a little. They can surely compensate for that."

"Only if the change stays small," Forsythe said tartly. "And since we don't know what's causing it, it's going to be a little hard to make any guarantees. Have them recalled to Seraph."

Pirbazari seemed taken aback. "You really think that's necessary?" he asked.

"Unexplained radiation surges and now impossible orbital shifts?" Forsythe countered. "I think we've gone slightly past necessary."

Pirbazari's lip twitched. "All right," he said reluctantly. "I'll talk to EmDef."

"Talk loud and firm," Forsythe said. "And while you're at it, see if they have any mechanism for moving Central into a higher orbit. Whatever's affecting Angelmass may hit the station next, and I don't want its orbit dropping just in time for Angelmass to plow into it."

"I'll check," Pirbazari said. "I know they stock some supplies for asteroid miners who sometimes stop by. Maybe they've got a few strap-on boosters aboard."

Forsythe grimaced. It would take a lot more than a few boosters to get something the size of Angelmass Central moving. But it would be better than nothing. "Just have that evacuation transport standing by."

"It is," Pirbazari said. "EmDef tells me—"

He broke off as Ronyon suddenly grabbed Forsythe's shoulder. Forsythe looked up, to find the big man staring wide-eyed down the corridor behind Pirbazari. *It's Ornina!* Ronyon signed excitedly, bobbing his head that direction. *And Chandris!*

Forsythe shifted his eyes down again, expecting to see the women walking through the front door on their way to see Hanan.

What he saw instead was the two of them hovering in the background as two emergency room techs wheeled in a gurney with a blood-soaked figure on it.

"Looks like Kosta," Pirbazari said, peering down the corridor. "What the hell happened to him?"

"An accident, maybe," Forsythe said, an odd feeling stirring in his gut. "Let's find out."

They arrived just as the group reached the elevator. It was Kosta, all right, his face puckered stoically. "What happened?" Forsythe asked.

"Oh, High Senator," Ornina greeted him, her own expression tight but controlled. "There was a—well—"

"Someone I used to know came by the *Gazelle,*" Chandris spoke up. "He had a knife."

"And showed Mr. Kosta how it worked, I take it," Forsythe said. Like both Kosta and Ornina, he saw, Chandris's expression and voice were under careful control.

But as Forsythe studied her, it seemed to him that her face had aged ten years since the last time he'd seen her.

"He was going to take me away," she said softly. Her eyes closed briefly; and when she opened them, they seemed to have aged another ten. "Kosta saved my life."

"It was actually the other way around," Kosta murmured.

"Save your strength, Jereko," Ornina admonished him gently. "Our first-aid bandages weren't able to stop the bleeding, High Senator, and the *Gazelle's* medpack was shut down with most of the rest of the ship's equipment."

The elevator doors opened. "You don't need to explain," Forsythe assured her. "Go get him fixed up."

"Yes, sir," Ornina said, as the techs got the gurney into the car. "Thank you, High Senator."

The two women got in with the others, and the doors closed. "Left arm and chest," Pirbazari commented. "Both of them slashes instead of penetration wounds. He should be all right, assuming he hasn't lost too much blood."

"I'm sure he'll be fine," Forsythe said, gazing unseeingly at the closed doors as all the question marks surrounding Kosta came flooding back. His mysterious funding source, his shadowy background, the anomalies in his manner and speech.

And all the questions now set against a Pax invasion of Lorelei.

And suddenly, it all came together. "He's a spy," he breathed. "A Pax spy."

Out of the corner of his eye he saw Pirbazari's jaw drop. But even as he turned to face him, he could see his aide's surprise turn to understanding. "I'll be damned," he said quietly. "Are you sure?"

Forsythe hesitated. Yes, he was sure. But at the same time, he also had no actual proof.

Which was, after all, the question Pirbazari was really asking. "Not yet," he told the other. "But I will be."

He glanced up at Ronyon, who was silently following the conversation with a puzzled look on his face. "I'm going to take Ronyon back to the office," he said. "As soon as Kosta is patched up, you bring him to me."

"Right," Pirbazari said. "You want me to bring the others, too?"

"Just Kosta," Forsythe said. "And watch him, Zar. Watch him very closely."

"Don't worry," Pirbazari said. "I will."

The stars emerged from the blackness, and the *Harmonic* had arrived.

"Seraph EmDef Command to liner," a tart voice came from the bridge speaker. "Identify yourself."

Captain Djuabi turned his head toward the bridge master screen, where the net and catapult ships showed in a tactical-type display. Each of the four catapult ships had three or four Empyreal Defense Force ships hovering watchfully nearby. "This is Captain Djuabi of the liner *Harmonic,*" he said, his voice stiff.

Far too stiff for Lleshi's taste. From his vantage point directly in front of the captain, carefully outside of the range of the visual comm camera, the commodore lifted a warning finger. Djuabi's lip twitched, just noticeably, and he gave a microscopic nod.

He would cooperate, all right. Not that he had many other options. With his liner's command areas all under Pax control, Djuabi had no choice but to comply with Lleshi's orders. At least, not if he valued the lives of his crew and passengers.

Djuabi shifted slightly in his chair, the movement sending a faint glint off the gold pendant and chain around his neck. Telthorst had wondered, rather pointedly, whether any number of human lives would even be a consideration for a man wearing an angel.

Perhaps they were about to find out.

"Point of origin?" Seraph Command asked.

"Balmoral," Djuabi said. Apparently it was still possible for a man to lie with an angel around his neck, at least under duress.

"Please transmit your papers," Seraph Command ordered.

Djuabi nodded to the man at the comm station. The Pax officer at the board set to work, fumbling only slightly with the unfamiliar control layout.

Lleshi rubbed his thumb slowly along the side of his index finger, striving to release some of the tension churning through his stomach. Everything was balanced together on this moment, a moment in which there was nothing he could do but watch and wait. The Balmoral papers the officer was sending out were as good a forgery as the *Komitadji*'s Crypto Group had been able to create, but nothing was perfect. If Seraph Command had a particularly sharp eye, or a particularly well-programmed computer, this gamble would crumble like soft stone under a mason's sledgehammer.

And if it crumbled, so would the entire mission. Plus, undoubtedly, the rest of his career. Telthorst would see to that.

For perhaps half a minute nothing happened. Lleshi gazed at the master screen, watching the slow drift of the catapult ships across the starry background and wondering about the capabilities of those EmDef ships escorting them. The defenders were destroyer sized; small but heavily shielded and undoubtedly well armed.

And this time around Lleshi didn't have any doomsday pods available to use against them. Still, they surely wouldn't be able to stand up against the full might of the *Komitadji*.

Assuming he was able to make such a confrontation happen.

The vector on one of the distant ships shifted momentarily as it moved to keep the *Harmonic* within the catapult focal area. They were playing this cautious, all right. Lleshi took careful, measured breaths as he kept his eyes moving around the bridge. Win or lose, there was no way he was going to show nervousness in front of the Empyreals.

"*Harmonic*, you're cleared for Seraph," the voice came. "Fly safe."

"Thank you," Captain Djuabi said. He touched a switch, and the comm light went dark. "Instructions, Commodore?" he asked calmly.

"You heard the man," Lleshi said. "Standard course toward Seraph."

A slight frown creased Djuabi's forehead. But he nodded and gave the helm the order without comment or question.

With a distant rumble of engines the *Harmonic* began accelerating. Lleshi kept his eyes on the master screen as the liner moved out of the net focal area, watching for any signs of suspicion from the EmDef ships.

But they were still just sitting there, drifting unconcernedly beside their assigned catapult spacecraft. Completely oblivious to what had just happened.

Telthorst would undoubtedly have called them fools. Lleshi couldn't help but feel sorry for them.

He gave the *Harmonic* five more minutes worth of distance before nodding to Djuabi. "Far enough," he said. "Open the lifeboat bays."

"Lifeboat bays open, aye," the captain said formally, gesturing the order to the appropriate station. "Acknowledge."

"Bays open," the officer at the station growled. Unlike his captain, this one was making no effort to hide his rage and shame. But then, he wasn't wearing an angel, either. "All bays show open."

Djuabi looked back at Lleshi. "Your move, Commodore."

"Thank you." Lleshi lifted his hand comm to his lips and clicked it on. "First wave: launch."

And on the board, the *Harmonic*'s outer hull erupted with drive trails as a hundred small spacecraft blew outward like spores from a flowering plant, using the liner's rotation to give them an extra boost.

But they weren't the liner's lifeboats. Those had all been offloaded at Lorelei.

These were Pax *Vlad*-class fighters.

"Attack pattern Alpha," Lleshi ordered. "All fighters."

The EmDef ships were on the move now, shifting to intercept vectors and accelerating to meet the enemy. "Remember your targets," Lleshi reminded them softly. "Not the destroyers, but the catapult ships."

In quick succession, the squadron leaders acknowledged . . . and as he watched the master screen Lleshi felt a tight smile touching the corners of his mouth. The gamble was still balanced on a knife's edge, but the waiting was over. Now, at least, he had some control over the outcome.

Taking a deep breath, holding the hand comm ready, he watched the ships prepare to engage.

CHAPTER 37

"They came out of the *Harmonic*'s lifeboat bays," Pirbazari told Forsythe as he held open the door to the Government Building's executive conference room. "The EmDef guard ships have engaged."

The conference room was surprisingly crowded, particularly for eight o'clock at night when everything was supposed to be closed and senior governmental officials were supposed to be at home. Either all of them had been working late, or else word of the attack had passed quickly enough for them to come back here to take advantage of the direct EmDef information feed.

Some of the officials were speaking urgently on their phones. Others were talking tensely among themselves or just standing in stunned silence as they gazed at the main comm screen at the far end of the room. The screen had been rigged with a multi-view array taken from the various ships and monitor satellites in the net region, giving them all a front-row seat to the battle.

"Tactics?" Forsythe asked quietly as he and Pirbazari pushed their way between the conversational knots. Ideally, a High Senator would have been instantly and deferentially ushered to the best vantage point in the room. The fact that no one had apparently even noticed him said a lot about the stunned state they were all in.

"Looks like they're going for the two closest catapult ships," Pirbazari said. "Numbers One and Three. Their first goal will be to disable the catapult so that the rest of their force can come in."

"Or so that we can't throw out the fighters," Forsythe said. "Or maybe they don't want us throwing out the liner?"

Pirbazari shook his head. "It would take some serious reconfiguration of the catapult ships to get to the liner now," he said. "You can see the *Harmonic* was careful to get well out of the center of the pyramid before launching the fighters."

"Then why is it going back in?" a short woman standing beside Forsythe asked. "I mean, if all the fighters are already gone?"

Forsythe frowned. She was right: the liner had shifted course and was accelerating on a vector that would take it close to the Number Two catapult ship. "Zar?" Forsythe murmured.

"The Pax must still be in command there," Pirbazari said. "On his own, a liner captain would certainly get his ship out of a combat zone as quickly as possible."

"Obviously," Forsythe said. "But what exactly is he *doing?*"

Pirbazari exhaled slowly. "That I don't know," he admitted. "EmDef counted a hundred fighters, and that's all the lifeboat bays a ship that size has. And the fighters are too big to have doubled up."

Forsythe rubbed his chin. "What about other weapons? Could they have loaded heavy lasers or other missiles aboard?"

"Where would they mount them?" Pirbazari countered. "There aren't any weapons bays or pods on a liner. It's got a couple of meteor-defense lasers, but those aren't big enough for anyone to worry about."

"EmDef seems worried about them," someone else said, pointing. "Look— there they go."

The EmDef destroyers guarding Number Two were indeed on the move. Leaving one of their number behind as close-support to the catapult ship, the rest were now accelerating to intercept the incoming liner. "A feint?" Forsythe suggested.

"I'd say there's a feint going on somewhere," Pirbazari agreed tightly. "They only need to hit two of the four ships to disable the catapult. Yet between the fighters and the liner, they're now threatening three of them."

And given the odds the Pax ships were facing, it didn't make sense for their commander to split up his forces more than he absolutely had to. "Maybe they're just going for insurance."

"Or as you said, one of them is a feint," Pirbazari said. "Designed either to draw off or pin down some of the defenders." He nodded at the screen. "The question is, which one?"

The battles for Numbers One and Three were burning fiercely now, the opposing ships lighting up with the faint flashes of laser and plasma weapons, or the brighter bursts of missile explosions. The EmDef destroyers were by far the larger craft, and with hulls modeled on those of angel hunterships they certainly had the thicker skins. In a straight slugging match, even top-of-the-line Pax fighters probably wouldn't stand a chance.

But the enemy commander was too smart to play it that way. His fighters were far more maneuverable than the destroyers, and he was using that edge to his full advantage. Dodging in and out of the EmDef defense formation, the Pax ships worked against the destroyers, worked the destroyers against each other, and systematically pumped small missiles through the screen at the two catapult ships.

Most of the shots missed, or were blocked by the destroyers, or were eliminated by defensive fire en route. But a few of them were getting through. Too many of them.

And as Forsythe listened to EmDef Command's running commentary, he realized that the situation out there was rapidly becoming serious.

Still, the Pax fighters were taking casualties, too. One by one, occasionally in pairs as a lead pilot and his wingman were caught in the same blast, they flashed and shattered and winked out.

But not fast enough. Not nearly fast enough. Through a red haze of anger and frustration and fear, Forsythe watched as the two catapult ships continued to take hit after hit.

And then, suddenly, the operational end of Number One flared with a blue-white fire. "What was that?" someone yelped.

"They got it," Pirbazari confirmed. "Not the whole ship, but the part that counts."

Someone else swore. "Then why don't they leave it?" he demanded. "Look at them. Isn't it enough that they knocked out the catapult? Now they want to kill everyone aboard, too?"

Forsythe ground his teeth together helplessly. The man was right: instead of veering off, the Pax fighters were still swarming around the crippled catapult ship. "Going for vengeance," he muttered.

"I don't think so," Pirbazari said doubtfully. "Vengeance in the middle of battle is a very unprofessional thing to do. And if there's one thing those people are, it's professional. My guess is they're still trying to keep that group of destroyers pinned down."

"So that their comrades will be free to take out Number Three," Forsythe growled.

EmDef had apparently come to the same conclusion. Abruptly, the destroyers guarding the fourth, unthreatened, catapult ship pulled away, heading for the beleaguered Number Three.

"Finally getting some backup over there," someone near the front said. "About time."

Forsythe felt his eyes narrow. The backup would certainly be welcome . . . but at the same time, drawing those destroyers into the fray at Number Three meant leaving Number Four completely helpless. "Zar, what in blazes are they doing?"

"They're gambling," Pirbazari said grimly. "With Number One down, they can't afford to lose any of the others—if they do, they can't catapult any Pax ships that come into the net. They don't see the *Harmonic* as being any real threat to Number Two, and Number Four is far enough away from the battles for them to have plenty of warning if any of the fighters suddenly turn and head that direction. So they concentrate their defense on Number Three."

"Sounds damn risky."

"It *is* damn risky," Pirbazari agreed. "The theory is sound enough; the destroyers can get back to Number Four pretty quickly, and the catapult ship itself isn't exactly defenseless."

He gestured toward the screen. "But there's that assumption that the *Harmonic* isn't a threat to Number Two. I'm not sure I buy that."

Forsythe looked over at that section of the display. The destroyers from Number Two had reached and surrounded the big passenger ship. Concentrating on that part of the running voice track, he could hear the EmDef squadron commander ordering the *Harmonic* to open its airlocks and accept boarders.

"They've been calling on the liner to surrender for the past couple of minutes," Pirbazari said. "So far, the captain has been stalling them."

Forsythe shot a glance back at Number Three. The destroyers that had deserted Number Four to come to its aid were nearly within close-point attack range, and in fact the front ships of the formation were already beginning to spark laser flashes toward the invaders.

But the Pax fighters seemed unaware of them. Still dodging in and out of the defending ships, they continued to hammer at the catapult ship.

He looked back at the liner, the hairs on the back of his neck prickling. The Pax fighters ignoring the incoming destroyers; the liner, still under enemy control, making no move; the Number Four catapult ship completely open to attack and the Number Two nearly as helpless.

Yet nothing was happening. Why wasn't anything happening?

And then, suddenly, he understood. "Call EmDef," he ordered, gripping Pirbazari's arm. "Tell them to shut down that net."

Pirbazari blinked. "High Senator, they can't do that. It's the only one still operating, remember?"

"I know that," Forsythe said. Any second now. It had to be any second now. "Call and give the order."

"If we shut it down, the whole system will be open," Pirbazari objected. "The rest of the Pax force will be able to come in anywhere."

"They don't want to come in anywhere," Forsythe snapped. "Don't you see? They want their reinforcements to come in *right here. Here,* where they can keep their advance force from being slaughtered."

"But then—?"

"What are they waiting for?" Forsythe jabbed a finger at the screen. "They're waiting for their clock to run down. They know that the second they knock out the catapult, EmDef will shut down the net. They'll have maybe a half-minute window; and that's what they're going for."

Pirbazari's eyes were darting across the screen, his lips half curled back from his teeth. Except for the running EmDef voice track, Forsythe noted distantly, the whole room had gone silent.

With a jerk, Pirbazari snatched out his phone. "Yes," he said, beginning to punch in a number. "You're right. *Damn* it."

But it was too late. Even as he punched in the last number and lifted the phone to his ear, the *Harmonic* finally made its move.

There was a flash from the liner's midsection, a burst of flame and curling smoke that resolved itself into the fiery tail of a missile. It was followed by another flash as the liner rotated beneath the departing weapon, the second missile bursting out almost directly into the exhaust trail of the first. Then came another, and another, and another, each new missile emerging just as the liner rotated into position and then dropping into line behind the others like baby ducks following their mother.

Pirbazari swore gently. "The airlocks," he said. "Of course. No weapons bays or pods on a liner; so they just loaded their missiles into the airlocks."

The surrounding destroyers tried to react, their own counterweapons blazing away at the line of enemy missiles. But the EmDef ships were too close to the liner, their antimissile defenses too slow to respond. And the destroyers were too far out of line to move into the missiles' path and take the hits themselves.

Abruptly, Forsythe realized why. The destroyers had, cautiously enough, arranged themselves in defensive formation between the *Harmonic* and the Number Two catapult ship, the closest and therefore most obvious target for an attack originating from the liner.

But that wasn't where the missiles were aimed. They were, instead, burning space for the more distant Number Four.

The ship whose destroyers were all currently at Number Three.

The EmDef commander saw it the same time Forsythe did. Orders were snapped, and within seconds the destroyers from Number Four were disengaging from their defense of Number Three and circling back around.

Or rather, they were trying to disengage. But with the trap sprung, the Pax fighters now abandoned their attack on the already crippled catapult ship and concentrated their fire on the destroyers. Even as the EmDef ships pulled free and headed toward Number Four the fighters moved with them, nipping at their heels like tigers attacking a group of fleeing elephants.

A sudden flicker of light caught Forsythe's eye. Number Four's defense lasers had found the range, and the lead Pax missile had been flashed into dust. Forsythe held his breath . . .

But no. The Pax commander had anticipated this one, too. The lead missile was destroyed, all right; but the cloud of debris it had become was still moving along its original vector.

And as Number Four's lasers continued to fire, Forsythe realized that the debris was actually shielding the missiles behind it from the attacks.

Again, the EmDef commander was right on top of things. Another series of orders, and two formations of antimissiles streaked out from Number Four's launchers. The first group swept through the dust cloud and converged on the next Pax missile in line—

This time the flash was bright enough to activate the telescope screen's sun filters, creating a brief dead spot in the view.

But not a circular one, as Forsythe would have expected from a normal explosion. Instead, this dead spot was triangular, stretching forward with the rear apex where the Pax warhead had been. Seconds later, when the dead spot cleared away, the second Pax missile was gone.

So were both waves of EmDef antimissiles.

"I'll be cursed," Pirbazari murmured, sounding more awed than angry. "A shaped charge. They had a shaped charge in that warhead."

Forsythe stared at the screen as Number Four's lasers opened up again and a third wave of antimissiles spat out. "I haven't noticed them use anything like that anywhere else today."

"They haven't," Pirbazari confirmed darkly. "Their commander seems to have done a very good job of anticipating our defense tactics."

Forsythe curled his hands into fists. Number Four's lasers caught the next Pax missile in line, sparking another of the brilliant triangular blasts. Again, the incoming antimissiles died in the explosion. "They're not going to make it, Zar," he said quietly. "They're not going to have time to destroy all those missiles before the last ones get there."

Pirbazari sighed softly. "I know."

"The ship's got shielding," someone across the room said, his voice sounding desperate. "Maybe it'll be enough."

"No." Pirbazari pointed at the screen. "See the ID they've attached to the last missile in line? It's a Pax Hellfire missile. Subnuclear warhead, extreme armor penetration, heavy electromagnetic scrambling. If it hits, the catapult will be gone. Along with the rest of the ship."

"Then why doesn't it get out of there?" someone else croaked. "Why the hell doesn't it get out of there?"

"Shut up," Forsythe ordered. "Can't you see it's trying?"

Number Four's drive had come to full power, driving it onto a vector perpendicular to the path of the incoming Pax missiles. Forsythe found himself holding his breath again as the catapult ship picked up speed. If the ship's electronic search-dampers worked—if the Pax missiles missed the fact that their target had moved out of their path—

"No," Pirbazari said suddenly. "*No!*"

"What?" Forsythe asked, his eyes searching the screen for a new threat. But there was nothing he could see. "What?"

"It's out of position," Pirbazari said, pointing. Somewhere along the way, he'd put his phone away. Now, abruptly, he was hauling it out again. "Don't you see? By moving away, it's now dragged the catapult focal ellipse completely out of the net area."

A cold hand closed around Forsythe's heart. "Which means if something comes in—"

"They can't throw it out again," Pirbazari said viciously as he jammed the phone to his ear. "Come on—answer. *Answer.*"

But once again, it was too late. Even as the next enemy missile in line was destroyed, a Pax warship appeared in the center of the net region.

But not just any warship. This thing was *huge*; bigger than any spacecraft the Empyrean had ever dreamed of creating. Bigger even than the original colony ships that had brought their ancestors to these worlds. A long, dark, monstrosity of a ship, bristling with weapons, everything about it resonating with arrogance and power and death.

The *Komitadji* had arrived.

Someone gasped a strangled curse, his voice stunned and awed and terrified. The big warship was already on the move, putting more distance between itself and the catapult focus as it lumbered toward the *Harmonic* and the EmDef destroyers surrounding it.

And, of course, toward the Number Two catapult ship.

The destroyers saw the danger, of course. But even as they scrambled away from the liner to turn to this new threat Forsythe saw that, for one last time, EmDef had been outthought and outmaneuvered. For the next few minutes, until the destroyers could get back in position, there would be nothing but Number Two's own defenses and shielding between it and the *Komitadji*.

The *Komitadji* didn't need even that long. Ten seconds later, a dozen high-power lasers flashed simultaneously from the warship's bow, all of them focused with surgical precision on the catapult end of the ship. With a roiling mass of vaporized metal and a flare of blue-white fire, the catapult equipment was gone.

And with it, the catapult.

"That's it, then," Pirbazari murmured. "The *Komitadji*'s here to stay."

"We have to stop it," Forsythe said, his heart thudding in his ears. "We have to attack. Slow it down, get more catapult ships into position—"

He broke off, staring at the screen in disbelief. Instead of attacking, the EmDef ships were turning away from the *Komitadji*. Not just the catapult ships, but the destroyers, too. All of them were turning away.

Turning away and running.

"What's going on?" Forsythe demanded. "Where are they going?"

"They're retreating," Pirbazari said. "The order just came in to—"

"Order?" Forsythe echoed. "What order? Give me that phone."

"Sir—"

Forsythe snatched the phone out of his hand. "This is High Senator Forsythe," he bit out. "What's going on?"

"The EmDef forces are withdrawing, High Senator," a young-sounding female voice answered.

"I can see that," Forsythe snapped. "Turn them around. All of them."

"Sir?"

"You heard me," Forsythe said. "Turn them around and attack."

No one replied. "Soldier?" Forsythe said. "Did you hear me? Soldier?"

"High Senator, this is General Roshmanov," a new voice came on. "Is there a problem?"

"Yes, there's a problem," Forsythe ground out. "Why are your forces withdrawing in the face of the enemy?"

"Sir, there's no way those destroyers can stand up against something that size," Roshmanov said. "It would be nothing less than suicide."

"It would be war," Forsythe insisted. "Isn't that the reason EmDef exists? To risk and possibly give their lives in the defense of the Empyrean?"

"To give their lives in battle, yes, High Senator," Roshmanov said. "But not to throw them away for nothing."

"And how do you know it would be for nothing?" Forsythe countered. Vaguely, he was aware that his voice was rising, but at the moment he didn't give a single damn. "How do you know until you try?"

"Sir, if you would just take a look at the size of that—"

"So it's big," Forsythe snarled. "So what? Do you always give up and surrender without a fight just because you're not sure you can win?"

Pirbazari was tugging at his sleeve. Angrily, Forsythe shook off his hand. "You listen to me, General," he said. "You're going to attack, and you're going to attack *now*. Get those ships back together and hit it."

"I'm sorry, High Senator," Roshmanov said, his voice icy cold. "This is an EmDef matter, and an EmDef decision. And I will not order men and women to their deaths for no reason."

"General—"

"Sir!" Pirbazari said insistently, tugging even harder at his sleeve. Forsythe threw a glare at him—

And what he saw made him pause for a second look. Pirbazari was staring at him, his eyes narrowed, his mouth slightly open, his throat muscles taut. Staring at him as if at a stranger. "Sir," he whispered hoarsely, his head jerking slightly to the side.

With an effort, Forsythe tore his eyes away and looked around him.

They were all staring at him. All of them. All of these high government officials gazing at him in astonishment or furtive disbelief or even out-and-out fear.

And not all of them, he realized suddenly, were looking at his face. Some of them were gazing in confusion at his neck, where his angel pendant glittered against his shirt.

Rather, his fake angel pendant.

Slowly, with a supreme effort, he lowered the phone away from his ear. Pirbazari was ready, taking it from him and tucking it quickly away. "It's all right, sir," he said. "This is just a retreat. It doesn't mean the war is lost."

Forsythe took a deep breath, let it out in a ragged sigh. "I know," he said, his voice sounding strained but mostly under control again. "How long till they're here?"

"From that distance?" Pirbazari's eyes darted to the screen, came back again. "Less than a day if they push it. No more than three even if they're not in any particular hurry."

"They'll be in a hurry," Forsythe told him grimly. "Trust me."

"We should know for sure in an hour or so, once we see what kind of vector profile they set for themselves." Pirbazari hesitated. "Which leads to the question of how we announce this to the public."

Forsythe looked back at the screen. "We don't," he said.

There was a ripple of reaction around the room. "Sir, I don't think we can do that," Pirbazari said carefully. "I mean, all of EmDef already knows about it—"

"EmDef should also know how to keep their mouths shut," Forsythe cut him off. "If we move quickly, we should be able to block all communications from the various off-planet stations and research platforms."

"You don't think someone will figure it out once that thing floats past overhead?" someone demanded. "Come on, High Senator, be realistic. We have to warn them."

"I am being realistic," Forsythe said stiffly. "I'm thinking that at this point all a warning will accomplish will be to precipitate a night of planet-wide panic."

"The people have a right to know," the other insisted.

"To what end?" Forsythe asked. "What's anyone going to do in twelve or fifteen or twenty hours? Grab a rifle and aim it skyward? Throw his family into a line car and try to escape into the hills? Do you really think that kind of chaos will do anyone any good?"

"Maybe the High Senator is thinking of trying to get a little more distance himself," another voice put in.

Forsythe didn't even bother to turn in that direction. "We will do everything in our power to prepare a proper military reception for the invaders," he said quietly. "Everything EmDef can put together will be waiting when they arrive. But it *will* take everything they have. I don't want any of EmDef's people or resources having to be diverted for crowd or looting control."

He looked back at Pirbazari. "There's nothing the general public can do to help," he said. "They might as well have one last peaceful night's sleep."

Pirbazari licked his upper lip, a quick swipe of his tongue tip. "Yes, sir," he said. He wasn't happy with the decision, Forsythe knew.

But he could also tell that the other realized the basic wisdom of it. "I'm sure you'll be wanting to get over to EmDef HQ as soon as possible to oversee the defense preparations," Pirbazari went on. "But right now, you have a visitor waiting in your office."

It was a second before the words connected. Right: Pirbazari was supposed to have brought Kosta here from the hospital. In all the confusion, he'd completely forgotten about the Pax spy. "Yes," he said. "Of course."

He started to turn away. A sudden thought struck him, and he turned back. "What happened with the Number Four catapult ship?" he asked, searching the screen for it.

"It's on its way back to Seraph with the others," Pirbazari said. "The Pax fighters abandoned their attacks when the EmDef ships began their retreat."

"Never mind the fighters," Forsythe said, frowning. "What about that Hellfire missile?"

"It self-destructed," Pirbazari said. "A few seconds after the *Komitadji* destroyed the catapult end of Number Two."

Forsythe felt his lip twist. "I guess they didn't want to damage any more of the spoils of war than they had to."

"Yes, sir, that's probably it," Pirbazari agreed. "Shall we go?"

Silently, Forsythe followed him out through the crowd, bitterness and guilt eating into his stomach. Pirbazari might believe that line about Pax greed. All of those who had heard it might believe it. It might even be true.

But he couldn't escape the sobering realization that, while he had been ready to order his own people into a suicide attack, the Pax commander had deliberately destroyed one of his own missiles rather than waste Empyreal lives.

And the Pax commander wasn't even wearing an angel. What did that say about angels?

More importantly, what did it say about Forsythe himself?

CHAPTER 38

The two guards Pirbazari had left behind to watch Kosta were big, competent looking, and very definitely not the talkative type. In fact, aside from telling him once to stop wiggling and shut up, neither had said a single word, not even to each other, since Pirbazari hurriedly handcuffed him to the chair and took off through the office door at a dead run.

They had all been sitting like that for nearly two hours when Pirbazari finally returned.

With a surprise visitor.

"Mr. Kosta," High Senator Forsythe said. "Nice to see you again. All recovered from your injuries, I trust?"

"Yes, sir, mostly," Kosta said, his initial relief at seeing a familiar face fading quickly into uncertainty. There wasn't a single hint of friendliness anywhere that he could see in Forsythe's expression, not even the abstract camaraderie that was supposed to develop when two people had shared deadly danger together. The High Senator's eyes were hostile as he gazed at Kosta, his face set in hard lines. "Thank you for your concern," he added.

"You're welcome," Forsythe said. The words themselves were formally polite; the delivery as cold and dark as a Siberian winter morning. "Zar, take the guards and wait in the outer office."

Pirbazari shot a look at Kosta. "If I may suggest, sir—?"

"I said wait outside."

Pirbazari's lips compressed briefly. But he nevertheless gestured to the guards, and the three of them left the room.

Forsythe waited until the door had shut behind them. Then, very deliberately, he walked over to his desk, shuffled a few papers out of the way, and sat down on one corner facing Kosta. "So here we are," he said, the hostile eyes boring into Kosta's face again. "Rather like a dramatic thriller you'd watch on a quiet evening, isn't it?"

Kosta shook his head. "I'm sorry, but I don't follow you."

"Oh, come now, Mr. Kosta," Forsythe said coldly. "The Empyreal High Senator . . . and the Pax spy?"

Kosta felt his lip twitch. He should have guessed. "Oh," he said. "That."

Something passed across Forsythe's face, leaving even harder lines in its wake. Apparently, for all his assumed confidence, he hadn't been completely sure of his accusation. "So you don't deny it."

"Not at all," Kosta said. "As a matter of fact, I was ready to turn myself in two days ago."

Forsythe snorted. "Of course you were."

"I was," Kosta insisted. "The only reason I didn't was because of Angelmass. Something's happening up there, High Senator, something very dangerous. We have to find out what that is, and fast. Before more people die."

"Ah," Forsythe said, folding his arms across his chest. "So you care deeply about Empyreal lives, do you?"

Kosta frowned. There was something simmering beneath the surface of the man, something that seemed far out of proportion to the simple fact of having unmasked a minor spy. "Yes, I do," he said. "I'm not your typical dramatic-thriller spy, High Senator. I wasn't sent here to sabotage or steal secrets or anything like that. I was sent to study Angelmass and the angels. That's all I've done."

"Of course you have," Forsythe said, his voice suddenly bitter. "And there was nothing in your orders about laying the groundwork for military action, I suppose."

"No, nothing," Kosta said. "The Pax believes the angels are an alien invasion—"

He broke off, the meaning beneath Forsythe's words suddenly penetrating. "What do you mean, military action? Has something happened?"

For a long moment Forsythe simply gazed at him. "You're an excellent actor, Mr. Kosta," he said at last. "Either that, or you truly don't know."

Kosta felt his stomach curl into a hard knot. "Please tell me."

There was another long silence. Then Forsythe stirred. "All right. Lorelei has gone silent. Something has shut down all its lines of communication; and that same something has also swallowed two investigating courier ships without a trace."

He smiled tightly. "Tell me again about alien invasions."

"Lorelei," Kosta murmured, his mind flashing back to his nerve-wracking entrance into that system, and to the unreasonably large asteroid they'd smuggled him in with. "That was where I came into the Empyrean. Hidden inside a fake asteroid."

"How many others were in there with you?"

Kosta shook his head. "They told me I was the only one," he said. "But the asteroid was pretty big. There might have been . . . maybe there were more."

"Was yours the only asteroid they dropped?"

"Again, that's what they told me," Kosta said. "But I don't really know."

"So in other words, they could have dropped off an entire commando task force with you and you'd never have known the difference," Forsythe concluded heavily. "Is that what you're saying?"

"I guess so," Kosta conceded. The pieces were starting to come together now, into a decidedly unpleasant mosaic. "It's interesting. Several times over the last few months I've wondered why they sent me. I'm not a professional spy, I don't know much about Empyreal culture, and I'm not good with social situations anyway. I didn't even have more than a few weeks' training."

"So why *did* they send you?" Forsythe asked.

Kosta swallowed. "I think they meant for me to be quickly caught," he said. "Probably thought that if you caught one spy it would quiet any suspicions about what the *Komitadji* had been doing at Lorelei."

"While the rest of the commandos planned to take or destroy the nets?"

Kosta shook his head. "I don't know what else they had planned."

For a moment Forsythe didn't answer. "No, I suppose not," he said. "The sacrificial lamb usually doesn't get to sit in on the wolves' strategy sessions, does he?"

There was a hesitant knock at the door. It opened, and Pirbazari stuck his head inside. "Sorry to bother you, High Senator," he said. "But you wanted to be kept informed of the situation at Angelmass."

"Go ahead," Forsythe said, his eyes still on Kosta.

"Its orbit has dipped some more," Pirbazari said. "Latest calculation shows that it could be close enough to threaten Angelmass Central in as little as four days."

"Four days?" Forsythe repeated, frowning. "I thought you said it would be a couple of weeks."

"It's moved deeper since then," Pirbazari explained. "That means it's picked up more speed."

"It also means it may have moved too deep to be a problem to Central," Forsythe pointed out.

"Maybe. Maybe not." Pirbazari's mouth tightened. "The thing is, the orbital dip doesn't seem to have been completely uniform. The astronomers think it actually moved out a bit at one point."

Forsythe turned to frown at him. "Moved *out?*"

"Yes, sir," Pirbazari said. "It was a little hard to tell—there was another radiation surge at the time that obscured some of the positioning data. But they're pretty sure."

"Which direction was the surge?" Kosta asked.

"You keep out of this," Forsythe ordered, throwing a brief glare back at him.

"I only thought that if the surge was inward, toward the sun, it might explain the outward movement," Kosta said. "Angelmass may have learned how to focus its radiation output and use it as a jet."

Forsythe had been looking at Pirbazari. Now, slowly, he turned back to Kosta. "What do you mean, *learned* how to focus its radiation?"

"An array of angels has certain characteristics of proto-intelligence," Kosta said. "Specifically, it shows the response curve of a classical Lantryllyn logic circuit. You can check on that with Che Kruyrov and Dr. Frashni at the Institute."

"What are you talking about?" Pirbazari asked. "What's a Lan-whatever logic circuit?"

"It was once thought to be the road to self-aware computers," Kosta said. "The point is that angels in a group show definite signs of intelligence; and over the past few years you've taken thousands of angels out of Angelmass. If you've left that same number of anti-angels behind, then it follows—"

"Hold it," Forsythe cut him off. "Anti-angels?"

"The angel anti-particle," Kosta said.

"Never heard of it."

"No one has," Kosta said. "But I'm convinced they exist."

He nodded his head toward the ceiling, in the general direction of Angelmass. "And if I'm right—and if anti-angels have the same potential for intelligence that angels do—then Angelmass itself may have become sentient."

Pirbazari shook his head. "This is ridiculous," he said. "We're talking about a black hole, not some two-year-old kid or even a well-trained chimp. How could it possibly be intelligent?"

"I know it sounds crazy," Kosta admitted. "But Angelmass's behavior is already defying all known black hole theory. This orbit-changing thing is only the latest example."

"So how would you go about proving it?" Forsythe asked.

"First step is to pin down the existence of anti-angels," Kosta told him. "I've put together some equipment that will hopefully be able to locate, identify, and capture one. While I'm doing that, we need Dr. Frashni's team to get busy on larger angel arrays, to work on the intelligence aspect."

"I see," Forsythe murmured. "Well, we can certainly get Dr. Frashni busy on the second part. As to the first part . . ." He cocked his head slightly to the side. "We'll see who the Institute can recommend for that."

Kosta felt his throat tighten. "Sir, I already have the equipment ready. It would take someone else days to design and assemble their own version."

"Why can't they just use yours?"

Kosta waved a hand, a truncated gesture with the wrist cuffs anchoring his arms to the chair. "Most of the planning and procedure is in my head," he said. "I didn't have time to write anything down. It would take as long for me to brief someone on the technique as it would for them to start from scratch."

"Then they can start from scratch," Forsythe declared, standing up. "First things first, Zar. Have EmDef order a transport to Angelmass Central. The station's got three hours to evacuate."

"Yes, sir," Pirbazari said, an odd look on his face. "Sir, under the circumstances . . . ?"

"We have to evacuate the station anyway," Forsythe said. "There's no reason we can't get the Institute busy on this, too."

Pirbazari grimaced, but nodded. "All right. Do you want Central's net left on?"

"Might as well," Forsythe said. "As Mr. Kosta suggests, we may want to get someone up there to check things out."

"High Senator, please," Kosta said in a low voice. "We can't afford to waste time."

"I'll be sure to mention that to Director Podolak," Forsythe said. "And when you've finished that call, Zar, you and the guards can escort Mr. Kosta to the EmDef military jail. I'm done with him."

"Yes, sir."

Pirbazari disappeared back into the outer office complex, closing the door behind him. "Ironic, isn't it," Forsythe commented, half to Kosta, half seemingly to himself. "For months I've been searching for a way to stop the flow of angels into the Empyrean. For a time, in fact, I even thought your research might be the key I needed."

He shook his head. "And so now you give me the key I've needed; just as the Pax begin their invasion. Funny how fast one's priorities can change, isn't it?"

He straightened up. "I'll give you one chance. Tell me what sort of Fifth Column arrangements the Pax has set up across the Empyrean, and I'll ask EmDef to be lenient with you."

"I wish I could, sir," Kosta said. "I really do. I don't want this war any more than you do. I can give you the location of the automated sleeper drop on Lorelei where I picked up my documents, but that's all I've got."

"Too bad," Forsythe said. "Normally, the court would probably hand down a life sentence for the crime of espionage. Considering that we're at war, I suspect they'll opt for summary execution instead." Turning, he started for the door.

It was odd, Kosta thought distantly, to hear a sentence of death being handed down to you. Odd, because at that moment his own life didn't seem to matter. In his mind's eye he could see the blazing fury that was Angelmass, moving impossibly about in its orbit, threatening hunterships and Angelmass Central.

Perhaps even Seraph itself.

Was Angelmass intelligent? Kruyrov's data certainly pointed that direction. Was it evil? They had only Ronyon's terrified reaction to go by, plus the vicious attacks on the various hunterships. But if the angels were influences for good, even imperfect ones, what else could a mass of anti-angels be?

He didn't have any answers. But there was one thing that *was* certain, and that was that they didn't have much time. Not with Angelmass only four days from Central. Not with the bureaucratic delays that would inevitably slow down any solutions even once the anti-angel's existence had been proven.

Not with the Pax war machine already at Lorelei.

No one else at the Institute could come up with an experimental procedure fast enough. It had to be Kosta's equipment, and the Daviees' huntership. And he could certainly not run any experiments from an EmDef prison cell.

Forsythe was reaching for the door now. "You're not wearing an angel, High Senator," Kosta said.

Forsythe turned back, a puzzled frown on his face. "What are you talking about?" he asked, tapping the gold chain and pendant around his neck. "What do you think this is?"

"It's a fake," Kosta said, studying Forsythe's face. The man was good, all right, every bit as competent an actor as he'd earlier accused Kosta of being. "Ronyon has the real one."

For a long moment the puzzlement persisted. Kosta held the other's gaze steadily, waiting for him to make his decision. "That's nonsense," Forsythe said at last. "You're grabbing at dust."

"I don't want to expose you, High Senator," Kosta said quietly. "I imagine this is something they can impeach you for, or whatever it is they do to elected officials here. But I don't care about that. All I want is to be allowed to go to Angelmass and find out what's happened to it. Let me go, and I give you my word that I'll come back and turn myself in."

Forsythe's mouth twisted. "Of course you will."

"It's the truth," Kosta insisted. To his mild surprise, he realized it really was. "We have to find out what Angelmass is doing—"

"All you want is to get free so you can bring me down," Forsythe cut him off harshly. "I'm the only one who can still function through this sheep-like fog the angels have everyone else buried in. If you can destroy me, there won't be anyone left to oppose the Pax."

"High Senator—"

"Forget it," Forsythe said. "It won't work. I won't let it work."

Behind him the door opened, and Pirbazari stepped inside, the two guards visible behind him. "Central's evacuation has begun, sir," he told Forsythe. "And we're ready to take Mr. Kosta."

"I've changed my mind," Forsythe said, his voice betraying none of the rage and paranoia that had been there five seconds earlier. "I'm going to keep him locked up in here for the night."

Pirbazari blinked. "Excuse me?"

"It'll give him time to think about cooperating with us," Forsythe said. "Tomorrow morning will be soon enough to turn him over to EmDef if he decides not to."

Pirbazari shot a look at Kosta, turned his eyes back to Forsythe. "Yes, sir," he said, still clearly confused. "Ah . . . you going to leave him cuffed to that chair?"

Forsythe glanced at his watch; automatically, Kosta glanced at his. It was nearly ten o'clock. "Have someone bring in a cot," Forsythe said. "Then disconnect or disable all the computer and communications systems, and pull everything out of the desk safe. Have someone reverse the door lock so that it locks the room from the outside, and post a couple of guards in the outer office area."

He looked at Kosta. "After that, go ahead and unlock him. There's nothing in here he can bother."

Kosta took a careful breath. "High Senator—"

"You have until morning, Mr. Kosta," Forsythe said softly. "I'd advise you sleep on it."

CHAPTER 39

The entire command deck crew was cheering as Commodore Lleshi crossed to the lift platform at the rear of the balcony. He acknowledged their acclamation with quiet nods and an occasional half smile, recognizing their psychological need for celebration but at the same time knowing full well that the war was far from over. Like all the other rebellious colonies that had defied Pax rule over the years, the Empyrean would resist to the end.

It was his job as commander to bring them to that end as quickly as possible.

Telthorst, as expected, was waiting for him as the lift platform reached the balcony. "The plan worked as you predicted, Commodore," he said as the memory-metal cage unwrapped itself. His voice and expression, Lleshi noted, were utterly neutral. "My congratulations."

"Thank you," Lleshi said, as if the other had actually meant it. "Campbell?"

"The Empyreal ships have scattered, sir," Campbell reported briskly. "Most of them are retreating toward Seraph. A few of the more damaged are heading off toward a small solar observation platform that's a few hours closer."

"The *Harmonic?*"

"Took off toward Seraph as soon as your boarding party left," Campbell said.

"I presume we can catch it again if we need to," Telthorst rumbled.

"I'm sure we can," Lleshi said, stepping past the Adjutor toward the tactical display, deliberately turning his back on the man. Telthorst had fought bitterly against Lleshi's Trojan Horse plan; and once it had succeeded, he had been just as vehemently opposed to Lleshi turning the liner and its shipful of potential hostages loose again. The man was never satisfied with anything. "Any signs of resistance?"

"Not yet," Campbell said. "There's a lot of communications traffic going on around the planet, but so far nothing in the way of ship movements."

"Except that one," Telthorst said pointedly.

"Which one was that?" Lleshi asked.

Campbell shot a look at Telthorst. "The system's main catapult is on the far side of Seraph," he said, touching a key. A flashing yellow light appeared on the tactical, trailing Seraph in its orbit. "So far, we haven't spotted any serious activity there."

"That will certainly change in the next few hours," Telthorst put in. "They'll surely try to evacuate some of their leaders and assets from the system. I strongly recommend we send a squadron of fighters ahead to try to cut off any such move."

"Recommendation noted," Lleshi said, mentally sending the suggestion straight to the shredder. He'd seen what Empyreal Defense warships could do, and he had no intention of putting any of his fighters outside the *Komitadji*'s defense zone on such a foolish mission. As far as he was concerned, if Seraph's leaders wanted to cut and run they were welcome to do so.

And if they wanted to stuff their pockets on their way out, they were welcome to do that, too. There were few things that demoralized a populace more than having their leaders run out on them in a crisis, particularly leaders who looted the public treasury before taking to the hills. In Lleshi's experience, a demoralized populace usually meant a quicker and more stable surrender. "Continue."

"That's the main catapult," Campbell went on, tapping more keys. The flashing yellow light vanished and was replaced by two flashing green ones: the first right beside the circle representing Seraph, the second much farther out in the system. "Again, no activity there. But we've also got a second, smaller net/catapult system in close Seraph orbit. We're not absolutely sure—the readings are odd—but Theory Group thinks it's hooked up in a binary link to a similar net/catapult out at Angelmass."

A binary link between net and catapult? That was a neat trick. "And you saw a ship head out from there?"

"Yes, sir, about fifteen minutes ago," Campbell said. "Angelmass is twenty-two light-minutes from our current position, so if the ship did indeed go there we'll be able to see its arrival about seven minutes from now. I've got a telescope watching."

He threw a sideways look at Telthorst. "Adjutor Telthorst's belief is that they've gone out to sabotage the Angelmass net."

"Really," Lleshi said, frowning at Telthorst. "To what end?"

"Obviously, to keep us away from it," Telthorst said tightly. "We've already agreed their best defense is those sandwich-metal hulls of theirs, and we know that all their angel hunterships are equipped with those."

"And you're suggesting that they're gathering the hunterships at Angelmass into an assault force?" Lleshi asked mildly.

"Is that so ridiculous a notion?" Telthorst shot back. "Or had you forgotten all those armed mining ships they threw at us in Lorelei system?"

"Though not very effectively, as I recall," Lleshi reminded him. Still, he had to concede it wasn't as ridiculous an idea as it sounded. Empyreal Defense might well believe that a group of armed ships popping through a net in low Seraph orbit could catch the *Komitadji* by surprise. "Campbell?"

"We've quartered the region looking for ships," Campbell said. "So far, we haven't found any indication that there's *anything* out there, let alone an organized task force."

"But you yourself admit that the glare may be washing out the view," Telthorst countered. "I still maintain that it doesn't make sense for them to not to have at least *some* working ships out there."

"Show me," Lleshi ordered, crossing over to his station and sitting down. He swiveled his chair around to the main screen just as Campbell pulled up the telescope image of Angelmass.

It was every bit as awesome as he had expected. He'd seen one other black hole in his travels; a much larger, much calmer one, sitting quietly in space like an invisible spider in an unseen web, content to draw matter spiraling into the darkness lurking behind the veil of its event horizon.

Angelmass was the exact opposite. A tiny pinprick in the fabric of space, it spat out light and radiation and particles with all the fury and power of a small star. The radiation drove away any bit of matter or solar wind that ventured too close, flashing or ionizing all matter farther away. With the sunscreens blocking out the brightest part of the central core, the visual effect was that of a large dead spot in space surrounded by a wide band of hazy light. Like the rings of Saturn or Demolian, perhaps.

Or like a halo. A halo around Angelmass.

With an effort, Lleshi drew his mind away from poetic images and back to the hard, cold reality of war. Campbell was right: there were no signs of ships out there.

Unfortunately, so was Telthorst. The halo glare of ionized gas was just enough to possibly conceal fighter-sized craft running dark or stealthed.

Fortunately, the solution was simple enough. "Do you have orbital data for the Seraph catapult?" he asked.

"We have the general data," Campbell said. "It's an equatorial orbit, a couple hundred klicks up. We can get it more exactly once we get closer."

"Do so," Lleshi ordered. "When we arrive we'll take up an orbit directly behind it, as far back as we can get without losing visual contact. Will that be acceptable, Adjutor?" he added, swiveling his chair to face Telthorst.

"I suppose so," Telthorst said. "At least, for now."

Lleshi glanced at Campbell, caught the brief sour tightening of the other's lips. Campbell knew it, too: Telthorst would never be satisfied. With anything.

"SeTO, put the tactical back up," he said, settling back in his chair. "Let's go in."

It was nearly 10:30, and the stars were shining dimly through the haze of the Magasca city lights, when Chandris arrived at the Government Building.

She made her way up the fifteen wide marble steps leading to the main entrance, grousing at each one along the way. It had been over two hours now since Kosta had pulled his disappearing act from the hospital, and a long and weary process of elimination had finally brought her here. If he wasn't inside, she was completely out of ideas.

But she had a feeling he was. A very bad feeling. Kosta, noble and idealistic and stupid, had already talked once about turning himself in. Now, still caked with his own blood from Trilling's attack, he'd apparently gone ahead and taken the plunge.

All of it to protect her and Hanan and Ornina, undoubtedly. Never mind that they'd all agreed he should keep his mouth shut for now. Never mind that the threat of Angelmass far outweighed whatever anyone might think the Pax could possibly be doing with or through him.

If there was anything left after High Senator Forsythe finished with him, she told herself darkly, she was going to personally feed it to the fish.

At this hour of the night, of course, the outer door was locked. One more annoyance to add to her list. She had it open in thirty seconds and slipped inside. The door leading into the main part of the building from the reception area was also locked. She got through that one even faster.

She had expected the place to be dark and essentially deserted. To her surprise, the lights were blazing, with a fair number of people still buzzing about the halls and offices. All of them seemed to be hurrying or talking together in urgent, hushed tones, some doing both at once.

It was highly disconcerting, rather like walking into a bank with a cutting torch and set of burglar tools, only to discover a police convention being held on the premises. But old habits quickly kicked in, turning on the air of arrogant importance that had gotten her into many places where she didn't belong, past people who should have known better. A glance at the directory as she passed, and she was on her way to the fifth floor and Forsythe's temporary office complex.

Deep down, she was still hoping that Kosta had somehow come to his senses in time and kept his identity secret. But the more people she strode past, and the more bits of conversation she caught, the more it became clear that these people weren't here so late just for the overtime pay. They were angry, worried, and frightened.

And the word "Pax" kept coming up.

Which meant that Chandris was too late. Kosta had indeed confessed; and chances were he'd already been transferred to some secure prison somewhere. Like the two hours of searching that had gone before it, this little side trip was starting to look very much like a waste of time.

Still, as long as she was here, she might as well keep going. At the very least, maybe she could shake loose some information from some gullible clerk. Arriving at Forsythe's office suite, she stepped up to the plate glass wall that separated it from the corridor.

She had expected this to be the center of all the activity she'd passed through on her way here—after all, unmasking a Pax spy was the kind of publicity coup that even a High Senator didn't stumble across every day. If Forsythe was any kind of politician he ought to be milking it for all it was worth.

But once again, her expectations turned out to be oddly off target. The office suite was only dimly lit, and virtually empty.

For a moment she stood outside the glass, peering in. The suite was arranged a little like Amberson Toomes's office complex: a large outer area with a handful of doors leading from the back walls into what were presumably private offices. Where Toomes's outer office had been the province of only the one receptionist, though, the room now facing her was crowded with a dozen desks and workstations. A common work area, then. Briefly, she wondered how much of the space was Forsythe's and how much was controlled by other local governmental agencies. Each of the doors at the back had a nameplate, but she was too far away and the light too dim for her to read them.

There were only three people in the room. Two of them stood flanking one of the rear doors, their postures and the guns belted to their sides marking them as guards. Chandris had never seen these particular men before, though the insignia on their jackets marked them as local governmental security officers.

The third person, however, was a very familiar face. He was sitting slightly hunched over at one of the desks, the glow from the computer display playing across a very troubled expression.

It was Forsythe's aide, Ronyon.

There was no way she could pop the door lock, not with two bored guards watching her every move. Fortunately, she didn't need to. She started to knock on the glass, remembered in time that Ronyon was deaf, and instead gave a sweeping wave.

The movement caught Ronyon's eye. He looked up, and abruptly the frown lines on his face cleared into a kind of eager hope. He scrambled to his feet, an awkward-looking motion with someone that big, and hurried across the room to the door. He unfastened the lock and pulled the door open, his free hand gesturing excitedly.

"Wait a minute," Chandris said, holding up a hand as she stepped into the suite. "Not so fast," she added, making sure to enunciate the words clearly. Ronyon could read lips, she knew, but she wasn't sure how well he could do in the suite's semidarkness.

Still, he would certainly be better reading her lips than she would be reading his hands. She'd leafed through a signing dictionary a couple of days ago, while sitting in the *Gazelle*'s storage room waiting for Kosta to try to steal the Daviees' spare angel, and she had all the signs memorized. But knowing all the words of a foreign language didn't necessarily mean she could understand a native who was speaking it. This was likely to be a long process. "Come on, let's sit down," she invited, taking his arm and coaxing him away from the door.

Okay, he signed, letting her lead him to the nearest work station. Chandris would have preferred to go back to his desk, so that she could see what he'd been reading on his computer, but it was a little too close to the guards for comfort. Even if they couldn't read Ronyon's sign language, they would probably be able to hear her side of the conversation from back there.

And she was beginning to suspect that this was one conversation she didn't want anyone eavesdropping on.

She sat Ronyon down behind the desk and pulled another chair up to face him, making sure her back was to the guards so as to muffle her words even more. "Now," she said. "Slowly, please. Tell me what's happened."

Mr. Pirbazari brought Jereko in here awhile ago, Ronyon signed, obediently moving his hands with exaggerated deliberation. *He said he was a spy!*

Chandris fought back a grimace. So she'd been right. "Did he say how they found out?" she asked.

I don't know, Ronyon signed. *I think Mr. Forsythe just figured it out. He's real smart.*

"Yes, I know," Chandris agreed. Half-right, anyway; it didn't look like Kosta had turned himself in.

And if he hadn't, then any noble statements he might have made about Chandris and the Daviees being innocent bystanders went straight out the window. If Forsythe came out of that office and saw her here, he was likely to jump to a completely wrong conclusion. "Is he in there with Mr. Forsythe now?" she asked, trying to sound casual.

Ronyon's face puckered in a frown. *No, Mr. Forsythe isn't here,* he signed. *Jereko is just in there by himself.*

It was Chandris's turn to frown. "He's alone?" she repeated, resisting the impulse to turn and look behind her. Forsythe wouldn't lock a Pax spy in his own office and then just walk off and leave him there for the night, would he?

But Ronyon nodded. *Mr. Forsythe talked to him for awhile, and then Mr.*

Pirbazari went in, and they took a cot and some food in, and then they all left. And one of the workmen came and turned the lock around on the door, he added, his face lighting up briefly with remembered interest.

The memory faded, his face creasing with concern again. *What are they going to do to Jereko? Are they going to hurt him?*

"I don't know," Chandris said, her mind still back behind her in that office. So those men were guarding a lone prisoner, not simply standing by while he was being interrogated.

But that still didn't make any sense. Surely Magasca had enough real prison space for even such a supposedly high-profile criminal like a master Pax spy. There was no reason Forsythe should have to turn his office into a makeshift cell.

Unless the High Senator didn't want him talking to anyone else.

And then it all fell together, and she found herself looking at Ronyon with sudden new understanding. Of course. Kosta wouldn't have wanted to go to jail—he wanted to get out to Angelmass, and there would be no chance of wheedling his way there once he was officially charged. He would have tried to talk Forsythe into holding off on an official arrest while he went and did his experiment, probably nobly offering to turn himself back in when it was finished.

And when that hadn't worked, he had played his trump card.

The fact that Forsythe wasn't wearing his angel.

"So Mr. Forsythe talked to Jereko," she said. "Did he say anything to you when he came out?"

He told me not to tell anyone about Jereko, Ronyon signed, his face suddenly going uncertain halfway through the sentence. *Uh-oh. I wasn't supposed to tell you this, was I?*

"It's okay," Chandris said hastily. "I'm sure he just meant not to tell anyone who didn't already know."

Ronyon blinked. *You already knew?*

Chandris felt her throat tighten, seeing a deep hole suddenly open up in front of her. Admitting to Ronyon that she knew about Kosta might get him to talk more freely, but it would also damn her as an accessory to espionage if he ever repeated that to Forsythe.

But she had no choice. Not if she was going to help Kosta. "Yes, I knew," she said. "He told me a couple of days ago, when we were discussing what to do about Angelmass."

Ronyon shivered, his shoulders hunching like he was trying to make himself smaller. *That's a bad place,* he signed, his eyes looking haunted. *It scared me a lot.*

"It scares me, too," Chandris assured him. "And Jereko, and a lot of other people."

She leaned toward him slightly. "That's why Jereko and I need to go out there. We need to find out some things about it, so that no one will have to be scared anymore. Can you help us?"

His face puckered even more. *I don't know,* he signed, the words starting to come out faster in his agitation. *Mr. Forsythe told me not to tell anyone, and now I have. If I help you, he's going to be real mad at me.*

"He'll be mostly mad at me," Chandris assured him. "If you get in trouble, I'll tell him it was my fault, that you didn't have anything to do with it."

He peered down at her hands, his face twisted almost like he was going to cry. *But that wouldn't be true,* he signed. *You aren't making me do anything. Mr. Forsythe says when somebody does something wrong they should take the blame themselves.*

"He's right," Chandris conceded. *Except for Forsythe himself,* she added silently, the thought of his fake angel pendant flitting through her mind. But it was no use bringing that up. Ronyon was clearly a willing accomplice to the fraud, which meant that Forsythe must have spun him some sort of story to make the whole thing seem legitimate. Trying to argue the point now would only confuse him.

I mean, I want to help, Ronyon went on, signing so fast now she could hardly keep up. *You and Jereko helped me a lot when we were out on the ship and I got scared. But Mr. Forsythe told me not to tell anybody—*

"Yes, I know," Chandris said, touching his hand soothingly. "It's all right. It's my fault—I shouldn't have asked you. I'm sorry."

He blinked. *That's all right,* he signed, almost shyly. *I'm not mad at you. I like you.*

She smiled. "I like you too, Ronyon," she said, and meant it. There was something about his earnest, childlike innocence that touched a chord deep inside her. She would go a long way, through a lot of pain, rather than deliberately hurt him. "Don't worry, it'll be all right. You and I will be fine."

And Jereko, too?

"Jereko, too," she said, nodding.

His eyes searched her face for a moment. Then, the creases vanished from his forehead and he smiled. *Okay,* he signed. *I believe you.*

"Good," Chandris said, feeling a pang of guilt. Did it count as a lie, she wondered uncomfortably, if you had all the good intentions in the world, but at the same time didn't have the foggiest idea how you were going to make a promise work? "Do you know when Mr. Forsythe will be coming back in the morning?"

He said nine o'clock, Ronyon signed. *Are you going to talk to him about Jereko?*

She reached out and took his hands. "Thank you," she said quietly, squeezing them once and then standing up. "I'll see you tomorrow."

He smiled up at her, exactly like a child who'd just been told he'd been a good boy. *Good night, Chandris,* he signed. *Happy dreams.*

She swallowed. "You, too, Ronyon."

He was still smiling as she left.

When Forsythe's presence on Seraph first came to light, just after the *Gazelle's* near-fatal brush with Angelmass, the Governor had offered the distinguished visitors top-class hotel rooms as well as temporary office space. Forsythe had accepted the office, but had turned down the accommodations. His ship was just as comfortable, nearly as convenient to the Government Building, and much easier to keep nosy media types away from.

He sat alone now in the control room of the ship, a drink gripped in his hand, gazing out the landing viewport at the starry sky overhead. It was nearly three in the morning, and he was as bone-weary as he had ever been in his life.

And, though he would never admit it to anyone, as frightened.

EmDef was doing its best—he had to give them that. In the seven hours since the Pax invasion they had pulled together an amazing assortment of fighting ships, armed patrol craft, and even a few research and weather satellites that could be modified into floating weapons platforms. Well before the *Komitadji* arrived over Seraph, all of the planet's defenses would be ready.

And none of it would do a single bit of good.

Forsythe sighed, a dark and lonely sound in the deserted control room. The *Komitadji* was just too big, too powerful, too indestructible. EmDef could throw everything they had against it and still not make a significant reduction in its offensive capabilities. When the dust cleared, the *Komitadji* would still be there.

And it would be sitting in orbit above a completely helpless world.

Forsythe sipped at his drink without tasting it, visualizing that bleak scenario. Earlier, at the battle by the net, the *Komitadji's* commander had destroyed a Hellfire missile rather than let it unnecessarily demolish one of the catapult ships. Would he show similar restraint and mercy toward a captured planet full of civilians?

Or would the level of restraint instead be tied to how quickly the vanquished were willing to surrender? Would the level of punitive action rise with each dent the EmDef forces put in the *Komitadji's* hull?

Forsythe had ordered that the people of Seraph not be informed of the impending attack, arguing in part that they might as well get one last good night's sleep. Would they understand his reasoning this coming afternoon when the truth abruptly rose up and slapped them in the face?

More importantly, would the EmDef men and women who would be getting no sleep at all tonight understand if he abruptly threw all their hard work away and surrendered Seraph to the Pax without a shot being fired?

What was a High Senator's duty here? To satisfy pride by allowing as much damage as possible to be inflicted on both sides? To present the money-worshiping Pax with a Pyhrric victory by forcing them to destroy much of what they had come here to conquer?

Or was his duty instead to accept the inevitable, present the enemy a fully functional world, and protect the lives of the people he'd sworn to serve?

Reaching to his chest, he fingered the angel pendant hanging there, his mind drifting back to all those High Senate meetings he'd attended on Uhuru. Irritating though he'd found his angel-wearing colleagues to be, he couldn't help but notice their overall calmness and assurance. They were utterly convinced that their methods were right, that the consequences of their actions would be what was best for the people of the Empyrean.

Had that calm been merely an illusion? A side effect of the sheep-like attitude the angels created?

Or had there been more to it than that? Did the angels in fact bestow a degree of genuine wisdom upon their wearers?

Forsythe didn't know. And it was looking more and more like he would never have the chance to find out. Even if he took the angel back from Ronyon tonight, whatever effect it might have on him couldn't possibly be fast enough to give him anything useful before the *Komitadji* arrived.

But it would at least short-circuit anything Kosta might say.

He snorted derisively under his breath. Who exactly was he kidding? Nothing would close Kosta's mouth. The kid had his own agenda—a Pax agenda—and the minute he got within squealing range of someone's ear, it would all come out. High Senator Arkin Forsythe, honored official of the Empyrean, had deliberately committed a felony.

There was no way he could conceal it. No way he could even bring it down to his word against Kosta's. Ronyon knew all about the scheme; and despite the pains Forsythe had taken to rationalize it for the big man, none of that would do any good once the questioning began. Ronyon was too honest, and too simple, to make any excuses or fabrications or spins. He would simply and straightforwardly tell the truth.

What would the people of Seraph think when they found out? What would Pirbazari think, and all the EmDef officers and troops still laboring out there in the night?

Unfortunately, he knew full well what they would think. Once, months ago, such a revelation would have meant the instant end of Forsythe's career. Now, here, the consequences would be far worse.

Because no matter what he ordered the people of Seraph to do now, it would be seen as nothing more than the self-serving manipulation of a corrupt politician. Surrender without a fight? He'd been bribed by the Pax to deliver an undamaged Empyreal world. Fight to the last man and ship? He'd been bribed to waste EmDef resources by throwing them uselessly against an obviously invincible Pax warship. Either way, the issue would be plunged into uncertainty and confusion, generating suspicion and hostility toward all their leaders.

And no matter when Seraph surrendered, before battle or afterwards, that same suspicion would likely spill over into the creation of a hundred different guerrilla units. Angry men and women would turn their anger and shame at Forsythe toward their occupiers, spilling more and more blood, until even the Pax declared Seraph not worth the trouble and destroyed it.

All that, because Kosta had somehow learned his secret.

Or rather, all that if Forsythe permitted him to reveal it.

The greatest good for the greatest number, the ancient measuring stick whispered through his mind. If Kosta had been a threat to Forsythe alone, it would be different. Forsythe had made his decision, and he was willing to face the consequences of his actions. If there was one thing his father had taught him, it was that.

But it wasn't only himself on the line here. Kosta had become a threat to all the people of Seraph, and of the Empyrean. The people Forsythe had sworn to protect.

And as an admitted Pax spy in time of war, Kosta had already forfeited his life.

From the direction of his office came the sound of gentle chimes as his father's old antique-style clock marked the three o'clock hour. It would be easy enough, Forsythe realized, the thoughts seeming as distant as if they were coming from someone else's mind. He would go to the Government Building at nine, as he'd told Pirbazari and Ronyon he would. He would go in alone to interrogate Kosta, with Pirbazari's spare gun tucked away out of sight beneath his jacket. A startled shout, an order to keep back, a single shot, and it would be over. The outer work area would be buzzing with clerks and junior officials at that hour, all of them ready to testify afterward as to what they'd heard.

And maybe Forsythe would get lucky. Maybe Kosta *would* try to jump him when he came in. It would certainly make the whole thing easier.

Wearily, he got to his feet and trudged aft to try to catch a few hours of sleep. By 9:05, he told himself, it would be all over. Kosta would be silenced, and he would be able to face the incoming *Komitadji* with a clear mind. The greatest good, for the greatest number.

On his way to his stateroom he drained the rest of his drink. It still had no taste.

CHAPTER 40

"Just relax, girl," Hanan advised, huffing a bit as he cleared the last of the fifteen steps and headed toward the main Government Building entrance, tapping the tip of his furled umbrella rhythmically against the marble as he walked. "You know the drill, and you've got all that native talent ready to call on. It's going to work just fine."

"I hope so," Chandris muttered, throwing a quick look at him as she got a couple of paces ahead and reached for the door handle. It wasn't Hanan's scheme she was worried about, in point of fact, but Hanan himself. Despite his loud and insistent claims that he was quite adequate to this little jaunt, she could tell that every step was sending a jolt of pain through him.

But you would never tell it from listening to him talk. "It'll be fine," he repeated soothingly. "Provided you got the names straight when you looked at the directory, it should go smooth as slippies. Ten minutes, tops, and it'll all be over."

Chandris hunched her shoulders beneath the unaccustomed weight of the short but heavy overcoat she was wearing. "Okay," she said. "If you say so."

"I say so," he said. "Just relax."

They stepped through the door and crossed to the receptionist's desk. "May I help you?" the middle-aged woman seated there asked.

"I certainly hope so," Hanan said gravely, handing her the elaborate business card Chandris and Ornina had designed and printed aboard the *Gazelle* two hours ago. "I'm Dr. Gridley Fowler, psychiatrist; this is my assistant Jacyntha Thinne. We need to see Office Manager Cimtrask immediately in Supervisor Dahmad's office."

"Ah . . . certainly," the receptionist said, looking taken aback as she focused on the card. "Let me call Mr. Cimtrask and—"

"Immediately, my good woman, immediately," Hanan insisted, stepping past her desk and striding toward the door leading into the main office area of the building.

He got three steps before the receptionist seemed to realize what he was doing. "Wait a minute," she said, swiveling around in her chair. "I have to call you in—"

"Supervisor Dahmad's office," Hanan called over his shoulder, pointing imperiously back toward her with his umbrella. "Immediately."

"But—"

Her protest was lost as Hanan pushed open the door and strode through. Chandris was right behind him.

"That worked," Hanan muttered as they headed down the corridor. "Which way?"

"Elevator's over there," Chandris said, nodding ahead. "We want the fifth floor."

"Dahmad?"

"Second floor," she told him. "We ought to miss Cimtrask just fine."

"Let's make sure," Hanan said, slowing his pace. "We don't want to bump into him coming down while we're going up."

They made a slightly more leisurely approach to the elevator and pushed the call button. The doors opened, revealing an unoccupied car, and they stepped in. Chandris touched the fifth floor button, and they were on their way.

In the silence of the car, she could hear the faint sounds of scratching and one or two tiny and very indignant squeaks. *It's a normal chop and hop,* she told herself firmly. *It's not going to go boff on us and fall apart. It's not.* Taking a deep breath, she set herself into her role.

Not surprisingly, Forsythe's office complex was considerably more lively than it had been the previous night. Ronyon was nowhere in sight, but the two guards were still on duty across the room. Two different guards, that is; there must have been a shift change sometime in the past few hours. That was good—the last thing they wanted right now was for someone to recognize her. Pulling open the door, Chandris held it as Hanan marched through, once again every bit the serious, overbearing, and rather obnoxious Dr. Gridley Fowler.

There was a receptionist seated at the desk just inside the door, working her way through a neat stack of mail. Hanan stepped to the desk and planted himself squarely in front of it. "I'm Dr. Fowler," he announced himself, tapping his umbrella tip on the floor for emphasis. As the receptionist looked up, he glanced down at the floor beside her and bent over. With her view blocked by the desk, he let a thick envelope slide out of his sleeve onto the floor and immediately picked it up. "Here—you dropped this," he added, straightening and tossing the envelope casually beside the stack of mail. "I have an urgent and immediate appointment with Mr. Cimtrask. Kindly direct me to his desk."

The receptionist blinked. "Mr. Cimtrask isn't here," she said, sounding perplexed. "He understood that he was to meet you in Supervisor Dahmad's office."

"In Supervisor—?" Hanan sputtered under his breath. "That ninny of a receptionist got it wrong. Mr. Cimtrask *and* Supervisor Dahmad were both supposed to meet me *here.* Get them back."

The receptionist's face set into hard lines. "Sir—"

Chandris didn't wait to hear the rest of the argument, which she was pretty sure Hanan would win anyway. Slipping around behind him, she crossed to a temporarily vacant desk and surreptitiously slid an envelope of her own from her sleeve onto it. She glanced at the nameplate—the man's name was Bulunga—and passed it by, heading for an older man scowling at his computer a few desks away. His nameplate, she saw, identified him as a Mr. Samak, Agricultural Affairs. "Excuse me?" she said hesitantly.

He looked up from his work with clear annoyance. "Yes?" he demanded brusquely.

"I've got a letter for you, Mr. Samak," she said, producing another envelope from the side pocket of her overcoat and handing it to him.

He shifted his scowl to the envelope. "There's no return address," he said. "No official markings. Where did it come from?"

Chandris spread her hands. "Don't look at me," she protested. "I'm just a page temp—I don't know anything. I didn't even know where to deliver it until he told me."

"He gave you *my* name?"

"How else would I have known?" Chandris countered patiently. "There's no address on it, either. He just pointed me to the door, gave me your name, and told me to deliver it."

"So it was someone already in the building?" Samak asked, peering suspiciously at the envelope. A man without much humor, Chandris decided, who had likely been on the receiving end of other practical jokes through the years. Her instincts had played her right; she'd picked the perfect target. "What did he look like?"

"Oh, gee, I don't know," Chandris said, shifting around far enough to glance behind her. Mr. Bulunga was back at his desk now, a slight frown on his face as he opened the envelope she'd left for him. "He had short dark hair, dark eyes, and a sort of round face," she continued, describing Bulunga as accurately as she could without being too obvious about it. "He had on a dark-blue cutback jacket with a gray scarf. Some kind of red pattern on the scarf, I think, but I don't remember what it was."

"Hmm," Samak rumbled, slitting open the envelope with a paper knife. "Very well. You may go."

"Yes, sir," Chandris said humbly, backing away. Picking up a stack of papers from another unoccupied desk as she passed it, she continued to move away, pretending to study the papers as she waited for the fireworks to begin.

It didn't take long. Samak's scowl grew deeper as he read through the letter Hanan had crafted, and his face was starting to turn an ominous shade of red. Four desks away, Bulunga was undergoing a similar transformation, only in his case it was from harried distraction to open-mouthed astonishment as his contracting grip made crumpled finger marks on the edges of his letter.

Samak fired the first shot. His darting eyes fixed on Bulunga; and then he was out of his chair, striding over to the other's desk. "Did you send me this?" he demanded, shoving the letter under Bulunga's nose.

To Chandris, Bulunga had the look of someone who was normally fairly easygoing. At the moment, with his own letter half crumpled in front of him, he wasn't in an easygoing mood. "Get that out of my face," he growled, glaring up at the other. "What in hell are you talking about?"

"Gray scarf with a red pattern," Samak said accusingly, hooking a finger under the edge of Bulunga's scarf and flipping it out of his jacket. "It was you, all right."

"I don't know what in stux you're talking about," Bulunga snapped, snatching his scarf back out of Samak's hand and standing up so abruptly that the movement sent his chair rolling back to crash into the desk behind him. "But while we're on the subject of letters, what is *this?*" he snarled, waving his paper at Samak.

"What in the name of holiness is going on?" a man in a neat gray suit muttered from a nearby desk.

Chandris glanced at his nameplate: Wojohowitz. "I was afraid this would happen," she said to him, letting her voice tremble a little. "That man—Mr. Samak—is an escaped lunatic."

"*Samak?*" Wojohowitz gasped disbelievingly. "But he's worked here for—well, nearly five years."

"That's his pattern," Chandris said, raising her voice just enough for Wojohowitz to hear her over the rising volume of the argument. Samak and Bulunga were close to blows now, from the looks of them, and the whole office had stopped dead in its tracks as they watched the show in stunned fascination. "He hides out somewhere for awhile, looking perfectly normal. And then, quite suddenly, he goes berserk."

Out of the corner of her eye, she saw Wojohowitz glance toward the two guards. "Somebody ought to do something," he said. "Why doesn't somebody do something?"

"We're waiting for the proper authorities," Chandris told him. Across the room, she could see Hanan whispering conspiratorily to another of the belligerents' shocked officemates. Weaving a similar story; only in his version, it would be Bulunga, not Samak, who was the escaped madman. Hanan glanced up, caught her eye— "Unless," Chandris added. "—yes. You go talk to them."

"Me?" Wojohowitz looked like she had just suggested he go swimming with crocodiles. "You must be joking."

"I'm a psychiatrist, Mr. Wojohowitz," she reminded him severely. "I never joke. You're one of his colleagues, one of the few people he trusts and looks up to. You're someone he'll listen to."

"No, no," Wojohowitz protested. "Not me. I mean, he hardly ever even talks to me."

"Don't argue," Chandris said sternly. "I know this man; and whether you realize it or not, he respects you. Go on—talk to him. He'll yell at you—he yells at everyone when he's like this. But trust me, he'll be listening."

"But—"

"Either you go—right now—or we have to wait for the authorities," Chandris told him. "He won't listen to them like he would to you, and they'll probably have to use physical force or even gas to subdue him. You want that to happen just because you're not willing to be a hero?"

She wasn't sure whether it was the thought of gas in his nice neat office or the magic word *hero* that had gotten to him. But one of them clearly had. Squaring his shoulders, Wojohowitz pushed back his chair and got to his feet. "Okay," he said. "You're the psychiatrist."

He strode toward the argument. At the same time, from the other side of the room, Hanan's chosen pigeon nodded his head in sudden decision and also started into the fray.

"What's going on here?" a voice boomed, loud enough to be heard even over the screaming from the middle of the room. There, standing just inside the door, was a white-haired man with the look of authority pasted all over him. Office Manager Cimtrask, undoubtedly, returned from his wild-snipe chase at Supervisor Dahmad's office.

Hanan was ready, stepping to Cimtrask's side even as the other started forward, taking his arm and starting to talk urgently to him in an undertone. Meanwhile, the argument in center stage, now expanded to a foursome, carried on without any of the participants paying Cimtrask the slightest notice.

And things were starting to come to a boil. Backing up all the way to the wall, Chandris sidled along to a position near the two guards still standing outside Forsythe's office door. Like everyone else in the room, they were watching the gathering storm with growing apprehension. One more good nudge . . .

At the doorway, Cimtrask angrily threw off Hanan's arm and stomped toward the fight. Hanan slapped him encouragingly on the back as he waded in, then caught Chandris's eye again and nodded.

Chandris took a long step to the nearest of the guards and clutched at his arm. "Watch out," she hissed. "That man in the gray suit—Wojohowitz—he said he has a knife! He said if they didn't shut up he was going to use it."

And right on cue, Cimtrask reached the argument and grabbed Samak's arm, half turning around as he did so.

Giving the guards a perfect profile view of the knife hilt Hanan had stuck to the back of his jacket.

The guard beside Chandris swore. Throwing off her hand, he charged forward. The other guard already had his phone out and had punched the emergency number. "Medical emergency—Suite 501," he barked. The first guard reached Cimtrask, spun him around—

And with a muffled crack, the smoke bomb inside the envelope Hanan had set on the receptionist's desk went off, blowing a pillar of dense white smoke toward the ceiling.

Someone screamed. The room's fire-suppression system had a more practical reaction: as the smoke cloud flattened out along the ceiling, the sprinklers went on.

The room dissolved into a chaos of shouts and screams and a panic-driven stampede for the door. The second guard started forward, shouting for everyone to remain calm. "Quickly," Hanan shouted, barely audible over the noise as he thrust his umbrella into the receptionist's hands. "Here—protect your desk!"

Automatically, she took it. Automatically, she pointed it toward the misty rain falling onto her precious papers and pushed the release button.

And let out a scream that momentarily drowned out the entire room as four small, brightly colored lizards fell out of the umbrella and scampered in different directions across the floor.

Chandris didn't wait to see any more. Stepping to Forsythe's office door, she opened it and slipped inside.

She nearly ran over Kosta in the process. He was standing just to the side of the door, listening to the noise outside his prison with bewildered nervousness. "Chandris!" he exclaimed as she closed the door to a crack behind her and wedged it into place with the tip of her shoe. "What's going on?"

"We're breaking you out," she told him, pulling off her overcoat. "You have anything you need to grab?"

"No," he said, his eyes widening in surprise at the medic's tunic she was wearing underneath. "What in—?"

"We've got medics coming, and rumors of a knife fight out there," she said. She turned the coat inside out, displaying the bright red bloodstain on the other side. "You're one of the victims. Put it on."

"I don't believe this," he said, shaking his head as he slipped on the coat. "How in the name of the laughing fates did you manage this?"

"I signed aboard a ship with a lunatic practical joker for captain," she said, running a quick eye over him and then pulling the door open. "Remember, you've been knifed."

They left the office, Chandris with a supporting arm around his waist, Kosta clutching at his side over the bloodstain as he shuffled along like someone halfway into shock. The pandemonium in the outer area hadn't diminished in the slightest; in fact, now that a couple more security men and three medics had arrived, it was that much worse. Chandris led the way around the back of the room toward the door, keeping them as far out of the swirling turmoil as she could.

They were nearly there when one of the medics glanced over and saw them. "I've got this one," Chandris shouted to him. "The rest are in the office back there. Hurry!"

He nodded, the movement shaking water off his forehead. Grabbing one of his fellow medics, he started bulling his way through the crowd. Chandris and Kosta reached the door and slipped out.

In the stairway they ditched Kosta's bloody coat and her medic's tunic. A minute later, they were out in the street.

Hanan was waiting for them around the corner in a line car. "Now, *that* was a masterpiece," he said with a grin as the two of them piled into the line car with him. "You know, Chandris, you have the makings of one of the all-time greats."

"I'll stick with the quiet life, thanks," she said. "What did you write in those letters, anyway?"

"Trade secret," he said. The grin was still in place, but as Chandris looked closely at him she could see the weariness setting in as the adrenaline-driven thrill of the morning's events faded away. The weariness, and the pain he'd been trying so hard to hide. "So, Jereko. Where should we drop you off?"

"The *Gazelle*," Kosta told him. "It should be ready to fly by now, right?"

"Right," Hanan said, frowning. "You realize, of course, that's the obvious place for them to start once they sort out the mess upstairs."

"Let's hope they think it's *too* obvious," Kosta said firmly. "But either way, the *Gazelle* it is."

He looked at Chandris. "I've got some experiments to run."

The sprinklers had been shut down and the more hysterical participants hustled out, but the scene was still one of chaos when Forsythe arrived.

"What happened here?" he demanded.

In that first flurry of responses he got five different answers, all of them mutually contradictory, none of them making much sense. But through it all, one fact became clear as a winter morning.

Kosta was gone.

Slowly, crunching through scattered papers and desktop equipment, he crossed the room toward his open office door, his feet making unpleasant noises as they squished through the waterlogged carpet. "When did this happen?" he asked the soaked office manager.

"Not fifteen minutes ago, High Senator," the manager said. He looked remorseful, embarrassed, and furious all at the same time. "This man called claiming to be—"

"Thank you, I heard," Forsythe said, dismissing the man with a curt wave of his hand. Stepping into his office, he gazed at the empty room, the weight of the gun hidden beneath his jacket tugging at his soul like a lump of frozen guilt.

The gun he had brought to use on Kosta. A gun with which he'd planned to kill a man in cold blood.

What in the world had he been thinking of?

He shook his head, wondering what had happened to him. His private refusal to accept an angel in the first place had been on purely moral and ethical grounds. Or so he had thought. And now, to conceal that decision, he'd been prepared to commit murder.

Could everyone else have been right all along? Was there something about the angels that politicians genuinely did need?

Could his father have been wrong?

There was a rapid crunching of wet papers from behind him. "High Senator," Pirbazari puffed, coming up beside him. "I just heard. He's gone?"

Forsythe nodded. "He's gone."

Pirbazari swore under his breath. "I'll get an all-grid alert out immediately. We'll get him back. Him, and the rest of his Pax team."

He spun around. "Don't bother," Forsythe said, catching his arm. "It wasn't any Pax commando team that did this."

Pirbazari frowned at him. "What do you mean?"

"Look around you," Forsythe said, waving at the office workers cleaning up the mess. "No one hurt, no real threats made, no weapons drawn except for a silly fake knife hilt. Not the sort of subtlety you would expect from people who would build a ship like the *Komitadji*."

"Then who?"

"Who else?" Forsythe said. "Our young liner stowaway and professional con artist, Chandris Lalasha."

Pirbazari's forehead wrinkled. "She could have been the girl," he conceded slowly. "But someone said there was a man involved, too."

Forsythe hesitated. It was obvious from the description that the man had to have been Hanan Daviee, fresh from his stint at the hospital. But Pirbazari apparently hadn't gotten the full story yet. "Probably one of her friends," he said. "She's been here for months now. Plenty of time to build up contacts."

"So where do we start looking?" Pirbazari asked. "Standard underworld hideaways?"

"As I said, don't bother," Forsythe told him. "We've got enough trouble as it is without having to worry about a minor Pax spy and his criminal friends. Do we have an ETA on the *Komitadji* yet?"

Pirbazari took a deep breath. "It should reach us about two this afternoon," he said, his voice heavy with reluctance. "Sir, I strongly urge you to reconsider. Kosta may indeed be only a minor spy, but he could still cause a great deal of damage. *Particularly* if he's hooked up with criminals. At least let me send someone to the *Gazelle*—they might stop by there to get some of the girl's things or clean out the Daviees' cash supply."

"No," Forsythe said firmly. "You don't think they would have planned this better than that? Wherever they're running, they're well on their way by now."

"Yes, sir," Pirbazari said, clearly still not happy but knowing an order when he heard it. "There have been some more developments with Angelmass, too."

Forsythe grimaced. "More trouble we don't need," he said. "Come on. You can brief me on the way to EmDef HQ."

All right, Kosta, he thought as they again passed through the lingering chaos Chandris and Hanan had left behind. *If you really want to go out to Angelmass and take a look, you've got a clear shot at it. I suppose I owe you that much.*

And if all that had been simply a ruse? If what Kosta had been doing was playing on Forsythe's sympathies and fears so as to break free and engage in the kind of sabotage Pirbazari obviously expected from him?

In that case, he now had a clear shot at that, too. Either way, whatever happened would be on Forsythe's head. Penance, as it were, for his sin of deception.

And for his sin of pride.

The police weren't waiting when the line car pulled up to the *Gazelle*'s enclosure. But there was a lone visitor pacing restlessly back and forth in front of the gate.

It was Ronyon.

He was at the line car's side even before the vehicle had rolled to a complete stop. *I've been waiting for you,* he signed, his hands again moving so fast in his agitation that Chandris could barely keep up.

"It's okay, Ronyon, we're here," Chandris said as she opened the door and climbed out. "Are you okay?"

There's big trouble. Oh—Jereko, Ronyon added as Kosta climbed out of the line car behind Chandris. *Mr. Forsythe let you go?*

"What's going on?" Kosta muttered as he turned to help Hanan out. "You can understand him?"

"Mostly," Chandris said, keeping her face turned so that Ronyon could see her lips. She'd always hated it when people talked behind her back; Ronyon probably felt the same way. "He says there's trouble."

Kosta snorted. "Yeah, I'll bet."

Trouble with Angelmass, Ronyon signed. *It's moving!*

"He says Angelmass is moving," Chandris translated.

"What's that?" Hanan puffed as Kosta got him out of the line car. "Moving how?"

"Rising and sinking in its orbit," Kosta said. "Forsythe's aide Pirbazari was talking about it last night. I tried to tell them about the intelligence experiments we did on angels, and what that might mean for Angelmass itself. I don't think they believed me."

Ronyon's eyes were wide. *Intelligence?* he signed. *You mean Angelmass is smart?*

"We're not sure," Chandris admitted, glancing around. Still no police in sight, but that could change any second. "Let's get inside. It'll be a lot more comfortable."

"And Ornina probably has the teapot on," Hanan added, limping noticeably as he headed for the hatchway. "Last one in has to wash the dishes."

Ornina did indeed have the teapot on. Five minutes later, they were all squeezed around the galley table, a steaming cup of tea in front of each of them. "All right, let's dig into this thing a little more," Hanan said. "I suppose I can accept this song and dance about how Angelmass could be intelligent—"

"Speak for yourself," Ornina murmured.

"—but even if I give you that," Hanan went on, ignoring the comment, "how can it possibly change its orbit? There aren't any forces acting on it, and it hasn't got any reaction mass it can throw away."

"Actually, in a sense it does," Kosta said. "Those focused radiation surges, remember? It may be that it's using those like a jet exhaust. Sort of like a natural ion drive. I tried to find out from Pirbazari whether that was part of it, but he never answered me."

"Part of it?" Hanan prompted.

"Problem is, that's a pretty slow way to go," Kosta said. "Ion drives just don't turn out much in the way of acceleration. For Angelmass to be making enough headway for them to evacuate the station, there has to be more to it."

"Wait a minute," Ornina said. "They're evacuating Central? They *never* evacuate Central."

It's already empty, Ronyon signed.

"Maybe not before, but they're doing it now," Kosta said. "Forsythe gave the order last night. I don't know whether or not it's been carried out."

"Ronyon says it has," Chandris said, watching the big man's hands as he continued signing. "They sent a shuttle . . . and as of four o'clock this morning, everyone was back on Seraph."

Ornina shook her head. "I don't believe it," she said, half to herself. "Central has been open continually since it first went online eighteen years ago. It's like the end of the world."

"You may not be far off," Kosta said grimly. "Ronyon, do you know if they shut everything down on their way out?"

I don't know, Ronyon signed. *I didn't see them say anything about that.*

"Let's hope they didn't," Kosta said. He was gazing into his tea, a haunted expression wrinkling the corners of his eyes. "We're going to need that catapult."

"You can't run that way, Jereko," Ornina said gently. "That catapult doesn't connect to anything but the Seraph huntership net."

"I'm not planning to run," Kosta told her. "And as for the huntership net . . . Ronyon, what else did they say about Angelmass?"

It's getting closer to the station, Ronyon signed. *The one that looks like a big spider?*

"How much closer?" Chandris asked.

Lots, Ronyon signed. *I don't know any of the numbers. But it's really strange. They said it was weaving up and down and shooting at the station.*

"Shooting at the station?" Hanan echoed, frowning, when Chandris had translated. "What has it got to shoot?"

"He must be talking about more radiation surges," Kosta said. "Aimed at Angelmass Central. It's already chased everyone off the station. Now it wants the station itself out of there."

It wants. The words dripped into Chandris's brain like drops of water off the edge of a roof. *It wants.* Up to now she hadn't truly believed Kosta's theory about an intelligent and malevolent black hole. Not down deep, anyway.

Now, suddenly, with those two words, she did. Angelmass was indeed alive and intelligent.

And it hated people. People on the station. Maybe the people on Seraph, too?

God help them all.

"Jereko, you said there was more to the course changes than just the surges," Hanan said. "Such as?"

"Such as brand-new physics," Kosta said bluntly. "I hate to fall back on mysterious forces mankind has never discovered; but in this case, I don't think we have a choice. *Something* is moving Angelmass, and it's not any force we've ever come across."

"Yes, but how could an entire force hide from us this long?" Hanan protested.

"How many black holes have we been up close and personal with?" Kosta countered. "All sorts of odd things happen near the event horizon, from huge tidal forces to variations in time. Personally, I'm voting on it having to do with gravity, either a polarization of the fields themselves or else something related to the time differential."

"I didn't know physics had become a democracy," Hanan murmured.

"It hasn't," Kosta said. "When I say I'm voting that way, I mean that's the theory I'm going to risk my life on. Maybe all our lives."

"Wait a minute, slow down," Chandris said. "Who's risking what here?"

"We can't just let Angelmass move around the Seraph system at will," Kosta told her. "Right now it's playing with gravity, figuring out how to use it. That's why it keeps bouncing up and down in its orbit. But sooner or later, it's going to get really good at it."

"If it hasn't already," Ornina said, a shiver running through her. "If it's attacking Central, it must be pretty confident."

Hanan shook his head. "A confident black hole," he said. "That sounds so strange."

"So what do we do about it?" Chandris asked.

"The only thing we can do." Kosta looked her straight in the eye. "We get rid of it."

She blinked. "What?"

"We use Central's catapult to throw it somewhere else," he said. "Somewhere deep in interstellar space, where the only gravitational fields it has to play with are tiny ones."

"How are you going to pull that off?" Hanan asked. "Like Ornina said, the catapult there is linked to the Seraph net."

"Then we'll have to disable the Seraph net, that's all," Kosta said. "There must be a way to shut it down from Central. We just have to figure out the codes."

"What if shutting down the Seraph net doesn't do it?" Hanan argued. "What if it just makes the catapult nonfunctional?"

"Then we're in big trouble," Kosta conceded. "But we have to risk it. I have to risk it, anyway."

"Suppose it all works like you say," Chandris said. "What then? Angelmass is a lot more massive than a huntership."

"I'm sure the catapult can be recalibrated," Kosta said. "It should be just a matter of feeding in new numbers and shunting the right amount of power."

"And if you can't do it?" Chandris persisted.

In the artificial light, Kosta's face seemed to have gone a little pale. "Then, again, I'm in trouble," he said. "It's still worth a try."

Hanan looked at Ornina, and Chandris could see a silent message flash between them. "All right," Hanan said briskly, starting to his feet. "I'll get the ship prepped—"

The end of the sentence became an agonized hiss as he froze halfway to his feet, his face twisting in pain. "Hanan!" Ornina exclaimed, scrambling up and taking his arm.

"No, what *you* are going to do is get back to the hospital," Chandris said firmly, standing up and taking his other arm. "Both of you. Kosta and I can take the ship out to Angelmass."

"Don't be silly," Hanan said between clenched teeth. "You can't do this alone."

"Well, we sure can't do it carrying you," Kosta pointed out, coming around behind Chandris. "Chandris, I'll help Ornina get him outside. You go ahead of us to the hatchway and call a line car."

A tentative hand touched Chandris's shoulder, and she looked over to see that Ronyon was on his feet, too. *I can call a line car,* he offered, looking at Hanan as if he were an injured puppy. *You could go and start the ship.*

"You sure you want to get involved with this?" Chandris asked, frowning at him.

I'm not very smart, Ronyon signed. *But I know that Angelmass is hurting people. I want to help.*

Chandris hesitated. She really didn't want to get Ronyon in trouble with Forsythe. But it would save them a few minutes; and if Kosta was right, they might need all the minutes they could get.

Besides which, if the police were scanning line car orders looking for her name or Kosta's, this ought to throw them off the trail a little. "All right, Ronyon, thank you," she said. "Go ahead."

"Where's he going?" Kosta asked as Ronyon turned and hurried out of the galley.

"He'll call the line car," Chandris explained over her shoulder as she followed him. "I'm going to go get the ship prepped. I hope they got everything put back together."

"Chandris?" Hanan called after her.

She turned back. "Yes?"

"Be careful, child," he said softly. "And come back. You hear?"

She managed a confident smile. "Don't worry," she said. "After all we've been through, you're sure not going to get rid of me now."

She turned again and left, careful not to look back.

CHAPTER 41

"They're starting to come up into orbit," Campbell reported as Lleshi stepped onto the balcony. "Looks like they're going pretty much all out to meet us."

"Yes, I see," Lleshi said, blinking the last bits of sleep from his eyes as he studied the tactical display. With roughly an hour to go before the *Komitadji* reached close-orbit distance, the Empyreals were emptying the planet, putting everything they had into space in preparation for the upcoming battle.

But unless they had a lot more in reserve than it appeared, it wasn't going to be nearly enough. "What about the communications and weather satellites?" he asked.

"They finished mining them about two hours ago," Campbell said. "At least, that's when the shuttles they had poking around headed back down. While they were at it, they put another hundred or so smaller casings in orbit, too."

"More mines."

"Firecrackers," Campbell said with a contemptuous sniff. "Even subnukes that size wouldn't be worth much, and the readings don't show any radiation telltales. Probably mining explosives like the ones those suicide ships in Lorelei system were using."

"Whatever else you say about these people, they're certainly single-minded," Lleshi said. "Anything else happen while I was asleep?"

"Surprisingly little, actually," Campbell said, tapping some keys. Over by Lleshi's station, one of the displays changed to a page full of numbers. "We've been monitoring their communications; and while there's been lots of traffic on the official and Defense Force channels, the civilian and media ones haven't shown any unusual activity at all. In fact, Comm Group says they don't think the people have even been told about us."

"Really." Lleshi rubbed his chin, frowning at the tactical. "Interesting. Either they're supremely confident that they can take us on, or else they simply don't want to start the panic before it's absolutely necessary."

"Most likely the latter," Campbell said. "Tactical Group's been over everything we've seen them do, and they agree unanimously that the Seraph defensive array is pitifully weak. We should be able to cut through it in no time."

"We'll soon find out," Lleshi said. "Keep a close watch for atmospheric craft lurking beneath clouds and in high mountain cubbyholes. They might be banking on our fighters not handling as well in atmosphere as theirs do."

"In which case they're in for a bad surprise." Campbell cocked his head slightly. "Speaking of fighters, sir, are you going to send a squad ahead to clear a path?"

"As Adjutor Telthorst wants, you mean?" Lleshi said sourly. "You're the tactical officer, Mr. Campbell. You tell me."

Campbell hesitated. "There is a certain logic to it," he hedged. "Depending on the strength and type of mines, they could pose a significant danger to the *Komitadji*'s hull-mounted sensors and weapons emplacements."

"Do you think that's what Mr. Telthorst is concerned about?" Lleshi pressed.

Campbell glanced down onto the main command deck floor, as if checking to see if Telthorst was on his way back from his own rest break. "Not really, sir, no," he conceded. "I think he mostly wants to keep the *Komitadji* in pristine condition for the victory flyover of the Supreme Council cathedra."

"That was my impression, as well," Lleshi said. "So that's agreed. We ignore him."

"Yes, sir," Campbell said, not looking particularly happy. "Sir . . . permission to speak freely?"

"Certainly."

Campbell seemed to brace himself. "Any Adjutor assigned to a ship like the *Komitadji* is by definition a highly placed official. He has a great deal of power; and you and he have not gotten along as well as everyone might have hoped."

"So far, you're stating the obvious," Lleshi said. "Are you suggesting I abandon my military duty in favor of watching my political back?"

"I'm suggesting it might be prudent to try to find some middle ground," Campbell said. "A compromise that allows him to save face while at the same time not putting our people at unnecessary risk."

"I see," Lleshi said, studying his face. "And all of this wise counsel is welling spontaneously from your own sense of decency and compassion?"

Campbell's lip twisted, just noticeably. "Mr. Telthorst called me into his cabin yesterday after we chased away the net defenses. He told me that you had brought the *Komitadji* to Seraph without orders, and said that if your irrational defiance persisted he might have to relieve you of command."

"And he offered you my job?"

"No, I think he intended to put on the commodore's tunic himself," Campbell said, a trace of disgust seeping through his rigid control. "He mostly wanted to see whose side I would be on if that happened. To find out whether or not I would join in mutiny against lawful authority, I believe is how he put it."

"Interesting," Lleshi murmured. "I appreciate your candor. And I won't ask what answer you gave him."

Campbell's face reddened slightly. "Sir—"

"Carry on, SeTO," Lleshi said, turning and stepping back to his station. Seating himself, he swiveled away from Campbell and called up the *Komitadji*'s fuel consumption for the past four hours.

So there it was at last. It had been a long time in coming; but Telthorst was finally preparing to challenge his control of the *Komitadji*. And for him to be sounding out Lleshi's senior officers, he must be feeling pretty confident that the time and opportunity were rapidly approaching.

Lleshi sighed, a silent lungful of air that seemed to come from the center of his soul, his thoughts drifting back to the day he'd been given his first commission and sent aboard his first ship. Then, the Pax Defense Fleet had been exactly that: a bulwark of protection for the people of Earth and her fellow worlds. The Supreme Council had been supreme in fact, not just in name, and the Adjutors simply an advisory arm of the government charged with watching finances and expenditures.

Now, nearly half a century later, it had somehow all turned inside out. The military's primary mission had become one of conquest, its strategy and tactics driven by money and profit and gain. Money to feed the Pax's hungry coffers, profit for the delight of the shadowy men who were the real power behind the Council; gain that was immediately turned around and used to finance the next conquest.

The *Komitadji* had been built for only one purpose: to be so huge and so terrifying that its very appearance would frighten wayward colonies into surrendering without wasting valuable resources on useless defiance. Perhaps even as they had reluctantly authorized the necessary funds the Adjutors had looked forward to the day when they could take the ship for their own, to control it without having to work through the military chain of command.

Now, it seemed, Telthorst was ready to make that move.

And as far as Lleshi was concerned, he was welcome to it.

It was a surprising thought, one that was almost as stunning to Lleshi himself as it surely would have been to Telthorst if he'd heard it. For a flag officer to quietly give up his ship to a civilian—especially a brash, inexperienced, coin-bisecting Adjutor—would have been unthinkable to the young Ensign Lleshi fresh aboard his first ship.

But the older Commodore Lleshi could see clearly the road the universe was taking. The Adjutors had been winning steadily for the past thirty years, gathering more and more power and influence to themselves. They had slowly and methodically trained everyone from the lowliest Pax citizen to the highest members of the Supreme Council itself to think solely in terms of costs and profits and losses.

And Lleshi was tired of fighting them.

Perhaps Telthorst would prove to be a competent commander. Probably not. But either way, at this point it wasn't worth a battle that would tear his crew apart in a power struggle. Certainly not in the middle of action against a hostile force.

Because no matter how incompetent Telthorst turned out to be, even he couldn't do anything to seriously threaten the *Komitadji*, not even with all the help the Empyreal Defense Force could muster. Perhaps if he embarrassed himself badly enough, it would at least slow the Adjutors down in their rush to total power.

So let the Adjutor have his moment of glory. In the meantime, the *real* commander of the *Komitadji* had an assault to plan. Signing off on the fuel reports, he keyed for the latest reports from Sensor and Tactical and began to read.

Chandris's familiarity with huntership procedure and personnel had gotten them a tow car without any questions being asked. It had taken a little more finesse to get them a spot at the launch strip, where an amazing lineup of ships was waiting, but she'd managed to pull that one off, too.

But it was quickly apparent that no amount of charm was going to get them past the Angelmass catapult.

"You must be kidding, *Gazelle,*" the operator said, his voice firm. "Don't you read your own agency's reports? All travel to Angelmass Central has been shut down. Period; end of comment; close file."

"Then I suggest you reopen that file," Chandris said acidly. "This is a rescue mission, set up and blue-three-coded by High Senator Forsythe himself."

"A what?" the operator demanded. He still sounded firm, but Kosta could hear a trickle of doubt now in his voice.

"What, your ears need cleaning?" Chandris said. "A rescue mission. Someone finally counted heads on the evac shuttle and realized they left someone on Central. We're going out to get her."

"Oh, hell," the operator muttered. "Who is it?"

"Comm supervisor named Jiselle," Chandris said. "You know her?"

"Met her once," the operator muttered. "Not worth rescuing, if you ask me."

"High Senator Forsythe apparently doesn't share your opinion," Chandris said. "Now, are you going to 'pult us, or do we have to drag him out of his meeting and have him *personally* explain to you what exactly a blue-three means?"

"Okay, okay, come on in," the operator said. "I'm calibrating now."

"Thank you. Out."

Chandris snapped off the comm and got the *Gazelle* moving. "Jiselle?" Kosta asked.

"The comm supervisor I talked to after we were attacked and I had to bring Hanan back in a hurry," Chandris explained.

"And the blue-three?"

"I copied the authorization codes from Forsythe's cyl before I gave it back," she said. "I figured they might come in handy someday. So, what do you think? Did he fall for it, or is he whistling up the watchdogs?"

Kosta shook his head. "You're the expert on human reactions," he reminded her. "What do *you* think?"

"I don't know," she said, peering at the displays. "He *sounded* convinced; but you can never tell with that sort. He might stay rolled over, or he might just as easily decide to check it out."

Kosta grimaced. "And if he calls Forsythe's office to check on that blue-three, we're dead."

"Only if he gets through to Forsythe himself before we 'pult," Chandris said. "If we can get aboard Central before the cord goes pop, we should be able to shut down the net and keep anyone from coming after us."

"So the plan is to get through as fast as we can?"

"Right, only without looking too obvious about it," Chandris agreed. "Of course, with a rescue mission we're supposed to be in a hurry anyway. I'd say we've got a pretty fair chance of making it."

"Okay," Kosta said. "I just wish the odds were better than just 'pretty fair.'"

"You want certainties, go into theology," Chandris said, studying her monitors. "*I* just hope none of these warships takes it into his head to take a look at us."

Kosta blinked. "*Warships?*"

"Sure look like that to me," Chandris said. "But hey, you're the expert on military hardware."

Kosta leaned closer to his displays, his fingers fumbling for the magnification control. Preoccupied with the Angelmass problem, he hadn't even focused on the other ships flying around them. But now that he actually took a good look at them . . .

"You're right," he said, the back of his neck tingling. Last night, Forsythe had talked about a suspected Pax invasion of Lorelei. Could Commodore Lleshi's task force have made it to Seraph already? "I don't like this."

"Just stay cool," Chandris advised. "They're EmDef ships; we're an EmDef rescue mission. Just one big happy family. But if they hail us, let me do the talking."

"Right," Kosta murmured, his eyes flicking across the various displays as he adjusted the views. If there was a Pax task force on its way, and if it was close enough to be in deceleration mode, there ought to be a set of visible drive glows out there somewhere.

He was still searching, wondering if the glow was being hidden by one of the ships blocking his view, when Chandris spoke again. "Okay, get ready," she said. "Here we go." There was the usual almost-felt jerk as the catapult threw them across Seraph system—

And abruptly a blaze of light exploded from the displays.

"What in—?" Kosta yelped.

"It's Angelmass," Chandris snapped. She did something to her board, and the light faded from painful to merely intense, then vanished completely into comfortable darkness as a small black spot positioned itself over the center of the blaze. "Sorry—the sunscreens hadn't been recalibrated."

"They shouldn't have had to be," Kosta said, his eyes flicking over the numbers. "At least, not this much. Oh, hell."

"What?" Chandris demanded.

"Take a look at the proximity numbers," Kosta said. "Angelmass is . . . friz. No more than a couple thousand kilometers out."

Chandris hissed between her teeth. "That close?"

"That close," Kosta told her grimly. "It's not only on the move, it's picking up speed."

"Then we'd better get this kickshow on its feet," Chandris said. From behind Kosta came the roar of the engines, and he felt himself being pressed back into his seat. "We'll go around and dock at the catapult end—that's where you'll be doing your work."

"Right," Kosta muttered. "Let's just hope they left the door unlocked."

"The ships are nearly in position, High Senator," General Roshmanov reported, crossing to where Forsythe and Pirbazari were sitting and pulling over a chair for himself. "Another twenty minutes, max."

"How soon until the *Komitadji* is in combat range?" Pirbazari asked.

Roshmanov shrugged uncomfortably as he sat down. "That depends on how destructive they want to be," he said. "We know the Pax has long-range subnuclear missiles that can probably take out a million square kilometers at a shot. A dozen of those properly placed, and there would be precious little left of Seraph for them to conquer."

Forsythe felt his stomach tighten. "Fortunately, that's not their style."

"Not their preferred style, anyway," Roshmanov agreed. "Though I suppose that if we make enough trouble they might switch to that out of pure spite."

"The Pax runs on profit, not spite," Pirbazari said. "Besides, I don't think we have to worry about being that much trouble."

"No," Roshmanov conceded heavily. "I'm afraid we don't."

For a long minute none of them said anything. Forsythe gazed at the tactical display, listening to the low background murmurs filling the EmDef command room, occasionally able to pull snatches of specific conversations from the general hum.

His phone, when it rang, made him jump. Pulling it out, he tapped it on. "Forsythe."

"High Senator, this is Lieutenant Hakara at Central Switchboard," a woman's voice said. "I'm sorry to bother you, sir, but Seraph Catapult Control has apparently been calling all around Shikari City trying to locate you."

"Me, personally?" Forsythe asked, frowning. He was hardly in the official chain of command here. "What about?"

"I don't know, sir," Hakara said. "I can connect you if you'd like."

"Yes, go ahead."

There was a click, a long pause, and another half dozen clicks at various pitches. "High Senator Forsythe?" a man's voice said tentatively.

"Speaking," Forsythe said. "Who is this?"

"Raymont, sir. Traffic controller on the Seraph Angelmass Catapult. It's—well, it's a little late now, sir; they've already gone through. I was wondering if you wanted us to send a backup shuttle along with them. Or behind them, now."

"If this is supposed to be making sense, it's not," Forsythe growled. He didn't have time for games. "Who and what are you talking about?"

"Why, the rescue mission, sir," Raymont said. "The blue-three code. The woman on the *Gazelle* said—"

"The *Gazelle*?" Forsythe cut him off.

"Yes, sir," Raymont said. From the sound of his voice, it sounded like he was suddenly having trouble breathing. "She said someone had been accidentally left aboard Central, and that you'd personally authorized a rescue mission even though the catapult was officially shut down, because a blue-three supersedes other orders . . ." He trailed off.

"I see," Forsythe said, his voice sounding calmer than he would have expected it to. Preoccupied with the incoming threat, he'd completely forgotten about Kosta and his theories about Angelmass. "When did they go through?"

"About two minutes ago, sir," Raymont said, sounding thoroughly miserable now. "Shall I send a shuttle after them? We could have something prepped in fifteen minutes."

Forsythe looked up at the tactical. "No, don't bother," he said.

"Or one of the EmDef ships could get there even sooner," Raymont offered. "We could recalibrate while it gets here—"

"I said don't bother," Forsythe repeated firmly. "Close down the catapult again, but leave your net operating. Sooner or later, they'll be wanting to come back."

"Yes, sir," Raymont said. "I'm . . . yes, sir."

Forsythe closed the phone, noting peripherally that General Roshmanov had disappeared sometime during the call. "Kosta?" Pirbazari asked quietly.

"And Lalasha, and the *Gazelle*," Forsythe confirmed, putting the phone away. "They've gone to Angelmass."

"I see," Pirbazari said, his voice gone suddenly hard and cool. "I guess I should have sent someone to the huntership yards after all."

Forsythe frowned at him. The other's expression matched his voice. "You have something to say, Zar?"

"We could have stopped him," Pirbazari said, his voice just loud enough for Forsythe to hear over the background noise. "Instead, you let him go. A confessed Pax spy; and you deliberately let him go. Way the hell out to Angelmass, where he'll be conveniently out of the way when the *Komitadji* gets here."

"What exactly are you accusing me of?" Forsythe asked quietly.

"I'm just wondering if you made some sort of deal with him," Pirbazari said. "If you did, shouldn't the rest of us be brought in on it?"

For a long minute Forsythe gazed at him, a part of him marveling at how rapidly it was all unraveling. A single decision not to wear an angel . . . and now it had come down to suspicion of treason. "I made no deals," he said at last. "But perhaps I should have."

Pirbazari's eyes twitched. "What's that supposed to mean?"

"The *Komitadji* is an impressive weapon," Forsythe said. "Very powerful, very dangerous. But as everyone is so fond of pointing out, the Pax wants conquest, not destruction."

He nodded fractionally toward the sky. "Angelmass is a different matter. It's already attacked several hunterships, and it looks like it's gunning for Central next."

Pirbazari snorted. "If you buy Kosta's theory."

"Dr. Frashni confirmed what Kosta said about his experiment," Forsythe reminded him.

"It's a long road from a nine-angel logic circuit to a mad killer black hole," Pirbazari argued.

"Agreed," Forsythe said. "And the first step down that road is to gather more data. Which is precisely what Kosta's doing."

"So he says," Pirbazari countered. "Maybe he just wanted to get himself out of the way of a fight."

"No," Forsythe said firmly. "Think about it. Every huntership in the yard has been grounded, which means he could have taken his pick of them. Why take the *Gazelle*, which would logically be the first place we would start looking for him?"

"Maybe because he knew we *wouldn't* be looking for him," Pirbazari said bluntly.

"He took the *Gazelle* because it had his test equipment aboard," Forsythe said. "He's there to find out what's going on."

Pirbazari's eyes were still hard, but Forsythe could see the suspicion fading a little. "And not because you offered him a deal to let him sit out the battle?"

Forsythe gave a snort. "If you think the vicinity around Central is safer right now than facing down the *Komitadji,* you're welcome to go sit out the battle with him."

Pirbazari's mouth tightened. "That was uncalled for, High Senator."

"So was yours, Zar," Forsythe said. "Are we clear now?"

Pirbazari seemed to measure him with his eyes. "For the moment."

"Good," Forsythe said. "Then let's see if the rest of the ships are in place yet."

Chandris had never been aboard Angelmass Central before, but she had studied the floorplans and procedures once during a quiet hour between angel hunts. Getting the *Gazelle* into the axis docking bay without inside personnel to assist was a challenge, but she managed it without too many false starts. The interface between the non-rotating bay and the rotating part of the cylinder was also a bit tricky, but again they got through without anything more serious than a bruised shin on Kosta's part.

"Quite a place," Kosta called down to her over the chatter of gamma sparks as they headed down a narrow access ladder toward the operations area. "Must have been fun duty being assigned here."

"I don't think it was usually this noisy," Chandris called back up, feeling her heart thudding in her ears. The gamma sparking wasn't nearly to the noise level that it had been during the radiation surges, but it was definitely heading in that direction.

"I just hope it doesn't get any worse," he called back. "These electronics can't take this kind of beating forever."

The station's designers had apparently had similar thoughts. The main catapult control complex, when they reached it, was considerably quieter than the approach had been. "They must have laid on extra shielding here," Kosta said as he turned in a slow circle, studying the softly glowing lights and displays. "Looks like they left everything on. Good."

"Including the net," Chandris said, looking around and then starting up the ladder again. "I'm going to go across to the other end and shut it down."

"Wait a minute," Kosta said, grabbing her ankle. "There must be a way of doing that from in here."

"I'm sure there is," Chandris agreed. "But it'll take time to find it. You want Forsythe and EmDef charging in on us while we're looking through manuals?"

Kosta let go of her ankle. "Go," he said.

She got back up to the cylinder's centerline corridor and made her way along it through the crew quarters and supply areas toward the other half of the station. Both sets of blast doors leading to the midway connection tunnel were sealed, but they opened quickly enough at her punched-in command. The midway tunnel itself was rather eerie: a relatively short corridor lined all around with red-rimmed hatchways leading to the double ring of escape pods she'd seen on her first trip to Angelmass.

She got the blast doors at the far end opened and passed through a mirror-image layout of supply rooms and crew quarters until she arrived at the proper access ladder and climbed down to the net control complex. A quick glance at the monitors to confirm that Forsythe and EmDef weren't yet coming through the net, and she began to go down the boards, systematically throwing every switch.

Two minutes later, the boards and monitors were totally dark. So was that entire half of the station. Groping her way along in the dim glow of the emergency lighting system, she headed back.

She reached the catapult control complex to find Kosta seated at one of the stations, gazing at a display and flipping back and forth between what looked to be at least three different instruction manuals. "Net's down," she reported. "How's it going here?"

"Slow," he said, not looking up. "In order to recalibrate for Angelmass, it seems I need a crash course in catapult theory."

"Great," Chandris said. "How long?"

"Call it an hour. Maybe a little less."

"And then we still have the actual reprogramming to do?"

Kosta nodded. "I'd guess another thirty to sixty minutes on top of that for the programming and the fine-tuning of the charge on the catapult's capacitors."

"So we'd better count on this taking a full two hours."

"Right." Kosta looked significantly across the room. "I just hope we've got that long."

Chandris followed his gaze, to a monitor showing the blazing speck that was Angelmass bearing inexorably down on them. Staring at the display, she could have sworn she could see the black hole visibly gaining on them. An optical illusion, of course. "What can I do?"

He rubbed his forehead. "How are you at electronic tech stuff?"

"I learned the *Gazelle*'s systems in three days."

"Close enough." He gestured to the chair beside him. "First thing you need to do is find out how to shut off the Seraph net from here—the last thing we want is to send Angelmass into a low planetary orbit. After that, start learning the mechanics of the reprogramming procedure. Once I've got the physics and math figured out, I don't want to have to wade through a tech manual, too."

"Got it," she said, sliding into the chair. Pulling up the procedures manual, she glanced again at Angelmass.

It *was* an optical illusion, of course. It had to be.

CHAPTER 42

"The moment has come, Commodore," Telthorst said, his eyes steady on Lleshi's face, his voice just a few stages too loud. "If you're going to launch a fighter screen to protect the *Komitadji*, you need to do it now."

"Thank you, Mr. Telthorst," Lleshi said, striving to keep the disgust out of his voice. As far as Lleshi was concerned, the decision had been made several hours ago. Telthorst's question was nothing but a pathetically obvious challenge, an attempt to make points with the command crew for his upcoming power bid. Who among them, after all, could possibly argue against anything that would help ensure the *Komitadji*'s safety?

But Lleshi wasn't going to play Telthorst's game. Not yet. Military procedure, as well as simple basic battle ethics, dictated that he first give Seraph the option of surrender. "Open a broad-spectrum comm blanket to the planet," he ordered.

The comm officer nodded briskly. "Channel open, Commodore."

"This is Commodore Vars Lleshi of the Pax warship *Komitadji*," he stated firmly, as if the Empyreals hadn't already figured that out. "I declare the Seraph system to be returned to the jurisdiction of Earth and the Pax. I call on you to withdraw your military forces to the surface and prepare to turn over the civilian government and infrastructure to my command."

He paused, but the only response was silence. "If you do not comply, my orders are to take control of this system by whatever means necessary, using whatever force is required," he went on. Telthorst's eyebrows twitched at the word *orders*, but the Adjutor said nothing. "You have ten minutes to respond. After that, I will take whatever action I deem appropriate."

He tapped off his microphone switch. "Mark ten minutes," he ordered.

"Yes, sir."

"Very noble," Telthorst murmured. "You don't really expect them to just give up, do you?"

"You had better hope they do," Lleshi warned. "If they decide to fight, you're going to have a much smaller collection of plunder to present your fellow poachers at the cathedra."

Telthorst's eyes flashed. "How dare you refer to the Adjutors that way?" he demanded. "And while we're at it, how dare you pretend you had orders to come here? This was nothing more than a blatant attempt on your part to steal some glory for yourself. Here, in the midst of—"

"*Komitadji,* this is High Senator Arkin Forsythe of Lorelei," a deep, measured voice boomed from a dozen command deck speakers. "What are your terms of surrender?"

"Unconditional, of course," Telthorst called before Lleshi could answer. "You will immediately remove your warships—"

"This is Commodore Lleshi, High Senator," Lleshi cut him off. "You misunderstand our purpose here. This is not so much a surrender as it is merely a return of wayward colonies to the Pax family."

"A fine distinction, some would say," the High Senator commented.

"Perhaps," Lleshi said. "However, that is the reality of the situation. Upon your acceptance, you will immediately gain the same rights and privileges as any world and people of the Pax."

"And the same duties, I presume?"

"No rights exist without corresponding responsibilities," Lleshi reminded him.

"No, of course not," Forsythe said. "I would like the opportunity to discuss the details before we make a final decision."

"What decision is there to make?" Telthorst put in contemptuously. "Your forces are outnumbered, outgunned—"

Lleshi snapped his fingers at the comm officer and gestured, and Telthorst's microphone was abruptly clicked off. "Commodore—"

Lleshi cut him off with a single glare. "My apologies, High Senator," he said. "I am quite willing to discuss these matters with you. An unarmed shuttle with yourself, a pilot, and no more than two others aboard will be permitted to approach. A fighter escort will guide you to the proper docking bay."

"And then?"

Lleshi smiled tightly. "However our discussion goes, and whatever your decision, you and your party will be permitted to return unharmed to Seraph before any action is initiated on our part. You have my word on that."

There was just the briefest pause. "Very well, Commodore. I'll be there within the hour."

"I'll look forward to our meeting, High Senator," Lleshi said. "*Komitadji* out."

He gestured to the comm officer, and the microphone went dead. "I trust you realize what a fool you're being," Telthorst bit out, his face flushed with anger. "He knows what the rights and responsibilities are—we laid it all out for them months ago, before they closed their systems to us. All he's doing is stalling, giving themselves more time to prepare."

"To prepare what?" Lleshi countered. "They have nothing down there that has a hope of standing up to us."

"Maybe they expect reinforcements," Telthorst said acidly. "Or didn't it occur to you that there are four more systems worth of Empyreal warships out there?"

Lleshi shook his head. "There will be no reinforcements. By now they know we're here, or at least suspect it, and each system is scrambling to prepare its own defenses. No one has enough ships or soldiers to spare for the others."

Telthorst folded his arms across his chest. "So you're just going to let this High Senator manipulate you into holding off your attack?"

"I'm going to try to set his mind at ease about the future of his world," Lleshi corrected. "If you don't like it, you don't have to sit in on the discussion."

"Oh, I'll be there," Telthorst promised softly. "I wouldn't miss it for the world. *Any* world."

They had been sitting beside each other for about twenty minutes, each deeply involved in their own reading, when Chandris finally finished her particular manual and came up for air.

The gamma clicks had become noisier. Much noisier.

Moving stealthily, trying not to break Kosta's concentration, she slipped out of her chair and crossed to the ranging section of the control board. On the monitor, Angelmass seemed brighter and angrier than ever, but that could still be just an optical illusion. Seating herself at the board, she keyed for some numbers.

It wasn't an illusion. Angelmass was indeed getting closer.

Dangerously close.

Swallowing hard, forcing trembling fingers to function, she keyed for a review and projection. Two hours total, Kosta had estimated, before they would be ready to throw Angelmass out of the system. Call it another hour and forty minutes on the clock, then. The question was, did they have that one hundred minutes left?

The computer projection was quick, precise, and unambiguous. They did not, in fact, have a hundred minutes.

They had exactly seventy.

She ran the numbers again, and again. But each time the projection came up the same. Long before they were ready to make their move, it would be all over.

She looked over her shoulder at the back of Kosta's head, leaning toward the reading display with oblivious intensity. He could have run once she and Hanan had sprung him from Forsythe's office. He could have vanished into the

Shikari City underground, or gone off into some wilderness area, and waited for his Pax friends to arrive in force, as they surely would eventually.

Instead, he'd risked everything to come out here. Risked his life to try to help the people of Seraph. How was she going to tell him that that sacrifice had been for nothing?

Abruptly, as if sensing her thoughts or at least her absence from beside him, Kosta's head jerked up. "Chandris?" he called over the gamma noise.

"Back here," she called.

He swiveled around in his chair . . . and she could tell from the look on his face that he already knew. "Angelmass?"

"Closing fast," she said. "Computer calls it an hour and forty minutes until impact. But thirty minutes before that happens the radiation will fry us even through Central's shielding."

His lip twitched. "You're sure?"

"I've run the numbers three times," she said. "We've got seventy minutes, exactly. How far are you on your reading?"

"Not far enough," he said grimly. "I've got at least another half hour to go, and it looks more and more like the programing will take a solid hour after that. Even with two of us working on it."

"Then it's over," Chandris said gently, or as gently as she could when she had to practically shout the words. "Come on, let's get back to the *Gazelle.*"

"No."

She sighed, getting to her feet and crossing to him. "Jereko, it's over."

"No it's not," he repeated flatly, his eyes flicking around the room. "We can do it. We have to do it. We just need to buy ourselves some more time."

"How?" Chandris demanded. "This isn't the *Gazelle,* where we can outrun the thing if we can find the right direction. This is a space station. It hasn't got any drive engines."

"Then we have to find a way to slow Angelmass down," Kosta said slowly. "Decoy it, maybe . . ."

He trailed off, an odd light suddenly in his eyes. "I hope you're not thinking what I think you're thinking," Chandris warned, her stomach suddenly tight. There was something about that look that reminded her of Hanan and Ornina, hell-bent on being noble and self-sacrificing, no matter what the cost.

And if that cost included the *Gazelle* . . . "May I point out that the *Gazelle*'s our only ticket out of here?" she said carefully.

"I know," he said, swiveling back to his board. "Is there any spare fuel aboard? Like for shuttles and hunterships that have run short?"

"I can check," Chandris said, sitting down beside him again and pulling up a floorplan and inventory list. "Jereko . . ."

"I know," Kosta said, leaning close to look at the schematic. "Trust me."

"And if you're wrong?"

His breath was warm against her cheek. "I'll try to have enough time to apologize."

The shuttle had been prepped, the pilot chosen and briefed; and Forsythe was looking over all the information the Empyrean had on Pax law and government when the word came that the Seraph huntership net had been shut down.

"What do you mean, shut down?" Forsythe demanded, frowning. "I left specific orders that it be left open."

"They say the command came from Central," Pirbazari said, his voice studiously neutral. It was a tone he'd used a lot in the past hour, Forsythe had noted with a growing uneasiness. "With Angelmass about twenty-one light-minutes away, that means the signal was transmitted within twenty minutes of their arrival at the net. Figure in maneuvering, docking, and debarkation time, and it looks like shutting down the Seraph net was the second thing they did once they got onto the station."

"The second thing?"

"Yes," Pirbazari said. "Shutting down Central's own net was number one. Seraph Control says the telemetry for that came through a few minutes before their own net closed down."

Forsythe forced himself to meet the other's gaze. "You still think I've made a deal with Kosta, don't you?" he said quietly. "Fine. Then tell me this: what does shutting down the net here gain him?"

"I don't know," Pirbazari said evenly. "But then, I don't know what going up there in the first place gains him. All I know is that the *Komitadji* destroyed one of Seraph system's main nets on the way in; and now Kosta has shut down two more. Coincidence?"

"He's been hanging around Angelmass and the Institute for months," Forsythe pointed out. "Surely he knows by now that the huntership system is binary linked. Those nets make no difference to traffic in or out of the system."

"One would think he'd know that," Pirbazari acknowledged. "But maybe he's a slow learner." His right eyebrow twitched. "Or maybe there's something else going on that I don't know about."

"If there is, I don't know about it either," Forsythe said, feeling sweat breaking out on his forehead. Pirbazari was, as best he could tell, about half a micron from breaking his self-imposed silence and announcing the whole story over the EmDef HQ loudspeaker system.

The only things that might be holding him back were a lack of proof and whatever residual loyalty he still might have for the man he'd worked with for so long. And neither of those were going to last forever.

"High Senator?" General Roshmanov called from the doorway. "Your shuttle is ready."

Pirbazari waved in acknowledgement. "That's it. Let's get to it."

Forsythe braced himself. Possibly not even through the next thirty seconds, he amended. "You're not going, Zar," he said.

Pirbazari had been looking down as he fastened his jacket. Now, slowly, he looked up. "What?"

"You're former military," Forsythe reminded him. "You know too much about EmDef procedures, personnel, and tactics. If Lleshi reneges on his promise, we can't afford for you to be in their hands."

"What about you?" Pirbazari demanded. "An Empyreal High Senator?"

"I know a little about military expenditures and far too much about council etiquette," Forsythe said with a grimace. "Nothing that's going to help with their war effort."

"But this isn't just a war effort," Pirbazari countered. "This world-swallowing technique of theirs is as much political as it is military. And you're the local expert on political matters."

Forsythe sighed. "What do you want me to say? *Someone* has to go."

Pirbazari's shoulders hunched fractionally. "So you're going alone?"

"I'm not *that* brave," Forsythe said. "No, I'm taking Ronyon."

"Ronyon," Pirbazari repeated, giving him that look again. "Interesting choice. I don't think we can expect to get sympathy votes from the Pax."

Forsythe stared at him, an odd feeling in the pit of his stomach. "Is that why you think he's still with me?" he asked. "For sympathy?"

"I didn't used to think so," Pirbazari said. "But then, I once thought I knew you, too. Now—" His eyes dropped to the angel pendant around Forsythe's neck. "I don't know what to think anymore."

"Then just trust me," Forsythe urged.

"I always have trusted you," Pirbazari said. "I've always believed that you wanted the best for the Empyreal people."

He glanced at Forsythe's chest again. "Now, I'm not so sure."

"That *is* all I want, Zar," Forsythe said, his throat aching. With the Empyrean threatening to come crashing down around them all, he suddenly realized that the friendship and loyalty of his people was all he had left. All, perhaps, that any of them had left. "It truly is. Give me this one last chance. Please."

Pirbazari took a deep breath. "I suppose I don't really have any choice, do I? Okay, High Senator. Just . . . good luck."

Forsythe touched his arm. "I'll be back soon." He started to turn away.

"High Senator?"

Forsythe turned back. "Yes?"

"When you return," Pirbazari said softly, "we are going to have a long talk about this. A *long* talk."

Forsythe nodded. "Indeed."

Triggering his call stick to summon Ronyon, he turned away again and headed to where General Roshmanov stood waiting for him, his back unnaturally stiff.

No, Ronyon wasn't going to be along for any sympathy his presence might be able to squeeze out of the ice-rimmed hearts of the Pax conquerors. But if there were to be any miracles of concession or compassion coming out of this confrontation, it would be Ronyon who held the key.

Pirbazari didn't understand that, of course. But then, Forsythe could hardly explain to him that Ronyon was the one carrying the angel.

Or perhaps an explanation wouldn't have been necessary. Perhaps Pirbazari already knew.

And as he followed General Roshmanov out under the hot afternoon sun toward the waiting shuttle, he wished darkly that he, the Empyrean, and the universe had never heard of angels.

"You're sure?" Telthorst demanded in that tone that always seem to imply he suspected someone of lying to him.

"Yes, sir," the sensor officer replied, his tone that of someone too far down the chain of command to take offense. "The telemetry was tight-beam, but we were close enough to intercept an edge of it. And of course, the power readings and noise leakage themselves confirm the net is down."

Telthorst swiveled his glare around to Lleshi. "Did *you* know an Empyreal ship had gone out to Angelmass?" he demanded. "Because *I* certainly was not told."

"We observed a ship being catapulted approximately forty-five minutes ago," Lleshi told him evenly. "I didn't consider it worth bringing to your attention."

Telthorst's eyes bored into Lleshi's. "Perhaps you've forgotten how things are supposed to happen aboard this ship, Commodore," he said. "As the Adjutor aboard the *Komitadji*, I'm to be informed of *everything* that could have an impact on our mission. *Everything*. You will then let *me* decide whether it's worth noting or not."

Lleshi inclined his head slightly in acknowledgment, trying to read past the fury in Telthorst's face. Why in space was the Adjutor reacting so violently to what was in reality a very minor situation? Yes, the nets had been shut down; but with the intercepted signal in hand, Crypto Group could surely turn either net back on anytime they wanted.

Unless Telthorst knew something Lleshi didn't. Something about Angelmass? Or about the ship that had headed that way forty-five minutes ago? He had access to private comm channels; could he have made some private deal with the Empyreals?

Or was this display of official outrage merely the first public salvo in his bid for command of the *Komitadji*?

"See that you remember," Telthorst said stiffly. "Now. You will tell me what exactly is going on."

Lleshi frowned. "What do you mean?"

"Don't play coy with me," Telthorst warned. "A mysterious ship you didn't think worth mentioning; and now access to Angelmass has suddenly been shut off?"

Lleshi's eyes flicked to Campbell, caught the other's equally puzzled look. "I'm sorry, Adjutor, but I have no idea what you're talking about."

For a long minute Telthorst just stared at him. Then, his lips twitched in an ironic smile. "Very well, Commodore," he said. "You want to play it close? Fine. Perhaps our guests will be more willing to talk when they arrive."

He stood up. "I'll be waiting in the conference room. You will inform me when the High Senator's shuttle has docked."

"You'll be the first to know," Lleshi assured him.

Telthorst nodded curtly and, without another word, stalked to the lift platform and left the balcony.

Lleshi looked across at Campbell. "What do you suppose *that* was all about?"

Campbell shook his head. "The man's crazy as a crane," he declared. "What does he think, that you've made some private deal with the Empyreals?"

"Certainly sounds like it," Lleshi agreed. "Should add a certain extra degree of spice to the negotiations, wouldn't you say?"

"We'll find out soon enough." Campbell nodded toward the display. "The High Senator's shuttle is on its way."

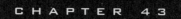

CHAPTER 43

The motorized wheels of Central's transport carts were useless in the low gravity areas of the centerline corridor. Fortunately, the designers had realized they would be, and had built in a system of running cables set into deep grooves that the carts could hook onto for motive power.

Unfortunately, the cables were set at a single, rather lumbering speed. Moving alongside the cart, shepherding the squat fuel canisters balanced precariously on top of it, Kosta listened to the gamma sparks and wondered bleakly if they were going to have enough time for this.

Or, if they did, if the plan would even work.

He reached the midway tunnel just as Chandris was coming in from the other side with a cart even more overloaded than his was. "There's about one and a half more cartloads left in this side," she reported, letting the transport coast to a halt beside the stack of fuel canisters the two had already moved in. "How many more do you want?"

"All of them," Kosta told her. "But I can go do that. You'd better start programming the escape pods."

"Okay." She glanced around at the collection of canisters. "I don't know, Kosta. If this doesn't work, we're going to be in big trouble."

"Like we aren't already?" Kosta countered, rolling the top canister off his stack and easing it carefully in the minimal gravity to a resting spot on the tunnel floor.

"Point," Chandris conceded, crouching down beside the nearest escape pod hatchway and punching the release. "What do you want me to set them for?"

"Better make it thirty minutes from now," Kosta told her. "We want to make sure we've got enough time to get everything else ready."

"Right, but we don't want to crunch things the other direction, either," Chandris reminded him as the hatch popped up. "We've only got forty-five minutes until Angelmass gets close enough to cook us, and that only if it doesn't speed up any more. Forty-five minutes minus your thirty gives us only a fifteen-minute margin for error. That's not very much."

"We'll make it," Kosta assured her, pulling off the next canister. "Don't forget, we'll be all the way at the other end of the station when they go off. The extra shielding should be enough."

"If you say so," she said, sitting down on the edge of the opening and finding the ladder with her feet. "Just remember you promised to have enough time to apologize if this doesn't work. I'm going to hold you to that."

None of the summaries of Pax governmental procedure had mentioned the full honor guard and fanfare that was waiting as Forsythe stepped through the shuttle door onto the cold gray docking bay deck. Slowly, automatically matching his pace to the beat of the extended trumpet flourish, he walked between the two lines of men, his eyes flicking from their black-and-red dress uniforms to their expressionless faces to the deadly-looking flash rifles held rigidly in front of them. It was a wonderfully balanced display of ritual pomp, official recognition, and implied threat, and he wondered if this was standard military procedure or something laid on specifically for his benefit.

Ronyon, walking at his side, clearly had no such thoughts or reservations. His eyes were shining as he looked around, his face lit up with a wide childlike grin as he gazed delightedly at the spectacle. Even with all the ceremonies Ronyon had attended through the years, he never seemed to tire of them.

There were several men and women waiting at the far end of the honor guard lines, with two of their number standing a pace in front of the others. A study in contrasts, Forsythe thought as he approached them, and not just because of their age or their garb. The elder of the two stood straight and tall in his dress uniform, his eyes brightly aware, his face calmly expressionless as he studied the approaching Empyreals. The other man, shorter and dressed in a drab gray suit, was also studying Forsythe; but his eyes and face were hostile and restive and vaguely frustrated. If the soldier standing beside him was a lion watching his approaching prey, the image flashed through Forsythe's mind, this man was a vulture waiting impatiently for something to die.

The musicians were good, timing their flourish to a dramatic finale just as Forsythe came to a halt three paces from the soldier and the vulture. "I'm High Senator Arkin Forsythe of Lorelei," he identified himself, his voice sounding oddly weak after the echoing brass. A nice little added bonus, he thought distantly, to the rest of the ceremony's psychological manipulation. "Currently representing the Seraph government. Do I have the honor of addressing Commodore Vars Lleshi?"

"I am Commodore Lleshi," the older man acknowledged, his voice as measured and intelligent as his eyes and face. He was older than he had seemed from a distance, Forsythe saw now, but he carried the years well. "Welcome aboard the *Komitadji*, High Senator. May I present my senior staff—" he gestured to the line of men and women behind him— "and our ship's Adjutor, Mr. Samunel Telthorst."

"Mr. Telthorst," Forsythe said, looking at the other with new interest. So this was one of the shadow-power group that allegedly kept Pax politics focused on the bottom line. "Officers," he added, letting his eyes sweep the group behind Lleshi. "This is my aide, Ronyon."

Ronyon touched his sleeve to get his attention. *Can you tell them I really liked the men with the guns and the fancy clothes?* he signed, his eyes still glowing with pleasure. *They were really neat!*

"What's he doing?" Telthorst demanded. He had, Forsythe noted, taken a hasty step back when Ronyon's big hands began their intricate dance. "Tell him to stop."

"He's just talking to me," Forsythe said. "Ronyon is deaf and mute. He communicates through sign language."

"What did he say just now?" Lleshi asked.

"He said to thank you for the honor guard," Forsythe said. "He very much enjoyed it."

"I thought you said he was deaf," Telthorst said, his voice dark and accusing. "How could he hear the fanfare?"

"He couldn't," Forsythe told him. "But he can see. He happens to like fancy uniforms and ceremonial guns."

"Really," Telthorst said, looking Ronyon up and down suspiciously. "So you're saying he's retarded, too?"

There was insult in the words, and for a moment Forsythe teetered on the brink of verbally blistering the man for it. But there was too much at stake here to allow personal feelings to intrude. "His mental development has been arrested, yes," he said instead, forcing his voice to stay calm. "But he's a good and conscientious worker, and an asset to my staff." He paused. "And, I might add, more pleasant company than many of those I meet in my daily activities."

Telthorst drew himself up—"We have a conference room set up over here," Lleshi said before the other could speak, gesturing to the side. Telthorst shot him an annoyed look, which the commodore ignored. "If you'll follow me, we'll begin the discussions."

The "conference room" was little more than a pilots' briefing room, plainly decorated and relatively small. The table was big enough to handle the group, though, and the chairs were reasonably comfortable. Lleshi took the chair at the end closest to the door, gesturing to Forsythe to take the far end. Telthorst rather pointedly sat down at Lleshi's right. Ronyon sat down at Forsythe's left, still gazing admiringly at the two guards who had stepped inside the room and now stood at attention flanking the door.

"Before we begin the negotiations," Forsythe said when everyone was settled, "I'd like to ask what exactly you've done to Lorelei and the Lorelei system."

"These are not 'negotiations,' High Senator—" Telthorst began.

"We destroyed the four nets in the asteroid belt," Lleshi told him. "Along, I'm afraid, with those defending them and manning the associated catapults. We also neutralized the small kick-pod catapult in Lorelei orbit and commandeered the liner *Harmonic*. Oh, and we were forced to neutralize several armed mining ships that launched suicide attacks on us during our trip inward. Aside from that, to my knowledge, we have harmed no one and caused no damage."

Forsythe felt his throat tighten. Mining ships. The ones he personally had ordered to be armed. "To your knowledge?"

"My task force commanders had orders to hold, not destroy," Lleshi said. "Up to the point where the *Komitadji* arrived at Seraph they had complied with those orders. Unfortunately, I have no way of knowing what has happened since then."

"I see," Forsythe murmured. It wasn't a very satisfying answer, but it was clear it was the best he was going to get for now.

Ronyon touched his sleeve. *Has something happened at home?* he signed, his forehead furrowed with concern.

"What did he say?" Telthorst demanded.

"He asked if something had happened at home," Forsythe translated, feeling a sudden flicker of guilt. In all the activity over the past few days, it hadn't even occurred to him that Ronyon had been left completely out of the information loop regarding the Pax invasion of Lorelei. "These gentlemen have sent warships to Lorelei, Ronyon. They've taken control of the system, but I don't think they've hurt too many people."

Ronyon looked over at Lleshi, a look of stunned betrayal on his face. *Why did you do that?* he signed. *We weren't bothering anybody.*

"Tell him to stop that," Telthorst snapped. "This is a surrender conference, not a children's tea party."

"That's enough, Mr. Telthorst," Lleshi said. "High Senator, will you translate?"

"He wanted to know why you invaded Lorelei," Forsythe said. "He asked if we were doing anything to bother you. Or anyone else."

"I see." Lleshi shifted his gaze to Ronyon. "I'm sorry, Ronyon, for whatever we're doing to your worlds. But we're soldiers, and our duty is to obey the orders we're given. I give you my promise that we will not hurt any more people than absolutely necessary."

"All of which depends on how much the High Senator is willing to cooperate," Telthorst added. "Which brings *me* to a question, High Senator. What exactly is that ship doing out at Angelmass?"

"They're doing a quick emergency study of the black hole," Forsythe said.

"What kind of emergency study?"

"Angelmass has been exhibiting strange behavior over the past few weeks," Forsythe said. "It started with radiation bursts, and has progressed to where it's actually changing its orbit."

"How?"

"I don't know," Forsythe said. "But I'm sure that if you ask nicely, Mr. Kosta will be happy to give you the complete story when he gets back."

Lleshi's reaction to Kosta's name was little more than a lifted eyebrow. Telthorst's was much more dramatic. "Kosta?" he repeated. "*Kosta?*"

"Yes," Forsythe said. "I see you know the young man."

Telthorst flashed a dumbfounded look at Lleshi, looked back at Forsythe. "Kosta," he muttered.

There was a tentative plucking at Forsythe's sleeve. *Mr. Forsythe?* he signed, an oddly intense expression on his face. *Jereko and Chandris didn't go to study Angelmass. They went to throw it away.*

Forsythe frowned. "What?"

"What?" Telthorst asked.

"Just a minute," Forsythe said, leaning toward Ronyon. "What do you mean, throw it away?"

"Throw what away?" Telthorst demanded. "What are you talking about?"

"Just a *minute*," Forsythe snapped back. "Ronyon, tell me again. What are Jereko and Chandris doing?"

Ronyon threw a furtive look at the other end of the table. *Jereko said Angelmass is going to try to hurt people,* he signed. *He said the only thing they could do was use the catapult to throw it out of the system.*

"That's crazy," Forsythe said. "He can't be serious."

"Bad news, High Senator?" Lleshi asked calmly.

Forsythe looked over at him, wondering what he should say. The truth? Or something that sounded at least plausible? "He says Kosta believes Angelmass is too dangerous to stay here," he said. "He says they're going to try to use Central's catapult to throw it somewhere out of the system."

Telthorst inhaled sharply. "Is that even possible?" Lleshi asked. "I was given to understand that the Seraph and Angelmass nets and catapults were linked together."

"They are," Forsythe murmured, the shutdown of the Seraph net suddenly making sense. "But if he shut down the net at this end . . . I don't know. He might be able to do it."

"And he *has* shut it down, hasn't he?" Lleshi asked. "He's shut down both nets, in fact."

Forsythe nodded. There was no point in lying; a well-equipped warship like the *Komitadji* would certainly have picked that up. "We were guessing he didn't want company."

"This is a trick," Telthorst put in, his fingertips rubbing restlessly against the table top. "He's making all this up."

Lleshi pursed his lips. "Mr. Campbell?" he called.

"Crypto Group confirms, Commodore," a disembodied voice replied briskly from one of the upper corners of the room. "He's using a dialect of the old Unislan sign language, and we've got enough for a baseline. Actual message: 'Jereko says Angelmass will hurt everyone. He says they must throw it away out of the area using the catapult.'"

"Thank you," Lleshi said.

"Nonsense," Telthorst insisted, jabbing a finger toward Ronyon. "An idiot like that? No one would trust him with that kind of information. I tell you it's a trick."

"Why are you getting so upset, Mr. Telthorst?" Forsythe asked, frowning at him. "I thought the whole reason for the Pax coming down on us in the first place was to protect us from the angels. You should be happy someone wants to get rid of the source."

For a long moment Telthorst just stared at him, his agitation and uncertainty coalescing into something hard and certain and vicious. "So that's how it is," he ground out. "You turned him. Kosta figured it out, and you turned him, and he told you."

"Told us what?" Forsythe asked carefully.

Telthorst turned to Lleshi. "Get the Angelmass net reactivated," he ordered. "Right now. We have to go out there and stop him."

Lleshi blinked. "What in the world are you talking about?"

"You fool," Telthorst bit out contemptuously. "Don't you understand? Angelmass is the reason we're here. It's the only reason we're here."

Lleshi threw an odd look at Forsythe. "But if the angel threat is removed—"

"To bloody hell with the angels!" Telthorst snarled. "What do the angels matter? What does *anything* from this flea-speck group of third-rate planets matter?"

He shot a look around the table. "It's Angelmass that we want," he said, his voice low and brittle. "It blazes out more energy in a second than this entire miserable world probably uses in a year. Terawatts and terawatts of power, just waiting for someone to tap into it."

"And *that's* what this is all about?" Forsythe asked, staring at him in disbelief. "Energy?"

"Why not?" Telthorst countered. "Energy is the road to wealth and power. It always has been. And free energy, like this, is nothing less than a gift from the laughing fates. Angelmass could run an entire floating colony, or give us a cheap way to terraform worlds—"

"Or power a shipyard?" Lleshi asked.

"Indeed it could," Telthorst said, his eyes suddenly shining. "You've seen what the *Komitadji* has accomplished already, in a bare handful of years. How much more could you accomplish with a dozen more ships just like it? Tell me that."

"The question isn't what *I* could do," Lleshi said quietly, his tone that of a man who has suddenly found the solution to a private puzzle. "The question is what the Adjutors could do."

Telthorst's lips compressed into a thin line. "Order the Angelmass net reactivated, Commodore."

"And if I refuse?"

Telthorst drew himself up. "Then I will be forced to take direct command of this vessel," he said, his voice suddenly stiff and formal as he pulled a folded sheet of paper from inside his jacket. "I have authorization from the Adjutor General himself."

Lleshi looked down at the paper, but made no move to touch it. "Mr. Campbell?"

"Sir?" the voice came again, sounding considerably more subdued than it had been the last time.

"Do we know how to reactivate the Angelmass net?"

"I believe so, sir, yes," Campbell said. "We have the telemetry readings from when it was turned off earlier, plus the signal it sent to deactivate its Seraph counterpart. Comm and Crypto say they can invert the instructions to turn either or both back on."

"Then do so," Lleshi ordered. "Both of them. If the Seraph net goes on, we can assume the Angelmass one will, too."

He looked across the table; and suddenly, it seemed to Forsythe, he wasn't carrying his years nearly so well anymore. "Unless there are special codes that would be needed, High Senator?"

Forsythe shook his head. "No codes, Commodore," he said. "No one expected any of this to be of military significance."

Lleshi nodded. "Mr. Campbell?"

"Signal sent," Campbell reported. "Seraph net . . . is up and running. We're painting a diagnostic, but it seems to be functioning properly. Time to Angelmass net activation, approximately twenty-one minutes."

"We'll want to be ready to jump the minute it's up," Telthorst warned. "We don't want Kosta shutting it down again before we can get through."

"Commodore?" Campbell asked.

"You have your instructions, Mr. Campbell," Lleshi confirmed quietly. "Prepare the *Komitadji* for catapult. You'll need to recalibrate their equipment for our mass."

"Already on it, sir."

"And make sure all weapons are standing ready," Telthorst added. "Energy weapons and missiles both."

He looked at Forsythe. "Because I doubt we'll be able to talk the traitor out of this scheme," he added softly. "In fact, I doubt it's even worth trying."

Blindly, his wide eyes fixed on Telthorst, Ronyon clutched at Forsythe's sleeve. *What's he talking about,* he signed urgently. *What does he mean?*

"He's talking about shooting at Jereko and Chandris, Ronyon," Forsythe told him. "He's talking about killing them without even offering them a chance to surrender."

Ronyon's mouth fell open, and an odd choking sound escaped from this throat. "Treason to the Pax has always carried the death penalty, High Senator," Telthorst said coolly. "Something you should keep very much in mind."

He again looked around the table. "And as long as we have a few minutes, let's discuss the disposition of the rest of Seraph system."

CHAPTER 44

The clock was down to fifteen and a half minutes, and the gamma-spark static was becoming deafening by the time everything was finally ready.

"This had better work, Kosta," Chandris shouted as she strapped into her seat, wincing as a particularly loud *crack* sounded from somewhere in the console in front of her. "If it doesn't, I don't think we're going to have time to get to the *Gazelle* and get out of here. You sure as hell won't have time to apologize."

"It'll work," Kosta shouted back from beside her. Chandris couldn't read his voice over the noise, but the hands clenched into taut fists in front of him didn't exactly inspire her with confidence.

"Well, if it doesn't, it was nice knowing you," she called, reaching over and putting her hand on his closest fist. "I mean that."

For a moment he seemed to hesitate, the hardness of his fist under her hand wavering. Then, abruptly, he unclenched his hand and wrapped it around hers, gripping it tightly as they watched the clock count down to zero.

And as it did so, an entire panel of monitor lights went solid red.

Chandris held her breath, straining to hear what was happening back there. But between the noise of the gamma sparks and the sheer distance from where they were at the far end of the catapult section she couldn't make anything out. She thought back over the steps of her reprogramming job, wondering if she could have frogged it up somewhere. If she'd missed a safety and the escape pods shut down . . .

"There!" Kosta shouted, squeezing her hand even tighter. "Feel that?"

Chandris frowned. And then she did: a gentle vibration running through the deck beneath her chair. A vibration that was slowly but steadily growing in strength.

She shifted her attention to the midhull visual monitor. Beneath the blizzard of radiation static, she could just make out the double ring of escape pods still attached to the midway tunnel. At the base of one of them, where the pod attached to the hull, she thought she could see a faint flickering of fire from a slightly imperfect seating connection as its drive tried to push it away from the station.

Its drive trying to push it outward, but its attaching clamps continuing to hold it firmly in place. If the pod was a sentient being, the odd thought occurred to her, it would probably be getting extremely frustrated about now. "What happens if the clamps break before the pods burn all the way through the wall?" she asked.

"It should still work," Kosta called. "That much heat alone—"

And then, without warning, the image vanished in a flash of white light. Simultaneously, the deck under Chandris bucked like a scalded cat, there was a bubbling roar from behind her, and she found herself being shoved gently but firmly back into her seat.

"It worked!" Kosta shouted. "Look at that! It worked!"

Chandris squinted at the snow on the monitor. But she didn't have to see anything to know that Kosta's crazy plan had indeed worked. The escape pods, all firing together against the relatively thin hull where they were connected, had burned through or heated through and ignited the fuel canisters she and Kosta had stacked in the midway tunnel. The resulting explosion had broken the station in two, giving their catapult end a solid push forward in their orbit as it simultaneously shoved the net end hard in the other direction.

The essence of a rocket, she remembered from her first page of reading aboard the *Xirrus,* was to take part of your ship and throw it in the opposite direction from where you wanted to go. Kosta had merely taken the definition to its logical extreme.

Only instead of throwing away the exhaust products of burned fuel, he had thrown away half their ship.

"Look's like we've picked up a slow yaw roll," Kosta reported, peering at another of the snow-covered displays. "Nothing serious, I don't think."

"I think the camera just went out," Chandris added as the faint image on the display was replaced by pure static. The acceleration pressure on her had eased back now, but the inertial readings indicated that they had picked up a nice bit of extra speed. "Either that or the radiation got to it."

"Probably the explosion," Kosta said. "Looks like it took out that whole emplacement."

Chandris swallowed. The camera position in question was a good ways forward of the midway tunnel. "Just how much of the station are you expecting us to lose here?"

"Not enough to worry about," Kosta assured her, swiveling his chair around to another station. "All that's back there is long-term supplies and crew living quarters. We can afford to lose those."

"I was thinking more about general station integrity," Chandris said. "There are only so many blast doors and supporting bulkheads in a place like this, you know."

"We'll be fine," Kosta insisted. "Hear that?"

"Hear what?"

"The gamma sparking," he said. "It's quieter."

Chandris paused, listening. He was right: the noise intensity had definitely gone down. "So we're definitely pulling away?"

"Looks like it," Kosta said, leaning close to one of the displays. "Not all that fast, really, but the difference in speed vectors is definitely on our side now. And of course, the upward bump in speed means we're also moving into a slightly higher solar orbit."

"That's going to make it a bit tricky to 'pult Angelmass out of here, isn't it?" Chandris pointed out. "If it's in a lower orbit than we are?"

"I think we can count on it to figure things out and change course after us," Kosta said grimly. "The point is that we've now bought ourselves some extra breathing space to get the reprogramming done. So that, hopefully, when it *does* come after us we'll be ready."

"Right," Chandris said, swiveling around toward a data display. "Let's hold onto that thought, shall we?"

Because there was still one tiny little problem that Kosta didn't seem to have thought about yet. Still, with any luck, she would have that one covered by the time it occurred to him.

Pulling up another of the station's operations manuals, she got to work.

"Ten minutes to catapult, Commodore," Campbell's voice came over the speaker. "We're ready to move into position."

"Very good," Telthorst called before Lleshi could answer, pushing back his chair and standing up. "Commodore Lleshi, perhaps you'd like to invite our guests to join us on the command deck."

Lleshi looked down the table at Forsythe. "Unauthorized civilians—"

"Yes, yes, I know the drill," Telthorst cut him off impatiently. "But High Senator Forsythe is hardly in the same class as someone's girlfriend who wants to be shown around the ship, now, is he?"

He gave Forsythe a hard look. "Besides, a tour might help convince him that these scare tactics of his are both pointless and ridiculous."

"They're not scare tactics," Forsythe insisted. "I've offered to turn over all the data we have on Angelmass—"

"I never liked ghost stories as a child, High Senator," Telthorst cut him off contemptuously. "I like them even less now that I'm an adult. We're going to Angelmass; and *you're* going with us to watch how we deal with traitors to the Pax. You might find it instructive."

He gestured to the guards at the doorway. "Escort High Senator Forsythe and his aide to the command deck. On your feet, High Senator."

"A favor if I may, Commodore," Forsythe said, his eyes on Lleshi as he slowly stood up. "My aide Ronyon had a bad panic reaction to Angelmass the last time we were in the area. Somehow, I think, he was able to sense what was out there. There's no reason to put him through that again. I'd like to request that he and my pilot be allowed to leave."

"Absolutely not," Telthorst said firmly as the two guards moved into escort position behind Forsythe. "No one leaves this ship until we have your signature on the surrender papers."

Forsythe's eyes hadn't left Lleshi's face. "Commodore?"

Deliberately, Lleshi stood up, looking at each of the two guards in turn. In his own mind, Telthorst clearly already considered himself the commander of the *Komitadji*.

It was high time he was disabused of that notion.

"Escort High Senator Forsythe and his aide to his shuttle," he ordered the guards. "They'll be leaving the *Komitadji* before we catapult."

Telthorst spun to face him, his mouth dropping open. "What in—?"

"I trust you'll make yourself available to continue this conversation when we return, High Senator?" Lleshi added.

Forsythe lowered his head briefly in a slight bow. "Of course, Commodore. Thank you."

Lleshi nodded back. "Lieutenant, you have your orders."

"Yes, sir," the senior of the two guards said, snapping a salute. "This way, High Senator."

The group circled the table and walked out the door, Forsythe looking grave, Ronyon merely looking troubled and a little confused. "That was foolish, Commodore," Telthorst said as the door slid shut on them, his voice rigid as an icicle. "Criminally foolish. You do not let a senior enemy official simply walk away when you have him in your hands."

Lleshi looked up at the hidden speaker. "Time check, Mr. Campbell?"

"Seven minutes to catapult, sir," Campbell's voice came.

"I presume you've run an analysis on Angelmass's orbit?"

"Yes, sir, but it's inconclusive," the other said. "We don't have enough of a data baseline to either confirm or refute Forsythe's claim that it's changing speed and orbit. If it is, though, it certainly can't be doing it very fast."

"So it should be safe for us out there?"

"Yes, sir," Campbell assured him. "We'll be well within radiation distance tolerances."

"Good," Lleshi said. "Then move the *Komitadji* into catapult position. I'll be right there."

He turned to Telthorst. "And as for holding onto enemy officials, Mr. Telthorst," he added quietly, "this ship is manned by soldiers, not terrorists. We do not take hostages."

"You'll live to regret this, Commodore," Telthorst hissed.

"Yes," Lleshi murmured, turning his back on the little man and striding toward the door. "I'm sure I will."

"Ha!" Chandris called, slapping her hand on the edge of the control panel in triumph. "Okay. I got it."

"Got what?" Kosta called from beside her.

"How we're going to 'pult Angelmass without getting fried in the process," she said, her throat aching with all the shouting she'd been doing. The gamma sparks had subsided now from painful to merely annoying, but she still had to speak loudly to be heard over them. "There's a remote-control setting here we can use to trigger the catapult. That way we can be out in the *Gazelle*, as far away as we have to be—"

"Don't bother."

"What?" She turned to look at him.

Kosta was slumped back in his chair, staring with dead eyes at the monitors and displays in front of him. "What's the matter?" she demanded, her heart suddenly thudding in her ears.

"We can't do it," he said. "We don't have enough power."

She followed his gaze to the displays. None of the numbers and graphs meant anything to her. "What do you mean, not enough power?"

"The station can't generate enough energy to 'pult Angelmass outward," he said. "The thing's just too massive."

She looked at the numbers again. No. Not after all this. This cord couldn't pop now. "What about inward, then?" she asked. "Could we send it inward?"

"Inward?" Kosta echoed, frowning at her. "You mean toward Seraph?"

"No, further in than Seraph," Chandris said, thinking furiously. "Whatever games Angelmass is playing with grav fields, it's got to be easier for it to move down a gravity well than back up one. If we put it into a low enough solar orbit, we at least ought to be able to keep it away from Seraph. Right?"

"But that'll just give it a stronger grav field to play with," Kosta argued. "It might still be able to work its way up that far. Or worse, it might just go straight into the sun where we'll never be able to get to it."

"I hadn't thought of that," Chandris confessed, wincing at the thought. "Could it eat up the whole sun?"

"I don't know," Kosta said. "Probably not—its cross-section is only a few atoms' width. But it could still do some nasty things in there, either accidentally or on purpose. We can't risk it without running some numbers first."

"So that's it? We just give up and go home?"

Kosta shook his head tiredly. "I'm sorry. I don't see what else we can do."

Chandris shifted her gaze to the forward display. The slow yaw rotation they'd picked up in the station's disintegration had turned them to face Angelmass now, though most of the black hole's blaze of light and energy was currently being blocked by what was left of the net section drifting toward it. After all this time and effort and sweat and risk; and now there was nothing they could do but run home?

"If we leave now, we won't get another crack at it," she warned him. "At least, not easily. Without a net out here, we're talking a mighty long trip to even get close. In fact, they'll probably have to build a whole new Angelmass Central and ship it out—"

She broke off. "Oh, my God," she breathed.

"What?" Kosta demanded, sitting up straight.

Chandris shifted her view to the telescope display, hoping her eyes had been playing tricks on her. But there was no mistake. "The net section," she said, hearing her voice suddenly trembling as she pointed to the display. "The running lights just came on.

"Someone's reactivated it."

For a second they both sat there, frozen. Then, simultaneously, both of them dived for their control panels. "We've got to stop them," Chandris said, trying to pull up the remote control program she'd just found. Her fingers slipped on the keys, stumbling in their frantic haste. "Oh, *God,* Jereko!"

"I know," he barked back, his fingers beating their own staccato across his board. "I'm trying to shut it down."

"What are they doing?" Chandris asked. There was the file; now access the system. "Don't they know what they're doing?"

"That's just it—they don't," Kosta bit out. "It's only been nineteen minutes since we blew the station. Twenty light-minutes out—they don't realize the net's headed straight for Angelmass."

Chandris bit at her lip, forcing her fingers to function. The display flickered with gamma sparks and threatened to crash; then it cleared, and she found herself in the system. She pulled up a list of commands, searching for those pertaining to net operations. It had to be somewhere in here . . .

Kosta folded his hand over hers. "Too late," he said quietly.

Chandris looked up . . . and felt her mouth fall open.

She'd expected it would be Forsythe coming after them, probably in one of the hunterships sitting idly in their maintenance yards. Or at the very most, one of the EmDef ships they'd seen crowding around Seraph.

But the ship that had suddenly appeared was something unbelievably and terrifyingly huge. Bigger even than the vast spaceliner *Xirrus,* its bulk filling the entire telescope display, utterly dwarfing the partially shattered half of the station lying beside it.

And as she watched in horror, Angelmass caught up with it.

The emergency hull-breach alarms split the air like enraged banshees screaming of death, their wailing only barely louder than the horrible hail-storm crackle that seemed to come from all around them. "Hull breach in Sectors G-7, 8, and 9," a voice bellowed from the speaker. "All three hulls have collapsed—"

Abruptly, the voice cut off, leaving only the violent chattering. "Seal all airtight doors!" Lleshi ordered, his eyes darting to G-Sector's monitor cameras. What in the name of the laughing fates was happening to them? The Empyreals couldn't have a weapon of such power. They simply *couldn't.*

But all the sensor nodes had gone black. *All* of them, over the entire starboard-aft quarter of the ship.

From the speaker came a sudden scream, just as suddenly cut off. "Engine control has lost air," Campbell snapped. "Main drive chambers all open to space."

"Do something!" Telthorst snarled. "Fight *back,* damn you!"

"Against what?" Lleshi snarled back.

A sudden and horribly familiar blare erupted across the command deck. "Radiation!" Campbell announced. "Lethal doses from starboard-aft quarter."

And then, suddenly, Lleshi understood.

It must have entered the ship near the stern, its blaze of heat and radiation charring everything in sight. As it did so, the gigantic ship seemed to twist aside, and Chandris's first impression was that it was making a desperate attempt to escape. But even as that thought occurred to her she realized that it wasn't so; that if anyone was still alive in there they were in no shape to bring the vessel under power. What was happening instead was that the once-smooth lines of the ship were bending and distorting as Angelmass traced out a leisurely path of destruction through bracing girders and supporting bulkheads, twisting and tearing them out of line and crumpling them like thin foil.

"Massive destruction in all aft areas," Campbell shouted. "Communications gone; power gone; sensors gone; air integrity gone. All personnel in aft areas presumed dead."

He was no longer barking the news quickly, Lleshi noticed with a sort of detached interest. There was no longer any point. Timely information implied that there was something that could still be done about a given situation.

But there was nothing any of them could do about this one. The *Komitadji* was sliding rapidly toward her death, and there was no power in the universe that could stop it. "Structural integrity is failing throughout the ship," Campbell went on. "Central-area bulkheads are bleeding air. Heat and radiation off the scale; firewalls collapsing from metal degradation."

"This can't be happening," Telthorst insisted desperately. His eyes were darting all around him, as if he were expecting to discover this was nothing more than an elaborate practical joke being played on him by a vindictive captain and crew. "It can't. Not to the *Komitadji.*"

He spun back to Lleshi, slamming a fist down on the arm of his seat. "This ship is *indestructible,* damn you," he snarled. "We built it that way. We spent *billions*—"

He cut off as the deck suddenly shook beneath them, a violent creaking sound screaming across the command deck as it did. "Forward structural integrity is failing," Campbell said. "It won't be long now."

"There's your prize, Adjutor," Lleshi told Telthorst bitterly. "There's your precious Angelmass. It's not waiting for you and the other Adjutors to go and milk it. It's coming to us.

"It's coming for you."

Another screech ripped through the room.

And on Telthorst's face was a look of absolute horror.

Beside Chandris, Kosta was muttering something wordless over and over again. A few seconds later, and the ship nearly vanished in the glare behind the sudden flash of brilliance as Angelmass burned its way out the near side. The station's sunshields activated; and on the telescope display, right at the edge of the artificial black spot marking Angelmass's position, Chandris could see the charred hull metal flowing like ash-filled water as Angelmass's tidal forces ripped apart its molecular structure. Again the big ship moved ponderously around in the grip of the black hole's gravitational field, the bow turning with a sense of fatalism back into its executioner's path. Again the metal of the hull broke and flowed, further forward this time, and again Angelmass casually burned its way through and disappeared inside.

Lleshi could feel the chair starting to melt beneath him as he looked across the bridge balcony one last time. Telthorst was sitting there, his face contorted almost beyond recognition. "You were wrong about one other thing, Mr. Telthorst," he managed over the screams of the *Komitadji*'s final death throes. "I won't live to regret it, after all."

It seemed to go on forever, a nightmare of death and awesome destruction. Angelmass went in and out at least three more times, like a needle tracing an intricate path for its following thread.

And when it finally emerged for the last time, the ship had been crushed and twisted and warped nearly beyond recognition.

Kosta's hand on her arm made her jump. "Come on, Chandris," he said quietly, his eyes still staring in dull horror at the view. "Come on. Let's go home."

CHAPTER 45

"The purpose of this meeting," High Senator Forsythe said, gazing steadily across the Government Building conference room table at Kosta, "is to figure out exactly what we're going to do with you."

His gaze shifted to Kosta's right, where Chandris sat beside him, then to his left, to Hanan and Ornina Daviee. "With all of you," he amended.

"I'm sorry, but I really don't see the problem," Ornina spoke up, a bit hesitantly. "Jereko has already said he wants to stay in the Empyrean. Why can't we just let him?"

Beside Forsythe, Pirbazari stirred. "It's not quite that simple, Miss Daviee," he said. "Mr. Kosta is a self-confessed Pax spy, and the three of you knew it. That can't just be swept into a corner."

"Why not?" Hanan asked. "I mean, he *did* help us figure out what was happening to Angelmass. Surely that alone saved a lot of lives. Not to mention that he and Chandris got that big Pax warship off our backs."

"Wrecking Angelmass Central in the process," Pirbazari murmured.

"It would have been destroyed anyway," Chandris pointed out. "You didn't see what Angelmass was doing out there.

"Actually, we *have* done a quick review of the monitor tapes you brought back," Forsythe said. "I think it's fair to say the station would indeed have been lost."

"So again, what's the problem?" Hanan asked. "Jereko's proved he's on our side."

"Are we not getting through here?" Pirbazari demanded. "The problem is that he's an agent of a government we're at war with."

"*Was* an agent," Hanan corrected.

"Legally irrelevant," Pirbazari shot back. "And unproven besides."

"Unproven?" Hanan echoed. "Then what—"

"Hanan," Ornina admonished him, putting a warning hand on his arm.

Hanan patted her hand reassuringly. "All right, then," he said in a more reasonable tone. "Why not let him defect? There must be provision for something like that in the legal code."

Forsythe made a face. "Actually . . . there isn't."

Kosta stared at him. "You're kidding."

"I've been through the whole code, edge to binding and back again," Forsythe said, shaking his head. "The people who wrote the Covenants a hundred eighty years ago never expected us to be anything more than a single confederation of a few worlds all alone in the middle of deep space. With nowhere to defect to or from, the topic somehow never came up."

"Well, obviously, that needs to be changed," Hanan said. "How do we do that?"

"*We* don't do anything," Forsythe said pointedly. "What *I* do is introduce a bill in the High Senate. Unfortunately, the process takes time; and meanwhile, Mr. Kosta is still an agent of the Pax."

"And the Covenants *do* make provision for enemies of the Empyrean," Pirbazari said.

At one side of the table, seated where he could see everyone's mouth, Ronyon began signing. "I would love to," Forsythe told him. "But that decision isn't up to me. Or anyone else in the Empyrean."

"What did he say?" Kosta asked.

"He asked why we couldn't just stop the war," Forsythe translated. "In that case, you wouldn't be an enemy and you could stay here."

"Makes sense to me," Ornina murmured.

"Wait a minute," Kosta said, frowning. "Is it really that simple? If we weren't at war with the Pax would that solve the problem?"

Forsythe gazed across the table at him, forehead wrinkled with thought. "Not entirely," he said at last. "But it would certainly be a start. The automatic categorization of you as an enemy of the Empyrean would become moot, and we could shift the focus purely to your various activities here."

"Why?" Pirbazari put in, his tone edged with sarcasm. "You know a way to make the Pax go away and leave us alone?"

"As a matter of fact," Kosta said slowly, "I do."

Forsythe and Pirbazari exchanged looks. "We're listening," Forsythe invited cautiously. "What do we have to do?"

"And how much is it going to cost us?" Pirbazari added.

"It won't cost you anything at all," Kosta said. "Do you have the coordinates for the Scintara system? It's in the Garland Group of worlds."

"I'm sure we can find it," Forsythe said. "Why?"

"That's where the operations for this mission are centered," Kosta explained. "Most of the top Pax commanders are there monitoring the invasion, plus probably a scattering of government officials waiting to take credit for your surrender."

"So what do we do, send them an ambassador?" Pirbazari scoffed.

"No," Kosta said quietly. "We send them the *Komitadji*."

Out of the corner of his eye he saw Chandris twitch her head around to look at him. "What?" she demanded.

"It was the glory of the Pax Fleet," Kosta said, a hard lump in his throat as his mind flashed back to his single brief trip aboard the massive warship. To the awe and excitement he had felt at being aboard a legend . . . "The ship that couldn't be defeated. To see it not just defeated, but completely wrecked, is going to shake them straight to their boots."

"But they'll know it wasn't actually defeated," Pirbazari objected. "Surely they'll be able to figure out it was destroyed by Angelmass."

"Doesn't matter," Kosta said. "Whether we've figured out how to use Angelmass as a weapon or whether we conned them into running into it themselves, the point is still that we managed to destroy it."

"No, the point is that dropping it on their doorstep is an invitation to dance," Pirbazari retorted. "They'll want to move in quick and slap us down hard before we can use Angelmass against them again."

Kosta shook his head. "You're thinking like a military man," he said. "Or like a politician, who has to worry about prestige and public opinion. But that's not who's running the Pax. The Adjutors give the orders; and all the Adjutors care about is money."

"That doesn't make sense," Pirbazari growled. "Are you saying they'll leave us alone simply because we've cost them a lot of money? That's not warfare. That's . . ." He groped for words.

"That's balance-sheet economics," Kosta agreed. "But that really is all they see. They'll leave us alone because the Empyrean has already become a negative number on the profit-loss scale. Because with the *Komitadji* destroyed, they've already spent more here than they could ever hope to gain. Why waste more time and money conquering us when they know they won't break even anyway?"

Hanan stirred in his seat. "I think our entire civilization has just been insulted," he muttered under his breath to Ornina.

"No, your entire civilization just has no idea how much the *Komitadji* cost to build," Kosta countered. "And if there's one thing the Adjutors simply do not do, it's throw good money after bad."

"Maybe not normally," Forsythe said. "But you're forgetting Angelmass itself. The Adjutor I spoke to—Telthorst—was spinning great and lofty plans for using Angelmass's energy output to build an entire fleet of ships the size of the *Komitadji*. That may be an asset they'll still consider worth fighting for."

"No," Pirbazari said thoughtfully. "Not any more. Not after they see what it did to their fancy birthday-cake warship. They won't dare risk putting a shipbuilding facility anywhere near the thing."

"He's right," Kosta said. "Even if they decide to rebuild the *Komitadji*, they won't do it here."

"What if they rebuild it in the Pax?" Ornina asked.

"They might," Kosta conceded. "After all, there are still a few other wayward colonies out there waiting to be conquered. But even if they do, you'll never see it in Empyreal space."

"You really believe this is how they'll react?" Forsythe asked, his forehead wrinkled uncertainly.

"I'm sure of it." Kosta hesitated. "But if you think it would help, I'm willing to go back with the *Komitadji* and spell it out for them."

"No," Chandris said firmly before Forsythe could respond. "You leave now and they'll never let you come back."

Kosta blinked. There had been an unexpected intensity in her tone. "That would bother you?"

For that first split second she actually looked flustered. It was, in Kosta's experience, a new look for her. "Of course it would," Hanan jumped smoothly into the gap. "It would bother all of us. You're our friend."

"He won't have to go, will he?" Ornina asked anxiously. "Please?"

"I don't think it will be necessary," Forsythe said. "The *Komitadji* should deliver the message clearly enough without Mr. Kosta's assistance."

"A recorded message from you might be useful, though," Pirbazari suggested. "Especially if they interpret it as you being turned to our side by the angels. It might discourage them from sending in more spies."

Kosta nodded. "No problem."

Hanan chuckled. "There's a potful of soul-searching for you," he commented. "Angels make people good; and now they've turned Jereko against the Pax. Wonder what the Adjutors will make of that?"

"You know what they say," Ornina reminded him. "The love of money is the root of all evil."

"That is what they say." Hanan leaned forward a little to look at Kosta. "So is that what angels do, Jereko? Take away the love of money?"

"Well . . ." Kosta paused, wondering if he should be talking about this now. But if not now, when? "Actually, I think they work one layer beneath that."

"You sound like you know something the rest of us don't," Forsythe said, eyeing him closely.

"I have a theory," Kosta said. "Not about what the angels are, exactly, but about what they do to people."

"I thought they made you be good," Chandris said, sounding puzzled.

"They don't *make* you do anything," Kosta told her. "All they do is *let* you be good. What I mean is that they help you turn your attention outward, toward other people, by suppressing the major factor that drives human selfishness and self-centered attitudes."

"What's that, the love of money?" Hanan suggested.

"Or basic corrupt human nature?" Pirbazari added cynically.

Kosta shook his head. "Fear."

There was a brief silence around the table. "Fear," Forsythe said, his voice flat.

"But there isn't anything evil about fear, Jereko," Ornina protested, sounding confused.

"I didn't say it was evil," Kosta said. "I said it tends to focus a person's attention inward and pushes away consideration of others. It tends to make you selfish; and selfishness, carried too far, is what drives most of what we consider anti-social and criminal behavior."

"Are we talking about the same thing here?" Forsythe asked, frowning. "Fear is a perfectly normal part of the survival instinct."

"Right, but I'm not talking about the kind of immediate danger that sends adrenaline pumping into your blood," Kosta said. "I don't think the angels do anything to affect that kind of physical response."

"So what *are* you talking about?" Forsythe asked.

"I'm talking about the persistent, nagging little fears that clutter up our lives and influence our day-to-day actions," Kosta said. "The small fears that keep us focused on ourselves. Fear of losing your job or your friends. Fear of not having enough money if you happen to get sick. Fear of being hurt. Fear of looking foolish."

"I know *that* one, all right," Hanan murmured.

"Do you?" Kosta countered. "Do you really? You took Chandris aboard the *Gazelle* knowing full well that she was there to steal from you. If she had, you'd have been the laughingstock of the Yard. Did you care?"

Hanan turned a frown toward Ornina. "But . . ."

"And *you* were afraid to trust them," Kosta continued, turning to Chandris. "Right? But you did, eventually, even though you knew it would hurt your pride terribly if you found out they were conning you."

He looked back at Forsythe. "As for me, I eventually got to where I wasn't afraid to turn myself in as a spy."

"So what exactly are you saying?" Pirbazari asked. "That all we have to do is give happy pills to the whole populace and we don't need angels?"

"Happy pills dull the mind and blunt the will," Forsythe murmured. In contrast to the others, his expression was thoughtful and reflective, as if certain things were suddenly starting to become clear. "As Mr. Kosta has pointed out, angels don't do that."

"They may actually help make you marginally smarter, in fact," Kosta suggested. "There's that small intelligence component, remember."

"Only when they're in large groups," Hanan reminded him.

"Or else it's only measurable in large groups," Kosta said.

"I was just thinking about the High Senate," Forsythe said meditatively. "All the straight-up trades and deals I watched them make, without any of the cautious maneuvering or self-serving manipulation that's always been a staple of political life. Full cooperation, full willingness to compromise. No fear of looking foolish or being taken advantage of."

Pirbazari shook his head. "I'm sorry, but I still don't buy it," he said firmly. "Even if this effect really exists, it's not going to do much if the person in question doesn't *want* to be a good boy."

"In fact, it might even make it worse," Hanan suggested. "Fear of getting caught is one of the things that's supposed to slow criminals down."

"Exactly," Pirbazari agreed. "So why haven't there been any High Senators like that?"

"There have," Kosta said. "Seven of them over the past ten years."

Pirbazari seemed taken aback. "Where did you hear that?"

"Director Podolak told me," Kosta said. "She said it had been kept very quiet."

"Well . . . all right, fine," Pirbazari said. "But there should have been a lot more than just seven who went off the wagon. Unless you assume most people basically *want* to be good, which I don't believe, either."

"Self-fulfilling prophecies, Zar," Forsythe said.

"What does that mean?" Chandris asked.

"Those are predictions that come true because everyone expects them too," Forsythe explained. "Remember, everyone firmly believes that angels make you act ethically. Once that's been accepted, only people who really want to serve the Empyrean will go after high office. Most of the self-serving types out to line their own pockets make very sure they stay away from anything having to do with angels."

Pirbazari shook his head. "I still don't like it."

"I'm not saying this is a hundred percent correct," Kosta conceded. "There's probably more going on that I haven't thought of. All I'm trying to do is find a theory that fits the behavior I've seen. Plus explaining Ronyon's panic attack out at Angelmass."

"Wait a minute," Ornina said. "Are you saying that Angelmass was attacking hunterships because it was *frightened* of them?"

"Basically," Kosta nodded. "If angels suppress fear, it follows that anti-angels are the essence of it."

"What in the world did it have to be afraid of?" Chandris asked. "We weren't going to hurt it. How *could* we hurt it?"

"Fear doesn't have to be reasonable," Forsythe said mildly. "In fact, for most of the fears Mr. Kosta listed earlier, it isn't reasonable at all."

"The point of all this is that we need to understand what the angels are actually doing," Kosta said. "To especially understand their limitations."

He hesitated. "Because I think you're going to have to learn to live without them."

"What's *that* supposed to mean?" Pirbazari asked suspiciously.

"That's right, you didn't hear about that," Forsythe said, gesturing toward Kosta. "Mr. Kosta thinks we should catapult Angelmass out into interstellar space where it won't be a danger to us anymore."

Pirbazari's eyes narrowed. "That's ridiculous. Besides, it seems to have settled down okay."

"Only because it's chased everyone out of its immediate neighborhood," Kosta pointed out. "There's nothing for it to be afraid of anymore. But suppose it happens to notice Seraph someday? No, we've got to deal with it before that, or at least have a plan ready."

"We definitely need a plan." Forsythe locked eyes with Kosta, an oddly intense look on his face. "The real question is whether kicking it out of the system will be enough."

And the expression on Forsythe's face . . . "Are we thinking along the same lines, High Senator?" Kosta asked quietly.

"If the interstellar void isn't far enough, I can hardly wait to hear what is," Hanan commented. "What do you want to do instead, give it to the Pax?"

"No," Kosta said, still watching Forsythe. "We have to put it back to sleep. We have to put the angels back in."

The stunned silence was broken by Hanan's low whistle. "You do know how to uncork political bombshells, don't you, Jereko?" he said. "You don't really think the High Senate will go for this, do you?"

"We may have no choice," Forsythe said quietly. "Catapulting Angelmass away postpones the problem, but it doesn't solve it. We can't take the risk of it popping up somewhere unannounced in the future."

"You're never going to sell this to the people," Pirbazari insisted. "They've gotten used to having ethical leaders."

"No," Kosta told him. "What they've gotten used to is being politically lazy. The angels have basically allowed them to let their government run on autopilot. Now, they're going to have to keep an eye on it themselves."

"Which in the long run may not be a bad thing," Hanan said thoughtfully. "Even ethics-based decisions can be wrong, you know. Maybe it's better to have a suspicious electorate looking over the government's shoulder."

"Fine, but don't forget that if the angels go, so do your jobs," Pirbazari warned, looking at Hanan and Ornina. "Yours too," he added, shifting his gaze to Kosta.

"We'll live," Hanan said with a casual shrug. "I was getting tired of space flight anyway. Food all over the galley every time we have to maneuver. Yuck."

"We're certainly not going to make any final decisions today," Forsythe said, starting to gather his various papers together. "But this gives us all something to think about."

"So what happens next?" Hanan asked.

"Nothing too dramatic," Forsythe told him. "I'll have EmDef put together a group of catapult ships and send them out to the *Komitadji*. It'll take them about a week to get there, and by the time they do Angelmass should have moved far enough away for it to be safe. Meanwhile, we'll have someone dig up the coordinates for the Scintara system. I'll talk to you later, Kosta, about recording a suitable message for them."

"Maybe we should send one to Lorelei, too," Pirbazari suggested. "In fact, we could send that one right now. Let the Pax forces know a pull-out order will be coming their way soon, and warn them not to mess with the planet and people until then."

"I can write something up," Kosta said. "We could also include a copy of the recording from Central's cameras."

"That should keep them walking carefully until the Pax pulls them out," Forsythe agreed. "Zar, you're in charge of getting that organized."

"Yes, sir."

"Then that should do it for now," Forsythe said, glancing around the table. "I'm releasing you all on your own recognizance, pending a hearing before proper legal authorities."

"Said hearing to take place after the Pax has run away with its tail between its legs?" Hanan suggested.

"We'll fine-tune the schedule," Forsythe assured him. "Thank you all for your time."

Beside Kosta, Chandris cleared her throat. "There's just one more thing, High Senator."

Forsythe lifted his eyebrows. "Yes?"

"I was the one who helped Jereko destroy the *Komitadji*," she reminded him. "In fact, if you follow the chain of events, you'll see that if it wasn't for me that ship would still be sitting over our heads."

"You want a medal?" Pirbazari asked dryly.

"No," Chandris said. "I want a reward."

Pirbazari snorted under his breath. "I think your reward comes in the same box as Kosta's," he said. "Namely, you don't get prosecuted for collaboration with a Pax spy."

"No, I don't think so," Chandris said calmly. "See, I don't think I ever knew anything about that. I'm pretty sure you can't prove it, anyway."

Pirbazari's face darkened. "Look—"

Forsythe cut him off with a gesture. "What is it you want?" he asked.

"The *Komitadji* was a really big ship," Chandris said. "A *really* big ship. I looked up some ancient privateer numbers in the old Earth history records, and the price for capture or destruction of something that size would have been right through the roof. In fact, salvage rights alone on what's left of the hulk—"

"We get the point," Forsythe interrupted her. "What is it you want?"

She looked him square in the eye. "I want an operation for Hanan," she said flatly. "Complete repair and reconstruction of his nervous system."

Hanan's jaw dropped, his eyes widening with amazement. Pirbazari, for his part, actually sputtered. "You must be joking," he insisted, clearly appalled. "You have any idea what that would cost?"

"At this point, two to three million ruya," Chandris said. "I figure that's around one and a half percent of what I could demand under privateer law."

"The Empyrean doesn't *have* any privateer law," Pirbazari growled, throwing a black look at Hanan. "This is extortion."

"Chandris, you don't have to do this," Hanan protested urgently.

"Shut up, Hanan," Chandris told him. "Look, High Senator. Like it or not, Kosta and I are the closest thing you've got to war heroes coming out of this. We could command a lot of public attention if we wanted to."

"Except that I hardly think you would want to," Forsythe pointed out mildly. "Certainly not considering your past and Mr. Kosta's current situation."

"Oh, I'm sure we'd prefer to keep a low profile," Chandris agreed. "Whether we actually do so is up to you."

Forsythe smiled faintly. "You would have made a wonderful politician of the old school, Miss Lalasha. Very well. Mr. Daviee will have his operation."

"Sir—" Pirbazari said urgently.

"*But.*" Forsythe leveled a warning finger at her. "Not because you've pressured me into it. Because you're right: you and Mr. Kosta have earned it."

He looked around the table. "Then unless there's anything else, this meeting is adjourned."

With a final nod to each of them, he stood up, and he and Pirbazari strode side by side from the room. Ronyon paused long enough to grin and wave a hand in farewell, then followed.

"You didn't have to do that," Ornina said, reaching past Kosta and half pulling Chandris out of her chair. Standing up with her, she enveloped the girl in a massive bear hug. "But thank you. Thank you so much."

"For me, too," Hanan said, stepping over and wrapping his arms around both of them. "Group hug, Jereko," he added, winking down at Kosta. "Want to join in?"

Kosta smiled. "Another time, thanks."

"You young people," Hanan said, mock sorrowfully. "Missing out on all the good things of life."

"Oh, be quiet, Hanan," Ornina chided as the hug broke up.

"Story of my life," Hanan said, mock-sorrowfully. "That was a brilliant analysis, by the way, Jereko. I'm with Mr. Pirbazari—I'm not sure I buy a single word of it. But it was brilliant nevertheless."

"You were wrong about one thing, though," Chandris said. "The angels *do* affect danger-type fear, at least a little. When Trilling attacked us, I was a lot calmer than I should have been."

"Come to think of it, so was I," Kosta agreed, frowning as he thought back over that incident. The adrenaline had been pumping, all right, but his mind had still been clear to function. Unnaturally clear. "Out at Angelmass, too. You're right, it *does* have an effect there."

"Maybe why the High Senate has always seemed so calm in the face of Pax threats," Hanan rumbled. "Even though they never seemed to be doing anything."

"They were, though," Kosta said. "That net-and-catapult setup of theirs is a terrific defense. They got that in place, then just refused to keep worrying about it."

"I wonder how the Pax got through," Chandris said.

"I don't know," Kosta said. "I imagine we'll find out once they've pulled their ships out and we can talk to Lorelei again."

"What will you do now, Jereko?" Ornina asked. "Do you need a place to stay?"

"No, I should be fine," Kosta said. "I've still got my room at the Institute."

"At least for another week or two," Hanan said.

"Oh, longer than that," Kosta assured him. "Mr. Pirbazari's dire predictions aside, the Institute isn't going out of business any time soon. Maybe not at all. Even if they agree to dump the angels back in, we'll certainly want to keep a few out to study."

"Will that be safe?" Ornina asked.

"I'm sure it will," Kosta assured her. "After all, it took an imbalance of several thousand anti-angels to make Angelmass what it is. A few or even a few dozen shouldn't be a problem."

"The question is, what will *you* do?" Chandris asked, looking at Hanan and Ornina.

"What do you mean 'you'?" Hanan countered. "Don't you mean 'we'?"

"You *are* staying with us, aren't you?" Ornina added.

"Well . . ." Chandris flashed a look at Kosta. "I'd like to, sure. But if there isn't any work, how can you afford to keep me on?"

"You mean how can we afford *not* to keep you on," Hanan said firmly. "Face it, Chandris, you're part of the team now."

"We wouldn't know what to do without you, dear," Ornina added gently.

"I wouldn't know what to do without you, either," Chandris confessed in a low voice. "But if there isn't any work—"

"There'll be plenty of work," Hanan insisted. "Shipping, transport, tourist rides—we'll find something."

"Actually, I don't think you'll have to worry about that," Kosta spoke up. "Forsythe strikes me as the persuasive type; and if he talks the High Senate into dumping the angels, they're going to need people like you for the job."

"What do you mean, people like us?" Ornina asked, frowning.

"Well, you can't just drop them in front of Angelmass like a row of space pops and expect it to gobble them up," Kosta pointed out. "All the outward radiation pressure will be pushing them away, especially if Angelmass is smart enough to figure out what's going on. They'll have to be basically force-fed down its throat."

"And the only ships that can get close enough to do that will be hunter-ships," Hanan said, his face brightening. "How wonderfully convenient."

"Don't get too excited about it," Kosta warned. "You won't be heroes any more, creating a better world for the ordinary people of the Empyrean. You'll be busily taking that better world away for reasons half the people won't believe in the first place."

"We all do what we have to," Ornina said quietly. "Besides, we didn't go into this business to be heroes."

"No," Kosta agreed. "I guess for some people it just happens that way." He stood up. "I'd better get back to the Institute and start working up a nicely threatening letter to send to Lorelei."

"We'll see you later?" Chandris asked.

Kosta reached out and took her hand. He'd always rather been afraid of Chandris, he realized suddenly. For that matter, he'd always rather been afraid of all women. Part of his general social ineptitude, he'd always thought, and had cursed the awkwardness and nagging fears of youth.

But that was before he'd faced death, out there at Angelmass, and suddenly all the fears of saying or doing the wrong thing had become utterly trivial. Maybe that had matured him. Maybe he had finally grown up.

"Sure," he told her. "Count on it."

Or maybe, the thought whispered through his mind, it was only the angels.

ABOUT THE AUTHOR

Timothy Zahn is the author of more than a dozen original science fiction novels, including the *Cobra* and very popular *Blackcollar* series. He has had many short works published in the major SF magazines, including "Cascade Point," which won the Hugo Award for best novella in 1983. He is also author of the bestselling *Star Wars* trilogy *Heir to the Empire*, among other works. He lives in the Pacific Northwest.